THE SKIN
BLACK HIND'S WAKE I

J E HANNAFORD

This book is dedicated to both my Nanne and my Dad.

Anne Hannaford, because you always wanted to write a book, this one is for you.

Dad, for introducing me to fantasy books, for always believing in me and for being my safe port in a storm. Thank you.

N

The Territories

Mynyw

Engad

Breton

THE NORTHERN BARREN

Kingdom of
Terrania

Terranian Sea

Orange

The Narrows

Jake's Port

Safe Harbour

Old Town

Respites

THE SOUTHERN
BARREN

The Everstorm

I am a child of the water; a soul of the sea. I grew up in a flotilla, born to a sea-folk family on a boat, and fully expect to die on a boat. As a child I played with a southern siren, and as an adult, heard fin-folk sing. So, yes I believe in the Old Ones.

— TIMOTHEE MARITIM

PART I
BEFORE THE STORM

MIDSUMMER

SELKIE

Sun shone through jellyfish clouds, bathing the golden beach with Midsummer's caress. It offered an invitation from our ancestors – one which Eryn and I eagerly accepted.

An entire pack's worth of flattened ledges protruded along the water's edge, enticing us to haul out and enjoy the warmth of the sun on our pelts. Once, they would have been filled with our kind. Now, they lay empty, their seaweed-covered surfaces a reminder that we were the first to visit for hundreds of years. I glanced towards home, a lump of grey blurring the straightness of the horizon in our blue-hued world.

I could think of a dozen closer islands I'd rather have visited, but I'd promised Eryn that we'd dance the ancient ritual together here on Midsummer's Day, and I had no intention of breaking my word.

My eyes were drawn, as my whole being was, back to the island. The pull of magic was strong, even here, far from the breaking waves on the shore. I glanced at Eryn, certain she could feel it too. She stared up at the crown of the hill, towards the source of the power – the ancient stone.

Sun warmed the shallow waters as we approached and I tried to push my concerns aside. It was a beautiful day and legends, though often based in truth, are stories of a past long buried; as dead as the humans who once populated this island. It had never been safer to visit. I let out a bark, trying to shout away my fear, to have it carried far away from us by the wind. After all, this was a celebration. I swam towards Eryn and nudged her playfully before speeding off towards the beach. Bubbles streamed from the air-pockets in my fur as I leapt out of the water. Eryn pursued me, her huge brown eyes gazing through the wave as she surfed past, joy emanating from every tail flick and fin slap. She slid on to the sand as a wave broke over her back, water running down her sides to reunite with the sea. She flung a fish into the air and caught it with a snap of her jaws, all the time glancing in my direction, daring me to join her.

The lure of frolicking in the shallows proved too strong to resist. I barked again and swam after her. We chased each other through winding sea caves and over soft sponge mountains, which flourished now they were recovering from the ravages of mankind at last. I took a deep breath, drinking in the scented coastal air before we dived to play on the starfish-speckled seabed. Eryn passed close to a cluster – teasing their long, brittle legs with a fin. They moved away as a single, writhing mass.

A flatfish flapped from their path, orange spots catching the light while its fins rippled. The fish tried to bury its body in the sand. I poked it with my muzzle, stirring it back into action, then flicked my tail and pursued it over the seabed. I could catch it easily, but the chase was half the fun. It looked as though it might escape into some rocks, so I snapped it up. Sated and ready to fulfil my promise to Eryn, I returned to where she played, gesturing for her to follow.

Born after the warming, we knew little of the days before. The grinding, whirring noises of mankind's ships had faded into history, and the crumpled, twisted towers protruding from the seabed around the coast had long since ceased working. Now, they provided homes for fish and eels or hiding places for playful youngsters.

When we were pups, our grandparents sat out on the high rocks as we bobbed in the water, eager to listen. They told us ancient tales passed down from their own elders. How once, before the oceans had swallowed the land, islands had risen higher above the tideline, and our coast had been different. How the pack's sun-bathing rocks had been claimed by the water and never returned to the sun. Yet, as we grew up, the land slowly began to rise again – or the sea fell. We didn't know which, only that these things were changing. Now, we had begun to recover our lost territories. Today, Eryn and I reclaimed the ancient rite of the midsummer dance before her mating.

Eryn was in love. In love with traditions and in love with her handsome selkie. His fur gleamed silver by moonlight, and she shone in his presence. They were made for each other, and at the next full moon, they were to be bonded. Inspired by the changes in our world, she had begged me to accompany her to dance at the stone.

We surfed onto the beach that day, barking with happiness, hauled ourselves up onto the soft sand, and waited as the sun warmed us until the splits in our skins eased open. The beach stretched back from the water's edge, rising to a hill above the tide line. Strands of green covered the land beyond the beach, as bright as seaweed in a high tide rock pool.

Colour bloomed all around us. I had never seen the land so beautiful.

I went first, sliding out of my skin, I rolled it carefully and hid it under the overhang of a rockpool. Eryn leapt free of hers, landing in an ungainly heap of giggles next to me. She shoved her skin under a rock and half stumbled, half ran up the beach, flinging herself onto the golden sand like a broken starfish. Waves of silver hair flowed down her pale back. Her belegged form was naked and mostly furless. I looked down at my own legs as I wiggled my toes in the warm sand. It felt much as the sand did at home – no terrible curse or tingle of power flowed through it. We were both pale, as most of our kind were. That kind of pale pink you find on the inside of a shell.

'It feels so good,' she laughed. 'But, it's scratchy without fur.' She rolled over, coating herself entirely in a shimmering layer of sand. She looked like a goddess. It was worth the long swim just to see her this happy. In fact, she glowed. I stared at her more closely. In her belegged form, a swelling in her belly was visible that her fur-skin had hidden.

'Eryn, you're in pup!' Selkie births were uncommon. The pack would be ecstatic with her news.

She blushed. 'Only a couple of moons. There's a long way to go yet. Don't tell anyone, please.' She pointed upward. 'The sun reaches its peak in an hour or so. We'll need to be there by then if we are to complete the ritual.'

She grabbed my hand and dragged me up the beach. Fragrance assaulted my sensitive nose, heavy and overwhelming as we walked through increasingly wild vegetation. Pink and purple bells hung silent on stiff, sharp stems and my toes bled from a multitude of tiny scratches by the time we reached the crest of the hill. I barely noticed the pain as the view over the other islands opened up. A larger island dominated the view to the south. Far on the northern horizon was our home.

'It has to be here somewhere,' Eryn said, running around looking for the standing stone our grandmother had described.

I collapsed onto a flat rock, my fingers searching through the foliage for its surface. They made contact, and the thrumming of ancient magic poured out of it. The thin hairs on my skin stood up with the sheer volume of power connecting to my selkie magic. I'd never felt anything like it.

'I have it, Eryn!' I cried. 'We can do it.'

She laughed then began to sing and sway, her body undulating in time with the tune. Even belegged, my sister was graceful. Her hair swirled around her face as though under water. She began to take small steps in a circle, creating the pattern we had danced many times at midsummer in deep waters far beyond the shore. I watched closely. When I recognised where she was in the dance, I joined her, weaving in and out of her patterning. The knotted path we wove glowed brightly with the power of the fallen stone.

We were so engrossed in our dance that we didn't see the boat slip into the cove.

We didn't see the lone human come ashore.

We didn't see him take Eryn's skin from beneath the rocks.

We did see him crest the hill, a greedy look in his eye as he realised he had trapped one of us. His sun-browned cheeks mottled red with the exertion, his bulbous nose textured and dripping in the northern breeze.

I cried out in dismay as I saw the skin hanging from his rough hands, my heart breaking like a sea urchin under a dropped rock. Eryn's scream tore my spirit to shreds. She had seen it, she knew it was hers. Through the pain, instinct took over. I would *die* to protect her and that unborn pup.

I turned and took hold of her shoulders, pulling her close as the man drew near. I whispered in her ear. 'For the sake of your futures, for the unborn child you carry and the love I bear you, take my skin. I will escape. I will find you.'

I didn't believe I'd see her again, and I wasn't sure it would work.

'Oh, bold sailor!' I cried out, running at him and falling to my knees. 'Please, please return my skin.'

He looked at the silver fur and Eryn's silver hair for a moment too long.

I reached for the fur, trying desperately to tug it back from his grasp and his attention switched. Piercing eyes stared at me, greedy and hard. I tried to wrestle the skin from him and failed.

Eryn took advantage of his distraction to flee. I moved as though to follow, deliberately stumbling. The man charged me, knocking my legs from under me. Then, he hauled me back up the hill by my arm.

He grinned as Eryn hurried away. 'I've done it! I caught a selkie.'

My head dropped in defeat. I watched her run. She picked up my dark skin and struggled into it. It didn't close at first, but then, with a gentle glow of selkie magic, it shut and she flippered her way out of the breakers. I saw her turn and look one last time towards the hill where I was held, and then she was gone.

Hatred roiled inside me as I spun to face my captor. I would find a way back to the sea.

He sneered, his roving eyes taking in every part of my naked form.

I lifted my chin and squared my shoulders. 'What will you do with me?' Ancient tales of forced imprisonment stirred in the depths of my memory. I expected to be taken forcefully. I braced for it, ready to fight him to my last breath.

'You are valuable,' he said simply. 'So I had best ensure that this,' he waved my skin, 'is secure from your clutches. I can't have you swimming away from me.' He stepped in close, the bitter stench of human filling my nose. He reeked of what I later learned was stale beer and sweat. Salty – the wrong salt. He gripped my chin in his hand and tilted my face. I wriggled free, but my legs, unsteady with inexperience, were not as agile as I would be in the sea, and I stumbled.

He laughed and swung his fist at my temple.

I awoke sometime later near the old harbour, tethered by my ankle to a post. My head throbbed, exacerbated by the buzzing banquet of fly-infested food in front of me. I had very little shelter, and I was alone, shackled and captured. There was no sign of the sailor or his boat.

'Valuable,' I muttered. 'So valuable you leave me tied up here with rotten food.' Maybe Eryn would come and untie me. I could try to escape – swim even – though how I would do that without flippers, I was unsure. Home was a long way.

The human food turned my stomach, its sickly scent nauseating. I tried to ignore it. There was enough food to sustain me on the foreshore if I could get there. I pushed myself upright and dropped from the dock wall onto barnacle-encrusted rocks. My feet throbbed, the earlier cuts stinging as they dipped into salt water, and new lacerations opened with every step. Near the full extent of the rope, I could reach a number of rock pools. Last tide's water still drained away, and the seaweed was moist and tempting. I plucked a handful, stuffing the thin, green sheets into my mouth. Small molluscs crawled enticingly across pink fringes of the pools. I smashed their shells on the rocks and sucked out the cool, juicy meat. Food was food, and I was starving.

A seal bobbed in the bay. He watched me for a moment, and I hoped desperately for a wind shift, for my scent to carry seaward instead of over the hill behind me, for him to realise I was not all I appeared.

He dived, and my hopes for rescue went with him. It had been a slim chance that he'd notice me. I swallowed hard as I accepted that I might never see my pack again. My parents taught me that hope remains alive until all options are exhausted, so once I had eaten, I dragged the rope back to the jagged rocks further up the shore. If I could find a sharp enough edge, I could cut myself free.

I know now that my efforts would have been in vain, I could have sawed at the rope for weeks, and it wouldn't have given way. Even had my pack found me, they could not have set me free. Spider silk rope, abominable treasure that it is, is too strong. The metal clasp around the spliced join would not break for me either. Not that day, or the next.

Sun heated my naked skin, and rain soaked me with refreshingly cool water. When the tide was in, I sat in what shallow water I could reach, my skin becoming wrinkled and soft. The brisk sea breeze chilled me faster than I dreamed possible. Without my blubber and fur, I was cold at night, and the rocks were impossible to get comfortable on. What should have been a perfect resting spot to relax or doze was a sharp, skin-lacerating surface of tiny barnacles. Daily, the number of cuts increased. I knew enough about this form to know that I wouldn't last long exposed to the elements naked and needed to protect myself somehow.

After two nights, a small boat crossed from the big island to leave water and a heap of foul human food on the rocks for me. The woman who brought it curled her lip in disdain at my naked form.

'Stupid creature. As stupid as the old tales. Letting yourself be trapped by that idiot of a human. You deserve your fate. You and all your filthy kind.' She spat at me and walked away.

The next time she came, I asked for clothes and wondered aloud how long I would be here.

She looked me up and down. My skin was red in patches, cut and damaged from the sun and rocks. I knew I made a sorry sight.

'He'll be back when he's back. He won't pay me so much for a ruined prize. I will get you clothes.'

When she returned, she dumped a pile of old clothes on the dock. They stank. I thanked her with as much grace as I could muster.

As soon as she'd gone, I threw the clothes in the sea and let the scent of home wash away the stench of the land, leaving the food, as ever, for the flies and gulls.

Once the clothes were cleaner and I could stomach their smell, I inspected what the woman had brought. Because of the tether, I would have to unpick the stitching on one leg and sew them back together with a fishbone, much like I'd stitch kelp leaves to make a bed. A rotting fish, dumped by gulls at the strandline had a few large bones left, so I fashioned a hook for the thread and donned the top. Its itchy fabric sat uncomfortably against my skin. How could humans wear this stuff? I set to work unpicking the knot on the trouser leg and carefully pulled the threads from the outer seam.

It took most of the day to restitch the trousers, the tiny stitches fiddlier than anything I had sewn before. Once the tethered leg was sewn on, I slipped my other leg in too.

I looked more human now. The clothes did a lot of the work for me, although I would still need to use a selkie glamour to complete the transformation. I tried to remember the shape of the old woman's teeth and carefully built an image of them in my mind. I dropped an illusion of them over my own sharp pegs. If I was going to pass as human, I was also going to have to eat their disgusting food, even if only to maintain my strength while amongst them. I stared at the pile and chose the least offensive item. It took a few attempts to chew it without gagging, but I persevered.

As I nibbled, the seeds of a plan began to form in my mind. I had seen some flint I could use to create a sharp blade and could tuck the needle amongst my clothes as a small protection against unwanted advances. I would be taken from here, of that, I had no doubt. But I would not go helpless into their world. There may only be a very small window to work in, a single chance for freedom, and I would be ready to grasp it whenever and however it came my way.

2

THE ART OF THE HEART

LADY GINA

There are many routes to power and still more methods
to hold on to it. In any power vacuum, there will always
be those who seize it with force, those who retain it using fear.
Self-styled kings who eliminate the competition and sow
discord whenever opponents rise to challenge them. The lands
north of the Terranian Sea were ruled by precisely that type of
king, his crown handed down as the result of an ancestor's
power grab. He'd reverted to ancient methods of intimidation
not seen in so-called civilised society for many hundreds of
years. Vanquished – or simply ambushed – enemies were
frequently mounted in pieces above his palace gates. It was
thought that many of his soldiers were loyal only through fear
of hurt to their loved ones.

The King of Terrania had two sons. The oldest, Prince
Anard, had chosen a life of seclusion on the island we now
approached.

I stood by my father's side at the rail of *Barge* as our

engines slowed, ready to drop anchor. Wind whipped stray
black hairs around his face as he stared ahead, a gentle tapping
of his fingers on the rail the only outward sign that he was
holding in excitement. Where kings on the land reigned over
small, hospitable areas of the coast, Lord Sal was the undis-
puted power on the water. His enormous, floating pleasure
palace, *Barge*, cruised around the ports, whilst his fleet of ships
plied the oceans, trading in information, illicit substances and
coin. Lord Sal had the power to make and break kings, and he
was excited.

He'd journeyed to Terrania many years ago in search of
adventure and pleasure, soon gathering a following of whores
and courtiers, entranced by his eloquence and beauty. Then,
something had happened, and his desires changed. Lord Sal
had taken full advantage of his newfound popularity, developing a network of information and secrets like no other. Yet,
despite his vast accumulation of power and knowledge, it was
not what he sought. My father planned to leave his mark on
the entire world.

He dreamed of restoring the balance, and he would use any
means at his disposal. Including me. Today, on this remote
island, we hoped to find part of the puzzle we sought to
rebuild.

We remained on the foredeck of *Barge* as we dropped anchor,
my heart pounding with barely concealed excitement as I
stared out at golden town walls rising from sparkling blue
waters. Today, I would go ashore on a mission with my father
for the first time.

We'd heard rumours about Prince Anard becoming even
more reclusive. It barely seemed possible, yet we knew he had

banished a number of female staff a few years ago. They'd all been dismissed on a single day, including our own informants. There had to be more to Prince Anard's secretive life than just a desire to avoid his family, and it was my job to try and elicit that from him.

'Go, get ready. I'll meet you down on our deck,' Sal said as he strode away from me, his glossy, black braid swinging with each stride. 'You'd better hurry. I've sent Seren to your room to help you prepare.'

I wound through the labyrinth of passages to my suite of rooms two decks below. A new painting hung on the wall at the base of the stairs. I paused to admire it, reaching for the dark-wood frame; it was subtle and delicate, a coastal scene from the Northern Territories. The centre of the image was dominated by a golden beach and the blue-silver leaves of sea holly. Anywhere else on *Barge*, it would have looked too simple and out of place – Sal must have had it painted especially for me. I lingered a moment, taking it in, imagining the scents and the sound of seabirds, then moved on swiftly towards my room. Seren waited for me, a mass of red fabric draped over her arm. It floated lightly in the air as she turned to watch my approach. Her wide smile grew as I hurried towards her.

'Don't rush. We need you to remain cool and composed. Keep practicing that effortless charm your father works so well to his advantage.'

It was easy for her to say, but I hadn't been around him as I grew up; she'd spent far more time around Lord Sal than I had. She had the keys to my room, but let me open the door and enter first. It was always so cool in here. The pale blue walls and cool air currents helped to make it a refuge from the searing heat of Terrania.

Seren waited quietly while I stripped, then began to pin the fabric around me as she constructed the dramatic statement we planned to make. Being naked didn't bother me. I was more comfortable that way. On *Barge,* however, and in polite society, clothes were necessary.

'When aiming to gather information from a prince, it's always worth dressing for the occasion,' muttered Seren, as she pinned another section of gossamer-thin fabric into place. 'Lady Gina, when you go ashore in Old Town, you need fresh air on your skin more than you need to keep eyes off it.'

She hacked and stitched the sea-anemone red tunic into its final form. Heavily embroidered cuffs hid venom filled needles. Slits in the sleeves of my over-tunic allowed air circulation and freedom of movement, while the high split was certainly not to show off my legs – they were weedy compared to other women. My breasts were barely covered, and the gilded sea holly clasp at my waist held together wisps of fabric so fine it could hardly be called a dress.

Once she was finished, Seren stepped back to admire her handiwork. She nodded contentedly, then opened my wardrobe and pulled out a pair of shoes.

My heart sank. I'd practiced walking in this pair for days now and still felt like a newborn as I wobbled around in them.

'It's not for the whole day,' she said, trying to stifle a chuckle.

My face must have shown too much. I tried to clear my emotions, focusing on replicating the serene countenance Sal wore and took the shoes from Seren reluctantly. I hated them. They had a stupid heel which made me tip forward as I walked. I was going to fall and embarrass everyone.

'I'll put them on when I get ashore,' I said, curling my bare toes into the sandy-coloured carpet before heading out and down several more flights of stairs to the small boat tied to the back deck.

Oak and Willow lounged in the sun, looking for all the world like any couple aboard who had found a private space to enjoy time alone. Willow glanced my way and gestured lazily towards the boat where Sal waited. I padded across barefoot and threw my shoes in as I boarded. I still wasn't used to their presence. Still, it was comforting to know they were taking care of *Barge* in our absence. Oak and Willow were part of Driftwood, responsible for guarding our borders, our privacy, and our interests.

Fish glinted in the clear water as Sal guided us alongside Old Town's dock. I leapt out, tying the bow-line around the cleat, then squeezed my feet into the shoes as I waited for Sal to tie off the stern rope.

Many parts of the world change with the seasons yet, this town remained the same, both confined and defined by the sea. I gazed up at the steep walls around us. Old Town was a secretive place, abandoned by most, and refuge to those who chose to live far from mainland politics. The dry heat exuding from the walls contrasted starkly with the coolness of the water we'd just left. My mouth was dry before we had walked halfway up the ramp. A colourful lizard darted ahead of me, stopping to raise its head and flick its tail at the casually reclining man waiting for us before dashing past him.

Sal sauntered by my side, tall and elegant. His long fingers rested on my arm for a second, asking me to pause as he took a step ahead.

'I'm here to see Prince Anard for a tour of his private art collection.'

'Who's your companion, Lord Sal?' the man asked. My fingers strayed to my cuffs as he leered at me, licking his lips.

'My daughter.' Sal drew himself up to his full height. He towered over most people we met. 'Lady Gina.'

The man stared a moment longer, now studying rather than leering, his expression slipping to practised deference as he nodded slowly. 'I've heard about you, Lady Gina,' he said. 'Didn't know what to expect. Maybe, your arrival will pull Prince Anard from his current state of mind. Follow me.' I gestured for him to lead on while I allowed my tension to quietly uncoil.

Once his back was turned, I tried to sashay up the ramp, swinging my hips as Seren had taught me, only to catch a heel in the cobbles. Sal grabbed my arm in time to stop me falling and raised an eyebrow.

'Maybe, just walk before you break a heel. Worry about embellishments on another day. Ladies who live on land wear shoes, and you cannot go into someone's house barefoot, nor would you want to walk on this hot stone without protection.'

'Shoes maybe, but this stupid design?' I hissed. 'I need something I can actually move in.' Stupid shoes. Why did people wear something so ridiculously impractical?

'We'll try to get you some new ones before we leave. Just get through today without falling over again, please.'

I ground my teeth and stumbled up the path after him with as much dignity as I could muster.

Once in Old Town, the mirage of timeless beauty melted away. Hidden inside the high outer wall, dilapidated houses crumbled. Nothing remained of their grandeur aside from piles of rubble, their walls plundered to rebuild elsewhere. Narrow streets ran between the footprints of houses that no longer were. Spires of white flowers poked through cracked mortar, and purple puffs of colour carpeted the ground.

The town was notably quiet. Aside from our guide, there

were few people around. I didn't blame them. I'd stay inside in this heat too, if I didn't have to be out.

Occasionally, we passed a pristine home, beautifully maintained and repaired, its window boxes a riot of colour. They looked out of place like intruders in a forgotten land. Children peered from one house, pointing at us as we strolled past, calling silently to invisible people further from the window.

We climbed onward through the town until we reached a more preserved area, our guide walking silently ahead. Canopies stretched out from doorways with tables arrayed in their meagre shade. Here, the residents relaxed, chatting amicably across the street, their accents as varied as their skin tones. Old Town was a refuge to all under Prince Anard.

We continued past them, a lull in their chat following our passage. I focused on taking one step at a time, on maintaining a calm facade despite my excitement. I followed in Sal's wake like a duckling learning to glide; my feet paddled frantically to keep up while he slipped smoothly through life. I yearned to stop under one of the canopies and take refuge from the heat, even to sit for a moment. When these shoes came off, there would be blisters.

The street opened up to expose a fountain filled with laughing children. Their water fight looked tempting, but I had a job to do. I revelled in the refreshing spray as we passed, the floaty fabric clinging to me damply. Beyond the fountain, topping a gentle hill, rose the huge building so much of this town had been plundered to construct.

It was decorated with the most beautiful mural I'd ever seen. Basking sharks swam through sun-dappled water, and the sea bed was blanketed with wildlife. Dolphins leapt from waves to breach with a splash, while tiny fish hid amongst corals, and crabs wandered the floor.

'It's quite something, isn't it?' Sal sighed. 'It's enough to make you homesick. Do you see the seal on the rocks?' He pointed to the far wall, where a fluffy seal pup rested on a beach near its parent.

'It's amazing. Whoever painted that knew the sea.'

'I've been asking for the artist's name, but all the Prince ever says is that she doesn't work for anyone else.'

The huge gates opened on silent hinges.

'Wait here,' our escort growled and sauntered off, scratching his arse. Clearly, the locals did not reflect the beauty of their surroundings.

'Lord Sal!' A small child flew across the open courtyard, wrapping herself around Sal's legs. Sal laughed and crouched down.

'Lila! I have something for you,' he said, and from somewhere inside his coat, he drew out a sea gooseberry. 'Go, put it in water quickly, and you'll see it glow.' The child vanished as fast as she had arrived.

'What will I be rescuing from my cousin's chamber this time, Sal?' asked a shimmering man.

His entire tunic was made from carefully stitched fish scales and it gleamed in the sunlight. Like the wall outside, it was a display of unparalleled craftsmanship. Aside from a collection of rare creatures, it was one of the most ostentatious displays of wealth I had seen.

The people you could draw on or the talent you could offer was a true measure of wealth. Most of the knowledge was long gone; the glory age of mankind well past. Many skills had been lost, and knowledge was held to ransom for the highest bidders. The people at the Prince's disposal must be in serious demand, for there was no question that this man could be any other than the Prince.

Sal smiled broadly. 'Prince Anard, may I introduce my daughter, Lady Gina.'

I inclined my head, just enough to show respect, not enough to lower my status and offered my brightest smile.

'A pleasure to meet you,' said Prince Anard. 'Rumours of your beauty do you no justice in the flesh.' He bowed deeply. 'You must be desperate for a drink in this heat? Let's get out of the sun to somewhere more comfortable where we can discuss . . . business.' He gave a thin smile and turned, leading the way into a room entirely bedecked in white.

Whereas the mural outside was a public demonstration of his wealth, in here, the focus was on him. There was nothing else to look at *but* him. A simple wooden table with three seats were the only furniture, and he took the seat positioned in a narrow beam of sunlight lancing through a window. Every motion sent rainbows around the walls. It was a carefully choreographed show.

I settled into the seat furthest from the door, grateful to take the weight off my feet and dreading having to stand again. Then, I watched him.

Prince Anard's eyes flicked across the courtyard repeatedly towards a pair of large doors. What was behind there that he could not keep his eyes away from them?

Sal took his seat, and silence stretched out as both men waited for the other to open the conversation.

Prince Anard shifted his weight and sent more rainbows dancing.

I decided to take the bait and break the stalemate. 'Your outfit is amazing,' I sighed. 'Where would I get something like that?' I glanced at Sal, hoping I had done the right thing before remembering I had to look un-coached.

Sal chuckled. 'Ever direct, my daughter.'

Prince Anard sat a little straighter as a wide smile broke, and with it came a slight release of tension from his frame. 'I prefer directness, Sal. It may have been a while since we last spoke, but you know that.'

I hate all the stupid formalities and fawning attention my father covets so badly. Prince Anard looked back to me and leant forward. Sparkling rainbows shot around the room. 'I am so pleased you like it. It's a new technique.' He twisted his arm to admire the sleeve. 'I'm worried it may be rather fragile, but the size of the scales makes it very flexible and comfortable. If you like it so much, maybe your father can arrange for you to have one made? I would be happy to lend you my tailor.'

'I might just do that,' Sal agreed, 'although Gina is more than capable of making her own purchases without my help. Speaking of which, why do *you* need me? Your message, though urgent, was cryptic.'

Tension returned to his shoulders, and the Prince shifted his weight nervously from side to side.

'My brother takes people without their consent. Women vanish into his home, to reappear over his gate if they fail to please him. I heard that another woman's body washed up ashore recently – he had captured her on a raid.' He looked at Sal, his hands gripping tightly to the edge of the table. 'Ulises took my artist. I don't know how . . . maybe he seduced her, maybe by force, but either way he took her from me, from within my home. My beautiful Sirena. There is not enough room in the world for us both any longer. I am no longer safe, even here. Our family bonds are snapped beyond repair. If he could get into my home and take her, what's to say he will not kill me next? He's always wished he was first born.'

'You want your brother . . . removed?' I asked, checking I had understood him correctly. Prince Ulises was several years younger than Anard but favoured his father in his approach to power. Ulises had a growing reputation for violence and would behead any who crossed him. A desperate desire to remain his father's favourite and gain the throne had lead to many acts committed in the family name. He had claimed swathes of land by force and was almost as hated as the King. Prince Anard was right – women he captured entered his castle and never left alive. I could understand why Prince Anard was concerned. Someone in his employ had been taken from within his home. It was an escalation of the tensions that he had no choice but to reply to.

Prince Anard nodded.

'How do you want it done?' Sal asked.

'What are my options?' asked Anard. 'I want her back, and safe, you understand.'

Sal nodded. 'I can arrange a public accident or a quiet poisoning. Possibly something more nuanced. Where do you want the blame to fall?'

'Let it be an accident. Terrible and unavoidable, something that I cannot be implicated in. How much will it cost?'

'I need to think on that.' Sal reclined languidly in his chair, his fingers drumming on the arm rest. 'Your brother's name has been circulating for a while now, associated with these atrocities. It would be a poor day for us all, should he take the throne in the future.'

He stared into the distance, deep in thought.

'Prince Anard,' I said, leaning forward eagerly. 'Do you have more work by your artist that you could show me? The mural outside was incredible.' Sal needed the space, and it was my turn to take the lead, to follow up on our hunch that there was something more going on in this almost empty palace.

'Lord Sal?' Anard asked.

'No, I'll stay here while I work out a few options for you. I need some time to think.'

'Yes, yes, of course. Please, Lady Gina, let me give you a

tour.' He offered his arm. I rose carefully, declining it. I didn't want him to feel how unsteady I was.

The Prince loved the sound of his own voice. I barely paid attention at first, taking a few moments to note the defences and the layout of the building as we wandered through. Aside from the guide and Prince Anard's cousin, I hadn't seen more than the shadow of anyone else. It occurred to me, that maybe this was why he was so talkative. Clearly, he was close to this artist. With her missing, maybe he had no one to confide in.

'Do you share your home with anyone?' I asked. It was time to follow the rumours.

'Not many, not while my artist lives – lived – here with me. Her privacy was more important to me than company.'

'You think very highly of her,' I said. Why was this woman so desperate for privacy that she wanted no one around? Who – or what – was she?

'I worshipped her.'

The frank confession mixed with past tense caught my ear. My instincts were screaming at me now that we had been right. His artist was likely one of the Old Ones, one of the forgotten races.

I turned on my charm, smiled, and tried to project as much of Sal's enchantment as I could. 'Worshipped? Not still worship?' I asked.

'I don't know.' The words spilled out, tumbling as though he had needed to confess it to someone. As though he didn't understand it himself. He frowned. 'If she walked in here now, I would prostrate myself at her feet. Without her here, I feel both free and bereft. I don't understand it. I just know I cannot feel whole without her. Yet – if I cannot have her, I want no other man to have her. I don't like feeling this way.'

That was more confession than even I expected, I pushed a little harder. 'So much, you would kill your own brother?'

He sighed. 'So much. Have you ever been in love, Lady Gina?'

'No, it is not my job to love.'

He looked at me sideways. 'You are indeed your father's daughter. I would like to show you a work. I haven't shown it to anyone because Sirena is a very private person. No one is allowed into her space normally, but, as she is not . . .' His shoulders dropped. 'You will bring her back to me. I can feel it. I will have a suit of fish-scale made as a thank you.'

'Black scale, just a vest would be wonderful,' I pressed. I knew just the person who would love to wear it. We arrived back in the main courtyard, in front of the doors that held so much of his attention. He took out a key from his pocket and opened the huge pair of doors.

Thick glass ran along one side of the room, revealing a view over the sea. The floor surrounded an enormous pool. Steps rose near the glass wall, and a waterfall cascaded over rocky grottos into the centre. The base of the pool was covered in fine black sand. Behind the grottos and the planted landscaping, the entire wall had been painted. My breath caught in my throat. The mural outside had been brightness and joy. Here, it was heart-wrenchingly beautiful.

Ice dominated the work. The sparkling blue of icebergs and the green of cold seas. Channels of clear water vanished into the distance. Narwhal rose, their horns protruding through the ice-holes drawn for them, their skins yellowed with age – not glowing with purity as an artist would normally portray them. A cream bear walked the ice under a fogbow, with terns circling above it. In a wall of white, she had managed to create a myriad of shades.

On a small island, a herd of walrus hauled out, protectively ringed around youngsters, as another bear stalked them.

'A polar bear?' I asked, walking towards it and reaching for the life-like fur. The detail was incredible.

'It's amazing isn't it? It makes me wish I could see it myself. She's made it appear so alive.'

'It is more than amazing,' I said. It was filled with so much detail, so much feeling, that I was certain the artist had been in the Arctic for a long time. 'You said this was her private place?'

'It is.' He gestured to a cave painted around a doorway. 'Her paints and her bedroom are in there. She never asked for much, once I made her this.'

The last pieces were dropping into place. It couldn't be this easy, not my first one. Sal would have picked up on this well before now. Surely?

'Did she have any staff?'

'Staff?' He laughed. 'No, she made me dismiss every female member of staff when she arrived. She made her own meals, and I didn't want the men seeing her, else their jealousy would have been unbearable.'

'So, your brother just walked in and took her with no resistance?'

'I left for a short trip, only a day or two. When I returned, the house guards said that he'd been here, overwhelmed them, and taken her.'

'Are you are sure he has her? She hasn't just left?' Might his artist have made a break for freedom and gone home to the ice?

'I am certain. No one who saw her could resist her. No one.'

3

FAILED TRADE

SELKIE

I knew my time on the island had finally come to an end when those blood-red sails cut across the horizon, growing ever larger as the strange vessel closed in. I picked up a sharpened flint and cut my hair. I cut it jaggedly to my shoulders, then threw the strands into the ocean – a part of me floating free with the tide. It was possible to fake hair with a glamour, but smaller changes were easier to maintain. So, I settled for two tiny, yet significant, changes, and the weather-marked, cropped-haired, broken-toothed woman with mismatched eyes that met the boat on the dock was not the same selkie left by the sailor.

Nor was this the same vessel that returned. This vessel was sleek, its central hull much wider than the two slender ones gliding smoothly on supports that protruded from either side. A mesh stretched delicately over the narrow strip of open water between them and the main hull. The vessel's tall mast was as black as night with thin, horizontally ribbed sails. Tall and powerful, they flexed rather than flapped. This was nothing like the small wooden boat which had left the island. I had rarely seen a boat of this style. If possessions represented people, this represented power.

The man who stepped ashore was not the one who had left me here either.

My eyes narrowed as I studied his approach. He was tall and slim, his sand-gold skin glowing with health, his hair ran in tight rows along his head. His muscles appeared bunched, coiled with tension, like a shark egg, ready to spring with the tide, then snap back into place.

We stared at each other. He was frowning, I was frantically calculating. Could this make my escape easier? Could I use this? Over his shoulder, a shape moved on the shore of the big island, and I saw the small rowboat launch from the old woman's home. I needed to get out of here fast, or she'd ruin this.

I dropped my arm and affected an exhausted pose.

'Are you here to free me?'

He smirked. 'Free *you*? I'm here to collect the selkie my master paid for.'

My insides churned. *Paid for?* I held down fear as the nausea began to rise. I had to remain calm. How I got off this island was irrelevant compared to retrieving Eryn's skin. He was staring at me now, still frowning.

'Paid for a selkie? That stupid sailor waved a silver seal skin at you, and you fell for it?' I forced a laugh. It almost came out as a squeak, I was holding so tightly to my composure. 'I watched him cut it from the seal. Everyone knows selkie match their skins. Do I look silver to you? Do I look like a dirty *selkie*?'

It was a risk. I had to hope he had seen the skin, that it was part of whatever trade they had struck. If I knew where it was,

I could steal it. I had to hope he did not know about our ability to use illusions. My minor glamour would hold if the old woman didn't get here first. So many hopes, such a slim chance.

'I don't know,' he muttered. 'If that double-crossing bastard has faked his way into this deal, I'll have his own fucking skin.'

'Why don't you just free me? Take me to him. I can prove it doesn't fit. You can kill him, and we can all go home?' I waited, still as stone as he narrowed his eyes, pacing the dock in thought. He bent down and picked up the rope tethering me to the post, running it through his fingers as he closed on me.

He raised his eyes and stared, a sly smile twisting his face. 'Or, you could be saying that to get it back and escape.'

'I could, but how would lying help me? If I was a selkie, I'd be exposing myself to you, and you'd just catch me again.' I held my breath. Oceans, he needed to be unsure. Unsure enough to take me off this rock.

He growled at his crew, who milled about on the boat watching us. 'Split up. Two of you search the other beach and the rocks in case there's another selkie and this is a decoy – yes, I know it sounds stupid. Do you want to answer to Icidro if we get it wrong? Sean and Craig, come and help me stow this wretched girl in the hold. If she's faking it, she's bloody good. If not, at least he will have something to sell at the market.'

'I'm tied to the—' I started, but he pulled out a key and unlocked the far end of the rope. The metal loop snapped open as soon as the key made contact. He took the end and passed me to one of the crew, who yanked on the rope – almost pulling me from my feet – and I scrambled to keep up before I ended up flat on the dock. I hobbled across the oddly textured surface of the boat, my sore feet feeling every ridge and groove. He dragged me below deck to a room where a tiny circular hole provided my only light. A clear glass filled the space; I pressed my face to it. As the crew member attached me to a ring sunken into the floor, I strained to see out the tiny window. Where was the old woman? Would we get away?

'Bed there,' he mumbled. 'Heads are down there.' He pointed at a small space exuding the worst stench I had come across yet. I must have looked confused because he laughed at me. 'You piss in it, then pump the handle. Your rope will let you get that far.' He turned to leave, then as an afterthought added, 'Don't pump it in rough seas. It tends to be a bit explosive. No one wants to be cleaning shit off you and the walls. It needs to stay clean, or we all get sick – right?' He left, and I sat alone in the dim light, waiting.

The island was small, the search party would not be long. They just had to be quick enough.

Stomping of feet, raised voices, shouting.

The boat vibrated gently, and we started to back out of the dock. The view from my window changed as we turned around.

More shouting and the vibration stopped. The boat began to tilt, as the sails filled and we gathered speed. The island started to recede. We were underway.

I pressed my face to the porthole as we passed her, the little boat bobbing wildly in our wake. The old woman's voice drifted across the sea.

'. . . my money . . .'

I smiled.

I watched many sunsets through the small port hole, as many as I had fingers – and more. I ate their disgusting food. Much of it stuck in my gullet, but I forced it all down, even their foul wood-imbued water. The fibrous texture of the chewy, burnt meat caught between my teeth, a taste worse than week-old dead crab. In their desperate desire to make it safe for their delicate bodies, they removed all flavour. Shrivelled up, dry, heated plants accompanied the meat. It was almost impossible to grind down with my sharp molars. I grew used to it, though I never grew to like it.

By day, I dreamed of hunting fish, of prising open a juicy clam. My nights were haunted by dreams of home. I passed the time listening to noises from the deck above, trying to guess what they each meant.

An enormous leathergill siren swam past one evening. Her sinusoidal swimming as graceful as her head was terrifying. The warmth of the hull under my hands told me that we must be well outside their normal range. I listened for her call, waited for the baited lure, but she chose to remain hidden from the sailors. I wondered what drove her so far from the ice. The warmth and my consistent view of sunset after sunset told me we had headed a long way south.

I learned to walk on sloped floors, that hearing certain activity above indicated a change of direction. Each day merely a sequence of noises and changes in the slope of my small world. Until one day, it all changed. The sea grew rough and choppy, the wind rising as a storm hit. We climbed, then crashed down the far side of the waves over and over again. Shackled as I was, there was no refuge or stability. Objects around the cabin merely swayed, everything too secure to fall – everything, except me.

I was bruised and battered by the time the waves calmed, and the sea gave up trying to sink us. Storms were so much easier under water.

A rancid stench filled the cabin, wafting past on warm air.

The heads stank and, although I was not responsible for whatever explosion of excrement had occurred during the storm,
the swearing of the sailors as they dealt with the mess was
vehement enough that I hid at the back corner of my cabin
until they were done. I had held my innards for the entire first
day, desperately resisting the need to use it, hoping we would
soon be ashore and I could find the land equivalent of a
seaweed clump. When land did not appear, I eventually gave
in, much as I hated the indignity of it. Once I had dealt with
the challenge of the heads that first time, it became less trau-
matic. I needed to be perceived as human, so this was merely a
whirlpool I had to overcome.

The winds shifted, and the boat accelerated, rocking gently
from front to back as it rode the waves, flying across the
ocean. The motion relaxed me. It reminded me of surfing the
currents around home, and I got my first real sleep that night.

I was woken by a scraping sound a few sunsets later.
Stamping feet and cursing filled the air on deck until finally,
the noise stopped. I peered through bleary eyes out of my
porthole. A huge expanse of land stretched across the horizon
as we sailed along low-lying coastline towards whoever had
bought me and, I hoped, Eryn's skin. The closer the coast
grew, the more the knots in my stomach tightened. All the old
tales passed down through generations of forced matings, of
being kept purely to gratify some human male … they all
crowded in on me that day. Crushed beneath whirling
thoughts, I stayed on the small bed until we stopped moving.

The sun was rising as they led me from my room, still tethered
by the ankle. The wooden platform I stepped onto swayed as
the crew followed, jostling to tie the boat alongside. My captor

tugged me toward an imposing building. I scanned the walls around it desperately, searching for an opening, or a place to run to. I hobbled across the uneven surface towards a pair of disfigured guardians, the remains of time-weathered carvings framing the wide entrance. I studied their grotesque forms, but whatever creatures they had once been were long eroded and streaked with ancient stains. Cool air flowed from the open door, and intricate patterns stretched out before me created by coloured squares, their shine marred beneath my feet by the mucky trail I created.

They led me into the presence of the largest man I'd ever seen. His folds of fat exceeded those of even a well-fed elephant seal. Greedy eyes peered at me from his rotund face, disappointment and confusion rippling through his features.

'What have you brought me? I paid for a raven-haired beauty, unsullied by man. A selkie, famed for their looks, not a skinny, wonky-eyed, snaggle-toothed adolescent.'

He rose from his seat, his clothes becoming trapped in skin folds and waded towards me, his bulk too huge for even the air to allow him easy passage.

'I'm no selkie.' I told him. My missing whiskers would have felt his face, he was now so close. The stench of alcohol poured from his body, making me nauseous.

'I'm inclined to agree. If that is the case, where is my selkie?'

'There never was one,' I lied. 'The man you paid took me to the island, tied me up and left me while he hunted seals.' I took an even bigger risk. 'He took more than one skin when he sailed away.'

His tiny gull-like eyes widened. So, I pushed on, seizing the chance.

'Do I look like I would have had silver fur?'

'You could have dyed it?'

'With what? I've been tied to a post on an island since that man' – I spat on the pristine floor – 'left me there.'

His cheeks flushed scarlet, and I heard a sharp intake of breath, but he held his cool. Power didn't come easily to a person without either intelligence or guile. He clearly had the second. I felt certain that his powers lay in the manipulation of truth rather than cleverness.

'I've paid for you. You will stay here, selkie or not, while we sort this *situation* out. His podgy fists clenched briefly as he turned to someone behind me. 'Get Jake back here, as soon as possible. Take her to get cleaned up. She will earn back what I have paid, one way or another.' He sneered at me, leaning in to whisper, 'And if I find you are hiding your true form, you will beg to reclaim a place as my consort over the work I'll have you doing.

I raised my chin a little, unwilling to be cowed by his threats. I'd get out of here as soon as his back was turned. Once I had the skin back.

A woman gripped me roughly by the arm, her fingernails talon-like against my skin. Caught like prey, I shuffled after her, hating my feigned helplessness.

She took me to a room where water fell from above me. I revelled in it for a brief moment. She gave me scented liquids, which I rubbed on myself until I smelt like them. While I washed, she tried to take my clothes away.

There were things I would need, hidden in the pockets I'd sewn inside the legs. I snatched them from her hands and promised to wash them myself, muttering about a connection to home or some other such nonsense.

The woman frowned, then reluctantly allowed me to keep them.

'You'll wear these,' she said, pulling out a set of plain

trousers and a matching top. Both in the same garish green she wore.

'It's the uniform. Mind you, I doubt you'll need it often. You'll be working on his tanks. You'll have three sets, one to wash, one to wear, and the other, clean and ready. Do not wear it twice, and do not wear it when dirty. You must wear it at all times unless you are working. In that case, you will wear the equipment provided.'

Working on his tanks. Oceans flood the man. His "tanks" were prisons of glass that filled a huge hall inside the building. I looked up at them in horror; each was crammed full of aquatic creatures. Nothing about them was natural. The entire set up of each was designed to show off the colours of the residents. Sad creatures floated around in them, some barely able to swim more than a few body lengths in any direction.

There were three of us assigned to their continual mainte-nance, though even as I say *us*, I mean there were two of them and one of me. Cowering humans cleaned the tanks brimming with snapping turtles and vibrant crabs, their speckled shells suited for a life in the littoral fringe of the sea. None of them belonged in these enclosures, stranded on gaudily coloured gravel, all so some idiot could admire them.

I first met one of the humans when she was cornered in a tank by a pissed-off looking shark. Pinned to the corner, her head was barely above water and far from the exit ladder. She screamed so loudly that it made me jump. I pitied them both. A predator enslaved for entertainment and a petrified, defenceless human.

At least I thought she was defenceless until she reached back and grabbed a device strapped to her belt. She pointed it at the shark, and it froze, its senses overloaded. Its cry of pain filled my soul. Before I thought about it, I ran and leapt into the water. Instinct crashed against reality. I couldn't swim well. These stupid legs didn't flap right. I flailed around, lost as a newborn pup until my feet found the bottom. The screaming of the shark still resonated through me, I needed to stop it. I waded through the tank and wrenched the object from the girl's hands, flinging it as far as I could, over the rim and into the room beyond.

She looked at me, stupefied.

'Why did you do that? How am I going to get out now?'

'You walk out. I'll do this tank in the future.'

'You're new,' she laughed. 'You take the stupid creature. See how long you last before you need the taser.'

Sharks aren't magical creatures, neither are their brains sufficiently advanced to be tricked by illusions. However, their scent receptors are incredible. This shark knew exactly what was in its tank and it kept well back from me. Most shivers of sharks and selkie herds maintained a respectful distance from each other. We avoid encroaching on their bays, and they leave us well alone. Here would be no different. I would treat her with the respect she deserved.

Once the human left, the shark swam closer. I sank my head under the water to face her. I didn't know if I could still hold my breath as long in this form, but I wanted to meet her as an equal, in our shared home. She swam up to me, and gently placed her nose in my outstretched hands, a true gesture of vulnerability and acceptance.

I did the rounds of the tanks after that. I selected the ones I wanted to work on and made myself known to their inhabitants. The gently pulsing jellyfish, tentacles caressing each other as they drifted through the water, their trailing nematocysts venomous to many creatures but not toxic to me. I liked that tank – their serene, rippling trails of death calmed my senses. A split-level tank where fire urchins coated the floor became another favourite. Many of the urchins had damaged spines where they had been tossed on rocks to clear a path for their torturers. All in all, it was a hall of horror, bathed in constant light and all bound in clear hard substances that may as well have been solid stone.

The others tried to give me the worst tanks. The ones they thought would scare me the most. When the humans were around, I had to keep up the act. To make the easy way the creatures allowed me to work around them look like coincidence. Slowly, I was accepted, and the jobs they used to torment me became a part of my daily routine; wake, eat their foul food, work, and sleep.

The day the sailor returned, they summoned me. The merchant gestured for me to sit amongst a row of other women while he stared at us appraisingly. I wondered if we were a line-up of failed selkie purchases? Or a set of diversions for the sailor? Icidro had gone to great lengths to get a silver-haired woman for this odd collection. Sylph-like and fragile, she stared at me, edgy as a blenny caught in the open.

I sat next to her, my stomach roiling at the prospect of seeing my captor again.

'None of you say a word,' Icidro commanded. 'Bring him in.' He gestured to the guards on the main door. The same door I had been dragged through several weeks ago.

This time my deliverer arrived, dragging the sailor with him. No longer cocky and proud, the sailor glanced at us. His eyes flickered back and forth along the line, sweat beading on his familiar, reddened face. He broke free of the servant and

strode towards Icidro, throwing a bag at his feet. It hit the
floor with a dull thud, and my heart skipped a little. Was it the
skin? Once I knew it was here, it was only a matter of time
before I found it and could return home. Maybe in time for
winternight.

'I see you have my selkie.'

He had to be faking it. Not a flicker of recognition crossed
his face when he'd looked at me. My twisted glamour hid the
selkie he'd caught. 'As agreed, I have brought you her skin.
Now, if you don't mind, I'll take the remaining money and be
out of here.'

Icidro pushed his bulk up from the over-sized chair,
waving his hand towards us.

'Which is your selkie?'

The sailor faltered – a split second, no more – and pointed
at me.

'I'm no selkie,' I barked a laugh. 'Do I look like a famed
beauty? You killed a silver seal to get that skin, you fraud!'

His face split into a sly grin, and he laughed. It was bitter
and mean, the sound of a triumphant hunter taunting his prey.

'Silver skin? Why, my selkie. I do not have a *silver* skin.
Why would you think I have? Your hair is as dark as the night
sky – much like your pelt.'

My heart pounded as his hand plunged into the bag, and he
brandished a black sealskin. The stench of death rode with it. I
gagged.

'That's no selkie skin,' cried the merchant, ripping it from
his hands. 'The blood still dries on it!'

I watched in horror as my chance of escape dissolved and
the future changed in an instant.

Icidro signalled a servant to his side. The woman stepped
forward and lifted a black item. She held it by a handle, her
finger resting across a small lever while a tube pointed

towards the sailor. She twitched her finger, and her arm jerked. A crack ricocheted around the room. The sailor crumpled to the floor, his life blood spilling across the immaculate surface, and the knowledge of where he had taken the skin, and any hopes I had of returning to my home flowing with it.

FISH PRINCE OF NOWHERE

LADY GINA

S al was exactly where we'd left him – relaxing in the chair, gazing out the window of the white room absently. He sat up as we entered, turning his attention fully towards Prince Anard. I remained standing near the door this time, uncertain if I should retake my seat.

'Your brother will not be a problem,' Sal announced. 'The price will be steep – if we are implicated, it would cost me my life.'

Anard sat heavily in his chair. He stared out the window gazing once again towards those doors, then raised his eyes to Sal. 'I will pay it.'

I wasn't surprised. Our conversation revealed just how deeply the artist had sunk her snare and how scared he was of his brother's next move. If my home had been violated, I'd want revenge too. I kept a calm face, trying to emulate Sal, who in turn surprised me with a rare public exhibition of emotion.

'You don't even know what it is yet!' Sal gestured expansively, shaking his head. He pushed to his feet and started to pace. 'Prince Anard, are you certain you wish to risk this for a woman you are not even bonded to?'

'I would risk my soul.' His head was in his hands as he stared at the grain of the painted table.

Sal glanced up at me. I'd moved out of Anard's direct eye line, and though I could say nothing – this deal was between them – I pursed my lips and nodded as subtly as I could. Would he understand me? Anard had as little choice in this matter as a netted fish. He could fight and struggle, but it was too late. Sal shrugged. 'Then, I choose a trade in favour.'

Anard looked up and offered Sal his hand. 'I accept. Whatever you ask, I will do it, if it is within my power.'

'Then, we have an agreement.' Sal pulled a roll of paper from his case. 'Sign here, and here,' he indicated. It was a simple contract, a favour swap signed and countered by me as witness. We were bound to the job. I just hoped that we could pull it off as subtly as Sal was implying.

Anard took the pen Sal offered him and scrawled his signature before passing it back. 'When?' he asked.

'I won't implicate you further by telling you,' Sal replied. 'We'll see ourselves out. Many thanks for the hospitality. The food was delicious as ever.'

He'd had food? We hadn't been gone for that long, had we? No wonder he was looking so relaxed. He winked at me. I really had to get better at hiding my emotions. Prince Anard moved to get up from his chair, but Sal shook his head. He rested a hand briefly on the Prince's shoulder before we left.

'If you change your mind—' he began.

'I won't,' Anard cut in, shaking his head. He returned to his contemplation of the table as we left him.

Outside the palace, I stopped to take another look at the huge mural. It all made so much sense. I was convinced my hunch was right and couldn't wait to share it with Sal. We strolled through Old Town's streets in silence, for town walls have ears and windows have tongues, neither of which needed to flap at either our presence or conversation. The people who noticed us on the way in would do enough of that without us adding any fuel to the gossip.

Once we reached the cobbled slope to the dock, I kicked my shoes off, resisting the urge to fling them into the water. Seren would kill me, and more than one murder would be sealed today if I brought them back ruined. I sighed with relief at the sensation of cobbles under my feet, flexing my toes and curling them over the stones as we walked. The ground was every bit as hot as Sal had warned it would be, but in that moment, I really didn't care. They felt a little like a beach and that was good enough right now.

'Blisters. I've got *blisters* from these stupid things. We aren't stopping to get new shoes, are we?' I muttered, as the novelty wore off, and the pain kicked in.

'We'll get Seren to fix them somehow – maybe you should start a new trend. If you, Lady Gina, are seen wearing flat shoes, you may just be ahead of the rest.'

Sal might have a point. I had seen far more scarlet, floor-length clothes in the last few weeks. 'That's a trend that I wouldn't mind setting.'

Sal smiled. 'I wondered if you'd noticed. Beauty and power wield influence. You have both now.'

'I don't enjoy the simpering men it also brings.' I laughed, still revelling in my freedom to move my toes.

'I know, sweetheart, I know.'

He climbed aboard our boat as I loosed the ropes, my shoes following closely behind. I untied us and pushed the boat away from the dock. Red fabric dropped into the water between us for a moment, flowing in the water beneath me like blood. I leapt aboard as the engine hummed quietly to life, and we shot across the sea back towards *Barge*.

Its sheer bulk loomed out of the water, immaculate shimmering sides reflected rippling waves between the water level lower decks. Several of these were open for residents to access, and laughter drifted across the water towards us. *Barge* was less a ship than a floating town. Individual huts rose from the top deck. The huts were mostly for show, to create an illusion of privacy for our guests and could easily be removed. The billowing tents adorning the lower section of the top deck were all dismantled from our recent voyage, their supporting structures protruding skyward like spines and garlanded with arches of jasmine. It was a world away from the coastal towns. Sal had even managed to grow trees on board. From our sea-level vantage, I could see a few of them now, waving their branches in the stiff off-shore breeze as we approached.

Barge was special – few ships this large still existed. When the population declined, no group had been spared. Knowledge was lost, and few could afford to employ or build machines that were once common. The gulf between the technologically rich and the rest of the population had never been wider.

We pulled up to our private dock, and Sal steered the boat between the guide rails. As we slid into the bowels of *Barge*, the door began to rise, water pouring from either side it as it sealed. Our boat was gently cradled in a sling as pumps emptied the remaining water. We waited quietly, until the dock was dry, then Sal leapt out and helped me down. Oak and Willow entered, their eyes searching silently for injury or change, before they waved us through. I knew that should we need it again, our small vessel would have been turned and ready to head back out to sea.

'Thank you,' Sal said as we passed them and headed to our private staircase. I hurried up the steps after Sal, excited to share my findings.

We locked the door, and Sal sank into his favourite armchair. He stroked the red arms, rubbing his fingers through the luxurious velvet as he got comfortable, then he leant back and looked up at me. 'Is it what we hoped? Do we finally have a lead?'

I sat opposite him, my own chair lean on the padding, designed to be a little uncomfortable, purposely hard to relax in – one of Sal's subtle tricks. 'It is. I am convinced that his artist was far more than she appeared – to him anyway. He was entranced, fully under her spell. Sal, you should have seen the space she had. He'd built her an enormous outdoor pool, and the paintings. Whoever was living there, knew the Arctic; they knew the details of the snow and the animals. They are old, much older than you or I. They painted a polar bear with such vividness they must have seen one. A polar bear! Just imagine.'

Sal sat up, paying close attention now. His eyes sparkled, and his breaths were shorter, faster. 'What do you think it is?'

I stood. The chair was annoying me too much today, and my very soul felt restless. 'I'd like to believe it's a siren,' I announced, pushing an irritating hair away from my face and taking a few deep breaths before I continued. 'The very fact he thinks his brother stole her for his own collection tells us she's not human, and he knows that, deep in his heart.' My own heart was beating with the revelation, my certainty growing with every word I spoke. 'I'm sure it's not a southern siren either. The ancient leathergill sirens are the only Old Ones who live in the ice. A full-grown leathergill could fit in that pool. Although, if he got her in there without noticing her real size, she'd have to be powerful. Why not just eat him, as most do? It's safer that way.'

I paused, thinking back on what I had seen. A leathergill siren fitted most of the clues, explained his behaviour, and I couldn't think of any other creature who would cause that type of visceral reaction from a human male.

Sal laughed, breaking the quiet silence that had settled. 'I think she discovered a new love. Where on the sea can you paint and not have it vanish with the tide? Maybe the chance to create eternal works was too much for her to turn down. She wouldn't be the only Old One to choose a life amongst humans.'

He might have a point. 'So, the chance to paint more murals, to have new, clean canvasses? Do you think that's why she went with his brother?'

Sal pushed himself from his chair and strolled around his pristine, white bed to the window. He stared over the sea for a while before he responded. 'No, Gina, I think she didn't want to be found out and had no choice but to use a full entrapment on him, and it's cost her dear. Those paintings of the ocean floor and its inhabitants and the ice you describe sound far from the paintings of someone in despair. They are a celebration.'

Did this leathergill choose her life with Prince Anard? If so, would she want to return home, to help us restore the balance? Or would she want to go back to her remote island pool?

'So, we rescue her and return her to the glass prison?' I asked. I didn't relish the idea.

Sal turned towards me, looking gently down into my eyes. 'No, we will rescue her and give her the choice.'

'I can live with that.' Freeing a legendary leathergill siren would be reward enough – a chance to prove to both ourselves and our crews that the rumours of entrapped Old Ones were true, that they truly existed. Finally, we would have evidence, coupled with an opportunity to seek revenge on the Prince who had refused our requests to dock in the capital for so long. I didn't think there would be many people mourning his loss. 'What's your plan?'

Sal turned back to his window. 'We'll send *Black Hind*. She's ready. It's time for Georgie to take her new crew on their maiden voyage and do what they've trained for. This task needs skills that Driftwood can't offer.'

'Zora too?' I asked, excitement fizzing in my stomach.

'Definitely. We need every advantage we can get.' He left his window and poured himself a drink from a dark bottle. Thick, syrupy liquid flowed into his glass, as dark as night.

'We are due into port tomorrow. If we have seeded the news well enough, there should be a number of influential men and women awaiting your arrival,' he said.

'What a delight.' The sarcasm slipped out before I could stop it.

Sal raised an eyebrow and sipped. 'I know, but it's part of the job. We keep them sweet; they think they have a chance, and we get to plunder their port for money and information. The secrets told in the throes of drunken passion to our crew are worth more than your hatred of the power behind them.

We cannot bring them down without the right things in place. You know that. Go and see Seren. As we sail into port tomorrow, I want you standing by my side as though this ship was already yours. See if she can do something about your footwear problem too. I can't always be there to catch you.'

He gestured towards the door. I was dismissed. I strolled up to the top deck, revelling in the evening sun on my skin and a cool breeze carrying the heady scent of jasmine. I wound between the tent uprights towards Seren's hut.

She reclined on cushions, her flame-coloured hair glowing in the sunlight as she soaked up the last rays of sun. I sat next to her and showed her my feet.

She laughed, a deep, hearty laugh, rich and melodious. 'Welcome to the world of fashion. We all suffer for beauty, Lady Gina. Did you manage to walk in them?'

I grimaced. 'You might, but I have no desire to, Seren. Surely you can design something attractive that I can actually walk in. Lord Sal might spend his time in fancy palaces and this floating pleasure house, but I grew up in the north.' I was pleading now, but I really didn't care. I would beg all night if it meant I never had to wear these shoes again. 'It's too hot here, my feet are sweaty, and I hate these shoes. They are pretty, I won't deny that, but *please*, can we create something more practical? Sal said that your designs start trends. Can we create a new one?'

Flattery didn't always work on Seren; however, today, she seemed happy to be persuaded.

She took the offending shoes from me and sighed. 'Let me see what I can do. You need to go and bathe those sore feet of yours in salt water to toughen them up. Go down to the waterside deck. I'll fetch some samples and ask Rupal to meet us there.'

I felt my shoulders loosen with relief. I wouldn't have to

wear them again. Today had been a good day – the possibility of a leathergill siren, and now, I was getting new shoes. I wandered barefoot down to the lower decks to follow Seren's advice and dangle my feet in the water, while I waited for her to join me.

5

THE BLACK HIND

GEORGIE

The boom cracked me on the head, and I sprawled across the deck, star-fished on its wooden boards while Zora laughed – again.

'When will you learn to duck?' she asked. Her eyes sparkled with tears and the smile tugging at her lips gave way to a grin before she collapsed in a fit of laughter. The rest of the crew watched on, none of them daring to so much as chuckle, although Theo's lips were twitching.

'When you learn to call it out? When the bloody boom is far enough above my head that I won't have to?' I retorted, rubbing a new bump already swelling on my tender scalp as I pushed myself up. I rested my hands on my hips and attempted to assume an authoritarian pose. It wasn't successful, judging by the number of crew trying to hold down laughter. I'd have said my pride hurt more than my head, but I had been whacked by that *thing* so many times now, that my pride truly was a boat well sunk.

'What are you all staring at?' I huffed. 'We are due at Lord Sal's yard shortly.'

They averted their eyes as one and tried to look busy. All except Theo. His shoulders shook with poorly disguised mirth. Had anyone else laughed, I'd have been insulted, but the man could sail a ship through the roughest seas. I had only been aboard for days before hearing the rumours.

'Theo Maritim's silver beard was from trips to the Arctic.'

'The colour was blown out by the winds of the Everstorm.'

Solo sailing exploits and voyages into the Everstorm – Theo was a living legend. Now, as he looked at me, barely salt-wet in his eyes, his grey-flecked beard twitched as he tried to hold the laughter in and failed.

'You'll get the hang of it or get wet,' he said between chuckles, then winked at Zora before returning his attention to the helm.

Black Hind had been hidden from me for weeks. Zora wanted to surprise me, and Sal had kept me busy with other assignments. I couldn't wait to see her. We had managed to get the panels fixed so, unlike this old hulk, it would have electricity. The last time I had seen it, the garish colours adorning the hull had hurt my eyes. Even then, the potential of the old boat had been obvious. Zora had loved it from the start, and truth be told, so had I. It felt like a home, and I sorely needed one of those. Somewhere I could be myself.

Zora had been charged with outfitting the boat. With access to Sal's unlimited coffers, I had no doubt it would be amazing. I scanned the boatyard, searching for her as we pulled alongside a pontoon. Zora appeared by my shoulder and pointed to a sleek boat on the furthest dock. Her hull was polished to a shine that reflected the waves. The mast and spars were a light grey, as was the raised rear deck and cabin.

She looked unremarkable compared to every other vessel; she looked as perfect as the woman next to me.

'Come on!' Zora dragged me onto the pontoon, leaving the rest of the crew to deal with the old boat. We ran around the gently bobbing path to the *Black Hind*.

We scrambled over the railing side by side and I stood aboard her, trying to take in all the changes they'd wrought in such a short time. Everything gleamed. The monochrome paint distracted the eye from her broad beam until you were aboard. Her narrow, blade-like bow was ready to cut through whatever we faced. All of the fittings and cleats, the winches and ratchets had been polished to a high shine, few had been moved. We had chosen this boat deliberately as she was designed and rigged to be run by a very small crew. Zora flicked a switch in the cabin, and the lower deck illuminated gently. It was enough light to move by – efficient, but we would not shine like a beacon on open water.

Down in the hull, two separate sleeping areas had been created. A narrow bunk squeezed into a small space alongside the galley, and another, slightly larger, room was set aside for the rest of the crew.

'I thought it better that our crew area was as small as we could handle to leave more room for what we need to transport.' Zora gestured around the empty hold as she held the solid door open. We both knew what we hoped this space would carry.

'Is there a water supply in here?' I asked. We would need one if we carried the creatures we anticipated.

She nodded.

Truth be told, sharing a room with Zora was unnerving me, and I wanted to be distracted from the idea. Having her sleep so close to me at night was terrifying. A beautiful, powerful sea-witch in my room. She turned to me, her dark skin shining in the dim light of the cabin, her eyes searching my face, and my breath caught in my throat.

'Do you like it? Did I get it right?' she asked.

'I love it. I love *her*. Is there another way into the large storage from above?'

'Yes, there's a hatch on the deck,' she said, pointing upwards.

'I hope we have the chance to use it. Thank you for all of this,' I said earnestly. She had done an amazing job, transforming the boat from the multi-coloured hulk that we had first found into this gorgeous vessel.

We stood awkwardly for a minute.

'Show me the rest,' I said, as the silence strung out for too long. We wandered around the boat as she pointed out each change.

'How long will we have before we need to collect the siren?' Zora asked.

'A few days, I hope. We need time to get used to each other and to work as a crew. Have you decided who'll join us?'

'Theo and Eden.'

I considered Theo, trying to ignore the legend his crews thought him to be. He'd been pleasant enough on the training boat. He was big burly man, though his bulk was deceptive and, despite being older, he had proven light on his feet many times. Theo was relaxed, willing to laugh at me and made no secret of having had some training in medicine before deciding the sea called louder than his patients, although he was quick to respond when someone was hurt. I liked him. Theo was less nervous around me than others I had sailed with.

'I haven't met Eden, I don't think?' I said, struggling to match the name to any acquaintance or face I had met over the past few weeks.

Zora smiled widely. 'No, they were busy finishing up here. I trust Eden with my deepest secrets. I have known them their entire life.'

That was enough of a recommendation. Not having to hide Zora's abilities on board was essential to my plans. If Eden could be trusted with her secret, then mine would be safe too. We climbed back up the short ladder to the deck and sat companionably as we waited for our new crew members to join us. Before long, two tall, slender figures approached from the village of Safe Harbour

Sal waved as he strolled down the dock. The man always looked so elegant, damn him. Every time I was next to him, I still felt ungainly and coarse. His companion also had an easy swagger, and my gaze was drawn to a pair of laughing sea-green eyes shining from a slender face. They'd shaved the sides of their head, which was topped with a waterfall of green hair. A single green feather hung from their left ear, echoing the shade of the flowing shirt its tip brushed against.

The newcomer embraced Zora with quiet mutterings shared below my hearing.

'What do you think?' Sal gestured at the boat, ignoring their reunion.

'I like it,' I said, still half watching Zora.

'I knew you would.'

'Your cousin knows how to make a boat disappear on the water,' the newcomer said, extending a hand. 'I'm Eden. Zora tells me you are Sal's cousin and my new captain.'

'Gods no. I'm in charge, I suppose, but Zora is definitely the captain. I'm just going to do what she tells me and try not to get hit by anything.'

'Like a boom – *again*,' Theo called as he strode towards us. 'So, is this us? The crew of the mysterious new boat.'

'*Black Hind*,' I replied quietly.

'What's a hind?' Theo asked as he vaulted over the rail and started to look around the deck, giving approving grunts and checking winches. 'Nice set up, more than the usual number of cleats, overly long winch ropes.' He stood at the helm and studied the deck appraisingly. 'This is fitted out for a very light crew. I could sail it alone if I needed to,' he said before looking at me expectantly. 'A hind?' he repeated.

'A female deer. The white ones are considered to be messengers from the old gods.' I watched him closely. No flicker of recognition, not a muscle twitched on his face. He just shrugged.

'Fair enough. So, why a black one?'

'Many reasons – mostly because we carry our own messages, and they are not sweet platitudes from the gods,' Zora told him.

'You do,' Sal said. 'You have a week or so until your first mission needs to be underway. Georgie has the details – Lady Gina has assigned you to a rescue mission. You may also need to kill the captor. I will let you discuss the methods you use between yourselves, but it has to look accidental.'

'Is Lady Gina going to tell us more about it?' Theo asked, visibly brightening.

'I doubt she'd totter down here in her floaty dresses.' Zora grinned at me.

'Completely impractical,' I muttered. 'Just like her shoes. No, Lady Gina is unlikely to set foot on this boat. If we are done drooling over the idea of Lord Sal's daughter, I'd like to get back aboard *Black Hind* now.'

'Of course.' Theo had the grace to blush. I suppressed a grin as he passed me and saw Zora doing the same. 'As human as they come,' I whispered to her.

'Yes, and we need him for just that reason,' she replied.

'Come on. I want to see if I can knock you overboard before nightfall, or whether you will learn to feel this boat.'

I was about to follow when I noticed Sal gesturing to me and pulled away from her grasp.

'I'll be with you in a moment, Zora. Let me have a quick word with my cousin.' I waited until Zora was preparing the boat for cast off, before we strolled out of their hearing.

Sal remained facing away from the *Black Hind* and her occupants when we stopped. 'Put out to sea and get used to your new boat. I'm trying to get details on the best date to retrieve the leathergill siren from a contact.'

'We need a bird's eye view to see the layout, or a map at least.' I said.

He nodded, 'That you do, but you'll find a way.' He clasped my shoulders as he spoke. 'Georgie, I have faith in you, I know you can do this discretely.'

We may need other doors opened in future, and that Fish Prince is the only one left to do it.'

This was going to be messy. I knew it had to be as subtle as possible, but faced with the imminent task of retrieving the siren, I was struggling to see how subtle we could be.

Sal squeezed my shoulders again. 'I trust you to do what needs doing.'

I nodded – the message was loud and clear.

Sal rummaged in his pocket and retrieved two bottles, handing me the first, 'Antarctic octopus venom, highly concentrated, it will work even when cold. Not fatal. It should give you time to get away.' The other bottle was much smaller and had a familiar blue ring on it. He offered it to me. 'This is full strength venom, Georgie. Remember, it's very effective when delivered in the right way. A scratch will cause paralysis, a puncture will be fatal – it will deliver sufficient venom to stop them breathing.'

'We're hoping that the information is right, that the facts you have been given match?'

Sal shook his head. 'We are hoping it's our first success. I've been working towards this for a long time. This needs to go smoothly.'

'I'll do my best.'

I tucked the bottles into a pocket and turned back to my new boat with a buzz of anticipation building on my skin.

'Georgie,' he called as I started to walk away. 'I've got every ear on *Barge* listening for unusual behaviour or bragging voices. We will find what we are looking for.'

We were a long way from shore when I finally called for the boat to be slowed.

'Is it shallow enough to anchor?' I asked.

'No, but there is nothing around for miles and very little breeze. If we head bow to wind, we can let the sails flap while we talk,' Zora said. She knew what I was about to do.

I stood by the mast, its strength fortifying me as I prepared to bare my soul.

'We need to talk. It is too late to turn back and too far to swim. You are all aboard *my* boat, even if you can sail it better than I.' I held the quiver in my voice as steady as I could.

Theo raised an eyebrow at me. 'Why do I suddenly feel that I should have turned down this job?'

I forced a laugh to hide my nerves. 'Trust me, Theo, you couldn't. If you'd heard our plans in advance, you'd beg for a place on the crew, a place in history. I am just saving you the humiliation of begging later.'

He chuckled at me. 'She's Sal's family all right, look at that attitude. We're listening.'

Even Eden's head was turned now.

'So, what mysterious mission are we on that needs a fully equipped boat, with expensive, legacy technology bursting at the gunwales, the dragon-wing rigging design – don't raise your eyebrow, Zora, I can see the catches for extra spars half way up the mast – and storage space enough to sail through the Everstorm and back?' Theo asked.

'Who's going first?' I ignored his question, knowing we had other business to attend to first and looked expectantly at Zora. To my surprise, it was Eden who spoke.

'I will,' they said, looking upwards with hands raised toward the skies. A gull dropped from the clouds, landing on the deck with a thud. It sat shaking its head in confusion and flapping its wings.

Eden stood over the gull and stroked its back. It climbed onto their hand and rested there calmly. 'I was born in the same village as Zora. She was always kind to me. When I began to show an affinity for animals, she supported me while others whispered behind my back. I am a bird-speaker, although my power is weak, and my abilities are limited, especially so far from home. I do have some talent that could help us, though. The ability to see through a bird's eyes can be used for watching people or seeing into places. Aside from that, I'm great at climbing. The sail design and rigging is mine. Just wait until you see the red set.' Eden grinned. 'You were right, Theo, we have to change the mast fittings, but I designed the rig to allow our entire outline on the water to change. When we use the red sails, we will have wings.'

Theo was very quiet. He studied Eden carefully, a frown building across his face as he watched the gull. He didn't comment on the rigging, and I waited nervously for him to speak. Eden raised their hand and freed the bird.

'No one has anything to say about this? No questions about

Eden's magic?' I asked, hopefully. I was grateful to have Eden's company and fully understood Zora's choice now. Eden would be a fantastic asset to the crew.

'I do have one,' Theo said slowly as he raised his eyes to meet Eden's. I braced myself for something ugly. I hoped Zora knew what she was doing, and right now, my faith in her character judgement was all that was keeping me still.

'Where did you get that amazing hair dye? Oh, and it's just birds whose heads you can see into, right?'

'Just birds.' Eden shrugged. 'Sometimes they don't want to talk to me, so maybe I should say *some* birds. The dye is from a plant. Next time I see some, I'll make it for you too?'

Theo touched his cheek and laughed. 'I've always wanted a coloured beard. A green one would be amazing. If you can teach me how to do that, I'd love it.'

I felt the tension in my shoulders begin to loosen. I hadn't expected Eden's revelation, but Theo took it so well I allowed hope to fill me a little more.

'Okay,' Zora stood next. 'I suppose I'm up now unless Theo has anything he wishes to share?'

Theo shook his head. 'Not really. I do snore pretty loudly. Who am I sharing with?'

'You and Eden are in the slightly bigger cabin. We may take on more crew in time. For now, you have all the space.'

'I stowed the spare ropes in one of the bunks. We have about as much room as you now,' Eden said. 'I didn't want them sliding around the hold and knotting.'

'If we are doing demonstrations,' Zora continued, waiting for our attention. I watched the others as much as her. Eden was grinning widely; clearly, they knew both what she was and what she could do. Theo leant forward, his hands resting on his knees as he stared at Zora intently.

An expanding ring of flat, calm water extended around us.

At its periphery, a wall of mist rose, until we were cocooned in a dome of fine droplets. A rainbow formed as Zora set it to spinning, and the sun caught it.

'It's beautiful,' Eden breathed. 'That's the biggest one I have seen you do.'

'It's amazing,' I said. 'Theo, Zora is a—'

'Sea Witch,' he replied, a wide grin splitting his face. 'Zora, every time I've sailed with you, we've had smooth seas and a fair wind. I'd just put you down as a good luck talisman of sorts – a lucky captain. This is so much better than luck! I am honoured to be trusted with your confidence.'

'Theo, how are you accepting all this so easily?' I asked, amazed at how relaxed he was, how well he took it. Zora had chosen him well. He was, after all, just human.

Theo smiled. 'Because I am a child of the water; a soul of the sea. I grew up in a flotilla, born to a sea-folk family on a boat, and fully expect to die on a boat. As a child I played with a southern siren, and as an adult, heard fin-folk sing. So, yes I believe in the Old Ones, as do all the sea-folk. Seeing the truth of Zora and meeting Eden validates everything I have always known in my heart. The Old Ones are still here, living amongst us. I have always been sure they were. I just hadn't found them.' His face lit up and he gesticulated wildly with every word. Rather than fear, or prejudice, happiness rolled off him. It was contagious and I felt the nerves building in my gut release their grip.

'Have you ever met a selkie?' I asked, when I felt I could trust my tongue.

'I think so,' he said, looking into the distance. 'Once, I went to a small island far north of here. There was a pod of seal pups on the beach, and I tried to get close. A herd of adults rose from the water and chased my boat away. I wasn't trying to harm the pups, but the coordinated way they worked – I'd never seen that before. It was different. Their voices were different.'

'You never met one in their belegged form?' I asked.

'Belegged?' he shook his head. 'That's an odd choice of words. All humans have legs. Do you mean without their skins?'

'Would you like to meet one?' Zora asked him, throwing me a wink.

'I would,' Eden interrupted. 'I hear their sexual appetites are quite legendary. They would take on our patron for voracity.'

I inhaled saliva as I tried not to laugh.

'Sorry. That was a vision I didn't need.' I spluttered, trying to rid unwanted images of Sal's sexual exploits from my head. Once my composure was regained, I continued. 'I'm glad you believe in the Old Ones, Theo. My family believe many are being held captive, even as their captors spout urchin dung in public about how science is everything, that there is no magic, and never was. We seek to return the guardians to their home regions and repair the damage caused by humankind. We particularly hope to locate a missing white hind – a guardian of the wild, without whom, much of our world will be permanently destroyed. Our first mission, however, is to attempt to recover a siren. We believe it's a leathergill.'

'They're enormous if legends hold any truth, and after the last few minutes, I'm inclined to believe them,' muttered Theo, rubbing his beard as he spoke. 'You were right, Georgie. This is a crew I'd have begged to be part of.'

Zora tilted her head towards the almost empty cargo hold. 'We have enough space,' she replied.

Theo stared at the closed trapdoor and shook his head gently.

I pushed on, aware that we could not sit here all day and conscious my disclosure was still to come.

'It is a two-stage rescue. First, we return her to her previous captor, where it appears she was content – if not happy. Once that's done, Sal hopes to uncover the whereabouts of the lost hind. Without her, the land her sister protects is dying. The trees will soon start dropping. Many others rely on that area, both Old Ones and wild animals. A single guardian is not enough. The wildlife is turning more feral, less inclined to listen to the gods. Nature's rules are being broken.'

'I can understand the need, but why is Lord Sal putting this in motion? Paying for this boat? Why *your* family?' Theo pushed.

Eden and Theo were both watching me now. Zora reached across and gave my hand a gentle squeeze.

'It's got to be now, Georgie,' she said.

I lifted my chin, trying to ignore the hammering of my heart and dropped my glamour, exposing my pointed teeth and true face to them.

'If I ignore the teeth, you are quite beautiful,' Eden said. 'But please, put it back on. Theo is having difficulty speaking.'

I replaced the glamour.

'That explains a lot, sort of,' Theo eventually said. His hands shook, and he had shuffled back from me. 'Your teeth are scary. Georgie, what are you?'

'I'm a selkie, as all my family are.'

'I didn't like that feeling.' Theo wiped his palms on his trousers. 'I wanted to own you. It made me feel a need to possess you. That's not who I am.' He stood and walked to the rail, to stare out over the water.

'Yeah sorry, that's the problem.' I replied. 'But, it tends to have worse implications for me than you. And, it's far less intense than anything a siren would elucidate in you. It's easier to hide my real face with a glamour, and less messy this way, in case I want to eat you.'

'Fish balls, no selkie has ever *eaten* a person. Have they?' Theo span toward Zora for confirmation. She shook her head and chuckled.

Eden was staring back toward Safe Harbour. 'Georgie, does that mean that Lord Sal is also a selkie?'

'It explains his interest,' Theo rumbled. His hands had stopped shaking, and he turned to rejoin us.

'It explains why he exudes sex,' Eden said, a smile twisting at the corner of their mouth.

'Now the introductions are finally over, shall we get on with teaching me to sail properly?' I asked. 'We have about a week before Sal gives us a direction and tells us to go. By then, I need to look like part of this crew to anyone observing us.'

They sauntered back to their positions as I watched. This felt right – the boat, the crew, and the task. We'd get that siren out of Prince Ulises' palace somehow. Then hopefully, Sal would get wind of the real prize.

6

A WINDOW TOO HIGH

SELKIE

With the sailor dead, I returned to my room feeling utterly broken – I'm not ashamed to admit it. See the skin. Find the skin. Go home. Sadly, it wouldn't be that simple. I was foolish to think it might be. Now I had no plan. Where in all the world's oceans was the skin now? That man, Jake, I reminded myself – I needed to remember that name in case I ever got out of there – I would need to hunt down where he'd been, search the places where he might have hidden it. *If* I ever got out.

I was certain he'd taken it for himself, maybe to trade it again? It was clear that he had never planned to give it to Icidro; he'd defrauded us both. Icidro had only lost coin and bragging rights, but I had lost my freedom – twice. Icidro had proven a powerful enemy to make, and a fatal mistake.

In the first days after the sailor was killed, I let myself swim in pity. I drowned in it and allowed it to flow through my veins. Then, I let it out and prepared to move on. I reopened my eyes to the world around me and began to search for a way out. I looked after my fellow captives whilst hunting for a chink in the household routines. I was reliable and did my job well. Eventually, as humans tend to do, they closed their eyes to me. I was no one special anymore – I merely existed. My room and the tanks were all I saw. Even our food was brought to a small room adjoining the tanks, our lingering fishy odour meant that we weren't welcome amongst the other staff.

My small room was at the end of a long corridor. It was tiny but private, a small sanctuary of peace in a claustrophobic world of human creations. There was no decor in the staff halls, no glaring lights like the main chamber Icidro received me in. Here, all the light was channeled down from skylights or struggled in through dust-covered high windows. In my own room, I was lucky enough to have a single, low window that I could see out of, even if it was barred. I often found myself sat on the chair as I brooded, gazing over a sea of rooftops belonging to the small town beyond our high walls. The only reminder of my home in sight was a fish shaped wind spinner atop a tall roof. My chair had one leg shorter than the rest and wobbled – I didn't mind, its rocking motion soothed me. The only other items in my room were the bed, a box for my clothes, and a small number of belongings.

When the sun was up, if I wasn't working, I would search for a way out, imagining routes across the rooftops and dreaming of freedom. There was no gate to the town, just a blank patch of ground between the house and the wall, a dead zone of withered plants and dust. I was a prisoner in this grand building. The only way out would be via the water, which meant that I needed to keep trying to strengthen my legs and swim while I worked.

I ate and worked in the tanks. I even slept in them on occasion, seeking a semblance of familiarity or comfort on shifts when I knew no one would disturb me. I moved in and out of that room as regularly as the tide. I'd noticed early on that my body clock was very different to that of the humans in the building. I worried that they might notice, but they are blind to the world.

Nature's rhythms elude their senses. The gods gave humans the abilities of invention and science, yet took away their capacity to exist outside their own minds. Maybe it was nature's check – to limit the spread of their noxious habits. If it was, it had failed. They'd grown too clever, altering the world we all shared and making it theirs alone. Yet, under their noses the wild continued. Rivers ran and tides flowed, unchanged, unabated. Only when the world fought back did they finally notice. But by then, it was too late – for them. Their deaths were a beacon of hope to all of the Old Ones, to all of nature on this planet.

Now, they lived in small numbers, clustered in settlements, for humans do not fare well in a world desperate to remove them. There weren't that many left, surely? Someone somewhere had to know where the skin was.

It took a few days of self-pity before the obvious struck me, and I was furious with myself for not having realised it sooner. The sailor had a boat. There was a slim possibility that Eryn's skin might still be on it. I tried to convince myself that Icidro wouldn't have already searched it, that maybe he'd believed me entirely. As he had not appeared triumphantly, bearing the real skin and claiming me, it was a sliver of hope I could cling to.

On the return journey to my room that night, I tried every window, and found them all locked. All that is, except one too high to reach without help. Stars shone through its dusty glass as fuzzy points of light. If I dragged something under it, then maybe I could reach the sill, pull myself up and get out. It was near the ceiling, so maybe I could get onto the roof. It wouldn't be impossible. A small smile crept across my face as I searched the hall for something I'd be able to drag. My room wasn't too far from here, up a small set of steps and at the back of the building. It was usually quiet around now, and if necessary, maybe my chair would work.

I considered it for a brief moment. I'd have to leave it there, letting the entire place know someone had climbed out the window. Maybe I could leave something with it – a book! I could make it look as though it had been taken there for the light.

Distant snoring floated through too-thin doors. From a passage nearby, the grunts of fucking humans echoed. Their enthusiastic search for pleasure would cover my footsteps.

The search for an object that I could drag at a more opportune time took me past their door, each step accompanied by culminating grunts loud enough to wake the dead. I smiled to myself. They should sleep well after that, hopefully well enough to allow me to keep exploring. I could smell a faint waft of salt water in the air and quickened my steps. If there was a door, I might be able to slip out. If the boat was there, and my skin was in it, I'd be gone by sun-up.

My heart hammered in my chest as I reached the end of the hall. At first I thought it was a dead end, then, I noticed the small set of wooden stairs leading down to a door. I placed my foot gingerly on them, waiting for a creak to give me away. Nothing happened, so I continued slowly. I was halfway down when I heard a voice call out.

'Who's there? Willow on the water.'

What was that supposed to mean?

I shrunk tightly against the wall, gently shifting my weight through my toes to move silently down the next step. So much for sleeping it off.

'No-one's answering,' the voice hissed.

Although I couldn't understand the muffled voice inside the room, the one at the door was clear as a rock-pool once the tide had gone out.

'I don't know! Should I risk it?'

Another muffled reply.

'Okay, I'll see you tomorrow, lover boy.' The ringing of boots against the stone floor told me that they were coming my way. I had nowhere to go now, except out. My palms sweated – a useful cooling mechanism in my seal form, it was simply frustrating when belegged. I gently gathered as much magic as I could, holding it close in case I needed it. I had no real idea what I would use it for. I could hardly make myself look like a wall. Still, it made me feel a little safer.

Footsteps closed in as I reached for the handle. My hand slipped. I wiped it quickly on my leg and tried again. It turned, and I hurried through, pushing it closed and checking it would open from outside in case I needed to get back in. I stumbled out into darkness, night-blind after the brightness of the house. Carefully, I edged along the wall, ducking under a window and heading for the front of the building and the dock. The moon was high in the sky; it must have been close to midnight. Did they have guards out the front all night? No voices floated over the water, no boots marched nearby. It was as quiet as I could have hoped for.

I ran towards the water as a pool of light spilled from the door I had just exited, then the light disappeared. I glanced back to see a large silhouette filling it.

I'd been found, but it was too late to turn around now. I reached the corner of the building where it met the water-front. Here, darkness was banished by bright lights mounted high on the wall. The carved guardians on either side of the entrance looked even more deformed when illuminated from above. The whole frontage was so well lit, that the moment I stepped forward, I would be visible. I tried to stay in the shadow, studying the vessels tied alongside.

There were two, the big, three-hulled one which I had arrived on, and a smaller, single-sailed craft tied alongside it. There was no one else in sight. I took one last look around and ran for the smaller boat.

'Oh no, you fucking don't.'

I felt the knife in my back, and stopped abruptly. I was grateful for its point, that meant it wasn't a gun. It didn't mean that he didn't have one. Icidro's woman swaggered around wearing hers on her belt. I knew what it could do now, and I had kept clear of her since. I tried to twist, to see who was behind me. Urchin dung, he must have come from inside the entrance. I took a deep breath and tried to force myself to relax. My only goal was to get home alive. If I was badly injured, I'd have to split my energy, and I doubted I could maintain this glamour and heal. For tonight, I had a win. The boat was here, I'd found a way out, and I could get back to it another time. How difficult could it be to sail when the sea and its moods were part of my very being?

'Don't do what?' I asked, trying to keep my voice steady and calm. My hands were sweating again.

'Whatever stupid thing you were about to do.' His voice was deep and gravelly, like he had eaten a bowlful of mussels filled with sand. It was very slightly slurred. I hoped that meant he was more relaxed than he might otherwise be and decided to push ahead with a story.

'I was getting river grass for the mirror carp,' I blurted. 'It's looking really unwell. And, it's Mister Icidro's favourite this week.'

'You needed it so badly that you were running, in the middle of the night, at high tide?' His voice rose in pitch. I mentally kicked myself, of course – I'd struggle to reach any grass at this time.

'I couldn't sleep with worry.' I'd started with this story, and now, no matter how ridiculous, I was determined to stick to it.

He dug the knife in, and the point cut into my flesh. A warm trickle of blood ran down my back like a crab nip – a warning not to get closer. A warning I heeded.

He leant in close. I felt his hot breath on my neck. Short, sharp breaths, nervous or excited.

'I don't like your ugly face, which is lucky for you tonight. Turn your scrawny self around and go back in whatever door you crawled out from. Mister Icidro is going to be a whole lot of pissed off if you get drowned collecting grass. I hear he was swindled out of a lot of money for you.' He shoved me towards the water, and I stumbled.

As I regained my balance, I looked around quickly. The roof overhung the water at the mid-point of the building, although the entire frontage below it was lit. If I could get on the roof, above the lights, I could get in the water.

'Please, I need the river grass,' I begged. Why on earth had that been my choice of cover? I could have chosen a million and one other reasons.

'No way am I letting you pick your own,' he sneered. 'Alvas, get the stupid cow some grass.' A slim man slunk out from behind a stone guardian and wandered to the water's edge.

'Alvas do this . . . Alvas do that . . .' he muttered as he reached into the water. With the water this high, he was struggling to reach any at all, and his disgruntled tirade continued. 'Sea cow. Maybe that was the problem. Jake didn't sell a selkie to Icidro. He sold an ugly bitch of a sea cow who needs grass at midnight.'

Gravel-voice shoved me again. I wanted to smash a fist through his face or bite him, but biting felt wrong in this form, so I held back. Showing my teeth was not a move that would end well for me. Alvas strode over, his arms drenched and a glower on his face dark enough to eclipse the moon. He shoved a handful of dripping river grass at me.

'Go eat the grass, sea cow,' he spat. They both took a step back, allowing me to return to the building. *I need to get home, I need to get home.* I repeated to myself, biting back a retort. *Need to get my sister's skin home.* Jake. I had a name. A boat I couldn't get to – yet – and a name.

I walked slowly back to the door, hoping that the owner of the shadow had returned to their room. I pushed it open gently.

'I've been waiting to see who was slinking around in the middle of the night.' Icidro's woman said as she leant against the stairwell wall. She looked down at me. My hopes sunk.

'Most girls try escape on the first night or within the first week. I'm surprised it took you this long.'

She didn't appear to have the weapon on her, but even without it she was far stronger than me. She was shorter, it's true, but she was solid muscle, and I'd already seen how little she valued life. Her body reeked of sex, and her eyes were hooded with post-coitus relaxation.

'I should take you to him,' she said.

'But you won't?' She looked relaxed, and I hoped that disturbing Icidro would be too much of an effort.

'Not tonight. Go, take that dripping mass of grass to wherever you were headed. Bloody idiot girls with your strange village habits. Fuck knows why you chose to tell them you needed grass. I suppose it's more plausible than "I needed a walk," which is what they usually say.'

Her arm snapped out, and she grabbed my wrist, drawing

me close. Her fingers dug into my flesh so deeply that there would be a mark tomorrow. I let out a yelp and dropped some of the grass.

She yanked me up the steps, letting go as suddenly as she had ensnared me. I dropped to the floor and scrabbled for the grasses. Now I had begun this lie, I was going to see it all the way through.

'Next time, I'll do more than just warn you,' she laughed, stepping over one hand and planting her boot on the fingers of the other as I grabbed the last strands of grass.

'Oops, did that hurt. I'm so sorry.' She laughed, grinding the heel as she lifted it off. She turned and stared back at me one last time before she strode away.

I hated humans. I hated it here. Easing my pain with a gentle flow of magic, I flexed my fingers carefully. Thank the gods, nothing was broken. Instead of returning to my room, I meandered back towards the tanks to put the grass in with the mirror carp. At least they had benefitted from my misadventure.

7

DEATH IN THE FAMILY

GEORGIE

Zora and I secured the sails while Eden coaxed our quietly humming motor to life. It was a grey sky, grey sea kind of day. One of those mornings that, when you look to the horizon, you can't see where sea ends and sky begins – perfect for a stealthy approach to Prince Ulises's residence. I stood, stretching out the muscles in my back as the brisk wind whipped my hair into my mouth and the waves into a short chop.

Sea spray rose high into the air adding to the light mist. Zora took advantage as we drew close to the cliffs – redirecting it to blur *Black Hind* and hide our presence from casual watchers.

The buildings perched precariously on the cliff top were a myriad of colours, each gaily shouting their presence to the world. Some were so close to the edge that after centuries of slow erosion below them, they remained in place solely by the sheer will of their stones. The largest, and our destination, sprawled across its own headland like a limpet sat atop a rock.

Sal had advised me to sail past the headland. On its western side, I would find a private beach affording us access to the cliff top. A long and winding path wound away from the beach, eventually reaching the opposing headland, where flashes of light reflected from the polished stone walls of a building hidden within the surrounding trees.

Sal kept many secrets, and secrets have a habit of slipping loose when unguarded. I wondered what Sal had over the reclusive owner of this beach and whether by sunrise tomorrow, they might come to regret their generosity.

Black Hind slipped into the cove. Theo pointed out the cave, and we turned towards it; our passage erased as Zora smoothed our wake to match the natural waveforms of the bay.

With Theo and Zora occupied, my eyes strayed to Eden, who stood with feet apart, staring at the clifftop. I watched as Eden rose both arms skyward, narrowing their eyes at a flock of gulls that rode the winds above us. The keen eyesight of a gull would be immensely helpful if we could persuade one to scout the layout for us.

I watched the birds carefully as they spiralled upwards, but nothing changed, and none of them flew our way. Maybe it would take longer than before. I kept watching, both fascinated and hopeful.

A fluttering thud on the deck made me jump. I turned to see what had landed and was greeted with a large heap of black feathers croaking unhappily.

'Not quite what I had in mind,' Eden sighed. 'But, it will have to do.'

The huge cormorant shook his wings out and waddled

across the deck, snapping his beak at Eden. I'd have stepped away from the irate bird, but Eden crouched to meet it.

'He doesn't look too happy with you, Eden,' Zora chuckled, turning to glance at the bird.

Theo studied at it too, a deep frown creasing his forehead, and he stroked his beard as he stared at it. 'It's a bit conspicuous. I mean, how often do you see a cormorant cruising above your house?' he asked.

The cormorant changed direction, its head tilted. Green, shining eyes stared at Theo's toes, where they poked from his sandals. He backed away, keeping his hand steady on the huge rudder to keep us heading towards the back of the cave and narrowly avoided getting his toes pecked.

Eden made a gentle cawing noise, and the cormorant stopped pursuing Theo, returning instead to Eden's side and allowed itself to be stroked.

'One willing bird is worth far more than an entire flock of grumpy gulls,' Eden observed. 'He's going to fly overhead a few times today, covering different directions and areas. By nightfall, we should have an idea of where we are going, if I can translate the findings.'

'We'll stay tucked into the cave while the bird scouts,' I said. 'No one except the bird leaves.'

The bird departed, and I went hunting for food. Shoals of fish darted through the water, and the clear light at the cave entrance sparkled from their tiny bodies. I dived into the shoal, trying to herd them into a ball. It was a fun diversion for a while. Eventually, they began to scatter and I let them go, grabbing a couple of stragglers before they all darted for freedom, then hauled myself out onto some rocks to eat my prize.

'God's above and below, Georgie.'

I looked up to find Eden staring at me from the deck,

mouth agape. They started to chuckle, and I heard the footsteps of the others coming to see what was so funny.

'I honestly thought you'd put your skin on to go swimming. I was not expecting – that!' Eden said.

'What?' I asked. I really didn't see the problem.

Zora emerged from the cabin. Her laugh echoed around the cave when she saw what Eden was pointing at. 'Sal is the same. You'll get used to it.' I tore a bite of flesh from the fish as she continued. 'Eating raw shellfish and whole animals with apparently normal teeth?' She grimaced. 'A naked selkie. I can cope with, but I can't get used to that. Georgie, can you eat further back in the cave? No cormorant is going to come in here while you deconstruct that fish like an apex predator.'

I spat out a bone, then dropped my glamour and gnashed my teeth playfully at them before diving into the water with a fish clenched tightly in my fist.

I'd returned to the deck and dressed before our new cormorant friend called across the bay. His dark plumage gleamed in the fading light as he skimmed the waves, rising up to land on the deck at the last minute.

'You didn't happen to bring a fish back with you?' Eden muttered. 'He's hungry and wants food before he'll communicate.'

I pulled a fish out of my pocket and handed it over. We needed whatever the cormorant would tell us. I could always catch another.

'Umm, thanks.' Eden chuckled. 'I wasn't actually expecting you to have one.'

'I like being surprising.' I grinned. 'Let me know when you two finish your chat.' I climbed below deck to find Zora. She was resting with a well-read book, its pages bent and creased so many times that its top edge was narrower than the rest of the book. I watched as yet another paper triangle lost its tenuous hold on the page and instead made a bid for freedom, floating to the floor. Zora huffed and folded the bottom corner up instead. Placing the book on the table, she gestured in Theo's direction. His snoring resonated around the hull.

'I told him to rest up,' she said between the rumbling snores. 'Whatever Eden finds, we need Theo to be awake and alert tonight. You un-glamoured is enough to cause him problems, and we expect to return with an adult siren. He needs to be ready to get us all away fast, and awake enough to keep his eyes away from trouble.'

Zora was right. As much as I'd have liked Theo's steady hand and calm manner up in Prince Ulises home, we needed our escape prepared. If the siren decided Theo was prey, it would make an already difficult mission worse.

Eden rushed into the cabin, flapping their hands in a fluster. 'Paper. Paper quick, before I forget the details.' I looked to Zora's book, but she narrowed her eyes and thrust a pencil and a few sheets at them from a pile I now realised she had been writing on.

Eden started to sketch immediately. Quick lines crossed the paper, their style clean and clear. I leant over the table, fascinated as boxes connected to rectangles. A map. Eden scratched their head and added more detail to one section. 'I can't quite remember this bit, but I don't think it's important.'

As we stood around it studying the layout, Eden explained what each shape represented. We were interrupted by the thudding of something tumbling down the steps. Eden clutched at their head. 'That hurt, bloody bird!'

'You didn't do anything,' I protested, but Eden was still rubbing their head.

'The cormorant won't get out of my head. If you check the stairs, I think you'll find the feathery mass at the bottom is him.'

'Who dropped a bird?' Theo wandered out, rubbing sleep from his eyes before peering at the paper. 'Ah, we have a plan then?' he asked.

'Not yet, but we will by the time it is dark,' I muttered, still staring at the map, trying to work out how we could get into the animal collection.

'It's definitely there?' I asked, glancing at Eden.

Picking up the pencil, Eden drew in a long snake-like shape in one of the enclosed areas. 'It's either a leathergill siren, or something else I desperately don't want to meet on a dark night,' they said.

About an hour later, we scrambled our way up the cliffs. My unpracticed muscles burned with fatigue as we neared the clifftop. We'd chosen our entry point, and Cor – as the bird had been nicknamed – had confirmed there was a door there. Cor had refused to leave the boat with us, so eventually, we left the stinking, wet, and bedraggled bird at the table to keep Theo company.

'He'll be gone before we get back, I'm sure,' Eden muttered, not sounding at all certain.

The cliff was steep, and if it wasn't for my lack of fitness and climbing experience, I'm sure it would have been easy. I hissed under my breath repeatedly as I struggled with uneven footing, made worse by the sight of my companions climbing swiftly ahead. Eden made the incline look as easy as a swim in a calm ocean. I struggled up after them, determined to be worth my place in the crew for more than just my species.

We were almost at the top when my foot slipped. I kicked out for a foothold and knocked a few small pebbles loose. The echoing rattle of their descent cut through the quiet night air like a knife.

'Did you hear that?' The speaker above was heavily accented.

'It'll be them shags landing on the cliff again. Don't worry.' A second voice, louder and booming echoed around the cliffs – this was not a voice I wanted to hear calling for backup.

'Shags, hah! Stupid name for a bird. What's cooking tonight?' accented man asked.

'How the hell would I know? With the King arriving tomorrow, whatever they rustle up today will be crap. They'll save all the good stuff for the weekend, as usual.'

I froze, balanced on a single leg at the steepest part of the ascent. Zora and Eden had flattened themselves against the cliff; their contours no more obvious than the rocks. Footsteps closed on us, thudding vibrations running through the ground as the speakers approached. Grateful that Zora and Eden would not be caught out, I quickly threw a large shadow over myself. It was huge, but as far as a glamour goes, very simple. If they knew the cliff face well, it wouldn't fool them. The darkness was our closest ally.

The feet stopped, as did my breathing. I held still, willing every muscle to hold its place.

'Told you, nothing there! Come on, we've still got at least an hour of our shift left.'

An hour. We had our window. As the footsteps receded, I refocused myself. It was time to climb.

I dragged myself over the lip and belly-crawled to Eden and Zora, now hidden in a clump of bushes.

'New plan,' I whispered. 'You heard them. We have an hour. If Cor's right, then we need to get through this gate and two

more spaces inside. Those two confirmed Sal's intelligence –
that the King is due tomorrow, so most people in here will be
preoccupied and distracted tonight.'

We crept closer to the entrance. The guards were restless,
pacing and muttering in discontented tones. I listened carefully to work out which was which. Even at that distance, the
bigger man's voice was clearly louder. He needed to be taken
out quickly.

'I'll take the one on the left,' I said. 'You two deal with the
one on the right.' I wriggled closer, using tufts of tall marram
grass as cover.

The big one should be an easy target. I slid a loaded needle
into the blow-tube and lined up my sight. He walked the same
pattern over and over, looking like a caged animal.

As he reached the apex of his arc, I let the dart fly.

A moment later, he swatted his leg. My practice had borne
out. Contrary to Zora's repeated admonishments, I *could* hit a
target at forty paces – well, thirty five, but who was counting?
A few steps later, his footing became unsteady, and he crumpled to the ground.

From my vantage, the shadows of Eden and Zora slipping
along the base of the wall were glaringly obvious. But the
distracted guard rushed blindly to help his fallen colleague.
Zora closed him down, then held a cloth over his mouth. As he
fell unconscious, Eden tied them both carefully, and they
carried them to the wall, lying both men gently on their sides.
We weren't here to kill any more people than necessary – an
accident, that was our brief.

I reloaded the pipe, slipping the cover over the end, then
joined them.

'Where next?' Zora whispered.

Eden pointed towards a narrow doorway. 'In there somewhere is a way to the next outdoor space, where Cor

showed me rare animals and a large pool containing the giant snake.'

We hugged the wall, reaching the small door with no further problems. The stench of cooking food and spices filled the air and turned my stomach.

'It smells awful in here, come on.' The coolness of the metal handle seeped through my skin as I pushed it downward, expecting to be stopped any moment by the resistance of a lock. It opened and we slipped inside, a small creak from dry hinges the only giveaway that we had left the courtyard.

The sudden plunge into light stopped us all for a moment as the bright artificial lights made me squint.

'There goes my night vision,' grumbled Eden, shielding their eyes.

'How in the Gods' names are we going to get a siren through this passage?' Zora spread her arms to gauge the width as she shook her head. 'I don't know if we can do it.'

Footsteps sounded ahead – that was the last thing we needed, being seen so early. I steeled myself to take them out, temporarily.

As soon as she rounded the corner, I shot the woman with a dart. By the time she reached us, her hand was limp and refusing to grasp whatever she sought to retrieve from her pocket. She collapsed at our feet, and Eden dived forward to cushion her head from colliding with anything.

'Georgie, we can't carry a house full of people with us.' Zora sighed as she studied the collapsed woman. She wore cheap clothes, a uniform maybe. She would be missed at some point; our timeline just got even tighter.

Eden scooped her up. 'Let's put her in a room or somewhere safe. Hopefully, she won't be missed while she sleeps this off.' Zora pushed hard at the next door on our left, and it opened, revealing a small cupboard filled with cleaning supplies.

Eden gently lowered the passed out woman to the floor.

'She's pretty small, I hope she survives the dose,' I murmured as I checked her pulse. There was one, feeble but regular, so I was confident that she would live. Yes, we had been seen, but maybe she would forget that in a haze of confusion when she woke. I tucked a pile of cloth under her head and closed the door.

A few moments later, we found ourselves at the base of a wide staircase ascending into the night. A dark, wooden door bound in ornate metalwork blocked the way ahead.

'It has to be through there,' Eden said, striding forward to try the handle. It was locked.

'I guess we're taking the stairs then.' Zora gestured to them with a shrug and led the way. Eden followed close behind. I sidled up last, keeping an eye out for further unwanted company. A breeze lifted my hair as we emerged into the night, the three of us crouching as we crept close to the edge.

'We've found her.' Zora breathed.

We stood atop a viewing gallery. Exotic creatures occupied small prisons below us. Many large predatory creatures prowled their perimeters, snarling. Their entire attention was focused on the man at the centre of the collection. His broad back was toward us while he was engrossed with the creature in the large, water filled enclosure. His hand stroked his swollen cock as he gazed upon her long, white body. The siren's skin glistened like an iceberg, her strong muscles rippling as she moved sinuously in front of him. He moved his hand faster and faster while she writhed beguilingly.

'Seriously?' Zora said. I could hear the exasperation in her voice. 'She's trapped. Why is she wasting energy encouraging him?'

The man was lost in his own ecstasy now, as the siren sang her lure in time with his movements.

Her head snapped around. She looked directly at me. In the midst of her song, she called to me with the voice of the Ocean. A roaring tide of feeling poured through my body carrying her voice in its wake.

'Get me out of here!' The siren stared at me, even as I tried to remain crouched.

I called back to her. 'What do you want?'

'His head.' In our shared language of ancient Ocean, I could hear the hiss of hatred, the hunger for death. Ocean allowed expression of primal emotions far more effectively than any human tongue. 'I want to eat this evil, tide-crawling, stinking barnacle that stole my life.'

Throughout our exchange, she worked him harder and eventually, the man's body convulsed. It took him a moment to realise that the siren was no longer dancing. Slowly, he turned towards us – his trousers still open. He reached for a gun; I hadn't seen it before, and it was too late now. He raised it towards me, his hand still quivering. The barrel of the gun was unsteady as he tried to gain control. The lights in the collection illuminated his face clearly, and the twisted grin, the cruel expression truly gave face to Prince Ulises' true nature, unmasked for us in that brief moment.

'Shit!' yelled Zora, flattening herself below the low wall and tugging at me to follow suit.

Instead, I stood tall and dropped my glamour as his finger moved to pull the trigger. He jerked his arm to the side, hatred quickly replaced by greed. A slow smile spread across his face.

'A matching pair,' he slurred, walking towards us, his trousers dropping as he walked. I gestured for the others to remain below the wall, but Eden couldn't resist a look.

'He's drunk. He's going to trip,' muttered Eden.

The events that followed unfolded so quickly, we could merely watch in shock.

He tripped, and as his finger gripped for purchase on the only thing they held, he pulled the trigger. The bullet hit the glass on the siren's enclosure, spidering a weakness across the panel in front of her.

The siren saw her chance and threw her considerable weight at it. The sound of smashing glass echoed through the night, a thousand shards falling like icy knives to the floor around her as they ricocheted from her scales. She emerged from her prison with her maw fully open, then reared up and descended on him from above, her jaws snapping clean through his torso. Blood poured from her mouth as she crunched down on Prince Ulises with obvious relish.

'Can we leave now?' she asked me as blood dripped from her mouth.

Eden was already clambering down the stone wall toward her. They crept closer, avoiding eye contact, and carefully negotiating the lethally sharp floor.

'I need to get something from the body to get you out.' Eden said. 'Don't eat any more of it.'

The siren eyed Eden curiously and asked, 'food?' I sent violent disagreement back, and she lowered her head. Eden searched the trousers of the Prince's remains, eventually raising a triumphant hand bearing a key.

'Come on.' Eden gestured for the siren to follow them. 'We'll meet the selkie at the door. It's a tight squeeze and you'll have to be careful.' The siren slithered across the collection behind Eden, unbothered by the glass or the trail of blood she left behind.

We ran downstairs to meet them. Eden came through first and stood boldly in the doorway, blocking her passage. It was brave and foolish, given what we had just watched. The siren still wore a necklace of blood, shimmering on her scales like gemstones.

'Where do you want to go? We will take you there.' I spoke in Ocean. At this point, there was little to be gained by keeping quiet, but we may as well hide our final destination from any hidden ears. I was certain we'd have company any moment now.

The siren looked deeply into my eyes, her own spinning, gem-like, reflecting the light from their many facets and gently replied, 'I want to get home to my friend. Then, I finish my art. Once my art is complete, I wish to return north. He promised freedom when I was ready to return home. I wish to honour his care with a completed deal. He sent you, am I right?'

It couldn't be better. In fact, it was almost too good to be true. Something – other than the siren – smelt fishy here. But with the likelihood of running into more of Ulises' people at any moment, we had to take her at face value.

'We get out and we get down the cliff. There is a boat waiting.' I replied.

'Let me go first,' the siren sung. 'He was not the only one who would debase himself in front of me, and I am still hungry.' She squeezed through the passage ahead of us, her bulk filling much of its width.

'They can't see her like that at all, can they?' Zora said wonderingly. 'They just see a woman.'

Eden nodded. 'If I squint, I can make her out. Come on, it saves our magic stores if she does the work. It may even look as though she escaped alone, dependent on who we meet.'

'I'm not about to stop her,' Zora muttered darkly. 'In fact, I can't say I blame her at all.'

We followed behind the siren, occasionally hearing a scream and crunch as she bore down on someone. The floor became slick with blood, and we followed as closely as we dared.

Finally, we emerged into the entry courtyard. Only one more set of guards to pass before we left this cliff top drowning in a sea of blood.

It was not to be. Weapons held high, three more shadows advanced on us. We emerged from behind the siren, and Eden pulled a gun out in retaliation.

'Where did you get that?' I asked.

'The floor.' Eden shrugged. 'Thought it might be useful. Can you take any down with your blow dart, Georgie?'

'Am full, no room to eat more.' The siren sighed. 'These ones are yours, sister. The small one looks tasty.'

'Thanks, but I prefer fish.' I raised the blowpipe and aimed at the largest. He took two steps towards us and crashed to the ground.

'Take the left.' I shouted as I broke from behind the siren and ran at the crouching woman now leaning over a still-twitching body. A woman . . . even if Prince Ulises had tried to keep the siren a secret from his staff – which I doubted – she would see that true form right now.

She turned too late. I leapt on her back, wrapping my arms around her neck. Gods, Eden had better hurry up. I flicked my wrist back exposing the needles, and delivered a full dose of the octopus venom into her throat. A shot rang out – too close. My victim fell to the ground, and behind me, someone fell.

Zora screamed.

I rose slowly to find the third attacker standing with their gun a hand's width from my head. His hands white-knuckled as he readied to pull the trigger again.

'What did you do to her?' he asked through clenched teeth.

'I killed her, and I'm going to kill you.' I dropped the aspect of my glamour that protected Theo from my pull, with my heart pounding fit to escape my chest and sweat beading on my hands. It was enough to make him pause.

I could see Zora moving around Eden's collapsed form from the corner of my eye. The siren sat bloated and sleepy in the middle of the courtyard, her initial thirst for revenge dampened by her full stomach.

I stepped forward, darting my hand towards his wrist, with as strong a grip as I could manage. He looked directly at me, confusion rippling through his features, uncertain for a moment.

'Or are you going to kill me first? Here's a dilemma,' I hissed as I tried to wrestle the direction of the gun somewhere else. 'You've never killed a person before, have you?' My partial reveal was working, uncertainty and fear rolled off him, and his scent reeked of adrenaline threaded with greed.

He pushed the gun back towards me. Strength was not in my favour right now. I glanced to the side and raised my other palm at Zora to hold her off.

'Want to live or die?' I tried to goad him, to draw his attention back to me. It worked until he glanced down at the corpse between us.

'Live.' He gripped the gun harder, and wrenched it from my grip.

'Good call,' I said, trying to resist the temptation to lunge at him. 'But then, you might talk.' I'd reached back inside his guard now. My needle hand so close to his arm that it would just take a little flick . . .

His eyes glanced to the two bodies and hardness returned. My spell broke.

'But first I'm gonna kill—'

I stepped back and ducked.

Crack. He crumpled, blood pooling around him.

Zora stood protectively over Eden, the gun in her hands and blood streaks on her face from trying to stem Eden's blood loss. 'We need to move, fast!' she called. I ran to them and carefully tucked the needles back in my sleeves.

Cor flew overhead, calling out in distress as he circled Eden.

'Use the witch,' the siren said. 'Can she not just drop a water cushion? Northern witches are very adept at water cushions. They are fun to play with. I might need a water cushion to get to your boat.'

Cor flew off again.

'Well, we know he's off the boat now,' I said, frowning over the siren's suggestion.

Eden groaned. A pool of blood was forming around their leg. Someone else would be out soon, surely. A huge siren sat in the courtyard could not be ignored for long.

'Could have been worse,' Eden said. 'But, I can't walk. I'd die for a set of wings right now. Have sent for help. Need rest.' Eden flopped back to unconsciousness.

'Tourniquet and run time,' Zora said, pulling her shirt off.

'Bite here, please.' She held it out and I ripped a section where she indicated. She pulled it apart sharply, splitting the fabric along the weave, then tied it quickly around Eden's thigh and pulled it tight.

'Can you carry Eden for a little?' she asked the siren.

'No. I don't carry humans. Which way?'

I slid my arms under Eden and picked them up. They were lighter than they first appeared, despite being a deadweight. Together, we ran and slithered out the gates. The original guards still slept where we left them. I had planned to untie them, but with bullets flying, there was no way this could be blamed solely on the escaping siren now. They might as well stay tied up. At least that way, they wouldn't be able to look over the cliff and see us leaving.

It took us a few moments to struggle behind the cover of the bushes at the top of the cliff. The siren stared at the drop intently.

'I can jump,' she said. 'It's no higher than an iceberg.'

If we let her leave without us, we ran the risk of her swimming off. But, with Eden critical and no other way down, we had little choice; I hoped she really did want to return to her paintings.

'Our boat is in the cave below. The only person on board is a human male,' I said. 'Don't eat him – without him, we will not be able to return you.'

'Too full to eat now. Will hide until you get there. I will wait. I want to keep my promise.'

'You know you could just swim free now?'

'Yes. But I will be hunted for this. I want to live. I will hide for a while first. It is worth it. The other home was nice. Kind. The human never did anything like this one did. He just likes my art. I will see you at the boat.' The last notes of her song faded as she slithered to the seaward side. We watched with awe as the silvery arrow dropped from the cliff into the sea, vanishing with barely a ripple.

'We freed her. Now it's her choice.' I whispered as much to myself as the others.

It was dark, we could see nothing, and we had no way to lower Eden.

'Could you do it?' I asked Zora.

'A water cushion? I have no idea what she means. I've never seen anything like that,' Zora replied. 'Isn't there anything you can do?'

I desperately wished there was, but I was a poor climber.

Zora was much stronger than me, selkie legs are not known for their muscle.

'If we can get Eden down to that ledge half way, then you build a really tall wave, I think I could keep Eden afloat while you dropped us.' It sounded stupid as soon as I said it. 'I'm sorry. That won't work will it? Water doesn't come from nowhere, and we still have to get Eden down.'

'I could raise the level some way.' Zora's voice carried a note of panic. We truly didn't have long. Any second we both expected to hear the sounds of organised pursuit. Voices rang out inside now, carrying on the wind. 'But you will still have to jump,' Zora added.

'If we jump together – holding Eden?' Storms, I just needed to shut my mouth.

'That has my vote. I don't think my help is coming,' Eden gasped, briefly aware of the conversation. 'Those poisons you carry. None of them stop pain by any chance?'

'Sorry.' I wished desperately that they did, but it was a terminal, final end to pain. 'Start building your tide, Zora.'

Zora furrowed her brow in concentration, and the tide began to rise on our side of the bay. Water moving, against all reason, upward to form a standing wave. If I leapt from the headland now, I'd comfortably survive the jump. Eden remained conscious and sat up.

'Sorry,' they said. 'We'd be away by now If I hadn't got shot.'

'We did it. Whatever happens now, just needs to be fast.'

Eden nodded and pushed to their feet. 'Agreed. So, we hold hands, jump and then you drag me to the boat. Is that the plan?' Eden looked pale, and the offered hand was clammy. The wave was a long way up the cliff now, I couldn't see how Zora could make it much higher.

'I'm ready when you are,' I said.

Wingbeats bore down on us as a trio of enormous white

birds grabbed Eden. They flapped frantically as they dropped towards the sea, somewhat slower than falling from a jump. Cor followed behind, shrieking at them as they fell.

Eden was dumped into the water away from the cliffs, and a silvery body rose beneath them.

'I won't carry, but I will support,' the ocean voice roared up.

Zora gently lowered the wave.

'I don't want to cause a travelling wave anywhere,' she said. 'I suppose that was the help? Maybe Cor can stay. Come on. We need to start climbing down and fast.'

Zora stayed close to me so I could cloak us both, and we worked our way down the cliff under a blanket of shadow. By the time we finally reached the base, my limbs shook with the combined effort of cloaking our presence and climbing. I swam into the cave with Zora's support.

Theo's voice reached us as we started to clamber aboard. He reached down and grabbed me by the wrist, his own clothes soaked. 'I found Eden,' he murmured. 'Washed up on the beach in here. Thought you'd all been chucked off the cliff. I could hear the shouts. I've treated the wound and put them in bed to sleep it off. Did you find the siren?'

'Yes. Theo, if you struggle to look at me, you are really going to struggle with her. For your own protection, I am going to blindfold you.'

'Sure.' He shrugged. 'I've seen them before, but it was an experience that leaves longing in your soul for years. Could do without that right now. Eden needs our attention.'

I wrapped his eyes and led him to the winch for the door to the storage deck.

'We are all a bit done in, can you wind this for us?' I asked.

Once the door was open, I called the siren aboard and she slipped quietly into the lower deck. The boat now sat low in the water from her weight. We closed the doors and unmasked Theo.

'Are we ready to go?' he asked.

I collapsed on the deck next to him. 'Yes.'

Zora gathered her last burst of strength to create a small cloud of mist around us as we slipped out of the cave and into the night.

SOLE HEIR

LADY GINA

'I have business up north. *Barge* is yours for a week or so.' Sal threw me a sea anemone. I caught the juicy morsel in my teeth and bit down hard. A salty explosion filled my mouth, my tongue tingling as the stinging tentacles discharged.

'This lady cannot be bought with tasty treats alone,' I replied, crossing my arms over my chest in imitation of a move I had seen Seren carry out many times, and stifling a laugh.

'No? But I imagine that she can be bought with new, fashionably flat shoes.' He grinned widely and drew a pair of flat-heeled, black boots from behind his chair. Ornate embroidery ran up the front of each – sea holly intertwined with a slender-stemmed, pink flower from the Terranian coastline. They were gorgeous.

'Beautiful and practical, if a little hot for this weather.' I turned them, watching as gold thread caught the light. 'Thank you. I consider them acceptable payment.'

Sal smiled back as he reclined in his chair. 'I've asked the crew of *Black Hind* to be on standby for you if necessary. I received urgent information that my contact has news from Jake's crew, as well as suggesting he has information on our quarry – for the right price.'

He was leaving me in charge, in title if not in reality. A fizzing of excitement grew in my stomach – maybe that was just the anemone.

'I can manage as long as Seren is here.' I tried to reassure him. 'Everyone will expect me to be left in change at some point. What use is the heir to an empire of sexual gratification and information dealing if she is unwilling to take charge herself?' I pulled the boots on to test them for fit, pretending that I hadn't noticed the colour drain from Sal's face. He pushed himself from his chair. 'Gina, I didn't mean you had to fuck the clients yourself!'

'I know. A sullied bargaining chip has little value.' I shrugged and stood to test the flexion of the soles. He had the grace to look shocked as I pushed on. 'I know you're only courting these idiots for money and information. I need to be seen as a viable choice and you as a respectable father – if one who continues to take his pleasures wherever he can find them. I don't have time to be dealing with fragile egos right now. These are really comfortable, thank you.' I tested them out on a stroll to the tank, eyeing up the contents as I decided which snack to choose next.

Sal paced the room. 'I expect that you will hear from Prince Anard. Our price remains a favour; I hope to have more details on what that will entail once I return.'

He stopped abruptly. 'Whilst I asked the *Black Hind* to be ready for you, I also suggested that they hide out. The loss of Prince Ulises has left his father incensed. I understand the staff were rounded up for interrogation to discover what kind of creature could have broken his son in half and left a swathe of blood and devastation behind them.'

'I still think it is strange that she wanted to return to Anard,' I muttered.

'Love has many forms.' Sal shrugged. 'Did she leave to help him gain a crown? Or does he have something of hers that she was desperate to get back? We'll probably never know, and if I'm honest, I'm happier not to. Now, I need to be on my way, and you need to be seen. Go, and get some food.'

He was right about both – he usually was – but it didn't stop me wondering about the siren as I wound my way down to the Ocean Bar. I wandered across it, lost in thought, trailing my fingers through the water of the low-sided central pool and sank into my chair.

I was admiring the way that pulsing jellyfish around me gently illuminated my drink when Seren slid into the seat opposite.

'He's gone. You're the boss.' She winked at me before waving to the bar for a drink.

'No, Seren, as always you're in charge. I am merely a stand-in figurehead. Although, please continue to feed any gathered information my way.'

'What about the clients?'

'No, thank you. I fear my desires would be difficult even for *Barge* to fulfil,' I replied.

'Information only. Got it. What about trade?'

'Seren, you know them better than I do at present. I'll trust your judgement. If you think it would be beneficial for us if they were to meet me, then send them in here. I will sit in public rather than be alone with any guests. My father has worked hard on my reputation, and I won't risk damaging it. If they want a private meeting, they will have to return once Lord Sal gets back. What time do we dock?'

'Midnight. It's a thing Lord Sal does. We travel on the midnight tide of darkest, deepest desires.' She blushed, and I couldn't help but wonder exactly when he had said that to her.

We enjoyed a meal together while she apprised me of the clients likely to board in this small town, then I took the opportunity to return to my rooms before we docked. I closed the shutter, plunging the room into darkness, felt my way to the soft bed, and sank into its cloud-like comfort. From the briefing I'd just received, tonight might be long and exhausting.

I sat alongside Seren as we opened that night. The queue of eager guests awaiting our arrival ran the length of the dock. Seren welcomed each guest and extracted payment before allowing them to board. Some kept their hoods up, silently pressing the required fees into Seren's hand. She accepted both their coin and the hungry gazes studying her generous curves with obvious pleasure. Once aboard *Barge*, they were escorted to the tented pleasure courtyard, which had sprung up shortly before we reached the town. The thin, blue fabric rippled in the gentle breeze. *Barge's* deck smelt of sea air and jasmine as the clients boarded. By the time the clientele finally left, even the arches of white flowers would not hide the scent of sex.

I listened carefully to their requests. Some clients were brazen, happy to declare their intent, while others whispered. All visitors received the same level of courtesy from Seren. Here, your status ashore meant nothing. As usual, while many wanted the sexual gratification of our services, others just wanted a neutral venue for meetings. Some guests sought illicit drugs or supplies and we supplied them all with the release or privacy they needed.

As the queue dwindled to the last few supplicants, a figure hovering in the shadows near the wall of the dock caught my eye.

'Have you seen them?' I murmured.

'Yes,' replied Seren.

The last of the queue pressed their fee into Seren's hand, and wandered towards the tent to be paired with their desire as our mysterious watcher crept closer. They turned away before our lights could illuminate them clearly, retreating into the shadows. I turned to Seren, and she shrugged.

'I wouldn't worry. That's not unusual,' she said. 'Probably watching for someone boarding. They know we don't divulge any private details.'

The hairs on my arms prickled. Something felt wrong about that observer but I couldn't put my finger on why. The way they moved felt too furtive.

'I'll be up here until they all leave or get put in the cooldown hall.' Seren nudged gently. 'Go, down to the Bar. You need to be seen.'

The Ocean Bar was quiet, much as it had been earlier. A couple sat opposite me at a private table surrounded by tropical fish. Every now and then, one of them would point excitedly at something in the tank. The bar staff were busy creating exotic and multi-coloured drinks flavoured with rare spices and flavours. This evening, Cypress was the Driftwood amongst them – here to keep the peace should it be needed. He called over a greeting before ducking through the doorway to the kitchen. He was so tall, I wondered how he could blend in anywhere. The only person I had ever met taller than Cypress was Sal.

The bar staff lined up drinks on the counter for the usual flood of guests; our entry fee covered everything aboard, food and drink included. I had thought it a strange system at first, but had come to understand the wisdom of it. In this relaxed atmosphere, secrets spilled more freely.

Intentionally delivered information would often result in the guest being offered a free return trip if validated as true and useful to us. I'd seen Sal petitioned directly almost every time we docked. To this end, my own drink was lacking the alcohol enjoyed by our guests, even if it appeared outwardly identical.

Before long, a shadow slunk along the edges of the ceiling-high marine tanks. I tried to suppress a laugh. This was the least effective place for that to work. Where you hid from one side, you were lit from another.

They slid into the seat opposite, hood still up. Something familiar about the way the person walked struck me. I shuffled back in my seat slightly so that my raised knee could hit the panic button if necessary.

Then, they reached deep into their cloak and dropped a black, scaled tunic on the table.

'With thanks for a job well done,' Prince Anard said. 'As I am now sole heir to my father's throne, you did an excellent job of gifting me something much bigger. Although, your crew did leave rather more mess than I would have liked. I will now have to mourn in public and probably call for your heads should it transpire that you were involved.'

It wasn't a threat, merely a simple statement of facts, and I didn't fault him for that. He had a role to play in hiding his own part in the rescue.

'We don't get bought for advancing politics or personal gain.' I replied. 'We merely supply pleasures on *Barge*.

However, I am pleased we could assist you on this rare occasion. Is your artist near to the completion of her work? I hear she was keen to return to it.'

'She was. I am distraught that she has now informed me of a desire to return to her true home. She claims her painting is almost complete.' I could hear the shake in his voice. He knew what she was now, even if he could never see her that way.

'That will be a truly unique piece, I am sure,' I replied gently. Entranced or not, his heart would be breaking once again, and this time she chose to leave him.

He leant forward, and the tank lights illuminated the inside of his hood. 'Which brings me to the purpose for my visit.' His voice was steady again now, and he stared intently at me. 'Can you arrange for a boat to take her north in a few weeks time? Once the official mourning period is over, I fear my father will seek revenge. I want her well away by then, and she agrees.' He leant closer. 'I'd rather lose her and live my life empty-hearted, knowing she lives than him get his hands on her. I will double my fee.'

Two favours from a future king. 'Of course,' I replied. It still didn't sit quite right. Why did the siren want this complex route? Why not just swim north when *Black Hind* had rescued her? I plastered a smile across my face.

'I will see to the arrangements personally. Do enjoy the rest of your visit.'

'You'll need this to get ashore. I've tightened security.' He slid a sealed document across the table, then rose and left without another word.

Less than five minutes after he had departed, feet pounded on the deck above me. Panicked shouts rose, and the relaxed atmosphere was shattered. Seren burst into the room, gasping for breath.

'We're being searched. We've never been searched before,' she panted.

'By?' I gestured for her to continue.

'The King of Terrania's men.'

Of course we were. Sal had run off and left me with the biggest political maelstrom that had been seen in Terrania in the last hundred years. I fiddled with my sleeves as I tried to work out what they would be searching for. Surely they hadn't found clues to our involvement already? Seren frowned at me.

'Don't do that, not in front of him.'

'He's here too?' I felt my shoulders rising and took a few deep breaths, focusing on trying to create a calm visage.

'Yes.'

It was time to put on that show Sal had been talking about. 'Get me a drink – the most exotic looking thing you can concoct,' I called to the bar. 'In fact – make it two of them.' I returned my focus to Seren as a nagging thought surfaced. 'Did my other visitor disembark unseen?'

'I don't know. I really don't.' Seren's fluster was putting me on edge. She needed to calm down and fast. 'Make it three,' I called. 'Is everything that should be hidden, being hidden?'

'Yes, but I don't know how long we can keep it up for.'

'We don't know what he wants yet. I want you behind the bar, where you can hear me, please, Seren.'

Our drinks shimmered with a rainbow of iridescence in the dim lights.

'They are perfect, thank you,' I said to the barman. I slid one to Seren. 'Thank you for the warning.'

She smiled shakily and gulped a few mouthfuls. 'I'll take it with me,' she said and wandered over to the bar, issuing orders as she went. The couple watching the tropical fish were moved further away as I awaited my uninvited visitor, and the barman slipped into the kitchen to be replaced by Cypress. This meeting would prove whether I was considered the heir to Sal's empire.

I didn't have to wait long. A half-dressed man was shoved down the stairs by some wary, gun-wielding men.

'Put those away in here, please,' I said, rising to my feet. 'For your own protection. Should you accidentally break a tank, the likelihood of you being killed by a venomous creature is exceedingly high. I am sure you would not wish to injure your employer either.'

They waved them toward me instead. *Idiots.* 'Who's speaking? Who is that?'

The dim light of our table afforded me the privacy for my hands to tremble slightly for a moment. That was all I allowed myself.

'We want to see Lord Sal,' the gun-wielding leader shouted across the room.

'I am afraid my father is away on urgent business. I am both his ears and mouthpiece. What you have come to discuss with him can be discussed with me.' My voice was steady. I raised my chin a little; it would not do to look at all cowed in this king's presence.

'Ahh, The infamous Lady Gina. Hidden child and famed already for your beauty, although your wits remain untested.' A man pushed through the protective ring encircling the exit. He looked so much like the Fish Prince that I had to look more than once to see the tell-tale wrinkles of age.

I gestured to the seat at my table and slid one of the drinks across. 'I took the liberty of pre-ordering your drink,' I said.

'What if you have pre-ordered my death?' He stared at it suspiciously. I'd heard about his paranoia and cursed inwardly that I had made the mistake of not letting him see it made.

I took a straw from the bar and sipped a mouthful from his glass. 'Is that sufficient proof for you?' I asked. He nodded and installed himself in the seat facing mine.

'Step back, please, I speak to The King alone.' I waved at his minders. They muttered amongst themselves for a moment until, eventually, the King himself turned around and gestured for them to move back.

My heart was hammering, but I had faked calmness and compliance for so long I could do it backwards. I slid back into my seat.

'How can we help you?' I inquired.

He looked over his shoulder, his fingers tapping out a rhythm on the table. He opened his mouth to speak, then closed it again. Eventually, he whispered, 'Do you believe in the Old Ones?'

I laughed. You should not laugh at a king, I realise, but the irony of the situation was just too much. I quickly grasped hold of my emotions and lowered it to a chuckle.

'Why, Your Highness, surely you don't believe in that sort of legend?'

'I don't know that I have a choice,' he said. His narrowed eyes staring intently at me. My mirth stilled. I positioned my knee against the button, hovering just below it as I leant in towards him.

'What do you mean, you have no choice?' I took a sip from the drink to hide the flutter in my gut – to steady my nerves. He wouldn't ask if I believed in myself, surely. Unless he had some information? Unless he was here to catch me.

I flicked a glance at Seren – she was poised. Apparently casual, but I knew that she and several others could be here within moments. The room behind her would be bulging with Driftwood by now, ready to swoop me to safety.

'I have reason to believe one of the Old Ones killed my son.' The admission tripped off his tongue lightly for a man who had loudly proclaimed the fallacy of magic to all who would listen at every feast day.

I feigned surprise. Prince Anard was right to worry. 'No! tell me more.'

'Witnesses, a few women, say he had recently captured a huge serpent for his collection, others – men – claim he had caged a beautiful woman. The accounts do not match up, even from his own staff. Then, there is the thick train of blood that followed his death. He was found in his own collection' – The King shuddered – 'severed in half. There were footprints too. Prints of people and gunshots. Someone else was involved both in the release of that creature and its escape, maybe they were also eaten. A witness to the raid can describe at least two of the group.'

'Why do you tell *me* this?' I asked. Having descriptions of *Black Hind*'s crew in circulation was worrying. I reinforced my glamour subtly to minimise the chance of him seeing the worry I knew would crease my brow, drew a slow breath, and exhaled gently before taking a sip of drink, wondering whose descriptions they were. Then, I pulled myself back into the moment as the King continued.

'I understand that my other son was on board earlier. He was seen boarding this vessel.'

Anard must have boarded with the rest. I'd assumed that he had used a private deck. That was a foolish move on his part. It was time to up the charm and distance ourselves from him. I tried to flash the King what I hoped was a bright smile.

'I would not deny any guest our pleasures, Your Highness. Sadly, as far as I am aware, he departed almost immediately as we did not have the person he desired aboard *Barge* today.' I leant across the table and whispered, 'Should I detain him the next time, Your Highness? I did not realise you were coming, and I am sure he didn't either, else surely he'd have been delighted to see you.'

His eyes scanned my face searching for something. My glamour was carefully reinforced, so he should see none of the emotions that flickered beneath the surface. Still, my skin prickled under his inspection. Abruptly, he snapped his head towards the bar.

'Get me another of these,' he called to Seren. As she walked down the bar to find the ingredients, he took advantage of the increased privacy.

'I didn't think Anard had the balls to put to use here. Maybe there is hope for him yet,' he muttered. 'Find me that bloody siren. I want its severed, serpentine head on a spike over my gates. Put out the news that there is a bounty on all Old Ones. I don't care if people think I am insane to believe they are real. I know what my own eyes saw, what the evidence says. Nothing human made that mess. As for my useless son, hiding in his island retreat, I doubt he will ever give me an heir, but I swear my line will not end with him. There's life left in me yet. I *will* have another son. And, when I do, you will spirit him away to wherever Sal kept you safe from my spies and eyes. For it must be the safest place on this continent.' He sat back and crossed his arms, his eyes flashing with barely suppressed anger.

'It was not of this sea or this continent,' I said truthfully. 'As for your other requests, I will endeavour to use all resources at my disposal to locate a mythical creature and free it from the bonds tying it to its current mortal situation.'

'I'm telling you, it's real!' The words flew across the table in a carriage of spittle, his cheeks flushing with the combination of alcohol and rage.

'You have my promise that I will treat it as such. I would not doubt the words falling so genuinely from your mouth,' I responded carefully. 'There is, however, a small matter of payment?'

He growled now. The flush deepened, and silver-streaked black curls on his brow bounced with each word he uttered. 'The payment is my not destroying *Barge* and the viper's nest of secrets and poisons you spread. The illicit nature of your business is well known, Lady Gina, and I could close you down with a single breath.'

I glanced at Seren. She'd heard him and shook her head gently, subtly signalling a lowering of hostilities was needed, but I was not about to capitulate Sal's legacy on the temper tantrum of a bereaved king. I sat up straight, trying to emulate Sal. Had we been standing, I would be taller and look down on the King. I spoke gently as I constructed a reply.

'Your Majesty, you could indeed close our access to your ports. However, I would remind you that you do not rule over us while we are at sea and *Barge* is not registered with any port that you own rights to or rule over. Mere threats will not pay for the risk my crews will take in hunting a beast as vicious as you are describing or the costs incurred in caring for a child until it is of such an age that you wish them returned.'

'You are in one of my ports now!' he retorted.

'True, however, it would be but a moment's work to cast off and be in international waters. I can do it from here.' I waved my hand in a pattern that meant nothing to a corner where no-one stood, and the King's head snapped around to look.

'He's already gone,' I said. 'He will ready us for departure. So, tell me again about the payment you are offering, before you are stranded on my floating kingdom in offshore waters and very much outnumbered.'

'Are you threatening me?' he hissed.

'Of course not. I would never be so crude. I am merely asking you to consider the terms of our agreement more carefully.'

A gun had risen from the holster of the man opposite me. He was sat on the table the lovers had previously enjoyed.

These people really didn't listen. 'I meant my earlier warning,' I called. 'Shoot me, and your King will be dead. Every tank around me is filled with toxic creatures and this glass is far from bullet-proof.' My mind was racing as I spoke. This could be the exact opportunity we had been searching for – presented in gift wrap at my feet.

'Do you not think, Your Highness?' I asked, 'that if your son had obtained what you believe to be one of the Old Ones, maybe others also have dangerous, unpredictable and feral creatures in their own illicit collections?'

I slid the drink Seren passed me across the table. She gave me another, and I sipped deeply while the idea settled into his rage-addled brain.

I pushed my drink to the side and gestured expansively around me. 'I dream of owning creatures I do not yet have. Therefore, I ask you for a payment that is in your interest as well as mine.'

Seren was grinning widely, reinforcing my hunch that I was headed about this the right way. I hid my slightly shaking hand under the table while I took a drink. She gave me a nod, and I powered on.

'Make a survey of the collections into law. Force every

collection to be registered. We can keep your records here if you wish them to remain in neutral territory, in a special safe which only you have access to. That way, you can find out if there are other dangerous creatures that should be disposed of and potentially prove you are not mad in enacting this hunt for a myth. I would, of course, request both the contract for that termination work and the opportunity to select two creatures as payment for it. The first as payment for the life of the siren who killed your son and another in down-payment for the care of your as-yet-unborn heir.'

I sat back and waited, desperately hoping that he would take the bait.

'It would take a while,' he muttered. 'How do I ensure all creatures will be truthfully cataloged by their owners?'

I smiled. 'Send your own men to verify the list when you collect it. Send women too, in case there are more sirens.'

'You only wish for this? Surely, Lord Sal can obtain any creatures he chooses?' He gestured around and laughed. 'Your father will think you made a very poor bargain. On the other hand, I fear you speak sense. I have not slept since I saw my son's body, and if there are others out there, then more people will die. If the Old Ones exist, they are far too dangerous to be kept as pets – no matter how pretty. They are feral, old, less intelligent than us, and surely must work on instinct alone. If any remain, they should be eliminated.'

Drink had fully loosened his tongue, and the diatribe continued to pour out. I sat with a fixed smile, nodding and agreeing as he slandered every being of power that had safeguarded this world from the plague of humans as best they could. I listened, and I was deferential. I listened, though every fibre of my being wanted to plunge my needles into his arm. They held a slow acting toxin; the effects would not be apparent for hours. By which time he would be far away from me.

But I didn't. I struck the deal. Seren wrote it out, and we signed, by the light of the pulsing jellyfish, a document that would potentially give me access to everything we had been searching for.

9

SWEPT IN ON THE TIDE

SELKIE

Many days later, on a morning when my hand no longer looked like a collection of sea cucumbers, I woke from an unsettled night, deep unease following me into wakefulness and leaving me on edge. I spent the morning looking over my shoulder, searching for something that would justify this feeling that would not go away. Dreams rarely bothered me once awake normally, but the sensation I had been left with was a fish hook tugging at my soul. Something had changed.

By midday, I began to relax, having talked my paranoia down and convinced myself that it was all in my mind. I ate the crab-guts the humans called food and, as I did every day, returned to the tanks. The depressed creatures in them called out to me for succour. One day I planned to free them all, if I could only free myself first. Then, there was still the not-so-small matter of locating Eryn's skin.

I was in the fire squid tank when Icidro appeared. His

scent wafted ahead of him as he waded at the head of a personal parade. He escorted a tall, elegantly dressed man with waist-length black hair that hung in a glossy braid. Delicate fingers pointed at various jellyfish in the tank on the far side of the room. An assistant scribbled down a list as he scuttled alongside them, looking for all the world like the crabs around my feet. Then, the visitor turned towards me, and for a split second, I saw the glow. A light hint of magic shimmered across his face.

I paddled closer to the edge of my tank, being careful to avoid damaging the sea life and wary of the squid as ever.

He looked at me and smiled.

He looked at *me* and smiled. The man stood a step behind the merchant and once he was certain I was looking at him, he bared his pointed selkie teeth. The glamour realigned, and he carried on conversing as they strolled around the tank room. A selkie, acting as a human, buying creatures? He had seen me. He knew what I was. My mind whirled . . . would he betray me? My instincts screamed in confusion. Should I run or seek his help? I decided to try and gain help – even if he lived amongst them.

Icidro was taking great delight in pointing out the most unusual creatures he had collected, rare and treasured specimens, while the assistant continued frantically writing as they passed tank after tank, the selkie picking out creatures from each. They stopped for ages at the tank with the antarctic octopus inside.

Then, they reached mine. I had finished and was trying to look busy when the selkie asked to see an incongruous mollusc from the back of the tank. Just its shell was sticking out of a hole in the coral. It was a delicacy at home, and not eating it had been one of my biggest daily battles.

'Get it, girl,' the merchant said.

I grabbed it by the shell and prised it reluctantly from its cave. The selkie's eyes burned into my back. He laughed when I returned. It was out of place, forced, and I wondered at first what was so funny, but hidden in that laughter he spoke – two words.

'Trust me.'

He used the language of the ancient sea, of Ocean, and met my eyes with his liquid brown pools.

'How much for the tank maid?'

How dare he try to buy me? I was not an object any more than these animals were. I roiled at the suggestion, but he kept eye contact. Trust him, he had said. At this point I had nothing else to lose, I lowered my eyes as they discussed me.

'She's a bit rough for your tastes surely, m'Lord?' Icidro raised an eyebrow as he spoke.

'Not for me. She fits the request of a client I have with rather . . . unusual requirements. They like subtle deformities.'

'This girl is talented. The best tank keeper I've ever had.' He shrugged, feigning helplessness. 'I don't sell people anyway. That would be slavery. And, we are in agreement on the wretchedness of such a business, are we not? After all, every one of the residents in your pleasure barge is there of their own free will, are they not?'

The selkie pursed his lips. 'You will need to send one with my new acquisitions anyway. I am spending a lot of money here today.' He rolled the words around as he spoke, fattening the thought-shrimp for eating. Were the merchant female, he'd have been entranced. As it was, he was merely amused.

'You are spending some for certain. But not enough to send her with them. Nothing you have chosen requires that level of special care. I could not part with her . . .' He licked his lips greedily.

The pregnant pause was an opening. I was for sale, at the

right price. My skin crawled at the thought, but I stayed still, allowing myself to be bartered over. *Trust him . . .*

The selkie didn't hesitate. 'Then I will have two of the antarctic octopus.' He glanced around. 'And, your full stock of the jellyfish. I needed a new display tank anyway.'

The glint was growing in the merchant's eyes, his stench filling the room and starting to roll over the lip of the tank. 'How about some fire urchins? Or a shark?' he pushed.

'I'll take both. Can I have the tank maid now?'

'Yes. You can take her as a gesture of my faith in your repeated custom and to look after the exceptionally expensive shark you are buying. After all, what sort of merchant would I be if your purchases were to arrive damaged? We both want the same thing in the end. Do we not?'

The selkie sketched a bow and held out his hand. They shook. Icidro took the list from the assistant, scanning it with an ever-widening smile. The selkie's gaze flickered toward me. He gave a tiny nod before returning his attention to Icidro and turning to stroll from the room.

'It is done. They will be prepared for transport tomorrow,' Icidro said, then handed the list back to the assistant.

The selkie stopped mid-stride. 'No. They'll be transported today. I have the money on board – in cash.'

I dared to breathe again as I heard the selkie speak. If the tide was with me, I would be out of here today.

Icidro shrugged. 'Then today it is.' Let's go and celebrate this deal.

I busied myself in the tanks, not daring to return to my rooms, in case I missed the selkie coming back. I was elbow deep in a filter change when our supervisor came in. She held a copy of the list, and her eyes sparkled with delight when she saw me.

'Yer've been sold to the pleasure ship,' she sneered. 'Can't fer the life of me think why they'd want sumun as ugly as yer, but there's all sorts down south. Make yerself useful. We've to get all the creatures ready fer transport. The weather is good, so yer'll be going by sea.'

A large sling was wheeled into the room moments later, its sides carefully padded and with water running over it, collected below, and recycled.

'Shark first,' the selkie called as he strolled behind it. 'We'll need to get her in the sling then over the side. It's not going to be an easy manoeuvre.'

His team began raising arms of the hoist, working together like a true pack. I searched their faces, but none wore a glamour. They were disappointingly human.

'How do I get in?'

He was stood right behind me. I should have smelt him, noticed his motion, all the time inside these walls had dulled my senses. If he truly intended me for a pleasure ship, then maybe on the way there, I could escape. I had been practising as much as I could. Being shore-bound but near my family was a thousand times more appealing than wretched humans fucking me. I still didn't know if I could swim far belegged or how I would find my way back home. After all, I didn't really know where I was – only that it was a long way south of home.

'Round here, Your Lordship,' I said, gesturing to the gap between the tanks that led to the ladder behind it.

'There's no need for titles,' he murmured. 'Consider me your rescue party. My true name is Sal Deepwater. I promise I'll answer everything you are desperate to ask later. Right now, we need to get you out of here before Icidro changes his mind. Help me get this shark in the sling. She should be swimming free, not in this stupid glass prison.'

Sal Deepwater; named for his birthing, not his looks, so he was from the South Territories. I had no idea why he thought I needed rescuing. I'd have got out on my own, eventually. But I wasn't about to turn it down. The shark swam to us voluntarily, allowing us to hoist her out. I can't really explain why she didn't fight, but somehow she knew.

They wrapped her in the sling, and half the team left the room at a jog, pushing her between them.

'What else did I ask for?' he muttered as we climbed out of the tank. 'Does anyone have the list?'

'Fire urchins, antarctic octopus, all the jellies…' The list went on. It took us the best part of the afternoon to gather up all the creatures and transfer them to the various containers lined up waiting. Each transport vessel was carefully designed to protect fragile species on a journey to their new home.

'And lastly, one tank maid,' he said. 'Let's go. Do you have belongings you need to fetch?'

'Only the clothes I arrived in,' I said.

Sal nodded. 'Then, you will leave in them too. You are no longer in this employ.' He poked the badge on my arm, frowning as he did so. 'I think I may escort you to your room and back – just in case.'

He seemed unsettled as if he were expecting to have his deal broken at any minute. The agitation rubbed off on me, and I jogged to my room with Sal following close behind. He waited outside the door as I changed.

'Hurry,' he hissed. 'Something feels wrong. This was too easy.'

We rushed down the halls, reaching the steps. People were moving around down here, and we slowed to a walk.

'We need another way out,' he said abruptly, taking a
device from his pocket with a flashing light on it.

'Window?' I asked. We'd stopped under the high one. Sal
glanced around us. The hall was empty now. He ran at it and
leapt upwards, pushing it open and pulling himself through it
as gracefully as though he were swimming in water.

'You'll get better at legs,' he whispered, reaching back down
for me. I closed my open mouth – his motion had been so
fluid! 'It's flat once you are up here. Come on,' he urged.

I struggled up the wall, hanging from his outstretched
arms, desperately afraid that I'd pull him back in at any
moment – or someone would see us. I was gasping for breath
as I reached the roof and dragged myself over the window
frame, its catch scraping against my skin.

Sal quietly pushed the window shut.

Staring out at the familiar rooftops from an unfamiliar
vantage, I tried to identify the right direction. 'That way' I
whispered, spotting the tower flying its fish wind-spinner and
orientating myself. There couldn't be two of those, surely?

We ran up the roof to the next level. Here, it was entirely
flat aside from carved drainage channels. We worked across
the roof, staying as low as we could. Sal checked his flashing
light regularly. We reached the point where the building
projected over the water and crawled on our stomachs to the
edge.

I expected to see some grand ship tied alongside to transport all the creatures he had bought. What I actually saw first
was a rabble of men charging off the deck of a newly arrived
vessel tied alongside Jake's boat. That boat itself now swarmed
with men – not one wearing Icidro's green uniform.

A group of the new arrivals sprinted towards the mansion,
waving a selection of long, pointed implements and guns.
They headed for the main door, taking aim at the men either

side. I wondered for a moment if it was gravel voice and Alvas. Sal had been right. We needed to get out of here fast.

To the right was a large sea-going ship. It sat deep in the water, and the sailors scurried about the deck readying for departure. I recognised a few faces from their ferrying of the transport tanks all afternoon.

Sal pulled the flashing object out again and pushed a button.

A shout rang out from his vessel, and immediately the crew cast off, moving the ship out into the river, departing without us.

'That's the animals away and safe,' sighed Sal. He glanced at me and grinned toothily. 'We'll catch them up, don't worry, but first, we need to get past those men.' He pointed at the crews swarming Jake's boat. 'They're here searching for you. I'm sure of it.'

'Who are they? And why would they be after me?' I asked, sweat starting to bead on my palms. I needed all the grip I could get, so I focused on the things I could control as Sal replied. I was on a roof, above them, none of them knew what I looked like.

'They're Lone Jake's crew. Pirates who plague The Narrows of the Terranian Sea. Jake is their figurehead, although he often sailed alone. He was as paranoid as you could get when sober, never trusted anyone with his secrets. When drunk his tongue loosened.' Sal grimaced. 'That ignorant scum boarded my ship, boasting about having caught a selkie. It's how I knew you were out here somewhere. I had one of my companions fill him with alcohol and try to get more details from him. He spilt where he sold you.' His lip curled as he spoke. 'But we didn't find out the location of the skin.'

Eryn's skin was still out there then, and if Jake had been

boasting about it, then maybe others in his crew knew where it was. I paused for a moment before my hopes ran away with me. They were waving guns freely. There was no way any of that crew would just hand it over.

'He brought a black seal one to the merchant to try to pass it off as mine.' I whispered. 'Do you have any idea where the real one is now?'

'I'm sorry, No. But, news that he walked into Icidro's and never came out was already filtering down river when we docked.'

'So, they know what I really am?' If they all believed it, then maybe Icidro would doubt me.

'You can bet your urchins they believe you're a selkie, yes. If I know that greedy lump of rotten whale blubber in there, he'll slither his way out of it, and you'll have two sets of people hunting for you. We need to get you out of here.'

'But, they know where my skin is. I need it back.' The words flew from my mouth.

Sal looked at me intently. 'He said it was silver. You and I both know that skin is as much yours as this is your real face.'

I shrugged. 'I'll agree that's true, but I need it to get mine back.'

He raised an eyebrow. If I survived this, I knew the unasked questions would need answering. He glanced up river. 'We'll get it back. First, we need to get on that boat.' He pointed at a small red boat racing down river towards us. 'How quickly can you switch glamour?'

'I don't know.' I really didn't. I'd been wearing this face for weeks now.

'You're about to find out. Follow me, switch before you get on board.' He ran for the edge of the roof, leaping off the edge with a graceful dive.

Could I swim that far? My legs shook as I pushed myself

upwards. Traitorous legs. I needed to believe I could do this – a chance for freedom was worth the risk. I stepped back a little, then ran to the edge and leapt off.

Sudden motion from below caught my eye. A group of the sailors had remained aboard their ship, and our appearance on the roof had caught their attention. As I fell, a loud crack rang out. Something missed my head by a mere hand's breadth as I fell into the water. The cool, enveloping sensation of home welcomed me. Sal was waiting on the bottom with his glamour dropped and natural teeth on show. I flailed my limbs to try and control my motion, but their long stick-like shape was useless in deep water. It was nothing like swimming in the tank. I needed my flippers. Sal saw my struggle, reached over, and hooked an arm under mine.

'*Hold on,*' echoed through my head as he swam strongly along the bottom.

I struggled to hold my breath, and bubbles of panic began to stream from my nose. He must have seen, as he changed our direction, bringing me to the surface behind one of the boats, gasping for lungfuls of air.

Small rowboats were being readied to launch; already, green liveried servants poked along the river bed with a pole, moving the reeds aside to search.

'Breathe,' he whispered. I did, then we sank below the surface, resting on the bottom as he searched upwards. I began to struggle again, but this time he pressed his lips against mine and filled my lungs with his air, much as a parent would aid a pup on early dives.

It bought us the time we needed. The red hull of the boat slowed above us. He gestured to his own face, now clouded by the silt we had disturbed, and re-glamourised himself. I tried to do the same, then we rose to the surface on the far side of the boat.

'What are you looking for?' A female voice called across to the mansion.

'Escaped servant, nothing to worry about. Short dark hair, wonky eyes, skinny,' I heard an all too familiar voice call back. My night-time nemesis. My fingers ached at the mere memory.

'If I see them, I'll let you know,' the voice above us called out. Her voice was rich and powerful. She sounded confident and relaxed.

'Yeah, you do that,' Icidro's woman called back.

'They're talking shit,' another voice interjected. 'They had a bloody selkie and now they've lost it. Their boss is mad, and our boss is dead. If you know what's good for you, it's Lone Jake's crew you'll be telling of any strange women.'

'I'll be sure to remember that too,' our driver called back, then quietly she said, 'Hold on to the ropes. We're moving along before they get closer.'

I grabbed the rope dragging from the front of the boat, wrapping it around my wrists several times. As we picked up speed, a wave broke over my head. I gasped for air whenever I could – eventually flipping onto my back to try and reduce the volume of water going up my nose. In this form, I could do no more than flow with the waves as kelp trees do.

We travelled downriver until the water grew salty and waves began to slap at the hull.

'Selkie express, all aboard,' she sang out as she cut the engine. 'The things I do for you, Sal! Do those fools really think selkies exist?'

Sal laughed and hauled himself out of the water, as a beautiful woman reached over the side to help me aboard. Her rich, brown skin was the shade of sea-smoothed driftwood decorating the shore after a spring tide. Her face was framed with a cloud of shining, black curls. She smiled at me, and it felt as though the sun came out.

'Hi, I'm Zora. Glad we could get you out of there. Sal tells me you are a distant relative.' She stared at me appraisingly. I had gone for a change in eye colour and a crooked nose this time, my teeth hidden under a more natural glamour. I was still imperfect, deliberately unthreatening.

She glanced at Sal, and a gentle smile tugged at the corner of her lips. 'I don't see much resemblance, except that you both look like you could use a good meal. Strap in. We have a long way to go and a boat full of rescued animals to meet.'

She pushed the throttle forwards, and we left the estuary and Icidro behind.

10

RECOVERY

GEORGIE

Cor rode the bow like a figurehead as we sailed for Old Town. Shimmering, black feathers fluttered in the breeze as he spread his wings. Eden hobbled around the deck, checking rigging and testing winches. It was good to see them up and about again, despite being less nimble since the shooting a few weeks ago. Theo had drawn the bullet out and stitched Eden back up. We'd used the tiniest dose of antarctic octopus venom to help Eden sleep as Theo worked, and it appeared the healing was progressing as well as any of us could have hoped. Although my selkie magic meant a slightly improved healing rate, Eden had no such bonus with their abilities.

Eden's vibrant green hair had been toned down to a simple brown braid after we'd heard the descriptions of those suspected of involvement in Prince Ulises's death. Given our destination, we needed to be careful. Dye had been procured from *Barge* for Eden while Zora had also changed her look. Her halo of tight curls had disappeared, and an intricate pattern of braids now swirled around her head. She saw me staring at it and smiled. I blushed, embarrassed that she had caught me out.

'Do you like it?' she asked, raising her hand and stroking the patterning.

I did. 'It's beautiful,' I replied. 'I didn't mean to stare, only I have never seen such intricate patterns created with hair before.'

'Eden did it.' Zora grinned. 'Maybe they can do yours too?'

I shook my head. 'No, it's beautiful on you. I would look like I had skinny eels writhing around my head, not a goddess.' I swallowed my words too late, she heard, and her smile widened. Zora walked away with an extra spring in her step. That woman always seemed to loose my tongue. I sighed in resignation and turned towards Theo, who held us steadily on course toward the island; he chuckled.

'She has that effect on us all, Georgie. It's no bad thing to speak your mind. Talking of which, how do you plan to get our large and seductive friend aboard with all these fools chasing her?' Theo gestured widely around us.

He had a point. The sea teemed with boats, as it had for days now. Like a shoal of mackerel, they twisted and turned, searching for the rumoured siren. News of the King's bounty had broken, and every sailor in the sea wanted a slice of money or prestige. Boats of every conceivable size took to the water. Surely they did not expect to capture, or even battle, a full-grown siren with some of these small boats.

We passed one crew full of women, their gunwales bristling with weaponry. Small wonder that Anard had asked for a quiet removal of the siren. If she flipped a single sail-like fin in this sea, she would be riddled with holes within moments.

Our specially adapted hold would get her safely out of the Terranian territories. Once we were much further north, in cooler waters, she could swim under our escort.

As we neared the port, it was even more evident that removing her through the main harbour under cover of darkness was not going to work. The luxury of her peaceful, artistic lifestyle was over. This truly had become a rescue mission, of life or death.

'How are we going to get in?' Eden asked, staring wide-eyed at the number of vessels. I didn't think *in* was the problem. What we needed to work on was out, and for that one of us needed to meet Prince Anard.

I wanted the crew away from sight, our boat inshore for the least time possible. As much as my face tended to slip the mind, we had planned for *Black Hind* to slip past notice as well. 'I'll go,' I said. 'Anard doesn't know me, and I can switch my appearance on the way in and out. Theo can't risk meeting her. We know she wants to get out, but he needs to keep his mind on the job, not his cock. You two can't set foot off this boat at present, Eden. Descriptions of you and Zora are being circulated far too widely for comfort.'

Eden nodded slowly in agreement. 'Let's say you can get in. How will you get her out? Escorting her up that slope in pitch darkness was bad enough without an audience.'

I had a sudden thought. It wouldn't be quiet, but it was the best plan I had so far.

'We're going to cut her out.' All three of them stared at me as though I'd lost my mind. 'Look, the prince doesn't want anyone knowing he has or ever had, a captive siren – especially now. He is going to need to get rid of the suggestion that her room was a captive location.'

'So, you want to take that glass wall down?' Zora glanced towards the top of the island.

'Yes, then the room looks like an outdoor pool, and he gets her past this flotilla by a side route,' I replied.

'A huge, silvery siren falling from the cliffs will still draw far too much attention,' Eden muttered.

'Not if there is a sea mist. How big an area can you raise?' I asked.

Zora's eyes were wide, and as she inhaled sharply. I realised I may have asked for something too big. 'Locally, I can hide us, possibly a small section of cliff, but that's going to look really obvious. I can't cover the whole island. I'm only a half-breed, remember.'

'You'll have to do what you can. Zora, you raised a tidal wave! You can do far more than you realise. That was a huge volume of water.' I hoped she could. If not, we were back to no plan.

She shook her head, 'Yes, but just in a small area. It's the range that's the problem. You want a small whirlpool, you got it. But want one over a larger area . . . it's only a fifty-fifty chance.'

'Hold up, did you just say you could possibly make a whirlpool?' I asked. Maybe the distraction could work. 'How far from us can you do it?'

Zora pointed at a wind patch on the water. 'About as far away as that.'

It was far enough from our ship that we wouldn't immediately be sucked in, but we'd still struggle to escape. Maybe I needed to speak with Prince Anard first.

Once ashore, the quietly enveloping nature of Old Town relaxed my senses. The siren-hunting sailors had encroached no further than the waterside taverns, the residents retaining the sanctity of their seclusion. A pair of guards stood by what appeared to be a hastily erected barrier on the steep cobbled ramp into Old Town.

I sauntered up to them waving a cheery hello; they looked as bored as I was nervous. 'Appointment with the Prince,' I said, waving the document I had brought from *Barge*. They took it to check the seal, then one stepped aside while the other opened the gate.

'The gate remains closed after sundown,' he said. 'We'll keep an eye out for your departure.' He gestured me through while his colleague held the gate, ready to close it should anyone make a rush up the ramp. He appeared tense, his eyes searching the water.

I reclaimed my papers and jogged through the quiet area of town. Once I reached the intact houses, I tried to wander along quietly, keeping my eyes on where I was going and resisting the urge to look around me.

At the main gate to the palace, a black liveried guard was propped up against the wall. 'Whaddaya wan?' he slurred as he tried to stand upright, with little success.

'I have an appointment with the Prince about a special commission,' I replied.

'At this time of day?'

I nodded furiously. 'Particularly because it is this time of night.' I held up a glowing vial of plankton I had scooped from near the hull. 'It's a special pigment he requested for his artist. I'm to prove that it does indeed glow before he orders any more.'

'I'll go 'n' call 'im.' Schtay 'ere. Wha' did you say y'r name was?'

'I didn't. Tell him it's the pigment he asked Lady Gina to acquire.'

He smiled at the mention of Gina's name and wobbled off. Security might be tighter down at the dock, but Anard's house guards were clearly not taking his fears very seriously.

The other guard walked more confidently. No scent of liquor drifted from his breath, and he narrowed his eyes under the artificial lights as he stared at me.

'He did say he had ordered something special from her. We were hoping she'd deliver it herself. But, what with her being a lady, I s'pose she can't be wandering around at night in other people's homes.'

'No, I am sure she couldn't be caught doing that. Not with her reputation to preserve.' I shrugged. 'On the other hand, some of us have no reputation to sully.' I laughed – with him, I hoped.

He chuckled. 'It takes all kinds of people to keep *Barge* afloat.'

I hoped a silent acceptance would stop further conversation, so I stared down the hill towards the fountain, its illuminated waters exposing a late-night tryst. The guard's eyes roved hungrily over me. If he thought I was one of the courtesans, he'd be in for a nasty shock. I deliberately shifted my stance to lean against the gate and attempt what I hoped was an absent stare towards the area I needed to reach. Those solid doors hid the most wanted creature in the entire Terranian sea right now.

I needed to persuade both of them to cut that glass out and somehow do it without an enormous shattering noise that would attract every boat in the vicinity, or else Anard needed to have a plan of his own.

The swishing of tiny scales drew my attention to a new arrival. He rushed across, extending his hand in greeting.

'Lady Gina promised she'd send help once the mourning period was over. Thank you for attending me so urgently. You are indeed prompt with my—'

I held up the glowing vial. 'Your paint.' I bowed deeply. 'Would your artist like to appraise it for its suitability, do you think?'

His grin tightened, and by the dim lights, I watched his shoulders slump.

'You are right. We should go and check with her before I order more.'

I followed him, watching his posture for a change, a suggestion of tension or sudden movement. But there was none. He drooped like kelp exposed to air. This was a man broken.

He closed the door, and the siren slithered towards me.

'Hello again, sister. Is it time already? Then let us be on our way.' She turned to the Prince and gently rested her head on his shoulder. 'He has been kind to me,' she said. 'He has shown no desire to be inappropriate. Will he be safe?'

'That depends. If we can get you out of here without anyone seeing you, then yes, maybe,' I replied. 'The sea is teeming with shoals of boats all searching for you. Although you could engorge yourself on them, there are so many, that eventually, one would kill you for what happened at the other palace.'

'Why? He was bad. Every species weeds out their own.' She radiated indignation.

The Prince turned towards the area she had been and gasped, then crossed the room at a run. By the time I caught up, he was gently reaching out to touch a patch of fresh paint.

'What's this creature?' he asked. 'I've never seen anything like it. It has a strange and powerful beauty with the shimmering scales. You've painted it so that this creature almost shines from the wall. But those jaws. That power . . . I fear the answer, although I suspect I know it.' He turned to the siren slowly. 'Why did you draw this?'

'My love,' she said. 'That is me.'

He looked at her with desperation etched across his face, begging her to change her answer. 'No, you cannot be that. You are the most lovely person I have met. I knew you were a siren, despite not wanting to believe it. But in all the pictures, all the paintings, they are as women.'

'All painted by men no doubt, who wished to boast of escape,' I muttered as I stepped back, trying to give them some space.

She again rested her head on his shoulder. I wondered what he saw, what he believed he felt. 'I am no person. I am Siren. You love me, yet with no desire. That has been both new and interesting. You have let me paint, and you have kept my waters icy cold. But now, I am weary. I need to go home. I need to swim amongst the ice. The vision on this wall is my home. Thank you for letting me go.'

He looked at me. 'If she is truly a siren, do you see her true?'

I nodded. 'She is more beautiful than that picture depicts. Her scales shine by moonlight like precious gems, and her eyes are hypnotically beautiful, ever in motion. You have been accorded a privilege few men ever are, in having a siren as a companion. Now, we need to get her out of here.'

He sighed. 'All this I understand, although it doesn't make it easier. Getting her out however, we can do easily. These flag stones cover an entrance to one of the many ancient tunnels that run beneath Old Town. They've been here for more than a thousand years. Over time, many have been lost through collapses, and they are mostly forgotten about, except by those of us who live here. They were both shelters and escape routes – a whole network of subterranean tunnels. I have always kept the one from my home intact. In case I ever needed to flee . . .' A frown crossed his face. 'Return to your boat. I will guide her down to the shore where you can collect her. Then, please take my love to safety.' He glanced back at the siren. 'Will my beautiful siren fly free? Will you promise to deliver her to the ice she has asked for?'

'I already did when I took this task on.' I was stunned by how well he handled the whole situation with no loss of composure, shouting or denial. Prince Anard exuded a serene calm in the face of what must be a heart-wrenching decision. He would make a good king, better than the current one – if his father let him live that long.

'Where is your boat?' he asked.

I studied the sea. There were so many that I could barely make out any defining features, especially in the darkness. By now, Eden should have raised the red sails, their speed essential in the escape we were planning. In the gentle moonlight, one boat with sails folded like a sleeping dragon's wings stood out. My heart swelled with pride at the sight of *Black Hind*.

'Over there.'

'Sail around the point of the city wall to below the arches. There is an inlet. It's small and the water runs under the walls there. Once, it would have emptied onto the beach. Now the sea fills it. Sirena will await you in the water there. Don't be late. She can't cope with warm water for long.'

'How long will you expect to take? Do you need an additional signal from us?' I asked.

He looked worried for a moment, but the siren caressed his shoulder with her tail tip. 'I can smell them. I know the boat. No signal is necessary.'

'How can you smell them? Surely they smell the same as any other crew of unwashed sailors,' the Prince asked.

'There are different scents on *this* boat compared to a normal crew, I assure you.' The siren's eyes spun lazily as she spoke. Light reflected from them in sparkling flashes around her pool.

'How long will it take you to get there?' I pressed again.

'An hour, maybe more. If no one is in the tunnels, then we can move quickly. If nothing has caused a rock fall in the last few weeks, then faster.' He nudged a large flagstone with his foot. 'We should get these stones lifted while you're here. They're heavy.' He looked around the pool. 'It is a beautiful place. I will miss spending my days with you here, Sirena.'

The siren's eyes span. 'Give it to your cousin.'

A small smile flitted across Prince Anard's lips. 'That's a lovely idea. Hopefully, she will think it was created as a special gift for her.'

We strained to move the flagstones, eventually, finding purchase on a corner. We raised it slightly, the Siren adding her force to the task once she could get her tail under it and together we lifted the first. The rest were easily raised after that.

Prince Anard stared into the hole. 'I really need to make sure these open more easily. I'll get them replaced in the future I think. There's another entrance inside the house, but this needs to be an easier escape.' He stared out to the moonlit sea once more. I wondered what he thought so deeply about. Once we both had our breath back, he strolled towards the door.

'Come on, I'll escort you back to the gates, and we will talk loudly of pigments and paints, then you will meet her by the inlet. Thank you. May your journey north be swift and safe.'

He was as good as his word, and as I rowed across the

moon-sparkled sea towards the *Black Hind,* I couldn't help but feel sadness for this man, who turned out to be more honourable towards our kind than any human I had met, aside from the crew of the *Black Hind.* I had hope for the future if he were in change. If it came to it, I decided, I'd remove the current king myself. This world deserved better.

11

A BAY A DAY KEEPS THE
SELKIE AWAY

SELKIE

Keening gulls rode the wind, dolphins frolicked in our bow-wave and for the first time since midsummer, as the sea spray danced my hair into knots, I let a thread of happiness creep into my being.

Sal's steady footsteps closed in, and he rested his arms on the smooth wooden rail next to me to stand in companionable silence as we watched the dolphins play. Once they dived and didn't resurface, he sighed. I felt the loss of their presence too.

Sal turned to face me, his direct gaze looking at the true me underneath the glamour. 'Jake's crews usually lie in wait at The Narrows. They will be searching for you on every ship that passes. It's easier to let them board and pay their toll, than fight, given the cargo we carry. I want you off this boat well before we run into them,' he said. 'It's a few days walk to Orange.'

He pointed at mist-topped hills rising ahead of us. 'If you cross those hills or travel around the coast, that's where I will sail to. If you choose to rejoin me, I can't promise you that we'll get the skin back, but I'll do my best to help. I have access to a range of contacts that no one else in Terrania can surpass.' He put a gentle hand on my shoulder – it felt like a genuine gesture of friendship. His face was earnest, and despite the glamour he wore around his crew, I could sense the honesty in his words as he continued.

'If you choose to go home, I'll understand. The choice is yours, and you are free to make it away from my presence. You need time to be free from any ties. I want to prove that I did not buy you, but your freedom. Zora will take you ashore, then continue ahead to let my main ship, *Barge*, know we are on our way.' He handed me a bag. 'Here's a map, some food – it's only dried fish – and a change of clothes for you. You need to secrete coins around you. Don't keep them all in the pouch. People are greedy and it will make you a target. Have some of this too.' He reached into his pocket and handed me a tiny bottle. 'It's for whatever you've hidden up those sleeves.'

'How did you know about the needles?' Had he been through my stuff?

'You keep fiddling with them. You really need to stop doing that. Otherwise, it is a really inventive idea. Although, you'll be far from the only selkie to have inventive weaponry.' He winked at me and pressed the small bottle into my hand. A viscous liquid moved sluggishly inside.

'What is it?' I held it up to the light, watching it move slowly as I tipped it.

'If you don't know what it is, then don't use it,' Zora muttered as she strode across the deck to join us. 'Or, it's not your target that will end up dead – it will be you.'

'I am sure you will be fine.' Sal smiled at me reassuringly. 'Some things run in our blood and playing with venom is one of them. Just be careful – you aren't invulnerable to all of them.'

But I am to this. Message received loud and clear.

'I'm not sure how to use the map you talked about,' I said, changing the subject quickly. 'Or why I have to walk alone instead of just staying aboard.'

'Where *have* you been living?' Zora laughed, 'that you have never had to use a map?'

I swallowed my pride and answered her. Sometimes the truth is easier to share, and in this case, it worked for my purposes. 'On a very small island, at least until that man captured me.'

She snorted. 'That explains a lot. Sal, are you certain she's going to make it on her own? I know she's your family, but she's so . . . ignorant.'

'Of course I can,' I spluttered, indignation running through my veins like fire. I would get there before them. I had no intention of failing in front of her.

'I'm going to prepare the boat,' she said. 'Don't be long.' With that, she spun away from us.

'I forget you are fresh off the isle.' Sal muttered once she was out of hearing. We both watched her shimmy down the rope ladder to the red boat below us. Every motion was graceful. She landed on the small deck with such light feet that the boat hardly moved.

'She's special,' Sal sighed. 'Right, let me show you the map.'

I pulled out the roll of paper he gestured to and unrolled it on the deck. Sal crouched next to me and realigned it.

'You really do need to do this. Free from being watched, you need to make a decision about your future. If you plan to hunt down your skin, you need to be able to survive. Crossing this land is only a small taste of what you may have to do. A map is a picture of the land you will walk through, as seen from above. Imagine you were looking down on a kelp forest on the sea bed, amongst wrecks and other waypoints. It's a lot like that. This is where you will land.' His finger slid around the curve of the bay as he spoke, and I looked up, searching for the shape on the coast ahead. Having located the bay we sailed towards, I looked at the map.

'What's this line?' I asked.

'That's a road, a flattened stretch of ground between two locations. Most are maintained well enough to walk on for a distance. People tend to stay on them. Especially now, especially here. They are so edgy away from the safety of their towns that it's likely they will attack long before they talk to you. If you want to stay off the roads, you will need to look at other features on here for your route.'

'I can use the sun, moon and the stars, like I would in the sea,' I replied. I was confident in my skills at navigating by the sky.

He nodded, 'You can, as long as you can see them. But look at those hills.'

He was right. If I chose that route, then I'd lose all sight of the sky. I stared down at the paper with renewed focus, trying to picture it as Sal suggested.

'You have to pass through a human settlement to reach *Barge.*' He tapped a group of marks. 'It's called Orange. Jake's crews are based south of The Narrows, but this town marks the edge of the northern kingdom of Terrania. As a valuable trading town, their presence is guaranteed in the area. Do not stop. Follow the road past the guards. Tell them you are headed to the dock for work. Remember, Jake's crews are searching for a black-haired, beautiful woman. Work your best glamour. It only has to get you to me. Then, we can agree on the next step, of whatever you choose to do.'

It was a fine speech, and for a brief moment, I felt sure I

could do it. But, as I stared at the map, other marks he hadn't explained stood out. 'What are these?' I pointed at a group of them.

'Trees.'

'These?' There were crosses drawn on the map. I ran my finger over them all, trying to commit each symbol to memory.

'Places to find rest,' Sal replied. One of those was directly between the bay and the town, towards the top of the hills. I still wasn't entirely sure I wanted to be beholden to Sal. He'd got me out of Icidro's, but living in a pleasure boat? That wasn't going to happen. I hadn't evaded Icidro, just to be groped and grabbed by drunkards for money.

I stared ahead, trying to match patches of green ahead of me with the areas of trees on the map. This coast was like nowhere I knew. The water was much warmer than home, while the sun was searingly intense. What I needed was time to think and a plan.

'If I walk straight to Orange, how long would you expect it to take?' I asked.

Sal shrugged. 'A couple of days, maybe more. It depends how fast you walk. I'll have someone keep an eye out for you. Tell the woman as you board that you are my cousin, and have come to be Driftwood. She'll understand. *Barge* will leave in about half a lunar month, which should give you more than enough time to join us – if you choose to.' He gazed out to the land, his eyes fixed on the top of the hills.

'Thank you. Sal, why do you live with them?' I didn't want to interrupt his thoughts, but I needed to know before I left.

'Truthfully? Because they are greedy and corrupt, because they love fucking, as do I, and because it has put me in a posi-tion of unrivalled power. The knowledge spilt in my rooms lets me do what I did today. Help out those who didn't choose this life. What I'd really like to do is use it a little more, to remove those who did and who abuse it.'

I looked down at the woman lounging on the boat, waiting for me.

'Will she be there too?' I asked.

'Sometimes.' He stood up, languidly stretching his limbs skywards. 'There's a needle and thread for you inside the front pocket. I'll see you on the other side. Whatever you choose, be safe.'

We parted awkwardly, and I climbed carefully down the rope ladder.

Zora coaxed the boat to life, and we sped through the waves towards the beach. She held the boat in shallow water as I clambered out. She leant over and enveloped me in an unexpected hug before passing me the bag.

'Be careful, Sal's cousin. There are strange creatures haunting the woods between here and our next meeting. I'll see you soon.'

The red boat slipped away from the beach, and it flew through the water, passing the lumbering vessel which transported my fellow marine captives. I watched her for a moment longer before taking a last look at the ship. I'd hoped to see the shark set free, but knowing that it would happen was good enough. I trusted that Sal would free it, but how much could I truly trust a selkie who had abandoned his own kind for the pleasures of life with humans?

I unpicked the seams of my top, then stitched gold coins around the hem. The paper money I split between the hem of my trousers and my waistband, leaving only a small number of valuable coins on hand and a couple of bits of paper.

I unscrewed the cap of the small bottle. The contents smelt a little familiar; maybe it was octopus. If this was as toxic as Sal had implied, while it wouldn't kill me I might still get decidedly unwell from a large dose. I needed to be exceedingly careful.

I'd refined the shape of my needles and given them a serrated tip with a small hook. Being caught by one would deliver as much venom as a small jellyfish or urchin. Stiffly curled spears of Marram grass would shield me from accidents, so I added a layer of it between the needles and my skin before dipping the tip of each in the venom.

Once I was satisfied with my work, I hunted along the sand dunes at the landward side of the beach for the path on my map. There, I laid the paper on the ground, and searched the skyline for a feature to navigate by. There was a dip in the hills that looked to be midway to the town, right about where that cross was.

The small path crested the dunes and wound down to the road. Plants pushed through the cracks in its surface, breaking through the hard layer and stretching for freedom. Their joyous flowers, bobbing atop dancing stalks invited me to follow. The boat had gone from sight around the headland, and I was now entirely alone in a strange land. Sal had gifted me enough money to buy passage back home should I choose to.

Now was the time to make that choice. I unfurled the map and studied it carefully now that I knew where I was on it. The road split some distance ahead, one fork heading towards what I now recognised would be north and the other continuing towards the hills, skirting the woods, and then turning south towards the town where Sal's *Barge* was anchored. The northern road wound like a kelp-stem on a dry shore towards a river and a small town or village. Maybe they had boats. Maybe it was a way home.

A way home, yet still without Eryn's skin. What would I do? Sit on the beach and watch my family play? See the pup born, but never swim with it? Reclaim my skin and force Eryn to that life, ever observing, never again truly belonging. Or, should I find human company and settle down? None of the options filled my soul with joy.

The other option was to accept Sal's help, to help him in return. I'd learn to sail for myself. This trip had shown me that being on the water was infinitely preferable to being in a human home. I could get my own boat, and when I found the information I needed – when the right guts were spilled, or lips loosened – then, I'd retrieve my sister's skin. If that day never happened, at least I would be on the water, and Eryn could live free and happy, unfettered by the guilt of seeing my face on a nearby shore. There was no choice really. I just had to see it for myself.

On that windswept shore, amidst a path of dancing flowers, I chose a different kind of freedom.

I wanted to see which Old Ones were still around and where they were living. I wondered if I could help them. Few had the opportunity to hide like we did; inland, and in the mountains and streams, I knew ruskies could walk where they pleased, or they used to.

Human religion had scarred this land. I found that I needed to know who had survived the millennia of human impact. Who – like the siren and selkie – had hidden in the far reaches of the north, taking refuge amongst inhospitable surface lands? Who had moved south as the heat rose to shelter in the desert? Were there still tibicena lurking in the deep caves around the islands now lost to the Everstorm?

I wanted to deal with Icidro too. If he was collecting us,

like some sort of living status symbol, how many other Old Ones had been caught? How safe were our families? Rejoining Sal might give me a new purpose in life. A reason to carry on fighting.

I began to walk down the flower-strewn road, towards the town, and Sal's ship.

12

WHEN WAVES COLLIDE

GEORGIE

Black Hind's blade-like bow sliced through the water. Our red sails were at full stretch as we approached The Narrows, their splendour matched by the incredible power generated through the stiff fabric. Despite our heavy load, we travelled swiftly towards inevitable confrontation with Jake's boats. They held the bottleneck as we flew towards them, spray bursting from our prow.

Cor sat in his, now customary, spot on the masthead, calling out the location of other vessels to Eden. His black wings spread as we closed on the fleet, then he lifted off to fly above us. We held our course. All four of us were on deck, to facilitate our flight from Terrain.

'Can I play with them?' Zora asked as she looked over my shoulder to the boats ahead.

'Please do. We need a clear run through. What are you thinking?' I replied.

'Watch and see – or should that be *witch and sea*?' That giggle . . . She sauntered to the bow, a smile playing on her face.

I waited as she worked through her plan, muttering quietly to herself.

'We need to go through there, as the wind is in this direction. So, that boat needs to turn. That one needs to change course and that one,' – she pointed at the biggest – 'needs to decide it doesn't want us to crash into it, more than it wants whatever we're carrying.' She studied the sea surface carefully.

I waved at Theo to direct his attention to Zora, and he nodded.

Soon, the sea rippled with white-cap waves. Zora extended her arms, humming to herself as the waves built in front of us.

'Hold course,' I called back to Theo.

'I trust our witch,' he said, his hand steady on the helm.

Waves continued to rise – they were level with the bow now and still growing.

'Looks a bit unnatural, us flying blood-red sails, riding on a tidal wave.' Theo called, 'Anyone would think we were using magic – Except they don't believe it exists.'

'It looks amazing!' Eden shouted. 'Cor is confused. I can see the wave from the front through his view. He thinks it looks like death-water after a kill. The wave is now high enough that the red of our sails is tinting it. I'd die to hear what they are saying right now!'

That was an image I was more than happy to cultivate.

The previously steady wind was now noticeably altered by the wave's backdraft, and our course was proving difficult to maintain. Theo wrestled to keep us directly behind the rising water.

'Are they moving? I can't see a thing,' he called.

'Yes,' Eden replied.

Zora built the wave a little higher, then released it. The water flowed with the outgoing tide carrying its momentum towards the flotilla ahead.

We flew freely now there was less backdraft and, as the wall of water crashed through the vessels, we followed – unscathed.

Zora fell, as the wave did, into a deep sleep on the deck. She appeared stable and the weather was warm, so I tucked a rolled blanket under her head to let her sleep it off while Theo sang lewd songs on the helm and turned us away from the devastation.

With Eden still out of action, I'd been designated temporary climber. I scrambled up the complex rigging to tweak the spars and adjust the angles of the dragon-wing rig. Whilst the normal rig could be adjusted from on deck, the spars of this sail set needed adjusting up here.

Cor plunged into the sea off our starboard side, returning with a fish.

'Can you ask him to catch me one?' I called down to Eden, hopefully.

'He says to get your own.'

I snatched a moment to glance back. The majority of Lost Jake's fleet were regrouping across the narrows, but the biggest vessel and two others had turned to chase us. I sighed. The others couldn't see me up here, and I allowed myself a moment of doubt. Knowing that we had the fastest boat and maintaining the pace with such a small crew for long enough to complete our mission – without jeopardising the bargain Lady Gina had made – were two different things.

Black Hind screamed along with the wind on our tail, flying like the dragon we resembled. We swooped down wave faces, rising as if to take flight from the crest of the next, gaining distance from our pursuers, for now. The fleet faded into the background as we turned north, holding course away from the coast.

Zora had recovered fairly quickly, although she would be drained for a while. 'The sea will make me feel better,' she said, after warning me that the next few days would be rough sailing. As much as I wanted a smooth passage, we needed all the speed we could get, and she needed the rest. I climbed down to the cabin, where Eden sat, poring over a chart. Cor had come in to shelter from the growing storm and perched over the end of the table, defecating into the bucket.

'Have you checked on our passenger?' I asked.

Eden shook their head. 'I'll leave you that pleasure. She isn't exactly enjoyable company. I don't know what I'm looking at half the time. She's too blurry.'

I knocked at the hold door, to warn the siren I was coming in.

'Into the darkness comes a cousin of sorts. A sister of the sea.' Her voice was invasive in this enclosed space. I sat far from her and stared at the pile of coils tucked in the back of the hold.

'I'm getting very dry, and this is uncomfortable.'

'I'm sorry, we'd hoped to sail alongside you soon. But, there are a fleet of boats chasing us, the ones who want to present your head to that human idiot.'

'I understand. When your pet witch is better, can she bring me water?'

'How about I open the hatch once Theo is no longer on the helm? This would all be a lot easier if you wouldn't keep trying to seduce him.'

'I can't help it. He is prey.' She slithered over to me. 'Do you not see him as prey? No, of course you don't. You selkies are full of curses and lust. It's hardly a surprise you won't hurt him.'

'We're hardly full of curses.' I laughed. 'One curse as I die, and we never get to enjoy the results. I won't hurt Theo because I need him. He sails this boat with an understanding of the surface and the winds I lack. He has knowledge of healing other humans that I don't have. Without the three humans on this boat, I could not have freed you, nor would we be returning you home. I have other reasons I need this boat.' I looked at her crystalline eyes. Whirling in the darkness, they were less hypnotic than in daylight. 'Are you hungry?'

'I have no need of food. Hunting is just a game I enjoy.' She started to encircle me and I laughed.

'You should be where you belong. Help the North return to how it should be. Leave me to try and work on the other areas.'

'You cannot fix this world alone, selkie.'

'I know. But, when we die, all that is left are shadows of our lives preserved in the memories of those who remain. I plan on leaving an exceptionally long shadow, filled with ripples of moonlight for those I helped and darker than the worst of nightmares for those who wronged us.' I turned from her and closed the door.

We rode the storm for two days, eventually reaching shelter on a tiny island. Narrow inlets with azure waters and golden beaches welcomed us. An old fortress, its high seawalls now crumbling in disrepair, sat alone, its long-drowned walkway visible as a light strip of blue under the sea surface. We tucked into the next cove, tying up alongside an old harbour wall. Under Eden's directions, Zora and I took the red sails down. We would raise them again in the far north, but a change in our appearance from a distance would be worth the decrease in speed.

Theo clambered ashore and scrabbled up the steep path to keep a lookout. Once he was out of direct sight, we opened the deck door. The siren slithered out, revelling in the water.

Sirena was beautiful without illusion. Her white hide shone back the reflected blue of the ocean. Along her back, her fins bore more than a passing resemblance to the sails on our boat. Strong supporting spines webbed with torn sails from her time in captivity, their damage achingly apparent once she was in her true element. Crystalline eyes whirled like those of the dragons from the deep golden deserts. She could not possibly be more beautiful as a human than in this powerful form – a true spirit of nature.

'We are doing the right thing,' Zora said. 'It's not that I doubted it, but seeing her swim freely – it gives me chills.'

'I know. Me too, and I'm like her, just less alluring.'

Zora glanced at me, dark eyelashes lowered and a corner of her mouth rose. 'You have your own allures, don't worry, Georgie,' she said, then sprung up the mast before I could reply.

'Pick your mouth up, Georgie,' Eden said, trying – and failing – to cover up a grin. 'You have work to do.'

And, work we did. The pristine white sails rose like shark fins. Stiff and unyielding, they flexed rather than rippled. On a slim-hulled boat, they would be incredible. But we carried the weight of a siren, and our hull was specialised in a different way. Boiling sun beat on our backs, and we dripped with sweat by the time we had completed the task.

'Eden, you need to get better,' I muttered.

'I told you, you should have left me on *Barge*. I'd have been fine.'

Zora snorted, 'We all know what kind of fine you'd have been, Eden. Anyway, we need Cor's eyes and your knowledge. You can still hobble about and turn a winch. Someone has to keep an eye on the other stuff too, like the panels and things.'

Things I knew nothing about. Despite Theo's best attempts at looking after Eden, they still limped badly. The wound was clean but healing slowly.

'This water is too hot.' The siren floated near the surface, basking in the sun. 'My pool was cold.' Her eyes whirred more slowly. 'I will miss that view, and my painting. I cannot swim far in this heat. I must be your passenger a while longer.'

'Sails!' Theo called down. 'Get her in the boat . . . Gods she is so beautiful . . . You have no idea how bloody annoying this situation is. I am perfectly capable of not losing my mind when I stare at a woman. I look at you all day, Georgie.'

'I'm a selkie, and you asked me to wear my glamour for your comfort.'

'I'm not having it,' he puffed, as he half ran, half fell down the cliff. 'I have never made an unwanted advance in my life. I'm not about to start now. It doesn't matter how alluring either of you are. I am perfectly fine to handle this.' He stood with his hands on his hips and legs apart on the beach, the sea lapping at his boots as the siren began to swim towards him. 'I am as much a part of this team as any of you.'

Eden popped their head out the cabin to watch. 'No one has said you aren't, but this, I have to see – even if it does mess my head up.'

The arrogance of human males never fails to astound me. He was challenging a siren who the rest of us had watched bite a man in half. We hadn't spared him the details either.

'We don't have time for testing your resolve now, Theo. You just claimed there were sails on the horizon. Once we're at sea, and I have the helm, you and the siren can have this discussion. For now, let's get out of here before they are close enough to recognise our hull.' Zora sighed.

Theo recalcitrantly climbed aboard, and the siren slipped into the hold. 'I could eat him?' she murmured as she passed.

'That would not help. He is not prey.'

We let the sails flap, and *Black Hind* hummed backwards, the engine slipping us gently away from the quay.

Zora gentled the waves to speed our progress and regain some distance. It worked, and over the next few days, the pursuing sails grew slowly smaller, retreating to a distance as we continued north. The lumbering vessel they hunted us with was rigged with cloth sails and the smaller one, was clearly unwilling to travel ahead alone.

The Territories were on the horizon by the fifth day. Engad side would be the narrower route, shaded from the worst of the weather. However, it also took us between the Territories and the mainland. The weather looked good enough to risk the fast route up the west coast instead. The seas were likely to be lumpier, and there was a chance of storms, but the weather was clear, and we could make it through in five days if we were lucky. We could stop to resupply in the Northern Territories. The waters should be cool enough to let the siren swim, and the others seemed to think there would be a welcome in the small scattered villages for both our coin and news.

Golden beaches and miniature mountain ranges of grass-covered dunes nestled between towering cliffs as we approached the southwest coast. Beaches stretched for miles. Occasional towns dotted the coastline, hanging onto the cliffs by a mix of sheer luck and determination. Some villages had clearly been abandoned, leaving glimpses of brick visible through encroaching woodland or on exposed cliffs where straggling buildings were decorated with the gold of gorse bushes poking through them.

The winds were against us here, and our slow progress became punctuated with tacks. With no sign of pursuit, we didn't worry too much. Eden lay on the deck, soaking up the sun, and Cor dived for fish from rocks near the shore. For a while, it was nice to relax, to enjoy the spray in my hair and the salt on my tongue again.

The daylight hours grew shorter as we drew closer to our goal. We changed our rotation to sail as far as we could each day, having eaten through most of our supplies. When we could anchor up, Cor and I would eat just fine. The humans on board weren't convinced by the fresh meat we chewed and crunched down so enthusiastically, but I wasn't sure we could supply them all for long had they wanted it.

The siren needed to stretch out and swim too – she was becoming dour and unpleasant. Despite Theo's bravado, we had refused to let him try his luck at resisting her. The mood she was in, we'd lose a helmsman.

We eventually rounded the headland and headed north between the Territories. The tide ran with us, for now. Waves rocked the boat, and we powered through with little challenge for a few more days.

Looming grey clouds filled the horizon as we approached a cluster of islands near the coast. The cliffs were breathtaking. Dark red sandstone, capped with a lace of yellow lichen and green – so very green – grasses. The entire coastline was scarred, bands of colour running vertically, as though great gods had fought here and the very land had been broken. And, perhaps it had.

The thrum of wild magic hung in the air, and the waters

teemed with life. I opened the hatch, offering the siren a chance to swim freely. She peered out at white-capped waves, building as they rolled towards the coast, then slunk back to the corner of the hull.

'It's not for me out there. This is your territory. I will not be welcome,' she said. 'Go, see your kin.'

I scanned the waters closely, and sure enough, heads bobbed. Curious faces looked up at us. Harbour seal skins adorned their bodies, all silver and speckled, their faces marked with patches and their bellies exposed to the sun as the selkies reclined on nearby rocks. A muscled bull seal, his huge size and the lack of many other males, a clear sign of his dominance, swam close to the boat. I leant over the rail to greet him.

'I see you,' he called.

'I see you too.'

'Come, swim with us.'

My heart broke. 'I cannot.'

'You value humans more than your own freedom? Or do they hold you hostage? I would free you,' he barked loudly. 'I can find your skin on a boat that small.'

Theo grinned as he looked into the water.

'Is that a selkie?'

'As much as I or Sal,' I replied.

'Why don't you join them? We can manage for a little while.'

'You know I don't have my skin aboard. It wouldn't be safe if we were under attack.'

I smiled at the bull seal, trying to swallow a lump in my throat. One day, I would come back here and swim with them. I would dive in the sea caves and explore this beautiful coast.

The winds grew, waves built, and the sea roiled around the

island. Foaming white blankets formed around the rocks. The selkies left to seek refuge, and we followed them.

I won't say that the storm had come out of nowhere, but it was a while since I had been in waters around the Territories, and the warmth of Terrania had softened me against the suddenness of the changes here. Large cloud banks marched across the sky, spearing lightning towards the islands as we prepared to ride it out.

We tied down everything on deck and hummed around the headland to a sheltered cove. I threw the anchor overboard and followed it, diving through the clouding water to check it was firmly wedged. It was as close as I would get to swimming with other selkies for a while. I checked the anchor and was greeted by a kind face. She was slim and young, brave to be out in storm waters. She touched noses with me in greeting, tilting her head. 'Have you seen my brother?' she asked.

I shook my head. No other selkies had been to greet me, unless she meant the big bull.

'The bull?' I asked.

She shook her head sadly as bubbles streamed from her sleek, well-fitted fur. I let go of the anchor line to meet her flipper with my hand and followed briefly, as instinct over-rode reality. Then, I simply hung in the water, watching her swim away.

I envied her the freedom of her skin without the confines of this belegged form.

I kicked out at the water, turning myself to grasp at the chain and haul myself aboard. My lapse in focus had cost me dearly. It was out of reach. I'd drifted away from it into increasingly strong undercurrents and now failed to make any headway as I was swept towards a tidal race. I surfaced, gasping for air, and waved for the crew's attention so that Zora might calm the waters for me and I could get back. She peered intently over the side into the waters below the boat. I opened my mouth to shout and got a mouthful of water.

The wind continued to rise, and waves crashed over me, dunking me under. I spluttered and coughed for air, struggling against mounting waves. One moment I could see the boat, the next, I was in a trough. I struck out again but, for all I swam forward, I was dragged back. Standing waves formed as the tide picked up and the rain began to descend. Greyness blanked out my vision. The boat was gone.

I stopped struggling and floated – feeling for the water's flow. I swam with it, and slightly across. If I could survive the tidal rip, maybe I could get to land on one side of the channel or the other. When the storm died, I could call the siren ... she might hear me.

A group of standing waves ahead showed the position of a chain of rocks and I narrowed my focus to surviving those. I took a deep breath and struck out toward the coast.

I crashed off a rock, my leg trailing behind me. Now, unable to kick with it, I was carried back to my original trajectory. I pulled as hard as I could with my arms, gaining ground for a moment, the strength from boat-work giving me the power needed. Water foamed red around me. If I didn't reach land soon, I was done for. My lack of concentration led me to another near miss, my head barely grazing a second rock, my shoulder taking the brunt of it. I flailed ineffectively, breathing in as much air as I could hold.

I thought I saw a black shadow above me, whirling in the wind, but when I next emerged, it was gone. An illusion of my traumatised mind.

Huge, spray-topped waves crashed against the cliffs, and I was dashed against another large rock. Its rounded, red form protruding from the water at the edge of the tide run. I wrapped my arms around it and hung on, my legs trailing

uselessly in the water. Something yelped as it crashed into my
arm. I let go, grabbing for the creature that hit me. They were
floppy, and we tumbled as I held it tight, trying to keep both
our heads above water, until I was thrown out of the waves –
thrown impossibly high into the air, to land onto the spray-
soaked cliff top. Broken but alive.

13

THE WHITE HIND

SELKIE

Forest-covered, cloud-shrouded hills rose steeply to the narrow pass. The coast road would take me to my destination more easily than this narrow path which climbed through the wild landscape and wound through a cluster of ruins, all crumbled walls and neatly abandoned piles of rubble. I considered the easier route briefly, but my skin grew searingly hot, despite the sea breeze. The pull of the shady trees was stronger than being near the water's edge, where the dry, barren coast rolled out below me, fringed by sun-sparkled sea. In the distance, Sal's ship closed in on the waiting flotilla. I ducked into the sparse shade of a straggly tree and watched.

Several vessels tacked into the wind as the large vessel rolled towards them. With the wind behind it, and sails bulging with power, it had more than enough speed to batter a way through – if Sal was willing to risk the lives of the animals on board. He wouldn't. As I watched, his sails loosened and flapped like fish in the shallows. The smaller boats surrounded Sal's ship. He'd been right to send me on foot.

Beyond the cluster of vessels, another coastline rose – dim against the waterline, yet my sea-eyes recognised it for what it was. Sal had guessed right. Lone Jake's men had been waiting in the narrow channel. I chuckled. At least if the boat went down, all the animals would be free, if a little lost. I pulled my eyes away, no more able to impact the events playing out than I could change the flow of the tide. It was time to move on.

I eyed the tree line, searching for a way through. The shade past the initial line of scrub looked to be worth a few scratches. Further up, there was a suggestion – a hint of a gap in the tree canopy where a path passed through the dip in the hills. The idea of sleeping both outdoors and unchained for the first time since I had been captured filled me with joy. These trees may not be tall, but I'd accept whatever shade they were willing to share with me.

As I turned my back on the sea, I sent it a promise of return. Having been separated once, I had no plans to leave my beloved water for any longer than necessary.

The climb to the skyline was far steeper than I'd anticipated. The gentle colours of the slope fooled my eyes as they masked the true gradient. Clothes clung to my body, growing damper with each step as I ascended into the cloud cap, their coolness against my skin so refreshing after the searing heat of the beach that I drank it in gratefully.

The trees grew taller here, and it appeared to be a good place to rest; night would fall before long. Tumbled towers – scattered, ancient, and long-abandoned – adorned the hill to either side of me.

Memories surfaced of swimming into the toppled base of one like them – of fish and eels making it a home now the tower had descended into the ocean. If these were the same, then they might offer some shelter.

I approached the nearest, fear and trepidation dogging my steps. If I saw them as potential shelter, they might already contain other animals. The closest one was a twisted pile of orange-streaked metal. The next was more intact, the door long fallen off and the space inside exposed. A slender sapling reached for the light, slicing through a narrow gap in the side of the tower. Mosses lined the remains of the sides, and webs strung from low branches to holes on the wall. Small, many-legged creatures peered out at me from deep in their woven tubes, their glisteningly round abdomens tucked far from my reach. I edged closer and they backed away, hiding.

The number of unbroken threads reassured me that this was not a place frequented by other – large – creatures. I settled down for the night, glad of the soft grass.

I awoke with a racing heart, my body alert to an invader well before my mind. Crunching of twigs and leaves as something moved around outside. I froze and listened carefully. The footfall pattern was wrong for a human – four beats, four crunches, sniffing. I reassured myself that I had the needles on hand. I wouldn't attack first, but I was not planning to be anything's meal.

A cloud bank obscured the moon, but my night vision could just make out the opening. I edged closer, coiled and ready to fight or run. It was unlikely that hiding in here was going to be the best option.

The sniffing stopped, and a rumbling growl echoed around my hiding place. Another responded, from further away, a snarl that built to a full howl – feral and chilling. The hairs on my arms rose.

The footsteps closed in. I was going to have to run for it, maybe climb. I needed to get away from the pack. One creature, I could fight, but if I was to be food, I'd struggle against a group.

I needed night vision, moonlight – anything to help.

I slunk out of the door. My scent now drifting freely on the air.

Gods, I wanted to be in the water right now. The limitations of evading pursuit on land were suddenly apparent. A break in the clouds lit up the small valley for a few moments.

It was long enough to see the trees.

It was long enough to see the silhouette of a deer and hear it call to me within my mind.

It was long enough for the creatures to see me.

The moment broke as the wolves did. As one, they turned. Eyes narrowed, their leader rose his voice, and the pack stalked towards me, their teeth reflected in a last flash of moonlight before the clouds reclaimed us.

I ran.

The deer had called me – that was no mere deer. Placing my trust in the magic of the Old Ones, I ran towards it. Scrub clogged my route. My feet caught under a low branch, sending me sprawling to the ground. I could smell the deer now, faint and tinged with fear.

I scrabbled to my feet as the first wolf landed on my back. Drool splattered my neck as its weight pinned me to the ground. I kicked upward with my legs, my heels connected with soft tissue under the beast's gut. Distracted, it shifted its weight backward, and I rolled over and stabbed a needle up into its jaw.

It yelped in shock. Teeth grazed my shoulder, then it snapped at my face.

I twisted desperately beneath it, praying for the venom to work fast.

The paws began to shake on my chest, and the creature collapsed. The remainder of the pack drew back – confused or scared, it didn't matter which to me.

Their whimpers drifted over me as a blanket of loss. When it came to kill or be killed, I couldn't afford sympathy. As a natural predator, I had no qualms about killing for survival. I hauled myself out from under the body. It still had the faintest of air movements from its nose. Maybe it would recover – its bowels were yet to loose, death had not grasped her final hold yet.

I staggered towards the edge of the wood, hoping I headed the right way. A small bark called to me from my right – the hind was still hidden in the undergrowth. She called again, and I altered my course.

Only the noise of a tiny twig snapping gave her away. I reached forward, and a gentle nose met my outstretched palm. I slid my hand down her neck, filled with privilege to be allowed so close to a messenger of the Old Gods. She withdrew, turning from me, and I followed her deep into the trees along a small stream. We followed it for several minutes, emerging on the far side into a softly lit clearing. The moon shone once again. Portentously, maybe. Had the dim light played me false? This was no magical messenger. Her sunken hips revealed every bone, and her – once white – fur was spotted with bloody sores. Black dust coated her, and she looked at me with liquid intensity in her eyes.

'Rest,' she told me. 'Safe.'

I sat, and she moved closer, hovering protectively over me. A Black Hind, as damaged as her land, her body reflecting the pillage and damage done to the lands she protected. I doubted she could transform anymore. Her spirit form was trapped in a physical body, enduring the pain.

No single spirit should take so much.

'Others?' I asked.

'Alone.'

She pressed her head against mine and shared a memory.

Another spirit, ensnared by a hunter then killed, skinned for her pelt. A third, her sister, captured – taken far away. No longer connected to their home. Tree spirits culled, The noise of the towers so loud it hurt to hear their sails spinning in the sky. Smaller spirits fled.

She shared an image of herself. *The sores were horrific, her body a patchwork of blackened scabs, oozing blood.*

This white hind had stood alone and kept the land alive. She had not seen another Old One for a long time.

The vision changed. Now, we looked down from this mountain. *The sea rose, and the land disappeared. The humans died. Silence returned. Some of her sores healed as the land was allowed to reclaim itself, but the spirits didn't come back. The land was empty of magic.*

The ocean rose in my soul, a swelling wave of loneliness until she broke physical contact, and the wave fell flat at my feet – no longer threatening to overwhelm me. The Hind's front knees buckled, and she staggered back upright, unsteady but proud.

'Rest,' she insisted again.

I felt inside, and the wave was still there. It was a mere ripple, but it would grow. I would feed it, and I would nurture it. Somewhere out there was a lost hind and a land in desperate need of her return. Whatever means I had at my disposal now had an additional aim. If Icidro was collecting Selkie, were others collecting Old Ones too?

Safe in her clearing, I fell into an unsettled sleep.

Burning sunlight woke me many hours later; daylight found me surrounded by tall, russet-trunked trees. Dark green leaves rippled in a breeze that didn't reach me on the woodland floor. A smaller, stumpy tree appeared at odd places between them, its trunk an intertwining growth of self. Sniffling and rustling in the undergrowth revealed a small black creature with a strange, stubby nose. It flexed its nostrils as it sniffed the air and emitted a startled 'oink' when it saw me, before turning its curly tail and bouncing away.

The Hind stood at the edge of the clearing. I sat up slowly, trying to hold her there with my gaze.

'What happens next?' I asked her.

'You,' she replied and walked towards me to place her soft muzzle once more upon my head.

A slender, dark-haired woman with sun-gold skin walked into fire, and the fire went out . . . A white hind walked towards me, and a figure clothed in red walked with her hand resting on its back, I strained to make out the face, but it was cloudy.

'You,' she said again. Then lifted her head and turned away. Flicking her tail as she sprang back into the shelter of the woods.

I collected my bag and left the clearing. Maybe, I could find it again in the future if I travelled from here in daylight. I walked towards the sun, keeping my shadow behind me. The slope gradually descended to an area with less tree cover, and I could appreciate the vista that opened in front of me.

A sparkling azure sea spread into the distance, beyond the town, that nestled where the land met the waves. Smaller ruins dotted the area between myself and my destination. To the right, towards the sea, the road wound along the coast. I turned around. From here, the trees obscured the peak, and I could see nothing that would guide me back into one part of the woods over another. Directly below me was a small ruin. I walked towards it.

I pulled the map from my bag, seeking the fallen towers and the hut. I lined the two up as I placed it on the floor, spat on a twig to coat it in dirt, then drew a line between the two points. It wasn't perfect, but it would give me a place to start. The line intersected the cross, marked as a safe place. It made me wonder if Sal knew about The Hind, but she hadn't shown him to me in her own memories. Finding Eryn's skin now seemed an insignificant goal, selfish in the face of The Hind's suffering. She'd asked for my help, and I would give it freely. Oceans, I'd tear the world apart to find her sister, to return magic to this land, and I knew just the person who could give me the power to do so.

I rolled the map up and tucked it away, striking out towards the road to complete this journey on the easiest route possible. If I pushed myself today, I could arrive at Orange and Sal's *Barge* tomorrow.

14

INTO THE ICY BEYOND

GEORGIE

A gentle breeze across my face woke me. The sky was clear, no trace of the storm remained and clouds scudded across my vision.

'You wake?' asked a small voice.

I rolled over to see who spoke, but a gentle weight pressed against me, holding me down.

'You not move alone. Broked'

A small, grey being stared at me. At least, I thought it did. Its incorporeal appearance made me wonder if my hand might pass right through it. Absently, I raised my arm to try, and it hit solid force at the being's periphery.

'Don't like that,' it said. 'Stay.'

My foggy brain struggled to recognise the creature. It was a spirit, that much was obvious, but it didn't have the feel of an Old One. It was fast, not lumbering through life. A fleeting energy – sharp and serrated – hung in the air.

I tried to recall the events of the storm, but aside from the

crashes and bangs on the rocks, little was clear. It was a blur of
foam and water. Except I flew higher than it was possible to be
thrown by a wave alone.

'Are you a wind sprite?' I asked as pieces fell into place.

'I'm Aria, yes.'

'Can you throw me back down?'

'Why you want to die? You save me, I save us.'

'My boat, my friends are down there.' I pointed over to the
island. I hoped they were still around that headland in the bay.

'That boat?' Aria pointed a finger of grey downward, gently
supporting me on an air cushion to sit upright.

Black Hind was indeed in the bay. Eden hobbled across the
deck, presumably checking for damage, and a black bird
circled Eden as they moved slowly from winch to winch.

'The bird pecked you.' Aria said. 'But you not taste good. It
left.'

If Cor had found me, the others would soon be here. While
I was upright, I checked my leg. The cut was small and already
scabbed over, the blood-streaked storm-foam either mislead-
ing, or not mine. I funnelled a little extra energy to the area in
hope of speeding the healing. If I could only use this skill on
someone else! What use was a self-healing Old skill, and the
ability to change an appearance, when others could take on
the world's pains?

I laid back down, watching the progress of the clouds
while I waited for someone to arrive.

Theo was first, his thudding feet gathering speed as he
closed in on me. I'd recognise the sound anywhere after
hearing it on the deck for so long.

'Georgie!' he exclaimed as he checked me over for damage.
'How in the name of all the Gods did you get up here?'

'Wind sprite,' I replied. 'Aria. Ouch!'

'They don't help people,' Zora retorted as she crouched

next to me. 'They build the winds, then release them. It takes a lot of aria to create a storm like that one, but it would have blown out once they were all flung from it. We used to get them in sand storms at home, tricky little creatures.'

'Let's get you down to the boat so I can treat that shoulder. It looks to be bruised badly. Your leg needs a proper clean too.' Theo stared at my head. 'Do you feel dizzy? That doesn't look like a big bang, but,' he gestured at my hair – 'you may have other damage I can't see until I check you over.'

'Bring Aria.' I gestured to where it was resting, the air wavering in a slightly denser fashion when I looked through it.

'How? Where?' Zora asked, looking around in confusion.

I chuckled; it hurt, so I stopped. I pointed with my good arm to where Aria drifted. 'Pick it up, the same as I did.'

Zora looked towards Aria, and her eyes widened. I watched her shoulders tense as she walked towards it, glad to see her pause. It was clear Zora understood just how carefully she needed to phrase her words. Zora was right to say they were tricky, for aria are sidhe, and like all their kind, words of trade are binding – for both parties.

'May I carry you, Aria?' Zora held open palms towards the sprite. It drifted a little, then stopped.

'Too weak. Like baby breath, not a breeze,' it sighed.

Zora scooped it up, cradling the dense air and walked off in silence. She held Aria at arm's length as though it might bite at any moment.

'Can you stand?' Theo asked. 'I probably should have checked that before Zora left.'

'I don't know. I could sit with Aria's support. Help me up, and we'll find out.'

I struggled to my feet, leaning heavily on Theo, and with

his support, began to walk. Slowly, we followed the winding, pebble-strewn path down the edge of the bay to the boat.

We found a very quiet and uncomfortable crew when we returned. Eden sat at one end of the deck, staring at Zora, who still held Aria. Maybe she was unwilling to let it loose on *Black Hind*.

Once aboard, I gestured for Zora to bring Aria to the hold with Sirena. Reluctantly, Theo opened the door, and I took Aria from Zora's hands. She exhaled in relief and smiled at me before they closed the heavy door.

The siren had been badly battered by the storm; dark bruises showed through her pearly hide.

'Help me, Sirena,' I asked once the others had left.

'You are here to help me. Not for me help you,' she hissed, tightening her muscular coils around herself.

'With both Eden and I injured, we cannot get you to the cool waters. The other vessels still hunt you. They chase us like you chase men, every day, they close us down. They may have missed the worst of the storm and be upon us at any time. We were in its heart, else how would Aria be here?'

'An aria, not The Aria,' hissed the siren as she edged closer for a look.

'We all Aria.' The sprite whispered so quietly I wasn't sure it meant me to hear.

'I will make you better, but it is for me, not for you,' the siren murmured as she caressed me with her coils, encircling us both. 'As soon as the water is cool enough, I swim. Then all you do is guard my fin.'

'Agreed.'

'My body cannot take another battering like that. I should have been in the ocean,' she continued. 'Next storm, let me out. I'll take my chances out there.'

'No more storms. Too many killed on rocks today,' Aria interrupted. 'It takes time for more of us to rise again.'

The siren stared at the sprite. 'Make me wind,' she demanded.

'Too weak. Blown out.' It drifted closer, a sly tone creeping into its voice. 'What do you pay? Every favour has a price . . .'

The siren's eyes spun faster, and she coughed up a ball of gelatinous goop. 'Use it. Get me home.' I grabbed it and thanked her. Collecting the sprite as carefully as I could, I hobbled from the cabin.

The goop stunk of dead fish and phlegm, combined with notes of acrid fat and something strangely astringent. My stomach heaved as I spread it on my wounds. Eden looked on, and I could see expressions of disgust cycling across their face.

'What is that stuff?'

'Siren fluid. Smells awful but has incredible healing properties.' I offered Eden a handful.

'On my leg?' they asked, gagging as they took some.

'Yes. One of us needs to be able to climb, or we're stuck here.' I offered the remains of the lump to the sprite who hovered nearby. It dived in, bathing in the stink. The goop-coated form that emerged dripping with siren phlegm was something I would struggle to forget in a hurry.

'Where you need wind for?' the sprite asked.

'We need to return siren to the ice, then get safely home to Terrania.'

'If I rest now, I can help. You saved me. I will help you. Then our debt is even.'

'You will help us until we reach the ice?' I asked.

'I can help you longer,' it whispered.

'That sounds good,' Eden offered, and Aria turned eagerly towards them.

I raised my hand to try and stop Eden saying any more and

shook my head frantically. I turned to the Aria. 'Until our debt is even only.'

From then on, our journey was smooth. The storms held their breath, and the sea was calm – becalmed for any but ourselves. Aria kept us moving with a gentle breeze, re-bathing in the remains of the siren goop each time it blew itself out. Slowly but steadily, we made our way through the Territories, stopping only for supplies at the islands in the far north.

We tacked north for days, maybe weeks, after that until even-tually, we saw the first of the bergs. A white sail, heavy on the horizon, impossibly large and drifting steadily. I threw the hatches to the hold open.

'Time to swim,' I called to Sirena, trying to hold back excitement, 'I see ice.' She reared upward, lean, dull, and slim compared to the effervescent colours and muscled body of our first encounter.

'Don't leave me yet,' she pleaded. Could she be nervous? It had been a long time since she was last here.

'We'll sail with you a while longer. Then, we need to turn back. It's late in the season. If we are not careful, we will end up ensnared.'

Theo watched her from the helm, gripping it white-knuck-led, with his jaw set and squinting hard.

'I still only see a woman. That thin fabric and lack of all sensible clothing are making me very concerned about her being cold,' he sighed, 'despite knowing it's an illusion.'

Eden sidled up next to him. 'I see both. It's strange seeing the huge body sway behind the image of the woman. She's unsettling in contrast – hollow. Those teeth and the eyes.'

Eden shuddered. 'They are more beautiful on her real face than her illusion. Her skin is like the inside of a shell. That purity of colour, with the play of rainbows. Her fins are like our sails, supported by strong spines but battered. The fins themselves ragged with damage.'

'I know she is big. Our volume of water disturbance shows me that,' Theo said.

I left them talking and strolled to the bow, keeping half an eye on the water ahead. I didn't notice Zora's soft, padding footsteps until she was next to me.

'It must be nice to go home after so long away,' she said quietly.

'It must be.' My voice caught.

She took my hand and squeezed it briefly, dragging me from the rim of a whirlpool filled with reflection and sadness, then flashed me one of her beautiful smiles.

'Come on, Georgie, we need our wits about us up here. If you need a big emotional unload later, we can deal with it then. We have to get closer to the true ice fields before we can consider this job discharged.'

She was right. The siren swam close to us, sheltering in our shadow, and occasionally diving for food but always returning to ride our bow wave.

We soon began to encounter more bergs. Greens and azures dazzled the eyes. The multitudes of colour possible on a berg composed purely from ice and snow were breathtaking.

The crystalline world we trespassed in soon began to encroach on our own. Frost grew on our exposed hair tips and hung from wet ropes. The sea slowed to a mire of slush, then cleared again, exposing dazzling, foam-crested blue waves. Bergs slid through the slush, leaving trails of clear water in their wake – for a brief while. Dazzling light, so bright it hurt the eyes, reflected back from all around us.

No pictures, no images, could have prepared me for the luminous beauty of this world. Here the siren was no more than a shining sliver of moving ice, reflecting the light much as the world around her did. Little wonder that her kind had remained undetected by sailors for so long. One of the few Old Ones who had slipped away from the ever-encroaching hunger of mankind's need for space.

In this supposedly deserted ice waste, a track down a berg caught my eye, large, long and straight. Just another chuck of ice I thought to myself. Or maybe, the very clue we are after. If we were seeing siren trails, then we would soon be able to leave.

But this was the Arctic. It was as dangerous as it was beautiful. Our boat's rounded hull would minimise the risks associated with traversing the area, but the weather was out of our control. The wind sprite shivered below deck, claiming we had reached the ice and its debt was discharged, that it was too cold and risked the very gas it was made from becoming crystallised.

The groaning of colliding icebergs reverberated through the water, waking me from a shallow and chilly sleep. When I opened the hatch, fog poured down, condensing on the boat's insides, and I was thankful for the well-insulated interior. Still, it made a feeble attempt to freeze before dripping to the floor.

Above deck, the world had been lost in a blanket of fog. We could no longer see whether we sailed into water or ice. Only the crunching of our narrow fronted hull gave it away.

I sleepily stared around, trying to locate anything that would guide us. The whiteness was complete. White sky, white sea, white bergs.

I held the rail to steady myself. Up could be down right now, and I wouldn't know any different. The siren called from near by. Her Ocean voice carrying faintly through the fog.

'I am home. This feels like home. You may go now. I hear more of my kind under the water calling for me to join them.'

A splash of slush landed at my feet, from her, I presumed. I slid across the ice-coated deck to peer over the rail. She reared up, her spinning eyes level with my own.

'Remember, selkie, you cannot do it alone. But, for all our sakes, you must continue to try,' she said before vanishing under the gently undulating slush for the last time.

I gazed at the spot where she had sunk. I'd miss the grumpy serpent. I was knocked off my feet by a heavy thunk from the opposite side of the boat. We drifted through the slush on an angle, ripples of it mounting by the bow until we thudded into another berg. The collision knocked us badly – our shallow keel rose up against the sides of the bergs, popping us out of the ice as it was designed to do. But the shelves of ice that had jammed together protruded quite a way up from the water.

Theo swore.

We were to all effect and purpose grounded. Ice continued to pack in around us. The speed of the travelling berg surprising us all.

The motor was out of the water, and the sails were useless. There was nothing we could do for now but wait, and hope that the bergs drifted apart again soon.

Eden turned off all non-essential processes, and we dropped below deck to allow us to remove our face coverings and speak without our words being frozen. I woke Zora and explained the situation as she sleepily joined us.

Theo began. 'We are either much further north than we realised, or there is an ice flow off course. Either way, we could be stuck here for anything from days to months.'

'Months?' Eden shivered. 'I suppose it's a beautiful place to die. We don't have enough food to last us that long.'

'We'll find a way,' I said. 'It was always risky travelling this late in the season. Zora, is there anything you can do?'

'I'll have to think on it,' she said – which I knew really meant, 'Yes, but you might not like the answer.'

We sat that night working through our stores and trying to come up with a plan. Eventually, accepting that much of it was out of our hands. Poor luck had grounded us, now we would have to use all the talents at our disposal and hope for an equally large blast of luck and fair weather to free us.

I stood at the bow the next morning and looked over the pack ice. There was motion of, if not water, then at least slush, to the South, at the ice-flow's edge.

Theo tied a rope around his waist to test the ice around us. It was thick enough to take his weight. We knew that before he tried because it would not release *Black Hind*, but some thin hope had made him try, and we had humoured him. We had lifted the keel as we had first encountered the ice, so we weren't trapped, merely grounded. We might slide over it, but our combined pulling force was unlikely to be sufficient to loosen us. After all, what are four people against a boat's weight? Even if we freed it from our icy pedestal, we would be left on the ice as it began to move.

'Where's a leathergill siren when you need one,' Zora grumbled as she joined me. 'It's possible I could do something, but it will completely exhaust me. Georgie, I can't guarantee I can get us out.'

'What if you melted enough of a channel to ease us down

and then soften the ice in front of us? If you can create fog you must be able to melt ice,' I said.

'It takes a lot of energy,' she replied. 'We need sun too; we need enough power for the engine to get us underway. The next time the sun comes out, I'll do it. Before we are too far from the edge. I'll take a small block of ice down to the cabin now and practise in there. I can't concentrate in this frozen madness.'

I didn't point out that she'd have to do it out here. If I had to give her every extra blanket we had, to allow her to stay warm and focused, I'd do it.

Whose stupid idea was it to sail all the way to the ice? Ahh yes, Lady Gina's. I'd made a promise to provide a full escort. It seemed so simple when the words had fallen from her mouth, a shame the reality proved to be more tricky.

We had plenty of supplies, contrary to Eden's suggestion. What we didn't have, was an endless supply of time. This might be a rogue ice flow but, as the nights lengthened, the sun would become useless to our panels. Before the moon became our only light, we needed to be well away from the ice. If we weren't, the distance between us and open water might grow insurmountable.

FISH'S BAR AND A BARGE OF DELIGHTS

SELKIE

Orange's town gates loomed in the distance. I wondered idly if they were to keep people in or wildlife out? The ground in front of the walls was razed to short stubble by a small flock of goats. With such limited cover, there was no doubt someone had already spotted the lone traveller heading towards them. I just hoped they hadn't looked too closely at me yet.

I dropped my bag under a tree, an ancient and twisted sentinel of the road. It was shady and cool as I leant against the seaward facing trunk and prepared myself. Maintaining a full glamour all the way through the town, as Sal had suggested, would be exhausting, but if Jake's men were in the town, it was a risk worth taking.

I tied my hair into a short braid and dropped the glamour over my entire body. I looked down and saw myself unchanged in any way – but if I'd got this right, anyone looking at me would see a young man. Should they try to touch me, their hand would pass through the illusion until it reached my body, so I needed to be careful not to talk to anyone for long, or get within arm's reach. I grabbed my bag and strode back to the road.

One of the men at the gate cast a lazy eye over me and waved me through.

'Where ya headed?' he asked. I found his heavy, unfamiliar accent hard to make out.

I opted for the deepest whisper I could manage, pretending I'd lost my voice. 'Ships, for work,' I husked.

'Sound like you could use a drink first, eh, Ernst?' the first man said, nudging his companion and chuckling.

'Head for Fish's Bar. They do a cold ale to warm your heart,' Ernst replied. 'Don't even try the Gilded Heaven on the other side of the road. Might be pretty to look at but the owner is mean as a bear trapped in a cave by a campfire.'

I tried not to think on the oddly specific analogy as I walked into the bustle of Orange.

The road divided the town as surely as a river separates her banks. On my right, small homes clustered together. They felt natural. Some even appeared to have grown rather than been built, if you looked closely. An array of bright colour filled the surrounding gardens, swelling with fruits and life. Children and animals played, and the air carried laughter. Dark tubes ran across the rooftops, weaving around them numerous times before entering the dwellings. These homes were somehow peaceful. Unlike many human dwellings, these simple homes did not impose their presence on their surroundings.

The left reminded me of an old painting from Icidro's home. Stone buildings loomed imposingly over the road with garish illumination spilling from their doors and shining through the windows. The hum of pumps and generators came almost exclusively from that side, and strange, hollow music echoed out of numerous doorways.

It was disorientating and foul. If this was the world the humans had lost, I was glad it had gone.

I struggled with the strange imbalance, gravitating towards the side that felt *real*. The road curved down towards the sea, and the Gilded Heaven filled my vision, its glowing sign flickering erratically. A flock of women attired in ridiculous clothes minced along the street towards it, giggling and laughing like seabirds hunting for prey. They swooped towards the entrance, shoving a young woman to the ground, causing her to drop everything she carried. She looked a few years younger than me. They sneered at her as she picked up the spilt contents of her tray, then swung through the doors, their voices raised in delight at something, or someone, they saw inside. I ran towards her, desperate to help, but she waved me away frantically, shaking her head. I backed off.

'Leave her be. You'll make a whole heap more trouble for her if you help,' said a friendly voice.

I jumped. Lost as I had been in my observation of the huge building, I had not noticed the unassuming tables set in front of a long, open wooden bar. A beautifully painted fish swung pendulously from the simple board across the front.

'Fish's,' I whispered.

'What'll you have? I'm telling you, lad, no point in wasting your coin or time on that one. If you're desperate for a piece of something, *Barge* is alongside for a few more days. We never know when it will be back, so make the most of its delights while you can.'

I hadn't planned to stop for food. Sal had told me to go straight to *Barge*, but something smelt incredible. For the first time since I had left home, I wanted to eat. I wasn't tiring yet, and I could smell the sea. I was close.

'What do you have to eat?' I asked.

'Only shellfish, I'm afraid, nothing fancy. We found a good stash of mussels this morning on the low tide. Want some?' he replied.

'They're really good.' Someone interrupted the man I assumed was Fish, waving dark shells, long and shimmering on the inside, which I recognised as the source of the mouth-watering scent.

'Please,' I said, desperately trying to maintain the deep whisper.

The mussels were delicious – slightly altered with use of flavouring, but it wasn't unpleasant. Even the fact that they were cooked was not enough to spoil them. I ate as slowly as I could, savouring the taste.

Quiet contemplation of my food was disturbed by a shrieking voice across the street.

'Why haven't you picked up all that glass yet? Table 3 has been waiting for five minutes while you have been dawdling, you stupid bitch.'

I turned my head slowly, trying to remain casual. The shrieker wore attire as garish as her customers. Her spider-crab-like limbs, all joints and no flesh, gesticulated at the poor woman still scrabbling on the floor before the crab-woman delivered a kick to her ribs, sending her forward into the glass once again.

'Now look, you are so clumsy you have blood on your hands. You'll be even later serving them. That's more money I'll be taking from your pay if you don't get them served quickly.'

I found myself on my feet, fingers toying with the needle tucked inside my sleeves. I could go over there, take the girl to the boat with me. I had enough poison on my person to take out that whole place if I was quick.

'I told you, lad. You're new here. Don't go causing trouble. Stay on our side of the street. Plenty have tried to get her out of there, and she refuses to leave. There's some hold old Mona has over her, and we haven't figured it out. I promise you though, we won't stop trying. Don't start a war on your first day in town, least of all one others have been quietly fighting for years.'

He placed a glass in front of me. The orange liquid it contained was tangy and sweet with a spicy kick. I swallowed it quickly and fished in my bag for some money. My hand closed around a chunky coin and I withdrew the gold piece. With no idea of its value, I placed it on the counter and looked up at Fish.

'Is that enough?'

'I don't know which boat you are fresh off, but that buys you a day's food on this side of the road and a seat on that side.' Fish smiled. 'You'd best get to wherever you're headed. Don't flash that kind of coin again, and no stopping for pretty girls. Free advice to go with your meal.'

'Thank you.'

I sat for a moment watching the woman across the road. Old Mona swung the door open and strode back inside, leaving the woman alone. She stood, pushed her shoulders back and narrowed her eyes after the departing woman, her fists clenching tightly. Then, she glanced over at me, and I saw her face properly for the first time. Dark hair fell in greasy waves, and she was thin to the point of being emaciated, but there was no doubt about that face. This was the woman in The Hind's vision – the one in the flames. I would have to ignore Fish's advice. This was a fight I would be getting involved in. Once I had Sal's support, I'd return to get that woman out of here.

My legs grew unsteady as I strolled down the hill, trying to resist the urge to run towards the sea. A set of guards at the far end eyed me considerably more warily than those who let me enter the first gate. Beyond them, rows of neat, white houses nested against the hill. Here and there, one was missing, a pile of rubble all that remained of a home. Most had flattened rooftops and people sat on them, calling across to each other. In narrow gaps, between the white boxes, I could see boats of all shapes and sizes anchored offshore, bobbing gently on the small waves of the Terranian sea.

'Looks like this one took his pleasures a bit too enthusiastically in the pleasure district,' one of the men muttered as I drew close.

'I don't recognise him. I know everyone,' the other said. His hand moved to rest on the weapon at his belt.

They peered at me, their eyes crawling over my glamour.

'No one gets in the pleasure district unless I let them through,' the first speaker said, stepping in front of me. He was broad and imposing. I still looked down on him, but something was wrong, and my ability to hold the glamour was fading fast.

'I travelled a long way – came in the other gate,' I said, my voice cracking.

'That's rare. You here for work?' he growled, stepping closer to me. I held my place, hoping that he wouldn't make contact with me and nodded. My voice had almost betrayed me. Whatever I had eaten or drunk was having an unanticipated effect on my body. I needed to get past these men and fast. I needed to find *Barge*.

'We don't usually let people through for free.' the first guard said, a sly smile growing on his russet bearded face. 'Have you got anything you can pay your way with?'

Fish had said not to flaunt my money. The one I had left

him was the only gold coin I had in the bag. The rest were less valuable, I hoped.

'I have a few coins if that will help,' I offered, reaching for my coin bag.

They nodded in tandem. 'Saves us asking for your papers. You know how it is. Pretty boy like you on your own – heading to the shore for work. You'll soon earn them back.'

I fished in my bag, making a show of trying to find coins, eventually pulling out a handful. I dropped them in red beard's outstretched hand, and their eyes widened. I'd messed up again. Too much.

'We never saw you. Don't go try'na join Lone Jake's crews with that kinda coin – go to the far end of the harbour.'

'Lone Jake?' The other chuckled. 'Heard he were shot. Should call him Lost Jake now!' Then he turned back to me and winked. 'Saw who?'

I breathed a sigh of relief as they turned their backs on me. No one else spoke to me or even seemed to notice me as I wound my way towards the shore. There were many small boats and a few much bigger ones resting drunkenly in the low water on their keels, but I could see nothing anchored out there that fitted my idea of a pleasure barge. I reached the edge of the town and searched the coastline. Most boats were far below the edge of the high harbour walls with the low water. Surely I hadn't missed it? I hadn't even stopped. He wouldn't have left without me . . . Would he? No, Fish had said it was there. A huge ship leaving the town would have been noticed.

I turned along the wall towards a set of shining buildings surrounded by lush trees. A railing fenced them off from the rest of the harbour, and they were just lower than the high wall. I climbed up the slope towards it. Maybe I'd see *Barge* from out there.

A voluptuous woman reclined outside a house. She was barely dressed; her generous curves would have attracted the most powerful selkie in any pack. She was beautiful. To be entirely fair, it was so hot I couldn't blame her lack of clothing. I found myself staring as I drew closer. She confidently returned my gaze, looking at me through long lashes from her side of the wall, as it gently rocked.

I blinked.

She laughed at me. 'You look confused. Is this the first time you've seen a woman with so few clothes on?'

'No.' I forgot to whisper.

She raised an eyebrow. 'You *are* young, aren't you?'

'I'm looking for my cousin,' I blurted. With my cover blown, I needed to find *Barge* and fast, I didn't want to give anything else away. 'They work on *Barge*.'

'Oh, they do, do they? And, what is your cousin's name?' she asked. 'Maybe, I can send you the right way.'

'I . . .'

I searched my memory, Oceans, what had Sal told me to say?

'I'm here for Driftwood.' I managed to dredge the word out eventually.

She looked at me with thinned lips, scanning me up and down. 'You don't look much like Driftwood material. Who did you say your cousin was again?'

I tried to swallow, but my mouth had grown so dry it was becoming hard to speak. I was so close, and I needed to find Sal before the glamour faded. I felt my mind fraying at the edges and struggled to stay upright.

'Sal, My cousin is Sal.' My voice sounded like my own, and I saw an eyebrow lift in amusement. She really did think I was young.

She opened her gate and gestured me through, 'We've been

expecting you. Come in.' She leant forward to support me as I wobbled towards her. That close, she again seemed to drop and rise before my eyes as she opened a small gate,

'Mind the step. It's bigger than it might look from there,' she said.

I stepped into her garden. The garden rose to meet me. I turned and saw what I couldn't from the shore – the step extended from the edge of the harbour wall and hovered above the garden.

'Your house is on the water,' I whispered. 'That's amazing.'

'Lord Sal's house. Welcome aboard *Barge*.'

Now, I could see it. All these small houses were one complex. She gestured along the deck to a long, central tent, blue fabric billowing in the breeze.

'If you head to the main hall, someone will attend to your needs.' The corner of her mouth twitched upwards. 'You can try asking for Sal, but I am not sure he'll have time. He's recently arrived with a whole ship-load of creatures for his beloved aquariums.'

I started towards the hall, then turned to wave my thanks, but she was already swaying back to her seat and waving coyly at a man strolling along the harbour.

More steps descended to the lower central deck, the smaller buildings raised on their own private gardens around the central hall. I was desperately struggling to maintain the glamour now. It took all my concentration to maintain both this appearance and forward motion. I staggered in the door. Do tents even have doors? It was floaty in here … Someone rushed towards me to catch my arm, but I waved them back.

'Private room,' I whispered. 'I'm Lord Sal's cousin. Please get him.'

One man ran off while another led me to an area where the

breeze rippled the floor length walls. They closed the curtain and left me alone.

I collapsed as the glamour dropped from my body. A click from behind a curtain and a swish of fabric alerted me to someone entering the space.

'I've got you.' Sal's Ocean voice washed over me. He picked me up, and as much as I wanted to fight, I didn't have enough energy left. I hated feeling useless. Sal carried me into the coolness, away from the noise and chatter of the hall, through a narrow passage. I don't remember much more of that day.

I awoke on a comfortable bed wrapped in a soft white cover, and I found myself staring into a glass tank filled with the most delicious food I had seen for at least two lunar cycles. Periwinkles crawled across the bottom and fresh seaweed swayed in the artificial current.

'You're awake?' Sal asked. I rolled over to find him naked in his chair.

'And you are . . .' I laughed nervously.

'Natural. I hate clothes. They are floppy and loose. No one comes in here without knocking.

I realised as he said it that there was just one window looking out over the sea – it truly was a private space. I sympathised with his dislike of clothes. Selkies were not meant to be dressed. I gestured towards the tank.

'Please, can I eat?'

'Help yourself. I keep it well-stocked in case I need a snack.' He smiled, and I tried to relax. I had made it this far on my own. He was still talking about the types of creatures he liked to snack on as I sprang across the room and plunged my arm in to grab handfuls of snails and seaweed.

I bit into them, delighting in the crunch-squish of the food. Gods, but I had missed this. Sal stopped talking and sat quietly as I ate, letting me enjoy my food in peace.

Once I was sated, I sat in a comfortable, large red chair.

'I need a boat,' I demanded.

'You will have one. But, if that is all you want, why did you come to me? I gave you enough money to buy one.' He frowned, staring at me or was it the chair.

'Because I need your help too.'

He raised an eyebrow. 'You need me, and I need someone who can get into places I can't. Someone entirely unknown. This could work.'

'Why?'

'I sometimes need people – removed. Most of the time, Driftwood deal with it, but there are tasks they do not have the natural talents for. Aside from sailing around the world on a random search for the skin, why do you want a boat?'

'I want to find the missing Old Ones of this region. They need to come home,' I said, standing and moving to the other chair in the room. Sal's shoulders dropped a little. It must have been something about that chair.

'You met the Hind?' he said. 'I hoped you would. She won't talk to me, thinks I have been turned to the wrong side. I was blinded by money and sex – so much sex! Human women throw money at you just for sex. It's a heady combination when you add enthusiastic men too. Sprinkle a little power in the mix and yes, I may have been corrupted. But, I was never blinded. I just needed the right tool. You fell into my lap. I gave you the choice. I always give freed Old Ones a choice.'

'How many have you rescued?'

Sal shrugged. 'Five or six. My money, all my resources and my network are now at your disposal. It's time to right things before they go too far. Did The Hind talk to you? Did she explain why the land was dying?'

I wandered across to the tank and spat the shell fragments into the water. 'Yes, she needs her sister. She can't hold everything together alone. All the other spirits have fled. She needs us to find the missing hind.' I was about to add my desire to rescue the woman I'd seen in Orange too, but something stopped me. If Sal was about to train and supply me, I'd rescue her myself soon enough.

Sal took a small shellfish himself, carrying it back to his seat carefully. He held it to his lips, then paused, gesturing for me to sit down.

'Before we proceed any further, and now we are alone, you need to explain how you lost another selkie's skin, and where your own is,' he said.

'That's easy,' I replied and settled back to explain.

16

WHEN THE NIGHT IS COLD, AND THE LAND IS DARK

GEORGIE

We huddled together on the deck, staring in amazement at the ripples of colour flowing across the sky. Purples and blues mingled with no consideration for each other's space. It felt like a message from the old gods. Human-kind insisted it was just solar energy, for to accept it was anything more was to throw every step of their progress into doubt. Could it even be considered progress, I wondered as I watched the shifting colours.

They reminded me of the waves on a particular beach at home. The clear, unpolluted waters green with cold and the blue warmth mingling with it. Eddies of light coiled across the horizon, caressing the stars.

We headed below deck reluctantly – the moon chasing us into the warmth, teasing us with her sparkling reflection from every exposed surface of the boat.

For the first time in days, Zora and I were headed to bed at the same time. Awkward shuffling ensued in the confined space as we tried to work around each other. I scrambled up to the top bunk before she could argue. Zora would be warmer in the bottom one, and I could handle the cold better than her. I wrapped the blankets tightly around me and closed my eyes to try and rest.

'Georgie,' her voice drifted up to me, quiet and gentle. I waited, intent on the next phrase. 'I'll get us out.'

'I know you will.' I listened for more, but nothing came.

Thin clouds drifted lazily over the boat in the morning, their delicate structures gossamer-light.

'Is it enough?' I asked, desperate for some good news.

'No,' Zora replied. 'Maybe by midday, it will be.'

Eden poked their head out. 'Breakfast, is served.' A theatrical gesture accompanied the words, but the effect was lost under layers of thick clothes.

'On our way,' I replied, staring up at the pale sun, willing it to brightness, before sighing and following Zora.

'I'm so hungry I could eat a boiled shoe,' she muttered as she sat at the small table.

'We've only been trapped a day. That's a little over dramatic, don't you think? We're hardly Franklin or the explorers of Old Earth.' Theo laughed, a true belly laugh, his breath freezing as it left him. I closed the hatch to try and retain the little heat we could.

'No, but there's not as much food as you might think. Lots of fruit has gone off, and the stored meat, whilst cold, is not great. We can use some energy, as the sun is out, to have a proper meal,' Zora said. 'Not much, though. We need to store as much as possible to propel us through the ice if I can melt a channel. Even if we get out, we don't have much food to get us to the first port for a restock.'

Last night, our meal had been dried meats and fruits – chewy, sticky and altogether foul. I could understand why the analogy of a shoe had sprung to mind. Eden had done better this morning, and I hoped I would be able to eat it with less difficulty.

Cor called out a greeting as I joined them. He looked a shadow of his normal self – the cold and confinement weren't doing him any favours. He pecked at a bit of food, rejecting it immediately. I sympathised. For as good as the food was to them, it would taste bland and salt-less to me.

At least I understood that I needed to eat to live. Cor reached my waist when he stood alongside me; he was a big bird who needed to eat a huge volume of food each day. He couldn't fish in the ice and was reluctant to fly too far from the boat. I tried to tempt him, but Eden shook their head.

'It won't work.'

'You have to get him to fish,' I urged. 'He'll starve himself if you don't.'

'Don't you think I've tried? I've even jumped fully into his mind to try and push him to eat. I might try to shove him out on deck tomorrow. He's too attached to his comforts for a bird of his size.'

'At least he stopped hacking up those gross pellets today,' muttered Theo.

The boat shuddered and creaked. I grabbed at the table as it shook again, now from the other side. Something had hit us. Had we worked loose? I doubted it – had the ice parted, we'd have noticed some bigger clue.

My heart pounded against my ribs as I eased the hatch upward to peer through. The stench of blood hit my nostrils with force. The deck was a freezing mass of red, with viscera strewn across it, clinging to every surface it touched, the source of the mess was entrails being dragged behind an enormous walrus carcass. The predator hauled the rapidly freezing body over the rail as I pushed the hatch up to get a better view. All I saw of it was a glimpse of shimmering white.

'What is it?' Theo asked.

I steadied my breathing, trying to sound as calm as I could. 'There's blood all over the deck. We have company – and I don't think it's Sirena. The good news is that there is blood all over the deck, so hopefully, it won't be hungry.' I forced out a laugh. 'Zora, we need to get out of here,' I said as I turned to face the crew.

'Give it an hour or two. As difficult as waiting may be, we still need to sit tight.'

I tried to calm my jangling nerves and closed the hatch, bolting it. Not that it would stop any siren big enough to take a walrus.

To help draw my focus away from the carnage above, I stroked Cor's head.

'You really do need to be out there. For you, to eat. For us, so you can tell us if there are more sirens and how far we will be trying to push this boat to open water.'

Cor croaked at me.

Eden shrugged. 'Maybe when you go up later, we can all head out on deck. If he's alone down here, it might be enough incentive to get him moving. He's definitely hungry. He might only need a small nudge.'

It wasn't. We stood on the southern side of the boat, looking across the windless white. The slim sliver of water on the horizon remained far out of reach. If we didn't get out of here soon, we'd be stuck for weeks – or longer. A shiver ran down my spine. I was not going to starve to death in this ice, nor were my crew. I'd dragged them up here. It was my job to get them back. Not for the first time, I wished I had my skin, then I could have dived for fish to sustain us.

Zora stared at the ice, engrossed in a battle of wills over its physical state. Blood-slicked snow stretched ahead, the darkness absorbing the sun's warmth a little, but not enough to help us.

Eden, Theo and I scrambled over the rail, dropping to the ice. We began to dig at the stern, freeing as much space around the hull as we could and heaping the ice away from us as we worked our way around the boat. Eventually, Zora called us back, and exhausted, we climbed aboard.

'How are we going to get it underway?' Theo asked. 'Even were the sprite to come out of its self-imposed hibernation, we can't sail down.'

'Then we'll pull it,' I said. 'If we can build enough momentum, maybe the bow will do its job and break the ice.'

'We could do with a flock of birds to tie to the boat and pull us.' Theo laughed. 'What's the point of a bird whisperer who can only talk to the sulking cormorant in the cabin?'

'Eden knows everything there is to know about this boat and how to fix it. You stick to your job of fixing people and steering us properly,' Zora snapped. I'd never heard her speak to any of us like that. Theo raised an eyebrow.

'Yes, boss!' he said and threw a mock salute before leaping overboard. 'I have a better idea – maybe,' he called as he slid down the berg. He stopped in front of a tall, crystal of ice down-slope from where we rested and began cutting a groove around it. Immediately, I could see what he was planning. Oh, that was clever, and it might just work!

I took the longest rope we had, fastening one end

securely around the bow, and slipped and slithered down to join him. Together, we cut a deep groove in the huge crystal and ran the rope along it. The sun shone on that side. Maybe if we moved fast, and kept it moving, this rope would not freeze. We returned triumphantly to the boat and readied ourselves to pull *Black Hind* down the slope when Zora was ready.

I was under no illusion that our weight alone was enough to pull us down. But, if we used the sail winches, we might be able to build enough tension that it would tug us the right way on the freshly melted ice while Eden stood ready to activate the motor. If we had enough momentum to break the sea ice, we needed to keep moving.

Things happened quickly. Zora focused her intent on the ice around the boat, turning it to water and convincing it in some magical way to remain so. There was a subtle shift in the deck beneath our feet. We wound the winch as though our lives depended on it, because they did.

Cor took off from the deck, distressed and calling loudly, shaking his head as he flew towards the edge of the ice. Something had upset him, but at least he was finally in the air. The boat shuddered a little, our shallow draft an advantage here. With the retracted keel up, the boat should slide on its belly until our momentum was enough to cut a path through the pack ice.

Click by click we wound, as Zora kept melting the ice. We shuddered again, our balance tipping slightly forward. A final pull, and we were freed.

As we slid past the tall crystal, we allowed the rope to play out over the side.

The crunch as we hit the pack ice at the base of the slope shuddered through the boat, but with the shudder came spray, and we remained in motion. Our bow had done its job. Eden engaged the engine, and we maintained our pace – slowly but steadily. Eden poked their head out and grinned.

'It worked. Next step; let's get those sails up and coax that sprite into helping. I want to get out of here.'

'The sails are damaged. We need the red set. Extra power will help us push through as well,' Theo replied.

Eden sprung onto the deck, happy to be underway and started calling out orders as they wrestled the helm from Theo.

'I need the detachable spars, the red sails and the other rigging lines,' Eden sang out.

'Theo, get whatever is needed. I'll try and persuade that sprite out.' I didn't like the idea, but it was our best chance – I just had to persuade Aria, that unless it helped itself, it would die.

'Don't bargain away your soul,' Theo murmured. I wasn't sure whether he was serious. The tone of his voice certainly implied that he believed it possible. He was right.

Down in the huge, empty space of the hold, the sprite huddled in a pile of blankets. We'd tried to coax it towards the warmth although, not particularly hard if I was honest with myself.

'We're moving,' I said. Simple phrasing was key here.

'I feel it.'

'We will stop moving soon. There is no wind.'

'What will you give for wind? My deal is done.'

I paused and considered my reply before I spoke. 'You are the one who needs wind.'

'I am wind. I do not need.'

I crouched down and reached for Aria. It was pale and thin; my fingers passed through its body easily. 'Do you want to stop being?' I asked. 'It feels as though you are stopping being.'

'I wish to blow again, from the big winds to the distant shore, to travel the world.'

'With more wind, this boat can carry you towards the Everstorm. With none, the boat will sit here, and you will either have to fly alone, weak and unable to make it, or stop being. Just like those who broke on the rocks, the day I caught you.' I paused to let that sit with it. We sat in silence for several minutes. I refused to be drawn any further. Aria had to see what it needed without me offering anything. Eden and Theo would make short work of changing the sails, so we needed movement soon – but not at any price.

Aria stopped flickering and flitted around the cabin pausing in front of me.

'Then, I will take myself home – with this boat. You will help me travel to the Everstorm, for bringing you with me, if we get free of the ice.'

I considered the response, turned it over in my head for double meanings and concluded that it was a deal I could make. It had no time constraint and no physical cost from the crew.

'I will help you to reach the Everstorm, if you help us to get free by creating the wind we need to keep moving the boat forward through the ice,' I agreed.

'Carry me,' it said.

I stuffed the squirming spirit inside my clothes to keep it warm and ascended to the deck.

'Have you got it?' Eden called from high up in the spars. The red sails now outstretched, our wings unfurled again. 'I'd die for some wind right now!'

'As you wish,' the voice under my chin muttered.

Eden fell.

They dropped over the edge of the boat, into the icy slush alongside us. Their body smashed against the ice before being dragged under. Theo moved to leap over, and I stopped him, throwing him a rope. He tied it around his waist and leapt off the boat. We were edging forward still, but only slowly without the wind.

'Gods, the motor,' I whispered.

Aria had extricated itself from my clothes and was beginning to blow.

I screamed for Zora, and she came dashing to my aid. We hung onto the rope as tightly as we could. Theo had only moments before we would have to haul him aboard, whether he had Eden or not.

His head bobbed to the surface, the bedraggled form of Eden alongside him.

The huge rudder swung with no one guiding it, and I hoped that it would at least protect them slightly from the motor.

We hauled as hard as we could, hand over hand, until we had enough length to wrap the rope around a winch and pull them aboard. The strength of the ratchets was more reliable than the grip of our fingers.

Theo flopped onto the deck, shivering violently. Eden was in his arms, blue and limp. They were both back on board in less than a few minutes, but in these waters – that was long enough to kill. Theo collapsed, then struggled upright, his training superseding his own need to survive.

He pumped on Eden's chest and tried to get the water out. At first it looked like he was succeeding but his own fatigue was apparent. I had seen enough of what he was doing to continue.

Zora dived into the cabin and returned with a pile of blankets. She crouched over Eden for a moment, placing her hand near their head. A globe of water rose from Eden's open mouth, and Zora flung it over the side. 'Keep going,' she snapped at me. 'Make Eden breathe again. Gods, selkie, do something! I'll get us out of here. We need to keep this boat moving. We need a chance of getting out of the ice,' she called as she ran back to the bow. 'Cor's returning.'

Cor landed alongside us. He stared at Eden, his head tilted to one side quizzically. There was an intelligence in those eyes I hadn't really noticed until now. He lay, not alongside Eden, but against the violently shivering Theo. Eden was still not breathing and had no heartbeat. I tried to ignore the creature and returned to what Theo had been doing, pumping on Eden's chest. Cor reached forward with his long beak and pecked me.

I tried again, and again he pecked me.

'I'm not trying to hurt them,' I panted as I worked. 'I'm trying to save them.'

Cor shook his head.

I started again, after checking for breath and again got pecked. Blood froze as it left the lacerations on my hands now. Cor waddled back to the exhausted Theo.

The wind sprite had produced enough wind to keep our momentum. Had Eden actually just slipped? Did I imagine hearing what I thought it said? No, Eden had bought our passage home with their life.

I didn't understand why Cor was still with us. One extra mouth to feed and no way of using it now – we'd gained a morbid mascot. I kept working, focused only on Eden.

'It's over, Georgie, stop.' Theo had been watching carefully, under cold-lidded eyes. 'Eden wasn't breathing when I reached them. I brought them back anyway, it was worth a try, and I couldn't leave the body for the ice. For the sirens.'

I didn't want to accept it, but Theo reached for me. 'You need to stop.'

'Can you get in the warm?' I asked him. I needed a moment to think. Zora needed time with her friend.

He nodded. 'If you open the hatch, I'll go down and warm up.'

'I'll be down in a moment,' I said, looking at the straight back of Zora, rigid with concentration at the bow.

I hesitantly approached her. She stared intently at the ice ahead, softening it with her willpower.

'Eden is gone,' I said, as gently as I could.

'I know.' Tears whipped from her cheeks, freezing as they left her eyes and hitting me like small bullets. I waited. I was good at waiting.

'They would want their body passed to the sea,' she said eventually. 'Why did they fall, Georgie? Eden never fell, not ever. I've seen Eden climb a thousand rigs and tweak many sets of sails. I've never seen anyone so surefooted.'

I wanted to tell her, but I was worried she'd say something stupid to Aria. It was safer for her not to know. This was a secret I needed to keep, for now at least. I was tied to a sidhe bargain, now worthless as another had superseded it.

I placed a hand over hers, my thick gloves reflective of the distance between us, and gently squeezed. Then, I retreated to take the helm, staring past Eden's immobile body to the open sea, beyond the ice.

Through the open trapdoor, I could see Theo and Cor huddled together under a blanket. Theo wasn't usually that fond of the cormorant but appeared to be accepting the warmth forced upon him by the determined bird.

Zora and I stood our vigil on the deck throughout the night. Theo warmed slightly and brought us food in the morning. I forced it down with my eyes near-closed from exhaustion. We broke free of the slush as the sun rose, bedraggled and exhausted. The ice ahead was now intermittent, and *Black Hind's* narrow bow more than capable of slicing through it.

Slow waves rolled out in our wake. Before long, a group of tusks protruded from the new air hole we had created in the ice as a herd of narwhal took full advantage of the extra breathing room afforded them.

Zora left her post in silence and scooped Eden up in her arms, carrying their frozen body below deck. We would release Eden to the waves when we were further from the ice, where it was safe to stop and say our goodbyes. Theo came up and relieved me of my role. I sat on the deck, not wanting to disturb Zora's mourning. I could rest later.

We had turned our back on the ice – for now. I couldn't shake the feeling I would be back one day.

17

OF DEATH AND DECEIT

LADY GINA

News of the *Black Hind's* return to Terrania had travelled through Sal's network at speed. He sent an escort boat filled with supplies to accompany *Black Hind* to his private harbour, along with a new set of blue sails. He wasn't to know that black would have better suited the crew's mood.

'You can't have too many sets of sails on a covert boat,' he'd said when I asked him about it. I failed to understand why they all needed to be so bright. Surely grey like the mast and spars would have made more sense. But then, my mood was hardly conducive to anything gaudy.

Black Hind limped back into Terrania with one less crew member aboard; Zora had insisted on dropping Eden's body into the seabird rich waters of The Northern Territories. The boat was headed into harbour for repairs, and Zora was in dire need of time to mourn her lifelong friend. Sal had told them to go. Safe Harbour was on the southern coastline, and from there, Zora would have time to go home if she needed to.

Not everyone gets the opportunity to rest I thought, as I watched *Black Hind* depart under motor with Zora on the helm and the brooding presence of Cor perched alongside her.

The Aria had emerged from the hold, tired and blown out. I'd found a safe place for it on *Barge*, somewhere no one would accidentally run into it until either *Black Hind* or another of the fleet's boats were ready to deliver it to as close to the Everstorm as they could safely get.

Sal stood beside me, staring into the distance. He chewed on seaweed with the slow, pondering motion that indicated his mind was not remotely on the task of eating.

'What did you find?' I asked gently.

'I found our old mutual acquaintance had acquired yet another resident he shouldn't have,' Sal replied.

'Did you free them?' I placed my hand on his, squeezing gently.

Sal nodded. 'I had to buy them, as ever.'

'Did you bring them back here?' I pressed, wondering what Sal had been tempted to save this time. Something so big, he had made a dash up the coast.

'Yes.' He paused. 'I was surprised to see Icidro alive, still trading in ideas and dreams abandoned as stories. I wish some days that we could remove him altogether.'

'If we know where he is, we always have a starting point. If he stops collecting, then someone else will only take his place. Did you gain anything we can use?' I asked. The image of Icidro seared into my mind. He represented everything that was wrong with humanity in my eyes.

'Maybe. How about you? Did the King offer anything we can use?'

Ahh, yes, the other human plague. I bit the thoughts down. You never knew for certain, once alongside a port, who's ears were listening. 'He had two requests. The head of the siren was the first; it's why he has been plaguing Seren weekly with couriers. He's desperate for news.'

'He was never getting that. I take it there is a token to give him?'

I nodded. 'Yes, hopefully, it will be enough.' I held up the bag that had been brought aboard from *Black Hind*. It contained a woman's head – a washed-up corpse whose head was to serve a greater purpose in death than life. Sal reached in to turn it around. He studied her face with a frown.

'It's not pretty enough. No one would believe this was a siren. Not even those stupid enough not to realise you'd be left with a serpent head, not a humanoid one.'

'How many humans alive now have ever killed one to know?' I replied. Our hopes rested on the deception lasting long enough to fool him. Once it was mounted on his gates, it would be feasted on by birds and become entirely unrecognisable within hours.

'I'm planning on asking Seren to work some magic with it,' I said. 'If we can fool him with this, he will be presenting us with two treasures greater than we could ever have hoped for. Two creatures of our choice from the overall list of all the illicit collections in his kingdom. Maybe we can find more Old Ones amongst them, maybe, the other hind.'

'Why does he offer two?' Sal closed the bag, tying it tightly. The smell was making my guts roil, and I was grateful for the relief.

'He wants us to hide a child. A child he doesn't yet have, who will inherit his throne. He wants them hidden where I grew up, where he believes you hid me.'

'Who's the mother? The Queen is far too old for pregnancy. He wants us to hide an illegitimate heir, so he can present them in the future. When? Once he has removed Anard from his line of succession?'

'I didn't ask either question. It seemed prudent to agree to his requests.'

Sal said nothing. His eyes roved the horizon again. The sound of his thoughts so loud, they were almost audible amongst the lapping waves at the side of the boat.

'If I were you—'

I raised a hand to stop him. 'You would wish your sole heir, your only daughter, to carry a half-human child, just for leverage.'

'Leverage and control of the future.' He sighed deeply. 'It should be considered. You are attractive. He would not turn you down.'

'I knew you'd ask this. It had occurred to me too,' I said and joined him in his contemplation. We stood together in silence for a long while, watching the schools of fish glide past *Barge*. Big ones, small ones, flashy bright ones, their confused mass a representation of the range of people who called *Barge* home. Sal didn't push. He was right; it would have been a plan for the good of all the Old Ones. I'd even considered it myself. But, it would not be the right plan, not for me, and not for now.

Sal eventually turned to look at me. I gave him a half-smile.

'I can't do it. I'm incomplete, and I would be ensnared. Never free, never myself. I can do more good out here than in his bedchamber. Completely aside from the fact that he is a despicable specimen of a human.'

He nodded, my answer accepted. 'Then, we will wait for a bawling infant to turn up and dispatch it to the furthest reaches of The Territories,' he said. 'Why are we getting access to this list?'

'I used my charm and offered to keep it safe for him. I sold him on our neutrality.'

'Then let's hope that we can appease him with this.' He hoisted the bag over his shoulder. A fly buzzed out.

'We'd better be quick about it, then. Or that will be bloated with larvae,' I said.

'Maybe some will infect his court.' Sal snorted with laughter.

I turned from my contemplation of the bag and gave him a kiss on the cheek for the benefit of any observers. After all, while we were in reality solitary creatures, to all our residents and human companions, it needed to look as though we'd missed each other. Sal gestured for me to walk ahead of him, and we returned to his rooms to meet Seren.

Seren looked at the severed head with narrowed eyes.

'You want me to do what?' she asked.

'We want you to make it look beautiful,' Sal replied. He was sat in his red chair while I had plumped for the bed over his uncomfortable audience chair.

Seren stared down into the bag again. 'Why would I want to make a bloody, severed head look beautiful? Sal, you've lost the plot this time.' She shook her head, but her eyes were studying the face. I knew that expression. I had seen it when she prepared me for meetings, the calculation in her eyes. A grotesque challenge had been set, and she would rise to it. If Sal asked, Seren would know it was important.

'We want to present it to The King of Terrania,' I offered.

She laughed, her hands wrapped around her stomach, a belly laugh like I had not heard in a long time. 'The King likes somewhere wet to stick his cock. Not the mouth of a shrivelled up corpse, no matter how pretty I make it.'

Sal choked on whatever he was eating, probably still seaweed. 'We said we'd kill him a siren. We didn't. But, we did find a body we now need to pass off as one. He may have something we really, really need right now.' Sal pleaded with her. 'This has to be utterly convincing.'

'I've never seen a siren.' Seren muttered. 'My parents used to talk about them when I was a child. Apparently, my father once saw one. It took all my mother's persuasive skills to return him to our flotilla safely.'

Sal looked into the distance. 'I have,' he said. 'Imagine the most beautiful woman you know, then add a little more perfection.'

Seren stared into the bag once more, her shoulders dropping in defeat. 'The King is not sea-folk. He won't know what we do. Fine. It's going to take me a couple of hours. If he turns up early, you're going to be caught out.'

'That's a fair point,' Sal agreed. 'Get the crew to cast off. Tell everyone we are going to retreat from the lights of the town for a starlit cruise, so they can fuck under the open stars and away from watching eyes. It's worked before.'

'I'll do that now. The sooner we cast off, the longer I have before he tracks us down.' Seren left, carrying her grisly charge with her.

'If anyone can do this, it's Seren.' Sal turned to me and leant forward, his hands clasping and unclasping with eagerness.

'Gina, we have some time to kill while we wait. Would you like to free a shark? I checked her over earlier, and she's fit to swim.'

We wound down to where residents of holding tanks awaited sorting into the animals he could free, and those he would hold onto until they could be safely returned home. A beautiful young thresher shark swam towards us, as eager for her own freedom as we were to give it to her. After the darkness of the last few days, I would take great pleasure in this.

18

A NEW DAWN

SELKIE

O nce all clients had left that night, the huge vessel slipped away from Orange. I didn't notice our departure. The combination of safety and exhaustion lead to the soundest sleep I'd had in months. Before the rest of the crew rose, Sal roused me gently and offered me food before suggesting we went outside.

It was a morning worth getting up for. A golden sunrise gently bathed the coastline in glimmering warm light, and the gentle calls of sea birds contrasted sweetly with the wind through the trees on deck.

'You'll need a new identity,' he said, breaking the contented silence.

'I know,' I murmured.

'We may never find the skin.'

I couldn't blame him for repeating that, for giving me another chance to say no; another chance to decline his deal.

'I know,' I replied. I gazed at the sun-soaked beaches in the distance and imagined the waves lapping on their shores. The warm rocks to lie on. I missed home – at least I was back on the water. I exhaled gently, consciously feeling the air leave me. We would find Eryn's skin one day I was sure of it. 'Won't people wonder what happened to the man who arrived last night?' I asked.

Sal chuckled. 'No. What happens on *Barge*, stays on *Barge.* No one will waste a moment's thought on you. Well, no one except Seren. She sees everything.'

'So, who am I? What have you told people?'

Sal smiled, and small wrinkles appeared around his eyes. 'I've said nothing . . . yet.'

'I don't want to be your lover.' I raised my chin as I spoke, meeting his eyes directly. I had no desire for that sort of pretence. I hoped he wouldn't take offence. He didn't strike me as someone used to being turned down.

'Oceans above, I didn't expect you to be. I am old enough to be your father.' His dark eyes widened. 'That would work, you know. Everyone knows I am . . . generous with my favours. It would give me legitimate reasons to be alone with you without suspicion of any commitment on your part. It gives you a way into certain places.' He rose, strolling over to the ship's rail and turned towards me. He leant back against it and studied me. 'We'd need to get your hair cut properly,' he said.

'I want to retain my own identity, separate from yours. If I am stuck here, I cannot hunt for The Hind.'

'Oh, but you can! We can hunt amongst the rich this way. So, why not have both?' Sal was gleeful. 'We can have it all if we but take it! And we'll work on that later, I promise.' He grabbed me by the hand, tugging me after him in haste.' Come on, let's get back to my rooms before we are seen. We have work to do before I introduce you to the crew as my new heir.'

'Heir?'

'Yes, it's a human thing. When they die, instead of scattering their collected belongings on the tide for others to collect, they give them all to someone. I'll be saying I'm giving it all to you. Rumours will get out; the residents of *Barge* will engineer subtle whispers into the right ears. Before long, you will have dinner invitations pouring in.'

I wasn't planning on eating more human food than necessary. That part of his plan seemed rather flawed. He tugged my hand again, and I followed.

Back in his rooms, he held up a mirror next to his face. I faced him, gathering what little magic I had regained overnight.

'Glamour your teeth,' he said, his excitement betrayed by a wide grin.

I placed a basic glamour on my mouth, making every tooth appear even and clean with all points removed.

Sal bared his teeth and glamoured them. 'Now, look at mine.' He pointed with his spare hand at a misaligned tooth. 'Can you see how I made that one look wonky? Do the same one.'

I copied it carefully, then studied his glamour more closely. I could see the lines of the illusion glowing gently as he showed me his work. Tiny tweaks had been applied that changed him subtly from his natural, selkie face – plumper lips, a rounder nose. I applied the same changes and looked in the mirror. It was getting closer. Sal's eyes marked him as a southern selkie where mine were clearly more rounded, more northern. I didn't want to change them if I could avoid it. The more detail I used, the more energy it would take to maintain.

'What about the eyes?' I asked.

'Leave them. They're the same colour,' he replied to my

relief. 'I doubt any human would see what you do. Can you change the line of your cheeks, raise the bone higher?'

I obliged, and he moved to stand next to me. We stared into the mirror. There was now enough resemblance to be beyond doubt.

'Hello, daughter,' he said, grinning widely. 'I make beautiful children.'

I memorised the tweaks and melded them into a single face. A change in physique was too hard to hold for any length of time yet. My journey through the town had illustrated that starkly. It was something I'd need a lot more practice in. My face was all we could work with – for now.

'Next, we need to get you dressed and groomed.' He hit a button next to the bed, and within moments there was a knock at the door.

The woman who had originally welcomed me aboard *Barge* cracked the door open. She glanced at me, then looked to Sal, entering the room and closing the door without saying a word.

'Good morning, Seren. Can I entrust you with sourcing clothes that will fit and be suitable for my daughter, please?'

Her eyebrows raised, just a flicker, then a huge grin broke across her face.

'Your daughter? Sal, when did you sneak her aboard? Is that why we left Orange so quickly last night? Of course I can. Would you introduce me properly?'

I stepped forwards and returned the smile. 'My name is Gina. It's lovely to meet you, Seren.'

'It's lovely to meet you too.' She beamed. I liked her immediately.

'Does this also mean you want an assembly called?' she asked.

'Please. How long do you think it will take for you to have Gina ready?'

Seren's eyes roved over me, pausing at my hair. Her lips thinned a little there, and I sensed I was in for the promised haircut. 'I can have her ready in an hour,' she said. 'You will, of course, want absolute secrecy until the announcement?'

'I know I can trust you, Captain,' Sal replied.

An hour later, I stood behind flowing curtains while the entire crew assembled below us. Sal's power was rooted in these people and their love for him. Once this was started, he had told me, we could not back down.

His voice carried across the ship. He talked of their recent stop and of profits and rumours. He spoke of the tanks being replenished. They cheered as he told them about freeing the shark. These people were on this ship by choice, and it was clear they shared – or indulged – his ideals.

Then, he moved on to me.

'I asked you all to dismiss your clients to allow our early departure. I appreciate your continued loyalty. There was an important reason for us to slip away quietly and without fanfare. A passenger came aboard – one I have awaited a long time. I wished to have complete security and privacy while we were reunited.'

A murmur rolled around the deck. It was so loud that I could hear the swelling tide of voices from my hiding place.

'I am delighted to present to you, Lady Gina, my only daughter and sole heir. It is time she learned how to run this ship. Please accord her the same privileges as myself.'

I stepped through the curtain to a sea of upturned faces. Seren had dressed me in fitted black breeches, tight to the calf. She covered it with a flowing, floor-length tunic, the colour of red sea anemones. Its draped neckline shimmered with streaks of gold, and each side was slit to mid-thigh. Long black cuffs, embroidered with golden sea holly, matched the gilded plant she had used to decorate my freshly cut, and styled hair.

Sal's clothes matched mine, a touch of black, red and gold around his own outfit. It was an image deliberately calculated for maximum impact. Silence fell as I looked at the upturned faces.

'It will be my pleasure to get to know every one of you,' I said.

Over the next few days, I wandered around *Barge* as Sal's shadow, trying to take in the layout – and failing – and trying to learn as many names as I could. We visited rooms that smelt of sex and spaces filled with drifting fabrics; chiffon swaying in the breeze, giving barely concealed privacy for guests. There were musician-screened rooms, where you had the enjoyment of the entertainment – yet privacy from player's eyes.

These were the spaces for the normal folk. Those who paid to board and leave from the dockside. Sailors in need of rest and relaxation, townsfolk who wanted some fun. Each area as opulently decorated as the last. The residents' area was quieter, the decor calm and restful. A lively hum filled the common areas with soft, open seating and expansive views over the ocean. Private apartments were hidden behind subtle doors and appeared almost invisible to anyone who didn't know where to look, ensuring no paying guests ended up where they shouldn't be. *Barge* was a wonder, and without a guide, I'd have been lost hourly.

On the third evening, we descended to the lowest deck, and I finally understood what Sal had done with the animals he had bought, when he paid for my freedom. Those exotic creatures from distant shores, the ones that would die upon release in the Terranian sea, remained on *Barge*.

In the dark room, each tank was illuminated and set out carefully for the species' individual needs. There was no garish gravel or decorations. It was a wonder we floated with so much water on board. Across the entire centre of the room, a low-sided reef teemed with life. Glass-bottomed tanks contained shoaling fish, swimming lazily above a sea bed they would never touch.

'If we visit waters that they live in naturally, I free them.' Sal said. 'In the meantime, I make their captivity the most natural I can.'

A large bar dominated the end of the room, and each table was intimate, isolated by the tank layout from all others.

Sal led me to a larger table than the rest, framed by a community tank containing an eclectic mix of organisms.

'Our table,' Sal said and sank into a comfortable chair.

It was beautiful and powerful; the statement it made not lost on me. Sal sat surrounded by the most poisonous creatures in the room.

'Tonight, we will dock and open our doors to exclusive visitors again. You will join me here for a meal. Should one of my more personal clients choose to visit, I may need to leave you.'

I laughed. 'Enjoy away! I'll just sit here and soak up the tranquility.' I leant in close. 'You aren't my real dad, you know? He let me go out scavenging as soon as I could swim.'

Sal ignored the jibe and carried on talking, just as my father would have. 'If you need help and I'm not here, then press the button under the desk. That will bring someone to you.' Sal showed me a large button just above his knee. 'There are many residents on *Barge*, most of them sea-folk. Some are here to entertain our guests, but this button will call a member of Driftwood, my personal security and problem-solving team.' He gestured towards the corner of the bar and a tall, black-skinned man stepped forward, his steps as graceful as a dancer and his eyes as lively as fish in the shallows. He exuded confidence.

'This is Cypress. When you are in Ocean Bar, he will never be far away,' Sal said.

Cypress flashed me a grin. 'I look forward to getting better acquainted, Lady Gina,' he said, then returned to the shadows.

Seren entered the bar, gliding towards us as I decided to go full petulant daughter.

'I won't need protecting! If you are busy, then I'll be just fine.'

'Hrm,' Sal replied, with a twinkle in his eye.

'I doubt any daughter of Lord Sal's needs protection.' Seren's smooth voice interrupted us. 'However, Lord Sal has suggested you talk to me about some specific tailoring you would like doing, something to do with your sleeves?'

'You can trust her. All jokes aside, I want you protected.' Sal insisted. 'I'll leave you to discuss the details. I have some other business to attend to. I'll be back for food later – did I hear there was fish on the menu, Seren?'

Seren laughed as she sat next to me. 'In a ship crewed by sea-folk, there's always fish on the menu.'

19

SELKIE EXPOSED

SELKIE

Sal was as good as his word, and, wearing the glamour I had used for my escape from Icidro's, I accompanied him ashore at the next port. Zora met us in the harbour, and her ready smile relaxed me instantly. As she strolled towards us, she held her hand on her heart in greeting.

'Sal's cousin!' she said. 'So, you decided to rejoin us. How was the long walk? That part of the coast is beautiful, isn't it?'

'It has its charms.' I said, thinking back to The White Hind and the food at Fish's bar. 'But, it was a long, hot walk.' I twisted my mouth into a mock grimace before returning her greeting gesture. 'It's good to see you again too.'

The three of us strolled along the busy quay, searching for the new vessel Sal had promised me, for my new life. We passed sleek courier boats, and dumpy ex-ferries, ultra-modern trimarans – like that owned by Icidro, and battered fishing vessels. None of them called to me. They were too bright, too bold, too big, or too small. I wanted something that could be run with a small crew, a group I could trust and be myself with.

A mid-sized boat caught my eye. Its once bright colours and unusual shape made it conspicuous amongst the flotilla of white, grey, and blue. It had a blade-like bow and an enormous rudder. I gravitated towards it, finding Zora at my side as we looked down on the boat.

'Smaller than that,' Sal said as he strolled up the pontoon. 'And, less conspicuous.'

He was right about that. It was red, orange, and blue, with yellow stripes. Zora looked at the sun-faded garish boat and shook her head.

'You're both missing the point. This boat is set up for a very small crew. It could even be sailed solo if necessary. Look at the positions of the cleats and the winches. The rigging is sound too. We can paint it any colour. In fact – this boat is so well known for its colours that a repaint would be worth doing regardless.' She clambered aboard, strolling to the cabin, gesturing for us to join her.

'Sal, there are *panels*. If you can pull in a technician, this boat is worth twice the money already.' She flicked a switch. 'There's a flicker on the dial. They aren't completely gone.' With that, she hauled up the hatch and swung down into the interior. Her voice echoed as we stood on the deck staring down.

'I thought so. It's huge. This poor boat has been used for all sorts; it stinks, but it's sound. There's room for your cousin, myself and a few more crew. I've seen this boat ashore when the old man used to have her – she's got a shallow draft, and she's thick hulled.' Her voice rose in excitement, and the hairs on the back of my hands stood up. I felt the same way she did. There was something special about being on this deck.

Zora poked her head back up like a hermit crab emerging from her shell. 'Sal, buy us this boat!'

'When did it become us?' Sal chuckled at her evident excitement, but, he hadn't said no. I watched from the side-lines as they talked, hoping he would buy it, trusting Zora to make her case.

'As soon as you asked me to help you look for a new vessel,' she replied. 'It's been great helping you rescue your family and all. It's exciting doing your trade runs but for once, I want to explore. Sal, you said that the boat I found had to be able to withstand all weathers. This is that boat.'

Having her on board would be amazing. I tried to keep my excitement in check. I'd liked Zora from the first moment when she helped me aboard her boat. The chance to develop a friendship in my current predicament was more than I'd hoped for. But, I found that I wanted, no, needed her to be aware of what she was signing up for.

'Zora, you realise that my work for Sal will be dangerous? That we will be in places we shouldn't, doing stuff we shouldn't.' I felt stupid saying it. This was someone who happily pulled a half-drowned woman out of a river without as much as blinking.

'That's just life around Sal. He has something big planned this time, I know it! So big, he's waited for his family to arrive before beginning it, rather than using Driftwood. Don't look at me that way, Sal. I've heard about your daughter. I know you're up to something.' She shook her head, tight curls bouncing as she continued. 'Bringing her out of wherever she has been hiding for years . . . You wouldn't expose a secret like that unless you thought there was a big risk to you, and someone else would have to take over your life's work. What-ever you're up to, I'm in.'

Sal ran his hand over the old panels on the roof, then

strolled across to the mast foot, pushing at it. He turned abruptly. 'Would you trust this boat with your life?' he asked.

Zora nodded. 'Yes. It's a forlorn, washed-out lump right now, but I saw this boat on the water many years ago. I know this boat.'

'Do whatever needs to be done – pay them in cash. I'll ready some crew to help you sail her to my harbour. Then, get her transformed, including new sails, and update the rigging, I want this boat to fly with the wind and hide in the mist.' Sal gestured expansively.

He ran a hand along her low rail and paced across her width. 'I want the boat out of the water to have her hull cleaned and checked. We don't know exactly where you're headed, but this boat needs to be ready to travel from the Everstorm to the Arctic. Fixing the panels might be an issue. There are so few technicians around, but if you think they might be salvageable, it's worth it.' Sal paused. 'Zora, it's really important that this boat looks nondescript when you are done. Everything needs to be subtle.'

'Got it, boss.' She laughed with delight. 'Don't worry about the panels. I know exactly who to ask. This boat will be as bland as I can make it and as swift as an approaching storm.'

I only half-listened to the rest of their conversation as I strolled along the deck, running my hand along the boat's side. It was smooth and well worn. The gentle lapping of water against the hull sang out to me. Her tall mast was old fashioned, the struts folded upward like a closed claw.

She felt welcoming. I felt peaceful stood here. It would be as close as I could get to being where I should be; I liked her and felt a smile growing across my face. My own boat.

Zora hopped over the rail and walked up the dock to the sales office as Sal strolled over to me.

'Do you like the boat?' he asked gently.

'I do, thank you.' I knew I was grinning like an idiot, but I couldn't help it. My heart sang. This was a way to make our plans happen, and one day, this boat would take me, and Eryn's skin home.

His mouth twisted in a grin. 'Do you like the crew?'

'She'll do fine.' I tried to underplay my excitement. 'Sal, does she really not know what you are?'

'She doesn't. She's never needed to. Come on. We need to be well away from here before they come back to make the deal. I don't want this boat associated with me.'

We returned to *Barge*, where Sal immediately arranged for Ash and Ivy to travel to the docks, then we retreated to the privacy of his cabin.

I grabbed a snail from the tank and crunched it while I let my thoughts run. I didn't want to jeopardise everything Sal had worked for, but I wasn't him. I wouldn't have a huge cabin to hide in and be myself away from prying eyes.

'We are going to have to tell her,' I said eventually.

'Why? I've managed for years.' Sal frowned.

'Yes, but you are being yourself. You have a cabin, where you can relax. I won't have either of those. How will we explain my absences – when I need to be here? I don't want to tell her, but I think we have to.' My insides had gone from joy at having Zora on my crew to fear of her reaction.

I pushed on. 'If we are going to be rescuing Old Ones, I need a crew who know what they are doing, who understand what we are, and aren't afraid of it. I'd like Old Ones on my crew – I know that's too much to ask for right now.' I stared out of his small window. 'Imagine what we could do then. How much easier hunting down lost guardians would be, if they understand what I can do.'

'We are only exposing you?'

'Yes. Just me. Just to her. You said you trust her with your life.'

'I do – while she thinks I'm human.'

Barge rested alongside the small port for a few more days. Visitors came and went, and rumours were sown while gathered information found its way to our ears.

This man was about to make a huge sale of land, that one was in the market for a particular rare fish, did Sal know where he could find one? Another visitor had heard that Sal had a new family member. Did anyone know who has bought the old boat at the end of the dock after years of her resting there? It was about to depart . . . and so it went. Rumours arrived, and our seeded rumours left, whispered in ears of the unwitting and drunk.

The day for our move onward came, and Sal pulled me to one side. We stood on the upper deck looking down on the last of the stragglers being persuaded to return to their homes.

'Are you certain you want to tell Zora?' he asked.

I watched a drunken customer weaving his way along the deck to where Seren checked them off as they departed, then turned to him and nodded.

'Zora is due to collect the supplies for the crew before we leave. I'll have her brought to my room. You can tell her there,' he said.

'How long have we got?' My skin prickled with fear, and I felt sweat beading on my palms. I wiped them on my red dress as Sal replied.

'Any minute now, let's go.'

My heart raced as we left and wound our way down stairs.

If this went as badly as it could, then we might have to detain Zora or . . . a knot began to form in my gut.

'What if she doesn't take it well?' I said finally when I could trust my voice to be steady.

'It would be a shame, but we may have to kill her. I think it's a risk we need to take, but I am prepared for a bad outcome. I do have other staff, if less reliable.' Sal's shoulders slumped slightly, and I knew that despite the bravado in his words, he was more attached to this particular human than he was trying to portray. In the privacy of his rooms, I changed both my clothes and my glamour to the one that Zora would recognise.

I felt sick when the knock came. Seren's voice called out Zora's arrival as Zora slipped inn and closed the door.

'Last chance,' Sal whispered, his eyes pleading as he met my own.

'No, we're doing it.' I walked to the door, twisting the key shut and putting it in my pocket. She turned, wide-eyed, as I tried to look less nervous than I was.

'Zora . . .' I couldn't say it. I knew I was fiddling with my sleeves again, the supposedly accident-proof needle ports carefully sewn along their thick cuffs. 'Zora, before we take our first steps as crew on the new boat, there is something I need to talk to you about. Please, sit down.'

She lowered herself into the lumpy seat, watching me through narrowed eyes. I remained by the door. In her position, I would have felt trapped and edgy too. I moved away from it to stand by the tank.

'Do you believe in the Old Ones?' Sal cut in.

Zora looked at him with her brow furrowed. 'I am not sure what I am supposed to say. It's a very odd question to ask after locking me in this room.' Eventually, she exhaled deeply and continued, looking down at her hands in her lap.

'When I was a girl, I met a desert dragon. It spoke to me. When I was a young woman, the trees showed their spirits to me. And, as I reached womanhood, the sea shared some of her secrets too. Yes, I believe in the Old Ones.' She raised her eyes to meet Sal's. She had spoken to a dragon. Surely, after that, our secret would not be so great or shocking. I dared to hope.

'You've never mentioned this before.' Sal said. He stood from his chair and walked towards her.

'You never asked.' She flicked a glance my way, met my eyes, and a tiny twitch of a smile flickered at the corner of her mouth as her eyes slid over the rest of my face. I resisted the urge to check my glamour. 'Why do you ask now?' she queried, still watching me.

'I would like to show you something.' I replied, taking hold of the moment and diving into it.

I released my glamour and showed her my true, selkie face.

Zora grinned. She didn't show a trace of surprise or fear; she just grinned.

'Thank the Gods for that,' she said, her shoulders shaking with repressed laughter. 'Sal,' she managed to get out, 'let me see your actual face too. It would make a nice change.'

This was not the reaction either of us had anticipated. I was delighted that we wouldn't have to lose her. There was a chance I really could have a friendship if she had known the whole time and still been kind to me, if despite it she'd still worked for Sal.

'How long have you known?' he asked, but did not remove his glamour.

'From the first day I met you.'

'How? Did I forget? Was my glamour not strong enough?' Panic overcame his features.

Zora stood and gently pointed towards his tank. Without

uttering a word, the water began to ripple as miniature waves rolled across the tank.

'Not all humans are magic-blind, and not all humans are fully human. When I became a woman, the ocean shared herself with me. I suppose full humans would call me a sea witch. I am, in truth, a cross-breed, human and ocean spirit. I have held your secret for years, Sal; in exchange for your truth, I offer you mine.' She dropped her hands, and the waves stilled, the tank as calm as it had been mere moments earlier. 'Now, where are we going with this boat? Can I meet Lady Gina, while we are doing introductions, so we have the whole family together?'

'About that.' I applied Gina's glamour.

Zora looked at me appraisingly. 'You're Lady Gina as well.' She shook her head. 'This is going to make things a little complicated. I mean, what should I even call you?'

'I am Lady Gina on *Barge* or wearing this face. At any other time, please call me Georgie. That's why we had to tell you, Zora. Sometimes, I will need to be here with Sal. I won't be on our boat.'

Zora nodded. 'I have one last question. Is Sal actually related to you, at all?'

I glanced at Sal reclining in his chair. He nodded his head, so I plunged ahead with the truth.

'My herd are from much further north than his. I had never heard of Sal until he walked into Icidro's. That's a fact, however, that no one else, ever, needs to know.'

PART II
AFTER THE STORM

20

BY ROYAL DECREE

We were eating in the Ocean Bar when word reached us that the King's boat was alongside with an armed escort. I fervently hoped that Seren had completed the corpse makeover in time.

I sat tall and unmoving as I prepared myself for his arrival. I'd kept my cool last time we met, and now, in front of Sal, I wanted to retain our advantage. If we pulled this off and the lists were actually useful – Gods, but it would be disappointing if the register of creatures turned out to be useless. If we had lost Eden for nothing. I couldn't let my mind drift there, not when we had a king-sized fish to fry.

I wandered to the central tank, noticing a particularly juicy starfish crawling across the rocks and imagined the squelch of its body, the taste of its flesh. I focused on the immediacy of now, trying to change the direction of my thoughts.

'I fancy that one. It looks plump,' I said.

Sal's eyes crinkled momentarily as the seriousness of his expression dissolved. 'Then, have it if you must. Later though, please. Starfish spines between your teeth might be a little distracting.'

'A fair reasoning.' I dipped my fingers into the water, caressing the tasty creature. 'Until later,' I murmured.

Footsteps rang out down the staircase – so many feet, in time and loud. Animals scattered around their tanks in panic.

'Here we go,' Sal murmured. He inclined his head and gestured towards the seat next to him. 'It's time to put on a show.'

I was settling myself when Seren ran through the bar door and deposited the bag carefully on the table. 'I've sprayed it with glue. It won't budge if he rubs it. She's been stored cold since I finished to keep it as fresh as I could.'

I opened the bag and peered in, stifling a gasp. The face was flawless. It genuinely was so beautiful that musicians would have sung her fame.

'She looks entirely real,' I said, closing the bag carefully and placing it under the table.

She sounded apologetic as she looked to Sal for his approval. It was very out of character for her. Seren knew something big rode on this, even if she didn't know what it was yet. 'I did my best Sal, really I did.'

He flashed her a broad smile, and she melted a little, softness seeping back into her tension-filled muscles.

'I'm confident that you are the only one who could have done this,' he said. 'While we talk to him, can you ensure the loc-box room is secure?'

'Of course.' She hurried away.

'She's amazing,' I said pointedly. 'And, devoted to you. You could do worse than taking her as a mate.'

'She is. Sadly, I like my freedom too much, Gina. Here he comes.' Sal sat straight, and the briefest glow passed across his face, giving away a gentle reinforcement of his glamour.

The usual armed idiots entered first. They lowered their guns when they saw the tanks – at least they remembered *something* from our last meeting. The King pushed through to the front of the group.

'Your Majesty, what a pleasure to host you here.' Sal gestured around the room, widely and effusively. 'Would you care for any entertainment while we carry out business? A drink perhaps – or I can provide you with a most discrete service.' He winked. 'Your lady wife would never know.'

To my amazement, The King blushed. In front of Sal he was different, less pushy, his power dimmed by the brilliance of Sal's presence, the sharp edge of his previous anger, blunted. A slender woman stepped out from his retinue to hover protectively at the King's shoulder. She glared at Sal through narrowed eyes as though she wished to strip the flesh from his bones.

'No, thank you, Lord Sal,' the King said, glancing backward. 'I have business of a different nature involving a matter your daughter undertook on my behalf.'

'Ahh yes, the Siren's head.' Sal gestured to me, and I lifted the bag to the table as Sal span his tale.

'It was killed in human form while attempting to entice another to his death. The crew of the skiff snuck up on it from behind.' He rose from his seat and mimed sneaking. I had to stifle a snort at the charade he put on as he embellished the tale. 'Avoiding its line of sight, he crept up, daring in his attack. While the siren was fully engaged with a hapless male on the beach, he leapt at it! He hacked off its head.' Sal swung an imaginary sword as he leapt on a table in a display of dramatic flair.

The King applauded. 'Let me see this evil that stole both my son's reason and life.'

Sal opened the bag and withdrew the head with a flourish.

Seren had worked wonders with makeup that I could barely achieve with a glamour. The King stared at her, mesmerised.

'I don't know what I expected,' he said eventually. 'But, it wasn't this. Surely, she is the most beautiful woman I have ever set eyes on. How could someone this gorgeous kill someone?' The woman behind him scowled.

As if beauty stopped anyone killing. Predatory animals moved with a lithe grace not afforded many prey, but that never impacted the symmetry of their faces. Again, and not for the last time I suspected, I wondered how humans survived so well when their ideals were so far from those needed for survival.

'How do we know she was not just a beautiful woman?' The slender woman asked as she peered over the King's shoulder.

Sal jumped lightly from the table and gestured to our booth. 'Come and join us, Your Highness.' Sal sat in his customary seat, his back to the large tanks, whilst the King was left exposed in the room.

'What value would there be in fooling you, a grieving father?' he asked. 'I'd gain creatures I could find with my own skills. It might take me longer to locate them, but nothing is outside my reach, should I choose to have it.' Sal leant forward, his elbows resting on the table and his fingertips touching. 'I would gain nothing by displeasing or fooling you. Did I see the kill myself? No, but I trust my crews with my life – theirs are forfeit should they cross me – much as your men would die for you.'

He stopped talking, leaving the implications hanging in the air.

Sal and the King stared at each other. In that moment, it was unclear who held true power; who would yield first?

I'd love to say I held my breath expectantly or some such dramatic statement but I didn't. I sat quietly, observing the face-off.

The King's eye twitched.

'If you say it is the siren, with your experience of exotic sea creatures,' he gestured around the room, 'who am I to argue?'

'Indeed.' Sal said no more. He didn't need to.

We sat with our drinks for a while, sipping them amidst an uneasy truce. The rapid scuttling of a crab's feet across the stones of the central pool punctuated the silence with their rhythm. If we were much quieter, we'd hear the snails scraping algae from the rocks. Not one of the King's men moved a muscle, aside from those of their ever-moving eyes.

'How has the survey progressed?' I asked.

The King placed his glass on the table, gently caressing the stem as he spoke.

'We've brought the first few with us. There is a glut of raids happening on collections – your idea may have had a degree of merit, aside from my own personal vengeance. This way, I now have the means to settle old scores, yet, stored here, they remain out of reach from those who call themselves my court.' By the narrowing of his eyes, I didn't feel that he meant to deliver fair justice. 'Few unusual creatures are listed, so far,' he said, glancing at me.

I nodded in what I hoped was a supportive fashion and dared to reach for his hand, inwardly cringing as I did so. In front of Sal, I felt bold.

'It must be reassuring to know no others will suffer as you have done,' I caressed him with my voice. 'It's the right move, and a quite brilliant idea of yours.' The woman had switched her gaze to me now. Her breathing quickened and a flush rose on her cheeks. Her hands clenched, white-knuckled.

The King pulled his hand away and glanced at the furious woman. If she was who he had chosen to carry his secret heir, this woman needed to learn significantly more self-control.

'It was,' he replied. 'Do you have the private loc-box you promised me?'

Sal nodded. 'I do. Shall we take you there now?'

'Yes. Dottrine, do you have the paperwork?' The woman stepped forward. She was mature and exceedingly attractive, now she had gained a handle on her jealousy. The King's eyes lingered on her for far longer than necessary.

She leant over him, ensuring her breasts were close to his face as she placed the papers on the table. Hunger for her oozed from his body, and her provocation was far from denying it. This display, added to the anger we had roused in her already, confirmed my suspicions.

I studied her carefully. It had only been a matter of weeks, so no swelling would be showing yet, even were they to have started straight after his son's death. Her possessiveness implied something much longer-term, deeper between them. The fact that she carried his documents even more so. This was a woman to watch.

'When we find more sirens or any other creatures, you will deal with them all as efficiently as this siren,' she said, staring at me.

I smiled back, inclining my head but not committing to anything.

'You may bring a single guard.' Sal said and rose.

Dottrine's eyes burned into my back as Sal led us from the room.

We travelled in single file through tight passageways to a quiet part of *Barge*, eventually reaching a small, unremark-able door. It was far from hidden to any trained eye although, I hoped it looked suitably camouflaged to the King.

He smiled widely as we entered a room with just three small doors set into the walls. Each was half the height of a man and they were the most secure loc-boxes currently in Terrania.

We opened the centre one for him. It took two sets of synchronised handles and a moderate amount of strength. The chamber inside was empty. The King bent down to inspect it, placing his head inside as he tested the edges. I had to resist the urge to shut him in. Maybe I could do that another day.

'I'm impressed, Lady Gina. As you suggested, this appears as secure as the ones in the Palace. There can be no question of anyone accessing these from within the court for their personal gain.'

'None whatsoever. Other than a handful of trusted staff, these are not even known about,' Sal reassured him.

I watched the King's eyes flick towards the other two doors. Both locked, one with a sophisticated eye scanner.

'Who else keeps valuables in here with that level of security?' he mused. Whether we were meant to hear it was uncertain, but I doubted this man did anything accidentally. I declined to acknowledge the comment, as did Sal. For to give anything away was a breach of trust.

He waited for a moment then placed his lists in the box. We closed the door for him, locking the heavy frame in place and simultaneously releasing the entire inner box to be retrieved from another door to the safe later on.

The King placed his own lock on the door. It had a display on the front and a small needle protruding from it.

'A blood lock? There can't be many of those left now.' Sal whistled in admiration.

'Three, and I own two,' the King said, pricking his finger to drive the lock's mechanism shut. Only he would be able to open it. Not even his son could succeed in breaking through this, had he wanted to.

'Shall we study the lists together when they are complete, to choose our reward?' Sal asked.

'You'll get access to both of your creatures only once my child, and their chosen guardian, is borne to the hiding place of Lady Gina,' was the hissed reply. 'I warned your daughter, that my reward would be to not sink your business to the seafloor. That position has never changed. However, you now hold lists I need secure, so until I have them all, you have a reprieve. Take me back to my men. Tell me, how many of the creatures in that room full of marine treasure could seduce or kill me? Lord Sal, I would like your own list ready for my next visit. I expect you back in one of my ports in six weeks time.'

There would be no list from us. I had made our position with regard to his rule clear, even if he refused to accept it.

We watched him depart *Barge*, more to ensure his entire retinue had left than from any sense of loyal reverence. Seren ordered the wakening of the revellers in the cool-down tent, and once we were satisfied that the King's boat was headed well away from the port and towards his home, we returned ponderously to the harbour, mooring alongside for our passengers to return home.

'Where to next?' Sal asked as we closed the gates.

'I'd like to return to Orange,' I said. 'There's something I need to do.'

'We have a permit for a two-week stay, and we haven't been back since you joined me there. If you are sure you are ready?'

'It's on the edge of his,' I gestured to the departing boat, 'jurisdiction. It's in trader waters, dirty money only waters, full of corrupt humans transparent in their greed. Is it wrong to want to vent my fury somewhere? I need to hunt, Sal. I am not so long amongst them that all my instincts are softened. There's someone there who could use our help.'

He snorted at that but did not repudiate my claim. 'As much as I like to pretend to human civility, I still possess instincts. Orange it is.'

21

GILDED PRISON

After months of practice, I could hold a full glamour for hours without losing focus. I pulled my hat low and strode with confidence. Weapons were banned from the pleasure district, so I placed my dagger in the safekeep and threw a few coins to the guards on duty.

'Gilded Heaven still open? It's been a while since I was last here,' I asked.

'Yes, but they won't serve pirates, mister,' one replied.

'Thanks,' I called back. My quarry was in sight, and this glamour was clearly working.

Many residents of Orange grew healthy and rich on the profits of illicit trade. I understood so much more about it now. Occasionally an electric vehicle would pass by, carrying someone fortunate enough to have access to one of the rare charging ports. I hadn't seen any of these on my first visit. *All for show*, I thought to myself. Why drive around at night when no one will see you?

We had tied alongside the tall harbour the night before, and *Barge* teemed with revellers. Several of Sal's wealthy clients maintained houses here, and we had welcomed them aboard through the discrete water level decks. They grasped at our presence, yet were repelled by our coin. Orange was a strange town, where on one side of the town, image was all. The divide between the lives, separated by the flattened dirt road, made so much more sense to me now I had lived amongst humans.

I strolled along feeling, as I had last time, the pull of the more natural side – home to those who chose a life away from Terranian tyranny. I let my thoughts drift back to that first visit so many months ago. So many lives ago!

The Gilded Heaven's illuminated sign caught my eye at the far end of the road, and other lights adorned the old building. Green pipes surrounded the windows, and a red light pulsed from a pole on the roof like a beacon. It was early winter, too cold for sitting outside, so the wealthy patrons would be hiding indoors, but I wasn't here for them.

I searched for a sign of the young woman, her furtive movements and the abusive treatment she suffered etched vividly in my mind's eye. I could recall the details of her scarred arms poking out of the tunic like fragile sticks, her muscles wasted away.

I paused for a moment, tugging my clothes straight, and pushed open the doors to the Gilded Heaven. In the bright light of the many windows and electric lighting, I spotted her immediately and sat on her side of the room. As she passed me, I reached out and caught her wrist gently. Oceans above, it was so thin that my hand encircled it, fingers meeting thumb on the other side.

Her eyes stared, dull and listless, as she looked down to see who'd caught her.

'Wha' ya wan'?' She blinked and looked me over again, her eyes briefly flickering with something else, something familiar. 'Owner won't lemme serve ya. She don't like pirates. Fish's bar's where ya wanna go.' She tried to remove her arm, and I gently opened my fingers to release her.

'Can ya see it?' she asked pointing outside. I turned to see what she was pointing at but saw nothing but an empty street.

'See what?'

'The red barrier, outside.'

I stared intently, and confusion must have shown on my face as she drew my attention back with a gentle touch.

'Go now, please.' she urged. I shook my head. I needed to find out more about her, about this place.

'Does she treat you well?' I asked, keeping a finger in contact with her. She tried to hide her tremoring by whipping her hand from my grip as she glanced over her shoulder, towards the owner.

'She feeds an clothes me, she gives me a roof, and lemme live here.' Her chin was raised defiantly, and her eyes flashed. 'She's like my Ma to me,' she said loudly. She looked directly at me, her eyes cleared for a moment and every word was perfectly pronounced as she spoke quietly. 'I wish she truly was like my mother.'

'Where is your mother?' I asked. Her choice of phrasing and the change in the tone of her voice in that wish set my senses on alert. I was pushing my luck now, but I needed to know if my instinct was right.

'My Ma is dead. The owner, she is like my ma to me. Do ya unnerstand?' The my in the second sentence was whispered, but the message was loud and clear. 'Do not eat her food, do not accept her gifts.'

I nodded. 'I understand you completely,' I replied quietly, only partially understanding her. Why would Mona give me a gift? 'You will never serve me,' I said loudly, checking that Mona was watching.

She was as I remembered, tall and skinny. Her opulent clothes unable to hide the protrusions and shadows of over-indulging in pleasure drugs. She smiled cruelly in my direction, reminding me of the fish my sister and I used to chase into crevasses for sport, with her gaudy hair ornamentation and unnaturally fleshy lips.

'Get out,' she spat across the bar. 'We don't serve your kind in here. Disease-ridden pirate.' She paused as something flitted across her face. Her expression hardened the longer she looked at me.

I wanted to take her out then and there, but that wouldn't work. Too high profile, too loud. I had no intention of getting a bad reputation with the guards in this guise.

Heads around the room turned in response to her voice. Men sneered at me, and women stared with interest, their hats bizarrely adorned with a veritable zoo of extinct animals made from grasses. I found myself regarded by the gazes of lions and elephants. The far side of the bar echoed their attire, coloured animals covered every available space on the shelves. The human concept of fashion was strange and, at times, baffling.

'My apologies, Madam. Your waitress already informed me I need to leave.' I sketched a bow and rose from my seat.

'Waitress! My God, did she call herself that?' Mona was flushed with rage. 'Street urchin's all she is.' Whatever thoughts had previously surfaced drowned under her hatred of the woman.

The waitress looked down and grabbed more mugs as she rushed past the owner. I saw the foot snake out. The mugs went flying, and the owner flew into a rage over the clumsiness of the woman.

I left.

If I stayed, I'd have killed her then and there. In that

instant, my plan changed. I'd originally intended to take the young woman with us when we left port if I could convince her to leave. *Black Hind* had joined us, and was anchored a good way from here. They would never trace her to us by the time we passed her through *Barge*. Now, I knew that wouldn't be enough. Not for me, and not for whichever poor unfortunate would be pulled in to replace this one. I'd told Sal I wanted to hunt, and I had found my prey. I returned to *Barge*, passing the guards with a smile.

'That was quick,' one said.

'I decided I'd rather spend my coin on *Barge*.' I winked. 'I hear they have some fine pleasures.'

They laughed, and one called after me, 'Prettier company than Old Fish, that's for sure!'

When Sal finally appeared in his rooms, he found me with a handful of sea lettuce and a mouthful of fresh fish.

'Damn it, again?' He laughed. 'One day, I'm going to stick something in that tank that will make your tongue numb.' He sat on the bed and took his clothes off. 'I hate these stupid things,' he said. 'I can't wait until we are offshore again and I can go for a real swim.'

I swallowed. 'If someone ever walks in on us they will assume—'

'Nothing, because they will see a glamour of clothes.' He stretched out. 'So, when are we expecting her?'

I shook my head. 'There's a change of plan. When do we leave?'

The corner of his mouth twitched upwards. 'I didn't like the last plan anyway. We are booked to be alongside for another week. What are you doing now? Will I make any money from this one?'

'You could if you plan carefully, I suppose. I'm going to kill the owner of the Gilded Heaven. In the confusion, I plan to take the girl. I think she is delirious with hunger, or maybe a little mad. She kept going on about a red barrier, but there was nothing there that I could see.'

I sat down, turning a shell over and over in my hands as I outlined my plan. 'I need a ridiculously fashionable dress, a companion, and I want spines from your fire urchins sewn into the cuffs of the dress. I plan to use them to scratch her with. My only real worry is that I may not be able to deliver enough venom slowly enough to get away.'

'How big?' Sal asked. I knew he meant the owner.

'As tall as your door guards, skinny, skeletal.' I held my hands up to illustrate her height.

'Are you sure you want her dead? Not just very unwell?'

'Yes.' It was the only way. If Sal had seen what I had, he'd not be questioning me.

'Then you don't want fire urchins. You need these.' Sal pressed a button next to his bed, and a panel slid open. In a tall tank floated a selection of jellyfish.

'Unless you have an extract prepared, no. Sal, this needs to be an in and out job. I don't have time for jellyfish soup,'

He sighed. 'But I have been wanting to use those for ages.'

'I know you have, but surely you want to be there to see the effects? I need to get this girl out of there fast. She's not one of us, but she does have an aura of a sort. There's something about her.'

Sal opened the drawer, lifted the false bottom and pulled out a vial. 'Here then. She'll choke and look as if she has something stuck in her throat.' The bottle had a single blue ring on it.

'You've given me this one before. We need to be careful.'

'I know, but I doubt any patrons of a bar in Orange will know the symptoms suffered by a guard in a palace across the far side of Terranian sea. You said timing was an issue. Use your needles, dip and seal the ends.'

I carefully pocketed the vial and grabbed one more mollusc from the tank, enjoying the crunch as it shattered. Salty, chewy and delicious. 'We need to get more of these.'

'And, you either need to stop eating them or dive for your own!'

I grinned toothily, confident that I had shell between my teeth. Sal rolled his eyes and laughed, then pressed the button on his table.

'You'd better finish that up before Seren gets here.'

The mention of her name was enough to get me moving. I ran my hands through my hair, detangling it as quick as I could. Sal watched me, bemused as I checked my clothes for seaweed.

'Clothes?' I asked.

'She won't be here long enough to bother.' He chuckled and dressed himself in a glamour instead.

'Sal! What if she touches you?'

'She won't be. She'll be touching you.'

What if she touched my face? My brain caught up to the racing panic of my pulse, pulling it back on a tide of sense. 'She's coming to measure me for the dress.' I said, feeling foolish.

'Yes.'

Two knocks at the door. She had been so fast, I wondered if she was waiting for the call. She had seen me rush past in Georgie's face a short while ago, so I wouldn't be surprised.

'Sal, let me in,' Seren called.

As he strode to the door, I had to admire his glamour. The

illusion of fabric even moved as he walked. It was still well beyond my talents to create something so intricate. I'd have to stick to faces and costumes for a good while longer. I fixed my own face and took a seat at the desk.

Seren lit the room with a smile as she saw me. 'Georgie! It's so good to see you.' She swept across the room and enveloped me in an embrace. Sal winked at me.

'No hug for me?'

I looked on, horrified, as Seren turned towards him. She planted her hands on her hips.

'Sal, I see you most days, and it would be entirely improper to hug my employer.' She looked him up and down. 'Really, Sal? What's wrong with the new clothes I ordered for you?'

'Apparently, it's perfectly acceptable to embrace my personal assassin?' He raised an eyebrow at her, and she blushed.

'I make her clothes, I keep her secrets, and I know where to avoid. No one else can hug her without dying. Someone has to, or she'd die of loneliness.'

Sal chuckled. 'Sometimes I feel lonely too.'

Seren blushed, and I turned away from the exchange.

'So what's the mission? What are we doing?' she asked.

'We are rescuing a young woman,' I replied. 'She's the whole reason I've come to this affluent urchin's arse of a backwater.'

Seren nodded at me. 'I saw *Black Hind* arrive last night. I'd guessed you were up to something. There are a few here I'd like to give a fresh start and a few who need a fresh end. Which establishment?'

'The Gilded Heaven. I need clothes for an escort too. Theo, I'll send him to you. I'm sorry, Seren, I also need one of those stupid animal hats. How long will it take to make one?'

She paused. 'I saw one of those on the dock. They came

into fashion in Terrania last year. I'm sure we have a base somewhere. I'll get the team on it tonight, but it might take a couple of days. It's not quick to make I'm afraid.'

'I know, I'm sorry. I can't guarantee its safe return.'

Sal was reclining on his bed again, watching the conversation. 'She needs needle pockets, the usual back-up knife, and a sleeve with a wet-pocket,' he interjected.

'Why a wet-pocket? I'm not aiming to kill that many people this time.'

'No, but it doesn't hurt to have a back-up plan,' he said.

Seren's fingers were sketching in the air, the way she did when she was visualising a creation. 'I agree with Sal, better over prepared than under. I have a plan. What colour wig will you be using?' she asked.

'The long, red one. Nice and distinctive.'

She looked at me appraisingly. I had hidden from her in Gina's flowing clothes since I returned. Their adjustable pinned gathers easy to alter to accommodate my loss of weight after the Arctic. In Georgie's clothes, I was exposed.

'You've been eating badly on your last trip,' she tutted. 'You look half starved.' Seren pulled a tape measure from her pocket and whipped it around me, quickly scribbling down the measurements she needed. 'I'll see you in two days for a fitting,' she said. 'Sal, I need to make a start if you want all this done in time.'

She left us alone, and Sal remained staring at the door for just a moment too long after her departure.

'She'd be good for you,' I said.

'So would fresh fish and seaweed,' he replied. 'Go, get changed, and I'll eat with Gina in the Ocean Bar shortly.'

'Only if you wear actual clothes.' I retorted as I left the room.

22

LOCKED IN TO HEAVEN

We strolled between the white harbour-side cottages of Orange with Theo's arm linked through mine. 'I've always wanted to see what was so special about the electrical side of the road,' he said as we dodged running dogs and children.

'It's loud, and it stinks of people,' I muttered. It must be strange for humans to see it, I begrudgingly admitted to myself. It was a nostalgic reminder of what they'd lost.

Zora slunk along in the shadows to our side, her face buried in a deep cowl. She was armed to the teeth – carrying extra weapons for Theo should the need arise.

'You don't look yourself tonight,' he said as we stared lovingly at each other. In truth, he was getting a good look up the street behind me, and I was checking that Zora had misted her way around the two guards at the entrance to the quarter. I returned my gaze to him, taking in the careful braids in his beard and above it, the ornately curled moustache and Theo's ever-twinkling grey eyes. He looked every bit the rich tourist but having declined Seren's offer of makeup, a careful study of his sun-swept cheeks would give him away. This man was no indoor dandy, but weathered and worn from many years on the water.

'All in,' I whispered as he returned his gaze to my eyes.

'Green suits you,' he murmured as another couple wandered past, snuggled into the deep hoods of their winter coats. We must have made quite a sight. The finery Seren had dressed us in, made us stand out – even here.

Theo waited until they were out of hearing before he continued. 'I'm not sure about all the paint on your face. One good rainstorm would wash it off, leaving a mucky mess.' He slid his arm around my waist.

'Not mine – I might be the only one in Orange whose make up won't run in the rain. Easier to change the way I look then,' I replied quietly. I hoped we would have no need for it. We'd gone over and over our plan with Sal until he was happy we hadn't overlooked anything.

'It's all right for some,' Theo grumbled. 'What about those humans like, I don't know . . . me, who have to walk in and out looking the same?'

The couple ahead entered the bar before Gilded Heaven as Zora slid into a seat at Fish's. I envied her the food, the mouthwatering scents of fish drifted across the road. I still remembered that meal as strongly as the woman we planned to free. Fish's words hadn't left me either. Maybe she had been waiting for her mother to die before she left. Maybe something else had changed and, tired of trying, the rest of the town had not noticed. Maybe she would just walk free if we opened the door and offered her a new life. The Hind needed her, or I did. Either way, we would kill to free her.

I gripped Theo's arm a little tighter, attempting to look uncertain, as light bloomed around us through the open door of the Gilded Heaven. I gripped his arm to slow my pace to his and resist the temptation to dive through the door.

That waitress was coming out of here today to join *Barge* or my crew – we could fit her on *Black Hind* if she preferred. There was a bunk spare, and we needed an extra set of hands on board. All I had to do was stay patient and stick to our plan.

Theo held the door open as I sashayed in doing my best imitation of Seren, my hips swinging and my eyes roving over every turned face. I smiled and nodded at each as they stared back at me, tossed thick, red hair over my shoulder and pointed at the bar with a flourish. 'Get me a drink, Miko, dearest, while I find somewhere intimate for us.'

Straw animals danced on heads everywhere, a true menagerie of madness. I selected a table near the window and sank into its sumptuous cushions, arranging my dress around me artfully. Garish lights cast their strange glow, illuminating me for the entire street to see. Red, orange, green; the lights were hot and before long, I'd be sweating. I picked up a strange, gaudy creature from the windowsill as Theo sauntered over with our drinks.

'Oh, you found an elephant toy. That's pretty, I've never seen a green one before.' He picked up another, a black and white bear with patches over its eyes. A small smile twitched at the corner of his mouth. 'A panda. My mother used to have one of these. We had a few that she had dredged up in her nets or found when diving. She told me they were children's toys from hundreds of years ago.' He turned the panda over to expose a broken foot before placing it back on the windowsill reverently.

'Have you spotted our target?' I asked.

He nodded, 'I could scarcely miss her after the way you described her to me. What's next?'

'Next, we get drunk,' I laughed.

Mona graced us with a long look, her eyes eating greedily into my clothes and lingering for an impolite period on my hat and face. I wore a bearded vulture in full flight, its claws just touching on the crown of my head. It had a lot in common with the increasingly predatory approach of the bar owner. Her arms were spread wide in welcome, and a sickening grin danced on her misproportioned lips.

'Welcome to the Gilded Heaven.' She waited for an introduction or a name, but I didn't offer one. Nonplussed, she continued – an unabated storm of charming poison. Like a lionfish, all show and much venom.

'My name is Mona. Please be welcome to my humble establishment. We are so glad you decided to stop for a while with us as a break from your busy schedule. Would you like the menu? I'm sure a meal would go a long way to assuage the hunger of a long voyage.' Fishing for details like that, she'd be trying for a while. I had no intention of filling in the blanks.

Seren had done an outstanding job with our clothes. The quality of fabrics quite outshone the rest of the room. They were like a flock of seagulls next to a pair of cranes. Even Theo's beard had been groomed to a shine before it was braided. In these artificial lights, his ruddy cheeks were less obvious. We could pull this off.

'That sounds lovely,' Theo said. 'Could we have table service? As you say, it *has* been a long journey.'

She fawned over us for a little longer, checking the drinks were acceptable and our purse heavy enough, then vanished into another room. We were left alone physically, but the entire place stared at us. Theo leant forward, pretending affection and whispered in my ear.

'Are you sure being this obvious was the right route to take? I'm doubting the wisdom of our decision now.'

'Of course,' I murmured back, grateful that it was him and not Zora. Being this intimate with her in public would have been too intoxicating to keep my wits about me. 'Here she comes.'

The waitress wandered over to us, stopping a careful distance away, and read out a list of options. We selected our meals and watched her as she returned to the kitchen.

'She'll have to get closer when she brings food,' I said hopefully. I wanted to tell her we were there to free her. To rid the world of her heinous employer, but I couldn't risk it. I glanced out the window. The lights ruined my night vision, but I knew Zora was out there waiting. Theo had to simply lure the waitress out while I dealt my justice.

There were only a few groups of customers, and we were patient as we played through our roles. After the Arctic, patience was a virtue I knew I had in bergs. To my surprise, Mona brought us our food herself, standing nearby to check the food was tasty before smiling and almost dancing off.

'She's an odd one,' Theo muttered, watching her cavort into the midst of her other clients.

We ate our meal, making conversation about people we didn't know and places we had never been. Made up names tripping from our tongues became a game. When the waitress came to clear the table, I reached across and grasped Theo's hand, looking up at her with wide eyes.

'Freedom is so underrated isn't it?' I babbled at her. I'd seen enough drunk people to have the slight slur down. 'I hear the owner is just like your mother. How pleasant it must be to work for a reincarnation.' Her eyes widened, and she flinched at my words. Then, that sensation of familiarity came back, along with her clear-eyed gaze. I looked straight at her and quietly added, 'Take chances when they come. They may be paths created just for you.' I switched back to a loud, tipsy voice to loudly proclaim, 'My Miko was a chance I took. Look how well I did from it.'

She looked at me more directly then and the colour drained from her face. Her hand flew to her mouth.

'No! I told you to go, to stay away. Why didn't you listen to me? Did you eat the food?'

I nodded enthusiastically. 'I did, and it was delicious. Did you make it?'

She leant closer to me as she bent to pick up something she had dropped. 'Look out the window, now can you see the barrier?'

This again? I humoured her and gazed out the window. What I saw made my skin prickle with fear and my palms begin to sweat. There was a glowing red dome surrounding the entire Gilded Heaven.

'What is it?' I asked.

She dropped her gaze to the floor. 'It is your new prison, and I am your cellmate. Whatever you are, you aren't human and Mona has spotted it. She's blood-bound you to this place.'

'This is why you can't leave.' It all made sense to me now.

Theo glanced between us, trying to follow the conversation. 'What are you talking about? I can't see anything out there, and I ate the food too.'

'I can, Theo,' I said. 'Urchin's arse, I haven't avoided capture, run from Icidro, and started a new life, just to be caught by some jumped-up blood-witch. I need to see if I can get through it.'

Theo pushed himself up. A huge sigh escaped him as he grabbed his drink. 'I'll have my dessert outside please,' he said to the waitress.

'Shall I join you?' I asked, making a show of checking my empty glass.

'It's a nice night for a star-lit drink, why not?' he said

loudly and planted a kiss on my cheek. We strolled out arm in arm, towards a seat at the edge of the dome. The closer we got to the barrier, the more the pain grew. A prickling at first, growing more intense as I neared, until I could shuffle my foot towards it, pushing my toes against the barrier. A searing, soul-rending pain ripped through me. I had to grip the edge of the table to keep from screaming aloud. I pushed harder, probing to see if I'd be able to survive breaking through it. As the arch of my foot reached the edge of the red, I knew that it would unpick me, that I would fall apart at the limits of my sanity were I to attempt to push through.

Theo sat patiently, gently stroking my hand, keeping me anchored until I stopped pushing and turned to face him. I could feel it at my back, uncomfortable but bearable. I could pretend it didn't hurt at this distance – for a short while at least. The longer Mona was uncertain whether she had snared me, the better.

'So,' Theo said, 'This barrier. Can we pass though it?'

I took his hand in mine and ran my hand up his arm, levering his hand into the barrier as I did so. He didn't flinch.

'You can.' I replied as calmly as I could. 'But, I'm trapped.'

'We'll get you out of here, I promise.' Theo whispered.

I threw my arms around him, maintaining our charade as I whispered in his ear. 'Get Zora. Get help. From *Barge* if you have to, but don't let Zora pass. I'm not risking us both being caught.' He squeezed my hand gently and rose from his seat, leaving me alone as he wandered casually over to Fish's and sat near Zora. Once he'd gone, Mona sidled out the door, and took the seat opposite me.

'I hear there is a large reward for anyone who catches a siren.' She licked her lips. 'And, as they are the only Old Ones I've ever seen with the skill of illusion, I'm guessing you will earn me a pretty pile of coins. Or, should I keep you for myself? Maybe I'll sell you to the highest bidder.

My fingers played with my sleeves. I could do it right now, kill her and be done with her. I raised my hand and narrowed my eyes as I drew my arm back.

'No!' the waitress called as she burst through the doors. 'Don't do anything, please. If you kill her, we are both trapped forever.'

Mona pulled her fleshy lips into a horrifying grin, her blackened teeth fully exposed and laughed.

'For once, that stupid bitch is right. I suggest you listen to her. Then, come back in and book your room for a long stay.' She was still laughing as the door swung shut behind her.

'Why haven't you just broken the barrier if you know what it is?' I asked the waitress, trying once again to push my foot through the redness. This time I managed to get it further, but the pain lanced through me, and I buckled, vomit spewing from my mouth.

Because I can't find the object it's anchored to. I've searched the entire place, under every floor-board and the entire perimeter. It's not inside the dome.

Theo rushed over, with Zora in tow, to rest a comforting hand on my back.

'You tried again?' he said.

'Uh-huh. I can't do it. I'm trapped,' I said, still trying to sound calm, trying to quell the whirlpool of emotions raging inside me. 'This woman – sorry, I don't know your name – this is who we came for. Neither of us can leave now.'

'Rialta. Thank you, but you should have gone. I told you to go! I'd have found a way out eventually.'

Her words echoed my thoughts in Icidro's when Sal had come to me, except that he had been successful.

'How long have you been searching?' Zora asked.

'At least twenty years,' Rialta replied. My heart sunk. The fact that this woman had trapped her here in a similar way to me, was one thing, but twenty years of fruitless searching, meant that Rialta was either trapped as a child, or she was a lot older than she appeared. And, if Mona had recognised me for an Old One, it was likely Rialta was one too, or at least part-blooded. The Hind's vision of Rialta walking into the fire returned to mind. Did she make it or put it out? Should we burn down the Gilded Heaven? Maybe that was the meaning.

'Can you set the building on fire, so the blood anchor is damaged too?' I said, feeling pleased that I had solved the puzzle.

'No, there are too many innocent people in there. I'll admit they suffer from greed, but they aren't evil. I won't kill them.' Rialta replied. 'There's no guarantee fire would break the blood anchor anyway.'

'Maybe I can try something,' Zora said. 'What shape is the barrier?'

'A dome,' I said.

'A sphere,' Rialta said at the same time.

'So the anchor point is near the outside of the sphere. It could even be underground.' Zora mused as she looked around us. 'How high does it go?'

'It reaches over the top of the Gilded Heaven but does not go as high as the light on its spire,' I said, looking up.

'I can't reach that light,' Rialta said. 'I have tried.'

'Leave it with me.' Zora replied. 'If I have to comb every part of this neighbourhood and dig half the street up, I'll get you out.'

Our gathering had begun to attract attention now. Faces peered out from the window of the Gilded Heaven and the couple who'd entered the building next door strolled towards us.

'You're supposed to be gone by now,' the woman hissed from deep in her hood. 'Why are you still here?'

'Ivy!' I could have hugged her. If Zora could find that anchor point, Ivy could scale any wall in existence.

'Do we have a problem?' Oak said as he took the seat next to her. I was mad that Sal had sent Driftwood as back up, but maybe he had foreseen more issues with my plan than I had.

'Yeah, we do,' Zora replied as Rialta stood over Ivy and Oak to take their order. 'There's a fucking blood-witch running this place. Now, not only is she holding Rialta hostage but she's trapped Georgie too.'

'Don't drink or eat anything' I grimaced. 'I was warned, but I forgot.'

'Fine, a cup of air and a plate of nothing, please,' Oak said to Rialta. 'Then we'll kill the blood-witch for dessert, easy. Like I said, what's the problem?'

'I'll have to take an order in, or she'll get suspicious.' Rialta muttered and rushed into the bar, leaving the five of us outside. Theo still sat with his arm around me while Zora stood a few steps away.

'No, it appears that we have to break the spell first, then we can kill her and get out – else I'll be here till I'm dead.' That was not an option. The Hind needed me – I'd get out somehow.

'I'm up for the new plan,' Theo said.' Who's with me?'

'Me,' replied Zora. 'Magic repels or attracts, right? It's never neutral. I have no idea what I'm looking for, but I'll know it when I find it. I need to go and sit down.' She walked back over to Fish's and ordered another drink. I saw the gentle motions of her hands that let me know she was drawing her magic around her.

Mona reappeared in Rialta's place, carrying two drinks for

Oak and Ash. 'Is this drunken woman bothering you?' she asked.

They shook their heads. 'No. In fact, that gentleman,' Oak gestured at Theo, 'was just saying just how delicious your food was.'

'Glad to hear it,' Mona said. 'Your room is ready,' she called over to me.

I offered her a smile. 'Thank you, but I think I'll just enjoy the night air with Miko a few moments longer. We'll be in soon.'

'As you wish. Enjoy it while you can.' A smirk twisted on her face as Mona crabbed her way back indoors.

Mist was gathering now, rolling towards the building, tiny droplets of magic as Zora collected every droplet of water in the area, then set them to circulating the building.

Given how little there was in the air, she must have pulled some from as far away as the water, costing her huge reserves. We wouldn't have long.

'Gotta love a sea-witch.' Ivy grinned. 'We knew Sal had one somewhere. He warned us once, in case anything happened on one of our boats. I just didn't realise it was Zora. These land-folk will have no idea what's happening.' She sat gazing upwards as mist pooled around the barrier. 'There's a gap! Up there.' She pointed up towards the red stone.

'I bloody knew it,' Theo said. 'I'll never get up there.' The mist dissipated, and Zora fell from her stool with a thud.

'I can.' Ivy said. 'It won't be easy. Theo, go and look after Zora. She'll need help. Georgie, accept her offer, and go inside. It might keep her in too. There's far less chance of her seeing us climbing. We'll get you out.'

'Or Sal will have our weapons as decor,' grimaced Oak.

Mona peered out the door, Oceans, but she was persistent.

'M'lady,' she sneered, 'it appears your beloved Miko has

abandoned you for another, better-looking woman. Come on in. Your room is prepared.'

Ria watched me through deep pools of sadness as I wandered drunkenly towards Mona.

'I'm quite sure you are mistaken.' I murmured, as I passed. 'My Miko will be up soon. We accept your hospitality grate-fully, however. It's been a long day.'

I gathered my self-control tightly, fighting the rising fear as I continued to sway up the stairs and faking my drunkenness to the other patrons. On the second floor, Mona opened the door to an overly opulent room. It stank of stale perfume and sweat – it was all I could do not to gag. Yellow stained sheets graced the bed, and the tired fabrics hanging from the window were threadbare.

'From tomorrow, you will work in here until I sell you. Use your talents and ensnare my customers. Take everything they have. If you do, you will get a better room, better food. If you don't you'll get this.' She swung her fist at me, striking me deep in the gut and I doubled over, winded. I thought of Sirena, and her lack of tolerance for humans. Mona was lucky I wasn't a siren, or she'd be dead by now. But then, I'd be trapped.

'Let me see your real face' Mona shrieked.

'Never.' I spat in her face. Urchin dung, but she could hit hard. I curled my fists ready to fight back, to defend myself from the next incoming blow. She kicked me instead. Then turned and left the room, locking it behind her.

23

A VULTURE'S END

The window was locked. The old glass far thicker at the base than the top, and there was no way I could punch through it. I searched the room desperately, but couldn't find anything solid enough to smash it with.

I wiped the grimy glass to peer out. If I threw myself at it, what were my chances? It was two floors up, and below my window was a generator, one of many I could now make out as my eyes adjusted to the dark. Behind the facade of wealth and opulence in electric row, was a stinking, noisy mass of machinery, their vibrations unlike anything I'd encountered with panel or cell-powered engines on *Barge.* Jumping was not an option – I had to get through that door.

Each building stood apart, separated by a wall. Small clusters of homes beyond gave out the dim glow of hard light, from humans desperate for whatever meagre trappings of Old Earth they could get their hands on. I wondered if their children played with the animals anymore. If they understood that these creatures used to actually exist – that their disappearance was all humanity's fault. Being trapped brought out the deep hatred for human society that Zora and Theo had softened with kindness. And yet, here I was, trapped by a human, awaiting rescue by humans. I allowed the storm to rage.

As I continued to stare out into the night, two shadows leapt onto a wall, a small one and a tall, broad one. If it wasn't Ivy and Oak, Gilded Heaven was in for more visitors tonight. I waved frantically at them, but there was no response.

How would Zora destroy the stone? Could Ivy or Oak smash it? Oceans, what if Zora didn't wake in time to break it? I hated being helpless. As soon as I knew there was a chance, that they'd got it. I'd need to get out. I fiddled with my cuffs to free a needle. I'd never picked a lock before. But maybe today was the time to start – after all, I could hardly make my situation worse, and at least I'd feel that I was doing something.

If Ivy could get there fast, if I could escape this room without help, we could still get out of this whole mess, poison Mona, and quietly slip away with Rialta. I laughed quietly at myself. That was a whole lot of if.

I wiped the venom off the needle with the curtain, then knelt in front of the locked door.

Several minutes later, I had achieved nothing and was resisting the urge to shout in frustration, to bark it away as I would in my seal form.

Pain started to encroach on me. Searing pain, familiar as the boundary grew more intense by the moment. This time I did not stop myself screaming. I scrambled backwards, pressing myself against the door. The boundary was closing in on me, the whole curve descending through the room as it encroached on my body.

Urchin's arse, Ivy must not have been able to destroy it on the roof. My heart hammered against my ribs. It had reached my feet now. I tried to make myself as compact as possible, and gathered as much magic as I could to ease the pain in my feet.

I could get no smaller, and when it reached my ankle, the pain grew unbearable. Although my leg looked intact, it felt as though my skin was being stripped from my flesh and my flesh from the bone.

Redness engulfed my leg, and I screamed in Ocean, pushing all my agony into the sound, before all I knew was blackness.

Hands shook me. I was pulled across the floor.

'Wake up.' A voice, was it Eryn? Was my sister trying to reach me?

'Eryn?' I asked.

'No, it's Rialta. Open your eyes. It's stopped moving. They've taken it to Zora, but she's still not awake.'

I rolled over, drawing my legs in close and rocking for comfort. Like a pup in the surf, I swayed back and forth for a few minutes. Rialta sat quietly at my side.

'I felt you,' she said. 'I couldn't hear you, but you shared your pain with the Old World.'

'Thank you for coming. How did you get in?' I hugged her.

She shrugged, 'I just pushed really, really hard. It's amazing what fear can do.'

I looked up at the door, its hinges were bent and warped where they'd been deformed and the door shoved through. That would have taken much more force than fear-lent strength. Maybe Rialta had some control of the earth, or was a metal witch. Now wasn't the time to ask.

'If they can wake Zora, she can do it. I've seen her melt icebergs.' I said.

A smile grew on Rialta's face as she looked past me.

'It flickered.' She laughed. 'Oh, Gods, in twenty years, I've never seen it as much as waver.'

I glanced round in time to see it happen again. 'Then, this lady will be checking out. Let's finish this.'

I stood up, flinching with the remnants of pain in my feet, straightened my dress and hat, then followed Rialta down the stairs. She moved off working around the customers as I strolled as best I could, towards the bar. I positioned myself so that I could see out the window and fished inside my bodice, hoisting a coin purse onto the counter.

'I've decided not to stay.' I declared loudly. 'The room is an utter mess, the view is awful and there are *bugs* in the bed.'

Mona laughed and leaned in close, her rancid breath drifting across my face as she spoke, low enough for only my ears. 'That bitch will pay for letting you out. However, I see no harm in taking your coins. I'd have had them all from you anyway once my customers had left.'

I smiled sweetly and began to count out coins. Her eyes widened as the pile grew. I added a few golds and a couple of silvers. 'Will that be enough?' I asked.

She chuckled. 'For your freedom, nowhere near enough.'

I wobbled and grabbed at my hat, collecting a carefully loosened straw in the process, then counted out more coins into her hand. I scratched her with the straw, and she flinched.

'Oh, I am sorry.' As the straw fell off my wrist, she glanced at it and smiled encouragingly.

'We're getting closer, but I still think I could get more from The King,' she said.

I fumbled in my bodice again and pulled out a gem. Her eyes were positively gleaming now. She gestured at it. 'Now, if you have a few more of those, that would cover it.' She smiled, her fat lip-slugs stretching to almost normal proportions.

I glanced past Mona to the window and saw the barrier disappear with a pop. She looked around in confusion.

I struck. It sounds dramatic, but it really wasn't. I scratched her again, this time with a needle. She ignored it, possibly assuming it was straw again. She still clutched the stone in her fist, but her attention was now fixed elsewhere. Presumably, she felt her spell break. She turned to see Rialta, who advanced on her with a grim expression and determination in her eyes.

Mona paled. Before Rialta reached her, she began to cough. I remained perched at the bar, pretending to be drunk enough not to move far and added a few sways for theatrical effect. All I had to do now was wait.

Mona started to grasp at her throat, and her eyes bulged. I was the closest to her, so *naturally* I felt it was important to help her out. Right out of life.

'She's choking!' I called. 'Someone, help!' She crumpled alongside the bar, her lips turning blue and her eyes wide with fear.

'I'll help you,' I slurred loudly as I wobbled from my seat towards her.

I hit her on the back – ostensibly to dislodge whatever she was choking on, and delivered another dose while I grabbed the rolling gem with my other hand and stowed it in a pocket.

Rialta stood at the other end of the bar and watched. She did nothing.

'Help someone, please!' I called again. 'She's not breathing. Oh—'

I was pushed out the way as someone shoved me clear to try and help Mona. Her back was pounded, again and her throat checked.

They'd find nothing. I watched her face purpling, her lips paling, and the twitches of muscle convulsions before she

stopped moving. Satisfied I had done my job, as the stench of
death-urine filled the bar, I staggered towards the door.

'She's dead, Rialta,' I whispered. 'Like your real mother.
Get out, go with Zora and you'll be safe. Sorry for pushing
you.'

'But you didn't push me?'

I shoved her through the door. It was harder to do than I
expected.

She grimaced. 'Sorry, I need to collect something before I
can leave,' she muttered and dived back in.

I continued through the doors. 'Miko? Miko, this place is
ghastly. Someone is dying in there. Please can we go home?' I
wailed and sobbed.

Theo crossed the road and gathered me in a rough
embrace. 'Let's go home. Where's Rialta?'

Zora slipped over from Fish's, and as Rialta emerged from
the Gilded Heaven, Zora grabbed her by the arm. A small fog
cloud rolled along the street, engulfing them.

I sat next to Theo for a moment as I let some of the tension
leave my body.

'When do we leave?' he asked.

'Any minute. Are you ready to escort this drunken woman
home to our boat?' I slurred jokingly. 'I really need to get this
stupid hat off. It's killing my neck balancing it.'

'Seren spent hours on it. You'd not be forgiven quickly for
wrecking it in one outing.'

A customer ran from the bar, ignoring us as they sprinted
unsteadily to the end of the street.

'Two coins they fall over before they reach the gate.' I
murmured.

'Three that they will make it there, but fall on the way
back, and it's a deal,' Theo replied. We rose from our seats, and
I leant heavily on his arm as we wobbled out to the middle of

the street to get a better view of the runner. He almost made it.

'Next time, I'll up the stakes,' I chuckled.

'Next time, don't get caught.'

The runner had picked himself up as we finally wound our way past, reclaiming our weapons from the basket under the watchful eye of the one remaining guard.

'Someone is *really* sick in that place,' I said. 'I really wouldn't eat the food.' I stuck two fingers in my mouth, miming vomiting, and shuddered.

'Yeah, we heard,' he said, narrowing his eyes. 'Did you see anything?'

'Hic... She went floppy, so I tried to help. But some men shoved me out. So, I left.' I pulled myself upright, trying to square my shoulders and deliberately failing. 'I know where I am not wanted!'

Theo wrapped an arm around me and rolled his eyes. 'If you don't mind, I think I need to get her back to our lodgings.' He shrugged apologetically.

'Where are you if we need to find you later?' the guard asked.

'We're guests in the last house on the dock.' The last few were owned by Sal, so any guest who paid enough could hire one. No one would be sleeping in the one we mentioned tonight.

I stumbled a few more times as we continued our unsteady way down the street.

'Stop it! I am either going either drop you next time, or you will fall the rest of the way,' Theo hissed after the third stumble. I smirked and went for an exaggeratedly weaving walk instead.

My erratic route gave me plenty of opportunity to keep an eye on other late-night revellers, and before long, I spotted a shadowy figure following us. I stumbled again, ducking us both into a patch of darkness.

'What are you doing? I just told you—'

I cut him off with a hand signal, and pointed up the street.

'Urchin dung! Will tonight's drama never end?' I whispered. 'Of all the nights, tonight would have been great for a clean getaway. I'm exhausted. Are you ready?'

'After you,' Theo gestured.

I turned as the shadowed form moved in. Theo dropped a knife into his palm from inside his sleeves. I sprinted towards the tail, hoping they valued information more than our deaths. They turned to run and found themselves facing Zora.

'I thought you might want some company tonight, Miko,' she called.

The tail paused, and I took my chance, leaping on them and knocking them to the floor. A small gun flew from their hand. When she rolled over I recognised the face but couldn't place it in the haze of the moment.

I sat on my attacker's chest and pressed my face up close. Zora picked up the gun and trained it on the now-struggling woman.

'I'm going to take my weight off you, and you are going to answer our questions,' I commanded.

She nodded mutely, gasping for air as I released my weight.

'Why are you following us? Who for?' I pressed.

She spat in my face and sneered as she kicked me.

'I *thought* it was him,' she said gesturing at Theo. 'When she' – pointing at Zora – 'turned up I was certain. We know someone on your crew ain't what they seem. I saw the red wave!'

She looked me up and down with a sneer.

'Fuck knows what your role is in this, you stupid bitch. Got yourself in deeper than you realised? This is the crew of the bloody *Black Hind*. You think you can just swagger in and take one of them for your own, did you? Who are you? What are you hiding that you are bribing and fancy dining them?'

She shoved me, and I realised, too late, she held a blade. She grabbed my wrist, twisting it behind my back until the dagger point was against my neck while she grinned venomously at Theo.

'It's poisoned. Best you don't push me, or I'll cut her. Won't matter to me, but if you want your bit of fancy stuff uninjured, best start talking. She's either brave or bloody stupid to tackle me.'

He laughed and shrugged. 'Take her. She was no fun anyway.' I could feel Zora's eyes on my back. Confident that the gun would still be trained on the tail, I focused on keeping my neck away from the blade's tip.

'I know who you are,' Zora said quietly. I could hear the sharp edge to her voice. 'I know who everyone in the Terranian fleet is. You're the harpoonist from Lost Jake's crew.'

'Yeah, what of it. We always get what we go after,' the tail retorted.

'All except that selkie he was rumoured to have caught.' Zora laughed, and I felt the harpoonist's grip tighten.

The rumours hadn't died with Jake, or his crew's invasion of Icidro's. I felt a whirlpool of fear growing. I knew they could still be searching, but it was easy to forget when I was aboard *Barge* or *Black Hind*. She held that knife too close for a easy strike, and I couldn't get the needles into position. What little venom remained in them was unlikely to do much anyway. I'd need to use the wet-pocket.

'Oh, we got it all right. Even hid the skin and ripped off Icidro.' The sneer in her voice made the ocean begin to rise inside me. I wanted to kill her, now, and get Rialta to the boats.

'Wasn't it Icidro who made Lone Jake into Lost Jake?' Theo pushed, edging closer to me, circling the harpoonist.

I could take her out easily if I worked to the right spot. A quick spin and I'd be there. I itched to pour the contents of the concealed wet-pocket down her neck, but she knew something about my skin. I needed to extract that information from her. My heart was pounding, and I was sure she could feel it through the silly dress I was wearing.

'How the tables are turned. Your little bit of side-stuff is scared.' Misreading my excitement at a possible cue for fear, she taunted Theo. It was a fatal mistake. If I twisted quickly, I could bite her.

Theo closed quickly, and as the harpoonist turned to avoid him, Zora crept up behind her.

I readied for the move, confident the others could handle her the second I was not at risk, when she spoke again.

'Of course, it wasn't our fault that the selkie must have died and Icidro's idiot brought the wrong girl back. That stupid old woman. I always knew she couldn't be trusted. She was supposed to hold the skin, then trade it for her money, but she never did. Went and died in the storm. Jake had to take a fake skin to try to appease Icidro.' She was shouting now. 'But the bloody selkie was real. He said it was, and I trusted Jake and I trust his brother. He still thinks the selkie is out there. So, I *know* this siren is real. If one is, they all are. Dragons, sirens, lamia, the lot.

Zora finally silenced her. A floating cloud of mist coalesced in front of the harpoonist's face and entered her mouth.

She spluttered for air and let go of the dagger as the water went down into her lungs; it clattered to the floor.

'Want her dead?' Theo asked. He was so calm you'd have thought he was asking if I wanted a drink.

'I'll do it. Hold her arms,' I hissed. Theo stepped in. She kicked him in the balls and, still spluttering, reached for the dagger.

'Fuck that,' Zora said and shot her in the leg.

She dropped to the dock. The gunshot would bring people running any minute, but I had something I needed to do first.

'Jake's brother is right. That selkie never died,' I said as I crouched to face her. 'That selkie is me. Thank you for your assistance. Goodbye.' I removed my glamour and watched her face slacken. 'Would you like to bleed out slowly? Or die quickly?' I asked her, licking my sharp teeth.

'I—'

'You don't really have a choice. Your crew took away mine.'

Zora grasped her hair and yanked the woman's head back as I cut the small, wet-pouch over her mouth, emptying the entire contents in. She tried to spit it out, but she'd have no chance.

Her eyes glazed.

'Throw her over the side?' Theo asked as he straightened up. 'Fishballs, that hurt.'

'No, carry her to the house. Sal will send someone to remove her later. She's got enough poison in her to kill all the local wildlife, and I'm not risking it. Zora, can you clean the blood off the dock quickly?'

Zora nodded, and I saw a small water spout form on the dock as I turned to chase after Theo who had hoisted the body over his shoulder and walked off.

We rushed to Sal's house, slamming the door closed, to find Rialta huddled in a corner of the room.

'You didn't run then? Come on, time to get away from

here,' Zora said, then turned to me. 'Sal's choice, remember. Always give them a choice.'

'The clothes chest is open,' Theo called from the room next door. 'But, there are no extra blankets to hide the body.'

'Just put her in it.' I replied.

Rialta tensed.

'Not you,' I laughed. 'We just ran into a little trouble on the way back.'

We locked the body in the chest, draped bed linen partly over it and exited via the back door of the house, slipping down the alley back towards the town and the end of the docks where we'd left a small rowing boat.

It was easy to reach the dockside in the darkness. Figures roamed, drunkenly weaving side to side, or silently slumped on barrels. At least one of them would be waiting for the harpoonist. It was surprisingly calm. Too calm. This wasn't going to work.

A dog barked at us from a window, and heads turned – too quickly for drunks – looking for the disturbance.

'Run!' I shouted.

We ran. We ran until our breath caught, and we were at the water's edge.

'Can you swim?' I panted.

'Yes,' Rialta replied. 'But, I've never swum in the sea.'

'First time for everything,' I replied. 'Stay close. Sorry, Seren,' I muttered as I took the hat off. I stripped the dress off too and threw it into the water, tossing the hat after it.

Theo leapt in, and Zora followed, emerging from her dive under the bedraggled hat.

'Go!' I pushed Rialta before she had time to change her mind, and the others escorted her away. Footsteps closed on me and again, I found myself leaping into water to escape pursuit from Jake's crews. This time, I leapt with hope. I had a clue finally, a clue to the location of my skin.

Theo swam alongside Rialta, cajoling her onward, while Zora followed, smoothing the ripples of our wake and masking us in a gentle fog.

Voices carried over the water as they tried to find us.

'Where did they go?'

'Who was that?'

'I saw two—'

'I saw five.'

I dived under the water, swimming for freedom, with a lighter heart than I had for many months.

24

UNLOCKED

Zora had anchored *Black Hind* offshore, leaving Cor aboard, alone. He'd leave the boat to fish regularly, and each time his broad wings vanished from sight, we thought he had departed for the last time. Yet, daily he'd herald his return with a croaking greeting. We'd all grown attached to him in our own way, I suppose. He reminded me of Eden at every turn, his bittersweet presence a constant reminder of the accident. Still, I'd been pleased when Zora brought him back with her, from wherever she had retreated to mourn Eden.

I didn't ask her where she'd been – we all needed our secrets and safe spaces. I envied her the chance to have had that time alone. Instead, I'd been keeping a self-important king sweet and plotting the recovery of the woman who now shivered on our private dock of *Barge*.

'I'm taking her to Seren,' Zora said. 'She'll get her fed and dressed.' She hauled herself from the water and sat next to the woman. 'Will you come with me, Rialta?' Zora waited, and when no answer was forthcoming, she continued. 'Anyway,

I'm sorry, but we need to hide you while we work out the best way to help you.'

'This is the pleasure barge?' Rialta asked. She looked up at me in horror, tears running down her cheeks. 'I'd rather have died, or been left in that hole than become part of this slave-ship. You're sex traders! I thought you were helping me, not about to make my life even worse.' With that, she leapt back into the sea.

Zora sighed as she slipped back into the water. 'Georgie, are you sure you want this one?'

A tight smile had grown on my face throughout the impassioned speech. I knew that level of passion, of hatred for being captive. Urchin's arse, but I felt her plea to the depth of my bones.

Zora took a second look at me. 'That's a stupid question, isn't it? I'll go get her before she ends up killed or accused of murdering her boss.' She slipped from the dock, the dock lights illuminating her powerful stokes as she easily ate up the distance between her and the exhausted woman. Theo, who had sat quietly during the exchange, rose to his feet.

'Let's get a boat ready,' he said. 'We should take her to *Black Hind* instead. Now they know we're in town, it might only be a matter of time before they try to board her.' He was right. The further from town we got, the better for all of us.

'I'd like to see them get past Cor.' I replied. He'd peck them to pieces if he was aboard, but the idea of Cor getting shot by an irate sailor caused a violent knotting in my gut.

'Still think she's special?' Theo asked gently. I wondered who he was referring to, but either way, the answer was the same.

'I'm sure of it. Get Rialta out to the *Hind*. I'll join you in the morning. There's something I need to do first.' I slipped through the doorway and called for Ash to ready the boat.

Before I could join them, Sal needed a report – especially as we'd left a body in his house. I wound my way up to my rooms to get dry and changed before meeting him. From the window, I watched the small, red boat slip away into the darkness with four figures safely aboard.

I could understand Rialta's reluctance. Zora may have given her Sal's choice, but clearly she had not explained it very well. In fairness maybe our little run-in with the harpoonist on the dock had stopped that from happening.

I pulled on Gina-styled clothes, the flowing fabrics drifting around me as I walked in a cloud of gently draping fabric and quickly styled my hair. Sal would have been informed of my return by now. He liked to pretend I did what I wanted, when I wanted, but he had grown to behave in a fatherly way. It reminded me of the solicitousness of my own father. I didn't mind. Oceans, I wouldn't be here tonight if he hadn't been so cautious. My skin still pickled from the calf downwards, and I curled my toes in response. No, I was pleased that he cared.

Sal had installed a food tank in my rooms while I was in the Arctic, and I munched on a shell fish as the dead face of the harpoonist floated through my thoughts. By now, she would be bloated and swelling in the heat. I found I still had no pity for her, even if she had given me what I so desperately needed – hope. If the King's lists also helped in the search for missing Old Ones, we'd be underway with both of our missions.

A sharp rapping at the door drew my attention.

'Come in,' I called. Sal wafted in, smelling of seaweed and salt.

'I know what you have been doing,' I said. 'You've been swimming.' Jealousy rose, and I batted it back down.

'The town guards seeking a young woman in whispers between the bed-sheets and openly in uniform, give me a clue to your success this evening.' Sal replied as he strolled to the window. 'I understand the crew of the *Black Hind* have departed already. It was such a brief visit . . .' He turned to me, concern etched onto his features. 'Are you sure you want to do this now? There's no need for a report. I've seen Ivy – blood-witches in Terrania is bad news.'

I shrugged. 'She's gone now, and I'm in one piece. This is unfinished business, I need to know if we are getting anywhere with our hunt. Afterwards, I need to get the *Hind* out of here for a while. Lost Jake's crew are watching the port. We ran into a little more trouble ashore.'

'I take it that the woman you rescued is with Theo and Zora?'

'Yes, she refused to consider staying. It's a shame, I can still feel a lot of *something* about her and she must be at least part Old One to have been captured. She pushed a door off its hinges with her bare hands! Your insight would've been useful.'

'We can discuss that later,' Sal said. 'If you are sure you have time now, let's go.'

I was bursting to tell him what I had discovered about the skin, but I didn't want him to start worrying about that when we had bigger and more immediate issues to deal with.

We reached the loc-box room and closed it from the inside. Sal strode to the door with the blood reader, checking it was locked securely, then joined me in front of the eye scanner. He dropped a different glamour over his face, one I hadn't seen him use before – his eyes had turned dark grey.

'It's words,' he said. 'I project a random section of a partic-ular book in them. One day I'll tell you what it is, and give you access. Right now, it's probably too intricate for you.'

I studied his eyes, barely able to make out a texture, let alone words. The complexity of the image must be incredible.

It was a stark reminder of how much more powerful he was than myself and, how much more capable I could become with practise.

The door swung open with a gentle click, exposing a passage. In its wall was a second box – a secret store inside a secret door. Even his loc-box was layered. I had to admire the elegance. There was no need to ask what was in this box. There was only one possession that would be this important to Sal.

We walked past it and through the thick walls of the room to the back of the King's loc-box. On this wall was another door, far bigger than the one in the room. It swung open easily, and the outer case of the lockbox came with it. The door, with its blood lock, remained untouched. The locking mechanism had, in fact, released this chamber to us.

Sal and I gently placed it on the floor and took out the sheaf of papers. The King had been so confident in their security that he had just dropped them in a loose pile.

'Here, you take one half,' Sal said and we sat in the dim light as he began to study the lists.

'Sal, I'm not exactly a reader, remember?' I said.

'I must find time to teach you,' he muttered. 'Pass them all here. You remember the names I tell you as we go through.'

We searched the lists for hours. Most of the creatures in the collections were of no consequence for their spiritual power, but there were specimens of creatures I thought long extinct. Sal drew a sharp breath at one point.

'Georgie, somehow, we need to persuade the King or their owners to match these up. Look.' He held out two sheets of paper, both entirely unintelligible to me, and pointed to letters in the same pattern on the two sheets. 'This one has a lynx, and so does this one. Only, this one is female. There is a deer listed here, and here, and a herd in this one, but no mention of colour. You will have to visit them all.'

'Me?'

'Yes. You are going to claim the favour bond we asked Prince Anard for. Be his guest on house calls. He's your ticket in.'

'I like him, but that's a lot of time to spend with one human, Sal. Surely tongues will begin to wave, and it will be hard to reconcile that with the King's request to protect some yet un-conceived child who may never exist.'

'You'll find a way.'

The sigh left me with rather more force than I intended.

'You can't hide on *Black Hind* forever, you know. You want to help The Hind, this is part of our deal,' he pointed out.

'No. But I could take it to go and retrieve Eryn's skin while you do the dinners and parties!'

'From where? The Everstorm? The Moon? That's as close as I've got. *Barge* staff have been getting Jake's crews drunk and otherwise pleasured for months now, and not one has spilt a single thing.'

'The one I left in the blanket box in your townhouse did,' I retorted.

'Why are they there, not in the harbour?' Sal honoured me with a reproachful glance. 'I just had everything in that house cleaned.'

'Because I filled them with the contents of the wet-pocket and I didn't want to poison you – or the wildlife. Dead animals floating around the dock suddenly would cause too many questions. Oh, and I left the rowboat on the dock too.'

'Great. I'll send a clean-up team tomorrow. Thank you for not spoiling my supper.'

'You're welcome.' I sketched a mock bow. He hadn't said no. I clung to that as he leafed through the remaining papers.

Finally, I broached the subject again. Saying it aloud would give it life, make it real, take me closer to going home. 'She said that the old woman had it. There was an old woman on the island next to the one I was held captive on. She used to row her tiny boat across and leave me food.'

The old woman bobbed on the waves of my memory. Her calls for payment as we left the port as fresh as the day we sailed. 'She knew exactly what I was. She was obnoxious to me. I'm certain they didn't pay her either. I saw her on the day they took me to Icidro, in her little wooden rowboat, staring after the trimaran.'

'So, they think she has it? They didn't return for it?' Sal had placed the papers down now and was giving me his full attention.

'The harpoonist said that the old woman is dead. Died in a North Sea storm.'

Sal was quiet. He stroked his neck, and I left him to his thoughts. Eventually he put the papers back in the safe, and we pushed it back, locking it again.

'She was either lying, or lied to,' he said finally. 'I'm sorry.' He placed a hand on my shoulder, laughter lines dimmed for the moment. 'The woman on the islands near you cannot have your skin. It was here, in Terrania, only a few days before I left to come and get you. I could smell it on Jake. He couldn't have taken it all the way back up to the islands and got to Icidro's in time for you to see him there. It's simply not possible.'

Although frustrating to hear, he was right. The harpoonist was either mistaken or deliberately misled, and I had killed her for it. I'd been so excited I hadn't even checked. The old woman – it could be any old woman.

'My enthusiasm got the better of me. It was there, in my reach, and I grasped at the assumption that I knew what she meant. Urchin spines and barnacle shells, I'm an idiot. I've been around humans too long.'

Sal rested a hand on my shoulder. 'We'll find it, Georgie. Old woman isn't a lot to go on, but it's more than we had. We just need to find an old woman who died in a storm, between here and Icidro's – assuming that what your harpoonist believed was a partial truth.'

My heart sank a little, but I raised my chin and tried to bury the feelings in a locked chest within my soul. After all, it was still more than we had to go on yesterday. I wanted the option to go home more than I wanted to leave the people who were fast becoming my new family. I wasn't entirely sure I wanted to return to the simple life I had enjoyed before. Sal remaining here was making more sense as time went on. Although, without someone who truly knew all sides of me, it might have been a very different situation.

We locked Sal's safe and left the room, each lost in our own thoughts.

'Go home to your boat.' Sal said eventually. 'Take some clothes for this woman and find out who she is. As you've lost Eden, I will find you a replacement technical crew member, but you'll need extra hands on board until then. Go. You should be with each other. I'll find a reason for Gina to have another short absence.'

Sal and I didn't really do private physical gestures, especially as most of the time when we were alone, Sal was natural, and I found it a bit disturbing. I must have been one of the only females around him not melting into his arms at any given opportunity.

'Thank you,' I said, and gave him an awkward hug. 'Okay, nah that feels weird.'

He laughed. 'Oddly enough, I agree. It feels good with a human because they know no different, but skin to skin with no fur on a selkie . . . it's just wrong.' He stopped walking and laughed. Short, embarrassed, barking laughs. 'Sorry. I didn't mean . . . Even if you had your skin I wouldn't . . . But you don't which is also . . . Oceans above, I need to stop talking. When in a tidal flow, stop swimming against it!'

I seized the opportunity to change the topic. 'I want to take Aria to its home. It gives us a focus, a closure, and a direction to sail in.'

'Now? Are you sure that you don't want one of my other boats to do it?' Sal asked gently, taking my offered life raft from his pool of discomfort.

I did; I truly wanted someone else to do it. Being near that thing picked at me like a crab pincer in my soul, but the idea of it fooling anyone else was far worse. 'Someone has to.'

'It doesn't have to be you,' he replied.

'It does. Sal, we are Old Ones. I can't fight it, but I know how to play its games. If you send a human crew without briefing them, how will you explain it? How will you avoid them falling into a snare? Even sea-folk would be rowboats in a storm – wrecked on the first rocks. Either you or I need to do it. You have been away too much recently. You need to be seen. Meet the King at the next rendezvous. Get his lists and start building plans for my tour with the Fish Prince. Let me do this. I need to. And, *they* need to. Even the kelp-whipped cormorant is sulking. We'll test the girl out on the sea.'

'What about your skin?' Sal asked. 'Georgie, the Lady Gina has been absent as well. You, as much as I, need to be here. A short absence is one thing – but a trip to the Everstorm is quite another.'

I stared past him. Eden may have been human, but I lived because of their innocent sacrifice. I wanted that creature as far from the other humans I liked as possible. 'When I get back, I'll be Gina for as long as it takes to find our hind. Sal, just give me a few weeks. Please.'

He nodded, and I knew I had his agreement. He'd cover my back while I was getting rid of the Aria. My soft bed on *Barge* would be waiting, but for now, I had a stubborn Aria to return and a crew to get underway.

I reached *Black Hind* in the early hours of the morning, carrying the Aria securely inside one of Sal's transport tanks. I'd been careful not to hurt it and explained that we didn't want it damaged or blown out before we could return it home, in order to coerce it into confinement. Flattering the thing was a necessary evil. Once it was safely in, I'd covered it for the journey out.

I gently deposited it on the deck and caught Zora's curled lip, distaste written clear in her features. After I'd secured the tank in the hold, wrapping it in the spare sails, I closed the door quietly and peered into the room Theo had shared with Eden.

It was newly divided by a makeshift curtain, with his bed at one end and a bedraggled Rialta sat in the other.

I passed her a bag. 'I brought you some clothes. You can get dry now' – I grinned in what I hoped was a friendly way – 'just in time to get wet again as we sail. You don't want to be on the pleasure boat, and I can't blame you. Just because Sal is my cousin doesn't mean I approve of all his businesses.'

She looked up at me and met my eyes directly. Her jaw clenched tightly, before she spoke. 'Then why d'you use it?'

'I don't use it like that! It's our base, a place to refuel and store things. We can travel light and fast if we have a safe port. It just happens that ours is a mobile one.'

She reached for the clothes, pulling out plain, practical deck attire. Tension began to fall from her shoulders as she saw nothing offensive or remotely similar to what *Barge* staff would wear.

'I'm going to let you get changed. We have a job to finish and need an extra pair of hands. It would be great if you'd come with us.' I left the question hanging and turned my back on her as she started to undress.

'I'll come,' she said, all trace of accent gone, her voice clear and musical as river water over pebbles.

'Good,' I muttered, thrown by the change in her demeanour. I wanted to turn around, but was determined to give her privacy and walked away instead. On a boat this small, there was only so long her secret could remain hidden.

'Thank you for rescuing me,' she called.

I stopped. 'Thank *you* for rescuing me!' I laughed. 'Rialta, I still don't understand how or why she caught you,' I said, hoping for a clue to the *otherness* of her, but she just turned her face away from me. I left her to get changed and returned to the deck.

Zora stood in her, now customary, position. We weren't even moving, and she stood like a figurehead in the bow, more beautiful than any carving. Cor perched on the rail alongside her, his wings dripping as pearls of water fell to the sea below.

I left them both to their thoughts and wandered along the deck aimlessly, gathering my own to explain my motives without letting Zora know what I did about Eden's death.

When Rialta emerged, she stood taller, her skin looked healthier, and she flashed me a shy smile before moving to stroke Cor. I was shocked at the lack of pecking and his calm acceptance of her.

I steeled myself for the impending storm of emotions I was

about to loose and called everyone over to inform them that we would raise anchor and sail for the Everstorm.

Theo accepted it without argument.

'This is why you brought that thing aboard again?' Zora growled.

I nodded. 'I want it as far away from people we care for as we can take it. I want that bargain fulfilled and the Aria gone. More than all of those, I want you all safe, away from Lost Jake's patrols.'

They fell silent.

Theo spoke first, breaking the tension that stretched tautly between myself and Zora. 'I'll lift the anchor. Zora, start teaching Rialta to raise the sails.'

Zora mumbled something I didn't catch. But she did as he asked, and before long, *Black Hind* was underway.

COR BLIMEY

The wind rose, whipping the ocean into a frenzy of white-capped waves. Foam swirled around the bow as we fought against the storm. Our red sails had been tightly reefed as the storm sped towards us unnaturally fast, leaving us no time to change them for storm sails. Slivers of sail flapped in a desperate bid to escape from the bound-up rigging. We rose and fell at the mercy of the ocean, propelled by the remaining section of small, lower sail. A cluster of islands on the horizon which should be growing closer remained eternally out of reach.

We were on the fringes of the Everstorm.

Zora stood in the bow. I'd asked her to expend no magic while we could cope without it. She'd tired easily since Eden's death and was barely recovered from her exertions in Orange. Aside from the exhaustion it caused her to use it, whatever well of magic she used had been weakened by her grief. We were a team, and between us, Theo and I would manage whatever needed to be done. As long as Zora and Rialta moved their weight as needed and Zora took her turn on helm, we'd stay the right way up. It was going to be a long and sleepless few days.

'How much further in do we need to go?' Theo grunted as he fought through another trough.

'The sooner this promise is discharged the better.' I agreed wholeheartedly. I wanted Aria off the boat. 'I'll go and check. Don't worry, I'll be exceptionally careful.'

'Before you go, I wanted to ask, this far south, do you think we'll see dragons?' Theo asked hopefully as he glanced at the sky between waves.

'I think they are all inland, in the great desert sunning themselves no doubt.' No chance any sane creature would be flying in a storm like this.

'I'm not sure I'd want to hunt in this either.' He swore through gritted teeth as he coerced us through another huge wave. 'I'll stop sky gazing and focus on the water.'

Cor shuffled onto deck, his feathers dusty and lacking shine from all the time he was spending in the galley. He stretched his huge wings wide, dull feathers fluttering in the rising wind, raised his beak and called out into the air.

'There's a creature that seems to relish a storm.' I shook my head as he took off into the wind, his wings beating hard as he rose above us. Cor circled above *Black Hind*, then flapped into the wind, towards the heart of the raincloud.

'He'll never see fish in weather like this. What do you think he's up to?' Theo asked.

'No idea. He's an odd one. Doesn't behave like any cormorant I know.'

Theo laughed. 'Do you know many?' Then, he looked at me, his laughter abruptly dying at the sight of my unglamoured, bared teeth.

'I only meant it as a joke,' he sighed and slapped me on the back. 'You really need to work on your sense of humour.' I parted my lips into a wide, toothy grin, exposing my canine teeth in all their shining glory.

'*I* was joking,' I muttered. It appeared I had once again misfired the humour.

The boat lurched down a wave, and I grabbed at the rail to stay aboard. I wore a belt clip – but being battered against the hull and dragged in the water was not in my plans.

'Go, see that sprite. See if we can be rid of it,' Theo called. I carefully worked my way across the deck as he shouted to Zora to move herself more usefully to aid him. Better him than me bossing her about in her current mood.

I opened the hold door. We'd all agreed that keeping it out of accidental earshot was safer, even without the dark knowledge I possessed. I opened the tank to speak to it, and Aria drifted around me. The once translucent body, now almost solid, its strength and power returning as the sprite rested.

'Where can we release you that will satisfy the deal?' I asked.

'There is storm. I feel it. Take me to heart of storm, then you returned me home. Bargain is done.'

'The centre of the storm?' I repeated, my hands growing clammy as I realised what it was asking. The Aria was trying to take even more lives. Determination replaced fear as I prepared myself to tell the others. I was not letting it win. We would deliver this Aria and remove its venomous presence from *Black Hind* – for good.

It nodded.

'Once you are in the centre of the storm, all bargains are finished and considered complete.' I left no room for argument.

'Agreed.'

'I will come for you and open the door once we get there,' I said calmly, keeping all emotion from my voice. 'I wish you a fair journey. May you explore new seas and fly freely on far away winds.'

The sprite looked surprised. At least, I thought it did.

'Thank you, selkie, for the old words.'

I left the hold.

'The centre of a storm,' I muttered as I wandered past the cabin and the control panel for the boat's power.

I was about to turn the panels off, and sink them to reduce the potential damage, when I realised it had already been done. Frowning, I scrambled to the deck.

'How long have the panels been off?' I shouted, the wind stealing my words, tumbling them into the water.

'Haven't touched them,' Theo replied. Zora was stood against the upwind rail and shrugged while Rialta looked at me blankly.

'I don't know how to turn them off,' she said. 'So, it wasn't me, but they were on less than an hour ago because I used power on the lights.' She shrugged. 'Maybe they've taken damage.'

'No one turned it off?' I asked again.

'It was probably Cor,' Rialta called across to me. 'He's always pushing buttons in there. I keep trying to see which ones, so I can undo his pecking, but he's insistent.' She showed me a cut on her hand. 'This morning – at that point when we struggled against the tide – I'm sure he was making it worse. Then he pecked me so hard I had to move.'

'He's been odd since Eden died,' I said. 'Normal birds don't mope around boats once a bird speaker link is dropped. They fly home.'

I looked at them all. We'd worry about Cor later; right now we had a bigger issue to face. The knowing was etched on every face. Even Rialta, who knew few details, was staring at her fingernails with more intent than one of the beauticians on *Barge*. I swallowed rising concern, pushing the roiling waves in my own gut back down with a firm thought.

'In order to get Aria off the boat, with no further bargains involved, we need to take it to the middle of the oncoming storm.'

'The middle?' exclaimed Theo. 'Bloody thing is trying to kill us.'

I nodded. Theo stared at me, shaking his head.

'For Eden,' I said. His chest rose, and the breath exhaled out almost as loud as the winds.

'For Eden,' he agreed. 'Rialta, please, don't as much as think anything while it's above deck. No matter how rough the journey or what it says. Just focus on positive things. As bad as this might look,' he said, as he wrestled another large wave, 'this is a small storm. If we work as a team, we can do this.'

Rialta nodded. Her clear eyes glancing at him, then sliding back to my own, as that undercurrent of familiarity prickled again.

An unknown but ancient quantity, like sirens have, like Sal has. Yet, until she revealed herself, I was reduced to pretending that I couldn't feel anything – utterly convinced that she was doing the same. Could we trust her? Should we? Oceans above, did we have a choice? Passing through the eye of a storm would be both a test of her willingness to live and her desire to help us do the same.

Theo swung the bow into the storm. Zora and I readied ourselves to shift our weight in response to his calls. It was going to be a rough few hours.

Warm rain fell in torrents. The tropical warmth that when ashore is so relieving after a hot, muggy day merely added more water to the deluge crashing over our bow as we battled through the waves.

My stomach churned, with nerves or the rolling motion, I

couldn't say – for both made me equally as unsettled. We struggled onward, tacking our way through the wind. Occasionally, a gust would swing us round, or a wave push us off course, but Theo stood firm, guiding us through the storm, his hand as steady as his nature. He stood alone, an island of calm amidst the tumult.

Zora threw herself into keeping the boat as level as possible. At times we stayed upright by sheer determination rather than skill, swept from our feet by water sluicing over the decks, the clips the only reason we remained aboard.

It was the first time I found myself wishing we had a cell engine like *Barge*. But the small panel-powered motor was all we could carry.

We fought the storm for hours, growing exhausted and battered, from stumbles and trips as we flew from one gunwale to the other. We were soaked and frustrated, but we pushed on. *For Eden,* I kept telling myself. I would not let the Aria claim any more of my crew.

A splintering crack caught my attention. I dived along the deck, shoving Zora to the side. The spar fell and crashed, a mere finger's width from my feet. A newly freed fold of sail started to flutter in triumphant escape, breaking free of its bindings now it was released from the confines of the tight spar. The ropes trailed out flapping in the wind, well above our reach in the howling gale.

Theo began to struggle, and the boat became even less predicable as still more of the sail un-reefed its self.

Could I climb up it? In this wind, I'd be stupid to. One of us had to release the Aria, and none of us should be off the deck when we did, but we would struggle to get to the heart of the storm in one piece like this. With one spar dropped, its twin was starting to waggle more actively, the tension on its restraints loosened by the flapping rope.

I tracked its end and was readying myself to make a mad dash up the rigging when a black shadow swooped past, catching the rope in its beak. Cor struggled against the wind to manage a bumpy landing at my feet. I took the rope from him and Zora joined me in pulling it as tight as we could. We tied it off securely, and I caught her staring after Cor as he tried to get below the deck hatch. Rialta opened it for him, and he hopped back down out of the wind.

I tried to speak, but the wind whisked the words out to sea, so I settled for a point and a shrug instead.

Rialta was right – something was odd about Cor. When we were out of here, I needed to find out what.

The wind dropped as suddenly as it had sprung upon us at the periphery of the storm. The boat levelled out. I rolled the tension out of my shoulders and stared upwards at the brief calm around us.

'Are we all ready?' I asked. It was time to free ourselves of the burden of the Aria.

Rialta wandered towards the bow, taking Zora's usual position, and Zora stood with Theo.

He reached for her hand and gave it a quick squeeze. A bolt of jealousy flew through me, much as sparks of lightning hit the sea in the distance. Why should she choose a selkie over a human male? I buried the sensation as something to deal with later. I needed clear thoughts for the next few minutes.

In the hold, the box containing the Aria was still stable and secure. I loosened the front strap and opened the door. 'We are in the eye of the storm, the middle, as agreed. It is time for you to rejoin your own kind and fly on the wind, to explore once again.'

The Aria faced me, its corporeal form of darkened air rippling.

'Let me out. I will go.'

As I carried it onto the deck, I could feel the sideways glances of the crew as they tried to look as busy and occupied as they could. The silence was eerie. Only flapping sails and the lapping of the large waves we still rode punctuated the quiet. No sea birds called, no voices rode the winds.

I opened the lid of the box, freeing Aria. It floated out, hovering near my face.

'You kept your deal,' it said. I nodded. Its form flexed in what I hoped was acknowledgement, and it flew past Theo, hovering close to his ear. He stood staring fixedly ahead, keeping our course steady, searching for a way out. It circled him, whispering gods know what in his ears. He flinched but maintained his silence.

Giving up on Theo, it tried Zora. After its second circle, she unceremoniously dumped a small blob of water on it and it passed her by.

Rialta faced it, her chin raised in defiance. Entirely as she has been told not to, she engaged it.

'I know you. I see you,' she said.

It stopped, hanging in the air an arms-length from her face.

'You will get no bargain from me, *Sidhe*. Your deal is done. Leave these people in peace. They are under my protection now.'

My breathing stilled. The Aria screamed a shrill call and flew off like a shark after blood, gone into the depth of the storm.

'Why did you say that?' Zora asked. She sounded calmer than I felt. Zora stared at Rialta with hands on her hips. Not as a posture of defiance; I knew her hands rested on the hilts of hidden weapons.

'Because it's true,' Rialta said as she returned to staring off the bow. 'Are we heading out of this stupid storm now? If I'd have known that little sidhe was the reason we were headed to here, I'd have sent it packing much earlier and we would have avoided this ridiculous situation.'

I felt my mouth gaping, my glamour slipping. I pulled it close and myself upright.

'If you'd have told us that you could have done that, it might have helped,' I retorted. But deep inside, I knew I'd have always felt that an incomplete deal with any type of sprite was a risk I had no plan on taking. We'd still have made this trip. I'd still have risked them all to save them from Eden's fate.

Theo was ignoring the whole conversation so diligently I wondered if he'd even heard it. Zora stared from Rialta, and back to me in turn.

'So . . . Rialta,' I said as I approached her. 'You were unable to escape from a blood-witch, yet you now claim to have the power to protect a crew who, if I am perfectly honest here, are more than capable of protecting ourselves.' I stopped, sat on the winch block and leant forward. 'So who, and what, are you?'

'I'd be more worried about your cormorant than what I am. I mean you no harm. You freed me. The cormorant, on the other hand, has a human soul trapped inside. They will both need help soon.' She smiled, and despite my reservations, it looked genuine.

'Eden!' Zora flew past me, down the hatch.

'Urchin spines, we'll not get out of this storm without a full crew on deck.' I felt the ocean inside me stirring, raising its own ire to match that which we had yet to battle our way out of.

Rialta shrugged. 'I can help. Tell me exactly what you need me to do.'

She was way too slim to be much use in balancing the boat, but I didn't tell her that. Once the waves built, Zora would return. She wouldn't leave us in jeopardy. At least, I had to hope she wouldn't. The wind-shadow on the surface grew ever closer.

'Starboard side,' Theo called.

I gestured for Rialta to move. 'Clip on again. It's going to be tough without Zora's aid.'

She nodded and crossed the deck, clipping onto the rail. The boat heeled the wrong way – it was dipping on the side we stood, even as the wind rose. Concentration lined her face as she planted her feet in the face of the oncoming storm.

'Let's get out of here,' she yelled as the wind caught us. Theo wrestled the helm, and I adjusted the sails as best I could, given their state, then worked along the deck to join her.

Huge waves continued to build, whipped into a frenzy by the storm, and we battled through them, rising skyward only to fall off the back end, crashing into the next oncoming wave. On the biggest, we slid down their face, to be surrounded by walls of water, on all sides. Tiny and fragile against the power of the ocean.

Had I been at home, I'd have been hiding in an undersea cave or hauled out on a remote wind-sheltered shore. This was the kind of storm we faced maybe once or twice in the winter, even less in the last few years – as though the weather had finally had enough and decided that the human scourge was reduced sufficiently to stop taking its ire out on them. I caught the fallacy in my thoughts. I was on this boat, crewed by one full human and a halfbreed. They were better people than I had expected.

'Hang on,' I called to Rialta as a huge gust hit us. The boat heeled, higher and higher we rose. I tried to reach for the winch, to let some power out of the sails, but as I leant forwards, the boat heeled further.

I heard laughter in the wind. Aria may have kept its word, but that didn't stop its kin from playing with us as a child plays with shells on the beach.

They pushed at us, to see how much we could take, tipping us to the extreme then dropping us back. Zora emerged from the cabin, able to reach what I could not, and as the power loosed and Theo wrestled us through the troughs, she clambered up the spray-soaked deck to join us.

'Bloody man could have taken a less dramatic tack,' she shouted over the storm, her words carrying back to him.

'The bloody man wants to get us all out of here,' Theo replied, though I wasn't sure that the others caught it as the wind whipped his words away.

We fought through. Exhausted and soaked, despite the best equipment Sal had procured, we were a group of bedraggled sea otters that emerged from the fringes of the Everstorm.

We headed for the small collection of islands north of the Everstorm. They had once had other names, but now, they were simply known as the Respites. We anchored in a deep harbour off the north coast of the northernmost island. The sheer will required to get ourselves to safety had drained all desire to argue with, or push Rialta.

Cor flew from the deck, he hadn't eaten for a while, and I suppose even the presence of another in his head would not be enough to override the instinct to hunt.

'Maybe that's why that bird sits out on the deck when we go to sleep,' Theo observed.

I hadn't noticed his approach. A sure sign of exhaustion if ever there was one. Theo was not known for his light feet, even if his healing touch was gentle.

I watched as the black speck disappeared into the distance, hunting for a good spot for his meal.

'Maybe you're right. Eden finds a way to keep an eye on us even now,' I replied.

Zora turned towards me. Was she crying? I wasn't good at this particular human emotion still. They seemed to get sad a lot more easily than I did. They did everything to an extreme – live faster, die younger.

'Do you think that Eden still knows us?' she asked. 'How much must it hurt to be severed from your body like that?' She turned from me, and I was spared the decision of how to deal with her tears for a while longer as she vanished below deck.

'Georgie, she needs your company,' Theo said. 'I'll bring you both some food in a while. Go, sit with her. We'll be fine stowing and tidying without you.'

I called her name gently from outside the heavy curtain, but Zora didn't reply. I heard a muffled sob instead. So, I pulled it aside and slipped in to sit with her. She lay on the bed, tears streaming down her cheeks.

'It's so unfair,' she said. 'Eden was – is the kindest person I know. They don't deserve to be trapped inside that grumpy bird.'

I bit back my desire to point out that at least Eden wasn't totally dead, and instead sat next to her as she sobbed, wrapping my arms around her. I held her as she cried into my shoulder. Eventually, exhaustion overcame her, and I laid her gently on the bed. Then, I sat on the floor, still holding her hand while she rested.

SOUL OF THE WATER

Cor returned our stares with interest while plucking mouthfuls of freshly caught fish from between his claws.

'Should we still call him Cor?' Theo asked. I understood his reticence. Would Cor care about a name that he probably didn't even recognise? I doubted he did. But Eden – could Eden hear us from within Cor?

'Eden isn't dead,' Zora murmured as she ran her hands down the bird's back, caressing his feathers with gentle fingertips.

'Not yet. But Eden can't survive in that body forever,' I replied. A misplaced soul was not something to be taken lightly. Both Cor and Eden would be warring for control of that small avian body. It worried me more than I dared to show, but I pushed the tide of concern down and focused on Zora. I tried to place what I hoped was a consoling hand on her shoulder. She didn't shrug me off. Despite all the time amongst them, I still had to guess whether I was doing the right thing. Humans were much more tactile than my own family. It comes from always having hands, I suppose.

'What now?' Theo asked. 'I don't know any medical treatments that could help this situation.' He dropped his head into his hands. Seeing the big man so lost, as unmoored as Zora, was a shock. He was used to being able to fix things. This was beyond him.

'You don't know much at all, really,' Rialta said, gliding into the cabin. 'I'm sorry if I appear ungrateful and for hiding what I am, but she' – she pointed at me – '*knew* I was not human. Just as she is if we are going for full disclosure.' She paused dramatically, but neither of the others moved or spared her a glance.

'Oh, they know,' I said, dropping my glamour and turning from the others to face her. 'What I want to know is why Zora hasn't spotted what you are.'

Zora shrugged, not taking her eyes from Cor-Eden for a moment. 'She's not an oceanic Old One. I don't see anything, not like you.' She glanced at me and flashed a quick smile. It didn't reach her eyes, but it was a brief respite from the sadness which graced her face most days, and I soaked it up.

Rialta paused in her stride and frowned. 'Zora can *see* you?'

I pulled my gaze from Zora and returned my attention to Rialta. I searched her face, her body for clues. But all I felt was that familiar tag of something old, someone *more* than human. 'What *are* you?' I asked, trawling my memory for a clue but coming up empty. Whatever Rialta was, she was not from the North.

'Rialta.' I rolled the word around my mouth. 'It means deep water, doesn't it? But, you can't be a lake nymph because that wouldn't make you a threat to the Aria.' I stared at her, willing her to open up to us.

'You don't want to know,' she said, and for a moment, a darkness floated past the clear eyes.

Zora interrupted us. 'Forget the what, I'm more interested in how you know about Eden – yes, Georgie, I know that's part of the *what*, but I don't care about the details right now – and whether you can help Eden.' She was staring into the bird's – Eden's – eyes.

'I can help, yes. But, it will mean the death of one of them.' Rialta walked past Zora to join us at the table, putting her hands gently on Cor's head. The bird shrieked in panic and pulled away, flapping frantically and leaping for Zora.

'He's not ready to let go, nor is the human soul,' she said as she leant back.

Zora snapped her head towards Rialta. 'I know what you are!' she cried. 'I've heard of Old Ones like you. They haunt the deepest desert and the river beds. The storm-ridden seas are too wide for you, the lives shed, spread too far apart. You live in the places where lives perish before their time.'

Rialta returned her gaze, unmoving.

'Death-snatcher, soul-stealer, spirit-catcher, life-sucker,' Zora chanted.

'I'm not particularly fond of most of those names if I'm totally honest,' Rialta sighed. 'They give children nightmares. I don't choose to steal fully body-anchored, unwilling souls, no matter how foul or tainted it might be. It's just an old tale. You aren't scared of me?'

Zora frowned. 'Why would I be? You are as essential as the sun, the rain and the sea. No one wants unhoused souls floating around. No wonder the boat has been lying low and steering calm.'

A mischievous grin played on Zora's mouth for a moment, and she looked over at Theo. 'Pick her up.'

Rialta actually grinned back at her, as though they shared a secret, a brief moment of togetherness. 'You're welcome to try,' she added to Zora's challenge and rose to stand in front of Theo.

Theo looked into his cup unhappily. 'I don't want to pick up a woman I don't know. I don't like picking up anyone I don't know. I know what sort of danger lurks around Georgie's person. What might you do to me? No, I'll not pick you up, Rialta.'

'You don't have to, Theo,' I said, remembering the oddly settled boat as we had battled through the storm. 'Rialta I have no idea what Zora is trying to prove here, but may I try to pick you up?'

She laughed, a clear, ringing laugh, and I relaxed a little more. 'I promise not to eat you. You are welcome to *try*.'

She was so slight I was gentle not to hurt her, but I couldn't raise her from the floor. Her weight was entirely disproportionate to her size. It was like lifting an enormous boulder free of the water. It should be easy, but it was deceptively hard.

'Gods, what did you do to yourself, Georgie?' Theo chuckled, having watched me struggle for a few minutes. 'A child should be able to lift Rialta.' He rose and traversed the furniture to reach us, his curiosity finally overriding his politeness.

'May I?' he asked, and Rialta giggled. She encircled her arms around his neck as he crouched to lift her. Try as he might, he could not lift her from the deck. Bent over and sweating with exertion, he finally backed off to sit heavily. His eyes were wide as he regarded her and he voiced my own thoughts.

'You carry the weight of that many souls?' he said in amazement. 'How many have you taken?'

She nodded and said nothing as she sat.

'Then, how were those women able to knock you over?' I asked. 'I saw you, outside the Gilded Heaven.'

'Acting,' she replied. 'Imagine what would have happened if they couldn't knock me down. It would have been far worse.'

'How did you even get stuck there?' I asked.

'Mona's spirit was so dark that I couldn't leave it to roam around causing havoc. She owned one of the darkest I have ever come across. I took a part of it, when she fell in a river. I discovered her and reached for her but as she died, she pushed her spirit into me – trying to jump bodies. Too late, she realised what I am and tried to withdraw. I backed off as she returned to consciousness, incomplete and weak. Then, someone was kind enough to save her. I had taken too little to stop it, but enough, I hoped, to avoid her being a whole spirit able to cause trouble or worse, to jump bodies as a whole.

'So, I followed her to Orange, certain she wouldn't recognise me and convinced that she wouldn't live much longer. I kept expecting her to die from drug use or any one of many other things she did, but she didn't. There was something strong about her, no matter how evil she was. I grew bold and visited her in Gilded Heaven. Like you, I ate the food. She recognised me as an Old One – I can only assume that she used her blood magic to do so – and, well you know the rest, It was worth the suffering.'

Had we stolen her away before she could complete her task? I felt nausea rising and swallowed hard to avoid asking the questions buzzing around my mind, but then I remembered what she had said as we left.

'The rest of her spirit. Is that what you went back for?' I asked.

'Yes.'

'You speak of evil so freely. Are you evil? Good? Do you see yourself as a judge?' Theo stood with his feet apart, his chin raised and his stare unblinking. She met his eyes for a brief moment, then her shoulders dropped.

Rialta stared at the cormorant and sighed. The type of sigh that leaves you weary just watching it. One of those sighs that would make oceans part with sympathy for the wielder, to allow them free passage.

'I don't wish to be. But, where I have a choice to make, then yes, I am a judge. One day you will ask me to choose between the bird and the human, because although you miss your friend, you will feel their pain too acutely. The bird will start to lose its sanity and take your friend's with it. Over time, the human will become feral, and rather than the bird becoming more human, it is as likely that the human becomes more bird. Then, we decide whether we need to free one of them – if one is willing to leave.'

'What happens to the souls if you free one from the body?' I asked.

'You really *don't* want to know the details. Suffice to say they become part of the swarm I contain.' She scraped her chair back. 'If you are done asking questions now, even spirit catchers need their beauty sleep. Sometimes a lot more than you do. It took a lot out of me keeping those stupid Aria at a distance through the Everstorm. I did take one that was getting too close, and it fought hard. I need to rest. You really wouldn't like me when I am tired or hungry.' She moved along the cabin to the bunk-room, her slender form hiding a huge weight. In more ways than one.

'What in all the oceans do we do now?' Theo slumped back in his seat, gesturing widely with his hands.

'We sail home,' I replied. 'Then, we work out what to do next.'

'We feed Cor decent food and keep them both healthy,' Zora said. 'And, I vote that we let Cor peck whatever buttons he chooses while we sail. I trust Eden to be guiding that.'

Cor croaked, and pecked at Zora gently before sitting on her lap. She flung her arms around the stinking bird.

'Georgie is right. Let's get back home,' she said as much to Cor as to us. 'Hug the coast and hope we get through The Narrows at night as easily as we slipped out.'

Cor hopped from her lap and waddled into the control cabin a little unsteadily, as though he was fighting himself, like a sailor trying to stroll down a street having drunk one too many. I didn't envy Eden the life or body they were tied to, but maybe it was better than death. For now.

TWO WET FISH

Theo and Zora wanted to test whether they could communicate with Eden while *Black Hind* was being repaired. Maybe Eden could somehow make themselves understood through Cor; I know I wanted to believe it almost as much as Zora did. The others weren't keen on Rialta remaining on board with them, and despite her assurances that she wouldn't interfere, I could understand their desire to have her far from Cor and Eden at this point. It made sense for her to accompany me back to *Barge* instead.

'You'll have endless rounds of tours and parties, drunken nights and idiotic humans who think money buys power,' Zora had pointed out as we chatted about the tasks Sal would have me doing.

Rialta had walked in at that point.

'I could come with you?' she offered, glancing at Zora. We both saw the release of muscle tension there, the uncrossing of Zora's arms. Rialta continued. 'It would give you someone with less base instincts for company. The others don't want me here as much as you do. Don't worry, Zora, I do understand. I promise I'd never touch either of them without discussing it. But, if I am not here, that temptation – and concern – is removed.' Rialta looked at me and shrugged. 'I'm a pretty good maid. I can be subtle. I'm very good at being unnoticed.'

I flinched as she said it. Taking her from one serving position and pretending she was my own servant seemed very wrong.

'I can see things you can't,' she offered. 'Why are you, a proud selkie, doing rounds of silly human houses anyway?'

'The land in the west is in danger. There's a single guardian left in place and she is struggling to keep it alive. You must have felt it from Orange. We believe that the current fashion for collecting rare animals and plants – Old Ones included – means that the missing white hind has been passed from collection to collection over the years.'

Rialta paced the cabin. 'I'd noticed something felt wrong beyond the walls, yes. This is a big task and worthy of our time. How will we get in?'

I noticed the we but didn't remark on it. 'It's a trade price for a huge favour, that I will be a guest of the Prince. He is an admirer of the Old Ones. You could even say a friend of ours.'

'The Prince is dead,' Rialta said. 'It won't work.'

'The heir is dead. The older son, Prince Anard, remains a recluse in Old Town. With his brother gone, he will be expected to become more publicly visible, and I plan to ride that opportunity like a breaking wave.'

'Seren is going to be pissed at you if Rialta can't work as well as her,' Zora said.

'That's true, but I probably should have someone of my own, rather than just rely on my father's staff. I can hardly take any of them ashore with me,' I replied. Rialta had senses I didn't – she would be a huge asset. I held back the smile that tried to break on my face. I had told Sal that I dreamed of a crew of Old Ones. We were well on our way there.

'Father?' Rialta asked.

I glanced upwards. Theo was unlikely to hear the conversation from on deck, but, I'd keep it quiet for now. 'I'll explain all that side of things when you have your stuff ready and in a dry bag. Bring anything you can fit in it. We will be there for a few weeks, at least.'

Barge was in the international zone of the Terranian Sea when we finally found it. Zora loosed the sails to slow us, and I dived over the rail, closely followed by Rialta, who, to my fresh surprise, floated remarkably well. It shouldn't have surprised me, I had watched her swim before but the revelations of the last few days had altered my perceptions of her. We struck out for the landing platform. No Driftwood were in sight, but we'd decided that to keep questions to the minimum, I'd swim aboard as Gina. I changed glamour half-way to *Barge*. If anyone was looking they would see Lady Gina swimming, rather than Georgie. Lady Gina could have met *Black Hind* anywhere, and Georgie would still remain aboard.

As I swam, my mind wandered. I truly didn't know how much longer I could split my roles. I couldn't believe we had got away with it as long as we had, but we needed to continue the charade for at least as long as it took to find the missing hind. Once we had fixed the West, I supposed I could pick one face. Maybe. The idea of leaving Sal without his heir and just sailing off home was tempting. No more floaty dresses or ridiculous demands from over-eager or over-powered humans.

We scrambled onto the deck, flopping like landed fish onto

the smooth, wooden boards, and I tried to bring my focus back to the tasks ahead. I drew myself upright, assuming the poise worn by Lady Gina despite puddles growing around us as we grinned at each other.

'Welcome home,' I said.

Ash peered around the door as Rialta hauled her dry-bag out.

'Lady Gina, are you hurt?' She rushed to help me to my feet. 'Who's that?' she whispered in my ear. 'Should I get your father?'

'Why would my father need to be called to meet my new assistant?' I smiled as sweetly as I could, to put the guard at ease. 'It's all okay, don't worry. Lord Sal told me where to find her. I just had to travel a little further than I anticipated.'

'How did you?' She looked out at the retreating *Black Hind*.

'They called into port.' I shrugged. 'Rather than hire a vessel, I joined them.' The guard looked at our soaked clothing and raised an eyebrow.

'We fancied a swim.' I grinned widely and stood, dripping further puddles with each step. 'Please follow me, Rialta. Ash, can you let my father know I'm home?' She nodded, and we walked off, leaving a trail of drips in our wake. Once the door closed, I released the held-in chuckle.

'I swear they think our entire family is mad.'

'Your father?' Rialta said, and I knew I wasn't getting away with it much longer.

'Lord Sal. We claim Georgie is his cousin, because it allows me the freedom to roam freely as a break from this place and carry out the less pleasant duties he requires of me.'

'Having seen the body you brought to the cottage, I can see why. It wouldn't do for his daughter to be an assassin. It cannot be good for his cousin either.'

I stopped, as a thought occurred to me. 'Did you take that spirit? The one we killed?'

She shook her head. 'It had departed long before you brought the body in range.'

'Do you remember what they remember?'

'No, I just feel the extra weight of their emotions.' She winced. 'It's often fear – especially with the untimely deaths of most I catch.'

I placed a finger to my lips as we reached the door that would allow us access to my rooms. They should be empty, but until we were in, I wouldn't assume that they were. We entered, and I quickly checked the rooms, locking the hidden door.

Dealing with the level of fear Rialta must have absorbed had to be difficult. I searched her face, but no flicker of emotion gave her away – just cool serenity. To process the emotions of hundreds of souls, and carry that throughout your life . . . I shuddered. it was a weight of responsibility that I didn't envy.

'What happens?' I asked. 'How is it that you aren't bitter, or jumping at your own shadow?'

Rialta shrugged and stripped her wet clothes off. 'I honestly don't know. It's just what I'm for. I'm part of the cycle of life and death. When I am killed, eventually, I fear that all these traumatised souls will go free.

'Can you not cross the veil and loose them?'

She folded her wet clothes up. 'I don't know. Maybe, if I had a guide. Without one, I don't know if I would ever be able to come back.'

Even Old Ones die eventually. Some of us live exceptionally long lives, most notably sirens and dragons. I felt that Rialta might be another, but I hesitated to ask her. Did I really want to know how old she truly was? Did I need to?

I put my sodden clothes with hers and rummaged in the wardrobe for dry ones. Nothing I had would fit Rialta well, but we managed to make a simple dress look presentable with a belt and judicious folding.

Floaty dresses swirled around my arms as I tried to select something that matched my mood. I slipped into one of my custom embroidered gowns. Red sea holly ran around the entire hem and cuffs. The fabric was, typically, gossamer-light and gold. I felt the fish-scale tunic for a moment, my fingers running over its shimmering delicacy. I carefully held it over the dress, and Rialta helped me do up the tiny buttons that ran down the back. It fitted beautifully.

'That's certainly a look,' Rialta said. 'I'm not sure what message you intend to convey, but it almost looks like armour of some sort. It's incredible.'

Armour against the world. A gift from Prince Anard worn in public. Both as important as each other. I was pulling my boots on when there was a knock at the door.

'Gina?'

I opened it to let Sal enter. He studied Rialta, his head slightly tilted and his fingers rubbing against his thumb. He wasn't entirely comfortable, and I wondered if he faced the same problem I had first encountered with her.

'A spirit-keeper,' he said eventually, still staring at Rialta. 'Gina, why is there a spirit-keeper on my ship?'

'This is the woman we rescued in Orange. She will act as my assistant while we hunt for The Hind.'

'You told her?' he spun around, a flash of anger marring his face, just for a moment. Then he regained control. The wild selkie was under that exterior yet.

I raised my chin to meet his flashing eyes. 'I did. The Hind showed her to me, I don't know why, but we need her. Rialta will help. She can see you and I. She couldn't tell Zora was different and she found Eden.'

'What do you mean?' Sal was still fuming, but I had caught his attention, and I watched him try to push it down, to quell the rising storm. He still kept glancing at Rialta, but with less outright hostility as I told him about Eden and Cor. As we sat down and caught up on the rest of the journey, I wondered why he was so strongly opposed to her. Once I had finished, Sal sat back in silence as he processed everything. I didn't disturb him.

Rialta busied herself around the room. I'm not sure she was achieving anything, but it served to remove her from the confrontation of sitting with us. I'd seen her look up as I mentioned The Hind, surprise on her face.

'Deal with the situation as you see best, for the crew.' Sal said eventually. 'If you think that there's a chance Eden may be able to communicate, I'll hold off advertising for their replacement for now.' He reached into his bag and brought out a sheet covered with small writing. He smoothed it flat and pointed at a line.

'We have three potential places to visit,' he said.

'Only three?' I was relieved that it wasn't more, but three meant possibly only three Old Ones had survived captivity in Terrania. If so, where were the rest?

'At my request, Prince Anard has drawn up a list of the events that he is invited to. Two of them cover locations of interest to us. With his brother *expired*, he needs to step up to rally support before his father creates another heir.'

'And, *we* have to look after it.' Babysitting a royal child was really not a task I wanted. I hoped Anard could claim the throne before it became one we would have to fulfil.

'Right. The first date, at the most hopeful of the collections, is next week. Can you be ready for then? Are you back?' Sal asked calmly, but I knew his tells by now. His fingers were gently tapping their tips against each other. He was more anxious about making this happen than he would let on.

I took his hand in both of mine. 'Sal, I promised you I would be. This is our priority now. We *have* to find The Hind. Tell me about these collections.'

'All three have deer herds. The first place we found on the original lists, and two new collections. There are other locations we will want to visit later, but as a priority we need to get into these. This first one also has seals.'

'Seals? Are you sure?' My stomach lurched.

'I've never had a way in to her collection. Whilst the son is happy to frequent *Barge*, many of the rich and powerful feel it is beneath them to have me in their home. You' – he squeezed my shoulder – 'are our way in. Remember, you're Anard's guest, not his woman, merely a friend he is introducing to society. I desperately hope that your looks and potential wealth, along Prince Anard's companionship, will grant you access to places I can't go.'

'I'll guard her.' Rialta said. I turned to see her eyes narrowing like a predator about to pounce.

Sal burst into laughter. 'I very much doubt that Gina will need much guarding. Every single dress she owns contains enough venom to kill most of the hosting party should they get too close.'

'That would be exceptionally messy,' I said. 'I'm not sure I'd get a return invitation.'

Sal looked at me.

'Did you just make a joke?'

I grinned.

'Oceans above, you are becoming more humanised each day.' He shook his head and walked back to the door, leaving the list on the table. 'Once you've had a look at that, I'll send

Seren to sort out your new friend's wardrobe. Come and meet me down in the Ocean Bar for supper. It's fresh fish.'

After he left, we leant over the list, and I sighed. 'He always forgets. Rialta, can you read?'

She smiled broadly. 'Please, call me Ria. I'm glad I have a real function in helping you after all.'

She read the names and each collection's inventory to me. There were several seals listed in that first destination, and they were accompanied by a dolphin.

Gods, the poor creatures, I hoped they truly were seals. The alternative didn't bear considering, but even seals would be traumatised. 'I want to get them out too,' I murmured.

'I understand. Remember, you need The Hind more. We can't just dive in freeing all these creatures after the Prince's first public visit,' Ria pointed out.

'I doubt that will be an issue,' I replied. 'They steal from each other all the time. Killing and theft means nothing to humans. They want what they want, and some of them will do anything to get it.' I stopped abruptly. Ria was looking at me intently.

'Do you think, with all the souls I contain, that I don't already know this?' she retorted. I felt my cheeks burning as she continued, more gently. 'What you say is true. But if all the collections start getting hit, do you not think some of the less savoury mercenary crews might start to wonder what money's in it, and whether should they be doing it too?'

She was right. After all, Jake's crews were now utterly convinced that the siren existed, as well as selkies. 'It's only a matter of time before they start hunting more Old Ones. We've been a commodity,' – I spat in disgust – 'for too long.'

'Should we warn the others?'

'How? We know a single leathergill siren. She will have encouraged others to hide in the far north after her escape.

You are here. You can hardly run around every lake, river, and mountain path hunting for your kin. My capture is known of within my community. Even if they do not know I am partially freed.'

'Only partially? You seem entirely freed to me.'

'Another day, Ria.' I was relieved that she didn't push me for details. We hid the paper in a locked drawer, and I helped myself to a few small fish from my tank as we awaited Seren.

Ria watched me eat for a few minutes, before she next spoke. 'Whatever The Hind showed you relating to me – I never want to know. If it's a prophecy or a vision, my knowing could affect whatever she needs me to do.'

Seren glided in, looking over my outfit with narrowed eyes, searching for flaws and issues. In her eyes, the daughter of Lord Sal had to be perfect whenever she was seen. Finally satisfied, she nodded her head in approval, then studied Ria.

'You're the new assistant?' she asked. In true Seren fashion, it was kind and gentle. Whatever disapproval she might hold privately about Ria appearing without her knowledge would never be voiced.

Ria nodded mutely.

'Hmm. You will need something much more dramatic than that if we are going to make you fit to be seen with Lady Gina. You need to catch the eye and then lead it back to her. I'll have something made ready for you tonight. Arms up.'

She bustled around Ria with her tape measure and left muttering about emergency sewing and sea holly emblems.

'So much for being an invisible set of eyes.' I laughed.

28

JELLYFISH SOUP

A week after Ria and I returned to *Barge*, Prince Anard slipped aboard by cover of darkness.

'Why are humans so melodramatic?' I yawned at Sal when he woke me.

He shrugged. 'It's *all* a bit over-dramatic if you ask me. He could arrive in daylight with his boat, so you can then board and sail along the coast to Lady Rene's home.'

'Do I need to be properly dressed?' I sighed, kicking the covers off as I scrambled for clothes.

He glanced past me to Ria, who was sleepily wandering back to her room, having opened the door.

'No, not if you bring her as a chaperone,' he replied.

'I'm hardly going to steal a prince's soul at midnight. That's even more dramatic than *his* arrival. We'll get dressed.' Ria said, rubbing her eyes.

'You have five minutes. He wants to chat and be back at his boat by dawn,' Sal called as he left.

I closed the door behind him, and grinned toothily at Ria.

'So, spirit-taker, let's have a clandestine meeting. I'm sure if

I was remotely attracted to human males, this would all be very exciting.' I yawned again, and she stifled a laugh as I rubbed the sleep from my eyes and opened the wardrobe.

'Something easy to get on,' I muttered as I flicked through the dresses.

'Or off?' Ria teased, as she reached past me to select a simple dress and a black shawl. Warm black wool was comforting. It was a good choice.

Ria struggled into one of the tunics Seren had brought her. They were sleeveless, something I was enormously jealous of, and grazed the floor. Tiny, sea holly designs were woven around the collar and hem. Subtle – but it was clear who Ria assisted.

'Let's go flatter the Fish Prince then,' I said, positioning my glamour carefully.

We sleepily wandered down to the Ocean Bar, pushing open the door to see Sal and Prince Anard drinking quietly together. They turned towards us. Sal was as calm as ever while the Fish Prince blinked rapidly, his hands tapping at the table like a seagull mimicking rain. No worms would rise to sate his hunger or calm his nerves here.

'Lady Gina, you remember Prince Anard, of course. Please, come and join us.'

I took a seat, and true to her word, Ria faded into the background. In reach but not included. I realised then how much more she might be able to do compared to me, and a tingle of excitement began to grow in my gut. Like a spring tide, it rose and emerged as what I hoped, was a genuine smile.

'Thank you for honouring your side of the deal,' I said, watching Anard shift in his seat.

'I miss her you know,' he blurted. 'Even though I know she wasn't truly as I saw her, I still miss her company. Do you think she's safe?'

'I am confident of it,' I replied. 'Our crew escorted her as far as the ice, even losing one of their own, to ensure her safety. You may be assured we could have done no more for her.' Sirena would be as safe as she could be, at least until the spring warmth started to melt the ice sheets.

'I am sorry for their loss,' he said.

A pang of pain about Eden's situation seared through me, and I turned towards Ria both to break his gaze and hide my face for a moment. I took a few deep breaths. Somehow, seeing Anard for the first time, knowing that we had gone there for him, made it worse.

Sal stepped into the conversation while I regained my composure.

'I do not wish to implicate you in upcoming events, so you may calm your nerves, Anard. You should know that we aim to use the information we gather for the good of entire regions. The Earth may feel as though she recovers to you, yet she continues to die. We seek to slow that decline. I fear you may have done too much as a species to stop it altogether.'

'You?' Anard asked. It was a rare slip from Sal. He must be more nervous than he appeared.

'We, of course, my Prince, I should not dream of including you.' Sal recovered as quickly as he had slipped, but Anard's brow furrowed. I was not convinced that he had bought the explanation.

'What do you need access to?'

'Lady Rene's collection. If not for Lady Gina, then at least for her assistant, Ria.'

Prince Anard glanced at Ria, then he leant over the table and whispered, 'Do you think they hide more sirens?'

'No, you know from the demands of keeping your own friend safe, that the behaviours needed to ensure that happens would have required such substantial changes in a household that we would have heard of it. No imprisoned women or huge serpents have been mentioned. What we do hope to find are other creatures of great importance,' replied Sal.

Anard sat back. His fingers had stilled, and his blinking stopped at some point in Sal's speech. He sat taller too – calm and poised as a slow smile grew.

'I always felt as though I had a job to do. Not being the first-choice son, the throne was never mine. But I've spent my life searching for a goal. Now, you have given me one. If there are others, other Old Ones like my Sirena trapped in captivity, I will help free them. Will they truly help fix this mess?' He gestured expansively, and I knew he meant far more than the walls of the room we sat in.

'They might,' I said. 'I cannot speak for them, but I hope they would wish to, and truly, I do not know what other chance we have.'

'Lady Gina, I want you to know that I would marry you if it gained us the access needed to curate our own collection. You could request the finest specimens from all of the private collections, then we could return them to wherever they should be. Would that work?' His face was illuminated with excitement.

'I . . .' I wasn't sure how to take the proposal, but he continued, and I had a moment to gather my thoughts as he concluded the offer.

'Of course, I would never love you – you know that? I will love her until my last breath.'

It was audacious. It might even work. But, it might not, and then I'd be tied to him. Anard did not need to know how my plans for him panned out, but I had no intention of becoming his queen.

'That is most kind and ingenious,' I purred. 'But, maybe one day, you will find another who you can love a little, and

I'd hate to deprive you of that happiness. We can make this work without a marriage. I'll have a public falling out with you after it is all over, leaving you free to move forward.'

Freer than he would ever expect. The plan grew in my mind, and the seed planted when he helped his siren to freedom was growing roots. Sal stared at me now, a single eyebrow raised in question. I'd have to explain later.

'Please meet us at the main landing dock in daylight, as public viewing of us together is important.' I continued. I would not be slipping away with Anard on a midnight tide like one of our staff.

Sal and Seren had been teaching me the intricacies of human etiquette all week, and the idea of eating large quantities of rich, chewy humanised meat in one meal, then leaping around at a feast, made my stomach spin like a whirlpool. It would be foul. Yet, it was less pain than The White Hind was in. In the long term, if we could put this prince on the throne, we might have a chance at influencing more than the bedroom thoughts and pleasures of the rich and powerful. Instead of picking the information from them like vultures, we could be the ones gardening it, planting more established seeds and feeding them carefully.

We went over the rest of the details; travel time, two days. Accommodations; a room for myself and Ria. How long he expected us to be ashore, and the return route. We agreed on a meeting point off the coast, and Anard left us, confident in his self-determined new direction. He slipped back aboard his silent boat and disappeared into the darkness.

'Do you think he is genuine?' Sal asked, as we watched him leave.

'You've known him longer than me. If it helps, my senses all shout that we can trust him. I hope they are speaking sense because I plan to replace the current king with a far more sympathetic one.' I grinned into the night. 'It might involve your jellyfish,' I said.

He chuckled, a low rumbling laugh that echoed out over the water as it grew.

'Jellyfish soup,' he said.

'Yes, jellyfish soup.'

29

A CHILD IN NEED

The meal was going about as well as I had anticipated. Drunken humans sprawled across tables around the room – several had even asked which services I was bringing to the party. I bit back answers referring to their death and destruction, instead opting to ignore the drunks and deflect the rest.

'I didn't realise you'd get this much hassle, Lady Gina,' Anard said at one point. 'They're so bloody rude.' He had barely drunk anything, yet the reddening of his cheeks reflected both his anger after the fifth such imposition and the soaring heat in the enclosed space.

'They certainly are,' I replied, holding my glass up for a refill. Unlike most of the guests, I was drinking water, and Ria was careful to keep me topped up, avoiding any other interference in our plans.

Our hosts sat at the top of a long table, but Anard, as a known recluse and who had turned up with me as his guest, hardly merited a table much higher than the middle of the room – at least until he was named the new heir.

I knew why the King had held off that announcement, and I was confident that the buxom assistant he had brought to our last meeting did too.

Our position worked well for me. Not too far away was a door in frequent use by a flow of house staff and giggling couples. A slender woman ran through the door, and a shadow slipped out in her wake. A few minutes later, Ria returned, now attired in house livery.

'What did you do with her?' I whispered.

'She's not dead,' was all the reply I got and likely all I would get. We were ready.

'Do you know where we are going?' I asked Anard. He nodded.

'I've been there before, a long time ago. If you take my arm, I'll escort you out for some air. Can you look faint?'

I sighed, and adjusted my face, slightly changing the tone. His eyes widened.

'Damn, that's one hell of a party trick. Do you actually feel faint?'

I shook my head and swayed slightly. Anard rushed to help me, calling over a nearby member of staff to aid us.

'I think she needs some air. Can you guide us back out for a few minutes?' he asked. I peered up to see Ria wink at me.

'Follow me, Your Highness,' she said, leading us from the hall as I leant heavily on Anard.

'I hate looking weak,' I hissed.

'I'm sorry, but it's the easiest way. We'll do something different next time,' he murmured. Next time. He was still on board at least.

'You can look sick,' I retorted. We followed Ria through the hall and out to a gently sloping hillside.

'Shouldn't there be some guards out here?' I asked. It was noticeably quiet. No voices, no footsteps.

'If I had to guess I'd say Lady Rene uses an automated system. This family used to be very proud of the cell power they had. But, nowhere near the same level of technology is running here compared to my childhood memories. Having fewer guards and talking up their remote systems feels like a thing Lady Rene would do – pretending it was all still working. He scanned around him. 'There, on the wall is a box, and there's no light on it. I don't think their system is working as it should,' Anard said, then muttered towards the hills. 'We can't rule it out, though. We could be being watched from somewhere in the house.'

I understood him well enough and continued leaning on him heavily.

'How will we get into the collection unseen then? It would have been useful to know this before we arrived.'

'I don't know,' he replied.

I clenched and unclenched my fists as I fought building frustration. 'You said that you knew the way?'

'I sort of do. Maybe this was the wrong door.'

I resisted the urge to knock him onto his royal backside and sighed heavily. 'Then I had better recover. Ria will have to go on alone. If they *are* watching, then you and I popping in and out of doors like moray eels on the hunt will attract unwanted attention.'

'Sit down,' he said, gesturing Ria over.

We sat with our backs to the house while he sketched the outline of the grounds in the mud at our feet.

'We're here. That wall there must be the perimeter. Ria, you'll need to get inside. I think they had paddocks out beyond the collection from childhood memory. Try to scout out as much as you can. Will you be okay without us?'

'I've been more than okay without you for my whole life,' she said, staring at the dirt sketch.

'The deer are likely to be well beyond the actual collection, near the woods,' he added.

'I'll be back at the dock before sunrise,' Ria replied, studying the mud-map.

'We need to leave before then!'

'Then send the small boat back for me. Lady Gina, what exactly am I after? A white or grey one? One that could be dyed grey, maybe?'

'No.' Anard shook his head. 'If this family have something special, it will be pristine. It will be well fed.'

'Not this one,' I said. 'It will be sickly, pale and unwell. It reflects the land. It may be hiding its own identity under muck. It should feel ...' I tried to recall how The Hind had felt. I remembered the wash of emotions, the calmness as she led me to safety. But overwhelmingly, the weight of the knowledge which she had shared. 'It should feel serene, almost calm, yet carrying a weight.'

'I know that feeling,' Ria muttered. 'If it's there, I'll find it. I have a feeling we may share a lot in common.'

I wasn't sure I could describe her as serene, but she was certainly capable of extreme calm.

Ria rose, rubbing out the sketch with her foot. We shuffled over it as we both rose. I stumbled again and smoothed out as much of the rest as I could.

Anard and I returned to the hall. This time, to try and gain an official audience with the seals in the collection from their proud owners. I needed to know. We entered the hall as the tables were being cleared, and a group of musicians took their places. Huge boxes to either side of them hummed with a noise likely inaudible to humans. I wanted to ask what they were, but as no one else was paying the slightest bit of attention to them, I assumed that I would be expected to ignore them too. The hum changed in pitch as the musicians picked up a range of instruments, some of which were familiar from *Barge*. Anard glanced over at them and sighed.

'Gina, we need to speak to them soon, else we'll never be heard.'

'If this is their highlight, surely they won't leave to show us around?' I saw his shoulders fall as he realised the same thing.

'We're going to have to stay a bit longer. I hope you can dance.'

'I can dance, well sort of.' I grimaced, recalling how hard it was on land. Seren's attempts to teach me these last few days had not been particularly successful, but I was ready to put them into motion. If only that hum would go away.

Then it did, and noise poured through the boxes. Louder than whale song in a cave, it rattled my brain. It was hard to think clearly in this din, let alone concentrate. The part of my mind that remained intent on maintaining the glamour, a part as fixed on its job as those sections that regulated my breathing, was struggling. I took a deep breath, feeling the beat of the music vibrate through every fibre of my body. The walls shook, the floor thudded, and the sensation was all-encompassing.

I opened my eyes to find Anard peering at me, worry creasing his forehead.

'Are you okay?' he asked. 'You looked a little odd for a moment, sort of blurry.'

'I'll be fine, but I'd like to try and get to the collection. I can't cope with this volume all night. It's impossible to think.' My glamour had almost failed. My heart raced, and I tried to remain calm, resisting the urge to flee. I focused intently on maintaining it as he spoke and trying to ignore the music.

He laughed. 'This is nothing compared to my father's parties.'

I felt a shudder run the length of my spine at the thought,

or was that the music? I was losing control of my faculties. I leant against a wall, instantly recoiling as the pounding beat passed through it. Our hosts remained seated, watching swaying bodies in the cleared space, twisting and turning around each other like shoals of brightly coloured fish. Occasionally, one would detach from their group and join another. Little conversation was happening, and they appeared entranced by the music. Maybe humans did make a kind of magic, a way to control each other. The rhythm accelerated, and the volume rose. The dancers continued to undulate in time. It was fascinating, and I could have watched for hours had the music not hurt so badly.

Anard tapped me on the shoulder. 'I don't think they will dance,' he said. Lady Rene has not danced since her husband's death and her son appears to be deep in his cups. 'Come on, We can try.'

He strode toward them, every inch a prince, while I followed. Mentally, I worked through Seren's checklist of poise. I added a little sway as we crossed the room. The shoals parted, none caring that we swam our own route. They simply closed after our passage.

'Lady Rene, may I introduce Lady Gina.' Anard gestured at me, and I offered her a polite inclination of my head.

Lady Rene had deep olive skin, wrinkled from years in the sun. This was not a woman who sat idly indoors like many of those who visited *Barge*. She was weathered and sharp. Grey-streaked hair coiled around her head like a silver-speckled crown. There was kindness in her eyes, and I felt a pang of guilt that we might be about to sabotage the tranquility of her home. She appraised me and gifted me a smile. It didn't quite reach her eyes, but the one she bestowed on Anard did.

'I've been regaling Lady Gina with tales of your wonderful collection.' Anard continued. He sighed, and his eyes glazed as the smile dropped from his face. He stared to the wall behind them for a moment, absent and leaving us all hanging on his next words. 'I have such fond memories of that visit when we were children, back when my brother and I . . .' he trailed off again and our hostess looked concerned as he hid his face in his hands.

'I am sorry,' Anard said. 'It's just too soon.'

Lady Rene stood and leant across the table to offer him a pristine, purple square of fabric, which he dabbed on his eyes.

If I hadn't been the one who took the order and arranged his brother's death, I'd have been fooled. I was secretly impressed. This prince could act. How much had he been playing us?

'It *is* very loud in here,' Lady Rene replied. 'My son likes to entertain at volume. Apparently, it's the fashion at the moment to be so loud that you cannot hear yourself think. I can see how it might be liberating for those of irrational thought, but for those of us with a little brain, it's rather too much. Lady Gina, do you have music like this where you have been living?'

I shook my head. It hurt, so I stopped.

'Shall we take a stroll outside?' She looked at Anard, who now stood taller, but was occasionally sniffing.

'Thank you, I'd like that,' I said and leant forward to whisper, 'We can't have everyone seeing the heir in tears now, can we?'

I hoped she would take the bait – a conspiratorial look, a friendship offered, a secret dangled. The Prince was still mourning. The Prince was the heir. She could ingratiate herself. She did.

'Shall we visit the collection, for old time's sake?' she asked him.

'I'd like that very much,' he replied.

Which was how we found ourselves surrounded by caged creatures, listening to a lecture on the positives of keeping them in captivity.

'Once, hundreds of years ago, these collections were called zoos,' she said. 'They were special places for protecting the rarest of animals from the ravages of the heat and the rising water. They protected them – and they bred them – aiming for reintroduction to the wild once the perils had faded. There are old texts showing how carefully they mated their specimens for the best, healthiest offspring. It was all a little primitive. Yet, because of that work, we are lucky to have the species range that we can see today.' She gestured around, her motion encompassing a huge array of creatures.

'What are you protecting them from this time?' I asked. It was a genuine question, but her eyes narrowed, just for a moment.

'The barren, the dry, the floods. Some of them, we saved from regions of the Everstorm before they were swept away.'

'Which exhibits are those?' I asked.

'Oh, they are not here anymore. Our hounds went to another collection, as they also had one. Maybe, one day, the storm belt will calm, and it will be safe to return them home.'

She truly believed she was doing the world a favour. Unlike Icidro, who collected purely for prestige, she genuinely believed she was helping. I could smell it on her. The misguided idea that human protection was the best form of preservation, instead of humans themselves leaving the wild alone. It was a misconception that, as a species, they seemed eternally blind to.

I looked around to distract myself and settle my voice before I spoke again. 'What oceanic creatures do you have?'

'Hrmph,' she replied. 'I suppose you *would* like those, being from a boat. We have the ocean tanks down this end.'

We followed her past mournful animals with nothing to stimulate them; neither grass nor plants grew beneath their feet. I doubted these *zoos* had breeding success with a strategy like this. Lady Rene was missing some important parts of her background reading.

We passed tanks of fish, lamplight glinting from their scales. We strolled past prowling wild cats, Lady Rene ignoring them as though they were of no consequence. To my horror, there was also a row of caged birds.

Eventually, we came to a huge enclosure. Swimming in tiny circles in the central pool was a faded porpoise, its ragged fin and sides scarred from encounters with the fake rocks in its watery prison. Hauled out on the rocks around it were seals. I reached my hand to the glass, staring at the pack. There were about fifteen of them, and the stench of that many enclosed pinnipeds is never a pleasant sensation, even for one as closely related to them as I.

'Do you still have the amphibians? I loved those.' Anard was turning the full force of his charm on Lady Rene now.

He looked over her shoulder at me, past the swept-up hair and the overly elaborate frills on her dress.

I mouthed, 'give me time,' and hoped he understood. He nodded and turned back to her. 'I seem to remember that you had a wonderful collection of frogs.'

Her voice sang with happiness, he had clearly found her passion, and she warmed to the subject quickly. 'Yes, we have some from before the warming. Ours are the only specimens I know of. Would you like to see them? We have had great success in breeding them. It's the family speciality.'

I wanted to see the frogs too, if they were successfully breeding, they could be species not seen in the wild for centuries. Sadly, now wouldn't be the time to release them.

Their slim chance of survival was probably higher here, where the risk of the dry, barren seasons had less effect.

Something kept pulling me back to the seals. Someone in there did not feel like a true seal. 'May I stay here?' I asked. 'I love porpoises.'

She smiled beatifically on me, the chance to get the Prince alone for a few moments, an opportunity she was willing to leave me alone with a porpoise for.

'Please do. We will only be a few minutes, unless Prince Anard wishes to see more.'

'I'll be back soon,' he reassured me.

'Let's get moving. It's a bit of a walk to the frog house.'

They strode off, Lady Rene's slim legs striding, in competition with his. Boots clicked against the path as they receded.

Confident that they were finally out of hearing, I turned back to the glass and called in Ocean, 'Who's there? Show yourself so I may know who needs my help.'

A tiny head poked out of an artificial cave at the back of the enclosure.

I gasped. He was a child. His eyes were bright as he stared at me and my heart shattered into a thousand pieces. He flippered forward, inching out of his shelter. Deep brown eyes filled with brimming tears looked up at me. His spotted fur lacked lustre, and I could see bones protruding. He could only be a few summers old. Sharp pain grew in my jaw as I gritted my teeth to resist shrieking in frustration.

I wanted to break through there, tuck him under my arm and take him to safety. 'I promise on the skins of our ancestors I'll get you out of here,' I said.

'Today? I miss my family,' he squeaked back.

'Not today, but soon. How did they catch you?'

His head dropped. 'In a net. Ma told me not to go out near the boats, but I was too curious, and now I'm trapped.'

'I have an important question. You need to be honest with me, little one. Have you ever taken your skin off?'

'No, I'm not old enough to walk on land.'

That was going to make this harder. Explaining how to do it was a mother's job, a rite of passage. Teaching him how to go belegged was taking a role and a moment from his family I could never give back. But I would give *him* back. I was sure we'd be forgiven for it.

'Eat as well as you can,' I said. 'You will need your strength. I must go. I need to look more interested in something else when they return.'

'You hide amongst them?' he asked, his eyes widening. 'I've heard of a selkie who does that. Ma says he'll never come home, not now he has everything and has been blinded to the treasures of the real, wild world.'

He had to be talking about Sal. All the pretence, all the fake relations and here was a youngster from his own pack. I knew at that moment we would move ocean currents to get this boy out.

'We'll be back for you,' I said, then as an afterthought, 'Is anyone else here who shouldn't be?'

'Every single creature,' he barked.

'I will rescue you.' I placed both my hands out, in a selkie promise and he mirrored me from the far side of the pool.

Then, I walked away, my feet growing heavier with each step. Leaving that child was one of the hardest things I have ever done. Killing a stupid human was easy. They were just like prey – most of them. I couldn't believe he had managed to stay hidden, but we didn't have long, judging by the condition he was in.

I was watching a pair of brilliantly coloured birds ruffle each other's feathers when Anard reclaimed me. 'Were the frogs as good as you remembered?' I asked, and Anard's face lit up.

'Yes, all manner of amphibians, they are quite the treasure. Lady Rene does an amazing job at preserving them.'

She glowed at the compliment. 'Do you like my birds, Lady Gina?'

'They're beautiful,' I replied. I wanted to scream about their cramped conditions, about how they could barely extend their wings. But, we needed to be in her positive graces. We needed to be so far above suspicion that we weren't in the frame when I returned. I hoped that whatever observational things they used, we would be able to get past them, that Anard was right about the failing cell.

We returned slowly to the main hall, where the party was in full swing. We thanked Lady Rene for her time and the tour, then settled back into our seats for a while. The volume was still excessive, and I focused on remaining glamoured by fixing a smile on my face and watching the dancers.

Eventually, the numbers began to dwindle, and we would no longer insult our hostess by departing. We took our leave, thanking her for a pleasant evening, and wandered out to the dock.

Back on the small boat, I searched for unwanted guests, evicting a small gull from the wheelhouse and a crab from our fender before we left the jetty to return to Anard's boat. It pulled away slowly, and he growled at it in frustration. As we ploughed the waves, I realised the cause of our weight and drag.

'Stop here,' I called as I hung over the side of the boat, looking below the water. Anard cut the engine. Ria almost capsized us as she clambered aboard.

'How did she hide like that?'

'I'm right here, Your Highness,' Ria huffed. 'I held the mooring line and swam out to the side of you. You just didn't spot me.'

'I didn't see you at all,' he said. 'How did you breathe?'

Now was not the time to tell him that Ria was what she was and that breathing was pretty overrated for a creature that sucked spirits and normally sat on the bottom of a lake. I was sure that Ria was glamourising her own appearance, much as I covered my teeth. Maybe she had gills.

'I got lucky, and I'm really good at diving,' she said. I bit my lip and left it at that.

The return trip was interminably long, with the news I wanted to share with her – and Sal.

We finally boarded Anard's ship, and confident that no one would overhear us, we retreated to our cabin.

'So?' I asked. 'What did you find?'

'Nothing,' she said. 'Not a trapped spirit in the entire herd. No off-colour deer or stags. All were healthy and as calm as you'd expect, given a stranger in their midst.' She stripped her wet clothes off, dumping them in a bag. I winced at the thought of Seren's response to that, but stayed quiet while Ria continued.

'I didn't see anything in the cages on the herd side either. There were some pretty unhappy creatures trapped in them. I wish we could free the lot.'

'One day – when the right person is sat on the throne, we will.' I sighed.

Ria raised an eyebrow and said nothing.

'We have to go back,' I said. Sal couldn't buy the freedom of another selkie. A sudden interest in one scrawny, unwell specimen would attract way too much attention.

'Why?'

'There's a selkie child in there. He is dying of malnutrition and I don't think he has long left.'

Ria pursed her lips. 'This is going to have to be a hit and grab,' she muttered.

I knew it too, but the question was, could we extract the child, with no clue left of our visit or was this going to be a big job?

I clambered into bed, grateful for the quiet. My ears still rang from the loud music, and my thoughts span and tumbled like a jellyfish in a tide rip.

'Don't worry. We'll get him out,' Ria whispered from her side of the room before I fell into a troubled sleep.

HIDE AND FOUND

My dreams were haunted by the tiny gaunt form of the stolen child.

When I told him, Sal's eyes had lashed with barely controlled fire, and his hands gripped his glass so tightly that I thought he would crush it into shards. 'We go ashore alone,' he'd said. 'Just you and I, wearing full glamours to mimic our way through. I don't care how bloody long it takes us. We are doing this.' He called for Seren straight away. She stepped back in surprise at the passion in his words; this was a Sal that neither of us had seen before.

'I want two skin-tight suits made up. Needle pouches in both.'

'For Ria and Lady Gina? That's going to cause some talk.'

'No, for myself and Gina. Seren, this has to stay secret. Utterly discrete – make them yourself. A young boy, a child, is being held captive. I think he may be a relative of mine.'

She chuckled. 'Another?'

Sal's face darkened. The humour fell immediately from her expression. 'Sal, how long do I have?'

'I need them as soon as possible. He doesn't have long.'

Once she had left, he began to pace. 'We'll take Ria. She can drive the boat, hold it off-shore and hide in the water if necessary. You need to rest and build up as much magic reserve as you can before we leave. Go to your rooms and drop the glamour, have Ria collect your food. Save every possible drop of energy you can. As soon as Seren is ready, we go.'

He studied the map we had tried to sketch between us, his finger tracing potential routes, only to return time and again to the dock.

'I wish I knew this building better,' he mumbled. 'How high is the wall around the collection?'

'Behind the seals, about three times your height.'

'Do you think it was an external one?'

'I'm sorry, Sal, I couldn't tell.'

'What about the paddocks? Did they join in to the collection?'

'I don't know. Ria might have more to add there, as she worked through them. The last time we did a blind entry, Eden sent Cor to scout.'

'How fast can you get them back?' Sal asked, his eyes widening.

I could feel his hope, thick and expectant it laced the room. But I had no idea if there was a way for Eden to communicate with us. I needed to speak to Ria before we dragged *Black Hind* from Safe Harbour into more trouble.

'Go, and rest.' Sal said, 'I'll think on this more and come to see you later.'

I returned to my rooms. I knew Sal would want the child freed, but the power of his determination, the passion that had been released by discovery of this boy, had been more intense than I had anticipated. I would not let them down in this, either of them.

I explained to Ria how we had used Cor previously and asked her about the chances of Zora having had success communicating.

'They felt separate,' was all she could tell me. 'I don't know if Eden was a true passenger or if they have any influence over Cor.'

We'd have to call them back. It was the only way to know. Sal was too busy, his mind engaged with plans he couldn't flesh out, so I ignored his instructions to rest and sought out Seren.

She was already sewing, black fabric flew through her machine faster than I thought possible.

Seren was a rare human. She ran the entire ship with efficiency and an eye for detail. She hosted and co-ordinated everything. Nothing that happened on board was beneath her attention. In short, she was almost so incredible that it seemed barely possible that she was human. Maybe she wasn't. But for now, she was exactly who and what Sal needed. She stopped the fabric at a seam edge and spun her chair around, brandishing the black item at me.

'Perfect timing. Put this on.'

I struggled my legs into the skin-tight fabric. It slipped over me almost as snugly as my fur used to, and for a moment, I thought that I would transform. The elation fell away as soon as it arrived. The reality of my lost skin hitting me, as ever, when I least expected it.

She pulled, and tugged at seams, scribbling down notes on a scrap of paper.

'Turn around please, Gina.'

I turned as she checked other details and drew new lines on the fabric with coloured chalk.

'You can remove that now,' she instructed.

As I struggled out of it I asked my favour. 'Can you arrange a boat to pick up the crew of the *Hind*? They are in Safe Harbour.

'Fast and discrete. I'll get one sent out today. The crew will be here soon. Are you wanting them all?'

I hesitated for a moment. 'Just Zora and Cor.'

'Cor? I don't think I know them.' She frowned.

'He's Eden's bird. I'm hoping we can find a way to use his eyes to help with the rescue.'

'That poor Eden. They were light and joy wherever they went.' She sighed deeply. 'Clever too.'

'That's what I'm counting on,' I replied.

She nodded. 'Maybe they trained that bird well enough that you can still use it. I've never seen Sal so fired up.' She patted me on the shoulder. 'I don't know how you plan to do this – but try not to let him empty every needle into the population of that house. It's too soon after you visited for obvious raids.'

She was right, but then Seren was always right. The selkie child didn't have the luxury of time. He was well-hidden and sickly. If we were lucky, they wouldn't even notice he was missing – or they would think the other seals or the porpoise ate him.

Seren had the suits made within days, and we were ready to leave. Sal was desperate to start the rescue, but I extracted the promise of one more day from him, hoping that Zora and Cor would come to our aid.

A small boat slipped into one of the docks with Zora at the helm. She waved, and Cor flapped his wings for balance as the boat bumped gently into position.

I tied the bowline off, and she leapt out with more lightness than I had seen in a while then thew her arms around me, squeezing tightly. Zora smelt of the sea. Her hair was freshly braided, and her eyes shone as she reached down and stroked the back of Cor's neck.

'Eden can hear us,' she said. 'They have limited control. As Rialta suggested, they are a passenger.'

'How do you know?'

She twisted her mouth into a grimace. 'It wasn't easy,' she replied. I think Eden can suggest actions and receive what Cor tells them. Like when they were separate – Eden can only see things as Cor sees or understands them.'

'So you talked to Cor, and Eden engineered a reply?' I asked, slightly confused.

'Yes, I suppose. I asked questions and gave yes or no options, with fish as a yes and squid as a no. Eden suggested which thing Cor wanted to eat in response.'

I had really hoped we would be able to use Cor's eyes, but it wasn't sounding very easy.

I crouched in front of Cor. 'Eden, if you can hear me, can you get Cor to peck at my foot?'

A sharp beak drilled into my foot moments later. It was the happiest I had ever been to be pecked. It hurt. I suppose deserved it though, for not telling Zora it wasn't a horrific accident. For keeping the secret safe – to preserve her life and that of Theo. Urchin's spines, but I wanted to tell her and Eden. The black bird was glossy and sleek again. A gloriously dressed, feathered host for Eden, at least for now. I watched Cor waddle across the decking and was filled with the kind of sorrow that can drown you. Was it worse to be trapped like that than it would have been to simply die? A human soul inside a bird. Free to fly maybe, but the frustrations, the limitations! And, sharing your thoughts. I reached for Cor, then withdrew my hand. I would not have stroked Eden, so I would not stroke Cor. I would treat the bird's body with the respect I would have given to Eden's human form.

'Eden, there is a child, a young selkie held captive in a large collection not far from here. We don't think they know what they have caught. At least we hope they don't. He's sick and close to death. Sal and I want to break in and free him.'

Zora's brow creased, and she crossed her arms.

'How will you do that?' she questioned.

'Full glamour,' I answered and the frown deepened.

'You don't use a full very often. It will exhaust you to search the place, and keep changing. Sal might be able to do it. He's been doing this for years. But you? What kind of reserves would you need to carry that out? Gods, Georgie, don't be stupid. You'll be too exhausted to get him out.'

I dropped my head and looked at my feet for a moment, trying to gather the courage to ask what I needed to.

'We hope that maybe there's another way. That we might not have to remain glamoured the whole time. Zora,' I rushed on, 'I don't even know when Sal used a full glamour for anything other than his clothes when he can't be bothered to get dressed.'

That raised a chuckle, but it meant I had to get to the point. 'I was hoping that maybe Eden could persuade Cor to scout for us – like he did before. That maybe there was another way in.'

'I'd rather not lose any more crew,' she said. 'Eden, get Cor to peck Georgie's foot again if you think you could do it.'

It took a long time for a response, and I was on the verge of accepting that it would not be feasible when a searing pain ran through my foot as Cor pecked at it repeatedly.

'There's not a lot of accuracy in this method, is there?' I muttered, trying to keep my feet away from a now persistent cormorant.

'I knew you could dance.' Zora's shoulders shook as she tried to hold back laughter.

'We need to leave soon,' I said. 'In the next two days. The pup won't last much longer. Can you work out a way of communicating the findings?'

'We can. Give us a few hours, and I'll work something out.'

'The back deck is all yours,' I said.

'We won't let that child down, Georgie. This is what we signed up for. Whatever our form – that's still the goal.' Zora squeezed my shoulder. Cor took off over the water, and Zora dived gracefully into the sea and swam towards the back deck.

When I dropped by to see them later that afternoon, Zora was sat cross-legged, a picture of *Barge* very roughly sketched out in front of her.

'How accurate is it?' she asked. 'It feels almost there, but I know there are details missing. Eden hadn't really been on board the top deck much – so this is mostly Cor's eye view.'

I studied it carefully, some of the buildings were the wrong size, and an entire upper deck was missing, but it would be good enough. 'I think this would work,' I said. 'How did you do it?'

She held up a pencil. It was attached to a stick, and she asked Cor to draw a line. Cor did a rough drag of the pencil.

'Now, I want you to think of *Black Hind*. Mark the front of the boat,' she instructed.

Cor made a mark.

'Mark the back.'

Cor made another.

'Now, the position of the main mast.'

Cor made a third mark.

'You see, a bird's eye view, we can do,' she said. 'But, if we try for anything more detailed, Eden can't direct the motion.'

I studied the map of the barge. 'In some places, it almost seems as though Eden can see it. There is much more detail over here, than here.' The difference between areas of the deck on the drawings were stark.

Zora nodded. 'I agree, it certainly feels that way – but Eden isn't seeing directly. Only the perception of what Cor sees or pictures. Then Eden directs Cor where to peck until we have a full set of dimensions. There's a lot of guesswork. I'm not sure it will be accurate enough to stake a life on.' She hung her head, and Cor snuggled up against her. They had managed far more than I had dreamed possible.

'That's my decision to make,' I replied. 'What you have given us is more than we had. Sal and I would have gone with or without it. Cor and Eden will improve our chances of survival ten-fold with this.'

Zora sent Cor-Eden out once more, and I stayed long enough to see them add the missing deck. We would get a very rudimentary outline of the house and collection. It had to be enough.

31

TONIGHT'S THE NIGHT

Zora took a small boat a few beaches away from Lady Rene's home, and Eden drove Cor to fly for hours until exhaustion overcame the bird and he was reluctant to co-operate further, refusing to fly. They returned with a rough map, and as thanks, we fed him the best fish Seren could procure from the Ocean Bar. Their incredible effort gave us more detail than we had dared hope for.

Sal and I had a route and a plan.

Our boat cruised close to the beach, the gentle waves of our passage lapping the sand no louder than the wind-driven wavelets already caressing the shore. Sal and I slipped out and swam underwater towards the dock. Shadowy forms rose around us; pillars and planks, boats bobbing gently on their moorings. We carefully scrambled ashore onto dark rocks, our black suits hiding us under the blanket of night.

We sidled along the outer wall. Eden had marked quite a few people in this area in daylight, but it was hard to know which were guard placements. We suspected very few, with what we knew about Lady Rene's desperate desire to appear affluent. More guards would imply their expensive security system wasn't working. I scanned the walls for the boxes Anard had shown me on the previous visit. Shadowy outlines indicated their presence, but only one had a light on. I pointed it out to Sal as we worked our way around to the entrance.

Thanks to Eden and Cor, we knew that the collection did not have an external wall on the shoreward side. The seal enclosure backed onto an open courtyard inside the main compound. If we could get through the gates and into it, we could climb over that wall instead of working our way through the house or navigating the entire perimeter. We'd still have to leave the long way, as no small child could scale a vertical wall – but this plan cut our time inside the grounds drastically.

We padded silently across the rocks, wet footsteps would dry, but sandy footprints were harder to hide in the dark. Clinging to the side of the building, we closed in on the main entrance.

Last time I had been here, it had been gaily decked out with flowers and berries. No trace of their scent drifted to me now. Instead, voices floated on the wind, two men in the dark guarding a gateway. It reminded me of the blood bath we had left after rescuing Sirena.

Lady Rene collected many species for the wrong reasons, but she was also keeping a small group of amphibians from extinction. Her work in that area gained her a measure of compassion I did not have to spare on Anard's brother. We would endeavour to disturb her home as little as possible.

Once we found The White Hind, and some semblance of normality could resume; when the land began to heal, then there would be a place for those precious frogs to return to.

At least I hoped there would be.

Ever since arriving on *Barge*, I'd been developing my magical stamina. Compared to my first attempt, back on first arrival in Orange, I could hold a full glamour far longer. Today would be different; mimicking someone recognisable would be challenging, draining, and I would not be able to maintain it for long if I came under attack or duress.

Sal and I had talked the plan through in depth. I'd copy their clothes, and their looks searching for eye-catching features to focus on. It would have to be enough.

'Stay here,' Sal hissed as he slid around the corner. Step one, take one guard out, replace them, then guide the other around to me.

I'd tried to argue that blow darts would be a better approach, but he was stubborn, and his impassioned argument for the necessity of speed won me over.

I counted to five hundred, then followed. Wet footsteps gleamed in the moonlight. If Zora were here, she could have fixed it, but she had another role tonight, and Sal had been gone longer than planned. I needed to move in.

Two guards sat in front of the heavy, wooden gateway under a dim light. Lady Rene might rely on surveillance and rumours by daylight, but by night, real eyes and ears were apparently her preference.

The closest man looked up as I neared, staring into the darkness.

His head tilted from side to side, like an owl trying to pick out a disturbance.

'I think something *is* there,' he said. 'You want me to go this time? Or shall we go together?' He stood and waited on his still-seated companion. When the other guard remained in place, he stomped off. 'I dunno what you saw, but you've not said a word since you got back,' He muttered as he neared me. I crouched behind a rock and watched him wander past, his hand resting on a weapon.

I followed quietly. Once he rounded the corner, I took him down with a dart to the back of his neck, catching him carefully before he hit himself on the rocks. Then, I gave him a second dose of a relaxant, dragged him into an alcove not far from the gate, and arranged him gently so he would awake safely in a few hours.

Starting with the long and pointed nose, I carefully constructed a glamour. His skin tone was golden tan, and he was missing a single front tooth. I noticed the significant mole on his cheek and decided to focus on the detail of that. It was likely that it drew the eye, much as it had my own. I hoped that if I got the mole close enough, then other features would be less important. When I had added the hair – jet black and curly, I didn't have to change too much there – I dressed myself as Sal had, in clothes of glamour over the black skinsuit, and returned to the gateway.

The seated guard glanced at me. 'Fancy shellfish for tea?' he asked in a low, husky voice.

'Only if they are raw,' I replied.

Sal laughed quietly. He pulled a key from somewhere under his glamour, and we opened the door.

Once through, we locked it, and slid the key back under for the guards to find once they awoke. We were now trapped inside the very house we were trying to break the child out of. Somewhere on our left was a route to the courtyard. We hurried along the darkened passage, testing each door until, eventually, we found one that opened. I peered around, listening for footsteps. In a home this size, I'd expect people to be up overnight. A quiet hall meant nothing of use to the night staff. Hopefully, it led to our garden.

We traded glances and took a chance on it. Swift and silent, we ran. Fresh air and the heady scent of jasmine drifted to us.

We grew it on *Barge* to help mask the scent of sex. I hoped it wasn't serving a similar purpose here, or any residents holding a night-time tryst were in for a rude surprise.

The moon had slipped behind drifting clouds when we emerged into the courtyard, their coverage dimming what little starlight speckled the sky. Conditions for climbing a tall wall unseen were good, as long as it remained quiet.

A light flickered on in an upstairs window. I pressed myself against the building. Maintaining the glamour took a lot of my reserves – we could not afford to wait long.

A silhouette filled the window, joined by another. Their shadows merged, and moments later, they began removing their clothes.

I counted on the fact that they were sufficiently distracted and began edging slowly around the garden. Thorns scratched my legs and caught on my suit.

Under the suit, I wore a rope coiled around my waist. I unzipped a small slit to pull it out, the sensation of the spider-silk weave sliding across my skin brought back memories of my time tethered on the island. So many months ago now. Had my family given up hope of ever seeing me again?

I pushed the treacherous thoughts away and wove through the bushes further. Sal was ahead of me, his back pressed to the wall as he stared at the lit room.

'We need them to leave the window first,' he whispered.

But the couple didn't. Naked flesh pushed up against the glass, silhouettes and laughter gave way to grunts of exertion. Finally, their frenzied passion reached its climax, and their shadows slid from view. My glamour was wavering as my nerves did. I could feel my face shifting slightly. *Focus.*

'Now!' Sal said, grabbing the rope from my hands. He tied

the hook he had carried to the end and launched it at the top of the wall. The clattering as it grabbed hold rang through the night.

I glanced at the window. Someone stood there.

'We've been heard,' I whispered.

'I know. Stay still.'

The silhouette vanished.

'Climb!' Sal urged and boosted me up the wall. I scrambled as fast as I could, shuffling along the top so that Sal could follow. I crouched low, searching for the roof we hoped was below. Eden had identified one, but we had no way of knowing how tall it was. I couldn't turn, I dared not stop, and as the roof came into sight, I eyed it up for a leap. My life had come full circle, running along a wall and roof at night with Sal.

I heard an angry shout from the garden and a gunshot.

I leapt, hoping this was the right roof. Only once I landed did I dare look back up. Sal crouched low, now trailing the rope down this side of the wall. He followed me onto the roof as a second shot rang out. More raised voices called as the house woke in response.

It was too late for tact now. Sal bellowed in Ocean, and a small voice shouted back from below us. Eden's map had been right. My heart raced with fear or excitement, maybe both. All I cared about at that moment was that we were in time – he was still alive.

'Hold this end. I'm going for him,' Sal said, thrusting the rope into my hand and dropping into the enclosure.

I studied our surroundings for the best route out. The small building I sat on straddled the glass enclosure wall. Probably the way Lady Rene's staff entered the seal pen. If we could get him onto this roof and down, we could get the child out without giving away what we had come for before we, ourselves, were collected.

Below me, they argued, Sal clearly not managing to persuade the child to remove his skin.

'Fine, I'll carry you like that!' I heard. 'We don't have time to argue. Do you want to go home or not?'

'Yes!' The child's voice wavered. I could hear the tears in it from here. I wanted to comfort him, to go in there and calm the situation. But Sal was right. We didn't have the time.

Light spilt into the far side of the collection, beams sweeping in broad arcs as they searched for us.

'Hurry up!' I hissed, 'they're coming.'

'There's one of those light things in that room,' the boy chirped. I heard a splintering of wood as Sal smashed a door, then he tugged on the rope. I hooked it over the roof edge and steadied it as they climbed, Sal bearing the small seal pup.

'Go!' he said, flinging the rope back down the other side of the enclosure.

I climbed only as far as I needed before dropping to the ground, the light tucked into my suit. Sal followed moments later and pulled the rope down after us.

He missed catching the hook, and it clattered to the floor.

Lights flicked in our direction.

'We need to run,' he said.

'It's too late,' I replied. 'We need to blend in instead.'

We tried to wind our way between oncoming lights that swept from side to side along each pathway, working our way between searching individuals. Finally, we were too close to the search party to hide much longer.

'Ready?' I asked, steadying my glamour.

'As I can be,' replied Sal. He was badly out of breath and now trying to hide the child inside his glamour, he would be unable to contribute much more. I turned the light on and started to sweep the area ahead of us, moving in a slightly different pattern to the others with Sal keeping close behind.

'Seen anything?' someone yelled at us.

I shone the light in their face, hoping to night-blind them. Anything to aid Sal at this point.

'Not yet,' Sal called back.

'Keep looking. Hold on, why haven't you both got a light?' The speaker asked, hesitating for a moment.

'Dropped mine, thought it better to have two sets of eyes and keep looking than to go back.'

'Remember, you're looking for two people,' the searcher said, staring at us again. I was beginning to think he was so tired, that he'd leave us to search. That his sleep – or drink-addled brain would accept the explanation, but something seemed to catch at him.

'Hey, aren't you supposed to be on the front gate tonight?'

I flashed the light in his eyes.

'Run,' Sal whispered in Ocean.

We ran past the other enclosures and wove between flower beds. Sal panted heavily, but he kept up. The thudding foot-steps in pusuit, spurring us ever onwards.

'Any face but yours,' he hissed as we turned a corner. I dropped the glamour with a sigh of relief. Our black suits would help us hide.

'I'm scared,' the small voice cried.

'We are almost out. Just hold on a little longer,' Sal panted.

We scrambled over a high gate and into open grassland. The wall still rose alongside us. If we could make it to the woods, we could get out. Ria had done it before. It was possible.

I was exhausted, each step taking more and more effort. My legs shook, and my muscles screamed at me to slow down, but I drove onwards. Sal's gasping breaths echoed in my ears, and the whimpers of the child pushed me towards the tree line.

Light flooded us. We had been found. The trees were not far now, but the pounding of a runner grew louder. A herd of deer startled ahead, running our way, then swerving at the last minute when they saw us.

'Something in the trees,' I called back.

'Or someone,' Sal replied.

I was caught . . . should we run on? I slowed for a moment as Sal levelled with me. He paused for a second, panting heavily.

'Keep running!' a voice rang out from ahead of us. Ria shot past me, heading directly for our pursuer.

I glanced back to see the runner stop in their tracks, crumpling to the floor at Ria's feet. She picked up the torch and began to sprint, but slightly away from us, heading to a different section of the woods.

'She's leading them away, come on!' I urged, trying not to think about the crumpled body that had dropped lifeless at her touch.

Zora met us in the trees. We stumbled into their welcoming branches as the clouds parted and moonlight bathed the field. Light glinted off the barrel of Zora's gun as she gestured for us to continue past. Ria's fleeing form slipped into the woods a few hundred trees away from us.

Other pursuing lights at the far side of the field slowed. We had to hope that we had made it difficult enough that they would drop the chase. After all, aside from a broken door and a dying seal-pup, nothing was missing from the collection. Not that they would know that yet.

We wound through the woods in silence, reaching the far side without any further noise of pursuit. The boundary inlet that Ria had warned us about stretched ahead. The wall dived into it on either side, towers stretching towards the stars mid-way across each section of wall illuminated the water. Anyone on a boat would be exposed and easy to spot. But we weren't anyone.

Sal untied the pup and placed him gently next to the water.

'It's a long swim, do you think you can make it?' he asked gently.

The boy looked out. His little voice quivered as he replied, 'If you are with me I can do it.'

'We'll both be with you,' I said as I crouched down and embraced him. 'I told you we would be back for you. Zora, are you ready?'

She grinned. 'I know we're running for our lives, but I have always enjoyed this trick. Stay close to me. The bottom will be slippery, and I can't make it too big, or we won't get past the midpoint before I run out of strength.'

'I'll swim with the boy,' Ria said as she emerged from the trees.

Sal crouched next to the pup. 'He isn't The Boy,' he muttered defensively. 'His name is Gar.'

Ria shrugged. 'Gar, swim with me. If you need a rest, we'll join Zora and Georgie.'

They dived into the water, turning to bob at the surface as we all watched Zora.

She stretched her arms forward, creating a path into the water. We walked in, and the waters flowed around, to rejoin behind us. It was, as she had warned, a small space. We followed Zora across the exposed inlet bed until the water was chest height on either side. A few steps later, we walked inside a bubble of air as she pushed the water away on all sides.

We moved slowly, dark waters swirled above us, and the even darker shadows of Gar and Ria passed close to us frequently. I lost track of time. Our slow pace allowed me to recover, even as Zora was using her own reserves. One step at a time, a gentle motion forwards. At one point, I thought that the water above us appeared lighter, but maybe it was the moon. Down here, we had no way of knowing how far we had come or when the sun rose.

Ria poked her head into the bubble eventually.

'You're past the wall,' she said. 'It's really deep here, though. You need to keep moving.'

'I'm coming out to swim,' Sal said and pushed through the walls into the water.

The air was getting thick and syrupy, the lack of fresh air starting to make my head pound. I wanted to swim too, but I would not leave Zora alone.

We continued onwards. I couldn't tell how long for. I was glancing up when I noticed the tendrils of water reaching through the bubble, drips falling from above. Zora's face was strained, and she collapsed to her knees. I wrapped my arms around her.

'Quick, take a breath,' she gasped, and the water flooded us.

I kicked for the surface, carrying her limp form, desperate to get her to shore. Sal swam close, tucking his arm under her. He took her from me, his clean-air filled lungs giving him more power than I could muster. Ria swam alongside me as I kicked upward. We had almost made it. The shore was closer than I had dared to hope.

'I'll be fine, help Sal with Zora,' I said, filling my lungs repeatedly to clear my head.

Ria swam off, and I was left struggling to shore, accompanied by a small selkie pup, who refused to leave my side.

'You promised you would come back, and you did,' he said. 'Thank you for being my friend.'

Tears stung my eyes as I swallowed the emotion. This brave pup had survived far worse than my imprisonment. I couldn't form any response to him. So I gave him a smile and kept swimming for the shore, where Sal leant over the prone form of Zora.

As my feet touched the bottom and dawn caressed the shore with gentle light, Zora sat up. Relief flooded me; we would all survive tonight.

We walked slowly from the water's edge across brush-land. Dry and desolate compared to the cultivated confines of the collection, the salt water inlet made the ground even more challenging for plants. Our bedraggled party struggled onward, taking it in turn to carry Gar until we saw the path in the distance.

'Any search party will be looking for two people plus a seal if they have worked out he is missing,' Sal said. 'No one is looking for four people and a small boy.'

He crouched down next to Gar and rested his hands on the boy's shoulders.

'You should take your first steps belegged, among family, with your mother's support and your father's guidance. To return you to your family, you must instead take those steps now.'

I could see where Sal was going, and he needed my help.

I removed my glamour and gestured for Zora and Ria to step away. They moved slightly ahead, giving us the space we needed to complete what was normally a private and significant ritual, one that welcomed the young selkie to the next stage of their lives.

I stood in front of Gar and held my hands towards him as my mother had to me, ready to catch him on his first wobbling steps.

'Gar, I will walk with you on the land. I will support your first steps,' I said.

Sal stood next to Gar and held his hands forward in the

selkie salute. 'I, Sal Deepwater, will walk with you on the sea bed, and everywhere you need my guidance.'

Gar raised his small head towards Sal, his liquid brown eyes seeking support.

'How do I do it?'

Sal crouched and showed him how to loosen the skin. I helped him to slide it off. He emerged, a tiny, perfect child. I had never seen a belegged selkie so young.

'You will ever be a citizen of the ocean,' Sal intoned, 'but you will have the pleasures of the land at your toes.'

Gar held his arms around his small, pink body and shivered.

Sal took his skin. 'I will guard this with my life,' he said.

Ria wriggled out of her clothes, removing a top and gently passed it to me.

I slipped it over his head.

'Thank you,' Gar said. 'That's warmer.'

We strolled the path, trying to look like friends and family on a walk. I held Gar's hand as he staggered along on his first steps. It was clear that we weren't going to get far with him on foot, and once the required ritual of one hundred steps had been completed, Sal picked him up for the rest of the way.

A pair of guards ran past us at one point, but as we had hoped, they paid us no attention. By mid-morning, we reached the small boat that Zora and Ria had hidden and gently started her up, humming quietly out of the bay. We headed away from *Barge* until we were far from sight.

Once she was happy we weren't being followed, Ria turned the boat towards home. I dozed, exhausted, in the bottom of the boat as Sal cradled a sleeping selkie child. We had done it.

32

EDEN'S GIFT

G ar was far too weak to take back to the Territories in his current state and would need to stay on *Barge* for a while, so Sal had set up a bed in his rooms. In belegged form, Gar's ribs protruded even further than under his fur; he was uncomfortable and awkward. His faltering steps across the room reminded us all just how close this rescue had been. I sat quietly, listening to Sal and the boy, deep in food and conversation.

They talked of red cliffs and blue seas, of golden rocks and islands. They talked of their home near a place they called Mynyw, and I realised that we had been there. The same island chain where that fateful storm gave us the Aria was their home. I left them reminiscing and slipped out. They needed this time together.

I was sat on the upper deck when the memory of the selkie I met that day resurfaced.

'Have you seen my brother?' It all made sense now. I felt the storm rising inside me, the growing dislike and hatred of much of humankind. That they could take a child like that, of any species, from its home for nothing but prestige. It took a lot to make a selkie feel sadness, but this young pup's plight had broken me. I couldn't help but think of my own family, of my own sister. Would I ever meet Eryn's pup? Would it grow up in a safe world now that humans hunted us again?

A gentle hand touched my arm, bringing my focus back to the moment.

'He's safe now,' Zora said. I didn't trust myself to speak. My thoughts were too agitated, my soul too stormy. So, I simply nodded and gestured for her to go ahead of me.

She led the way down to the back deck, where Cor dried his wings in the evening breeze. I followed in silence.

'You didn't know he was there,' she said eventually.

But I *had* known a brother was lost somewhere. I had forgotten – I should have asked more questions. We should have gone back to the island before we left to travel north.

I sat on the deck, running my hands over the wood grain, watching the sparkling sea.

'I'll be back,' I said. I stripped my clothes off and dived into the water. I needed to swim, to feel my home against my skin.

I cried, and the sea took the tears into herself. I swam until I was exhausted, then I just floated. I wanted to be myself. More than anything in that moment, I wanted to stop pretending. But I couldn't risk everything else, and without my skin I would be forever incomplete. I floated in a sea far from my home, wearing Georgie's face. A small laugh escaped me, as I wondered what the residents would say to see Lady Gina swimming naked. I turned away from the huge, hulking ship.

As I watched clouds scud across the sky, Cor flew over-head. He circled around and landed with a gentle splash to float alongside me. I had no doubt he was guided by Eden and sent by Zora.

We floated companionably for a while, watching the sun descend over the horizon. Before the light faded entirely, I returned to *Barge*. It was past time to fix what I could and find my sister's skin. I was ready to go home.

Zora helped me out of the water. She had found a towel from somewhere and I wrapped it around myself. It was warm, furry almost, and I snuggled into it.

'Zora, I want to go home,' I said.

She reached for my hand. 'We'll find your skin, Georgie, I promise.'

'I can't go yet.' Already the stars were peeking through gaps in the cloud. Glimmers of hope in a cloudy sky – like Sal was, like his ideas were. 'I need to help Sal find The Hind first. More parties, more night-time raids.'

I heard her try to hide a sigh.

'I hated it, Zora. It was loud, it was crowded, and it stank. You're part human. You're used to it. I worry that if Anard starts to go to more parties and we raid them afterwards, that he may come under suspicion.'

'Why is that a problem?'

I closed my eyes, leaning back against the wall. I knew the answer. But could I explain it to her? 'Because I think he is a solution,' I said. 'He cared so deeply about the siren. He sees us as real and understands we are needed. Even if he doesn't know *we* are part of that group. He is willing to help us hunt for The White Hind.'

'You've grown fond of him.' She withdrew her hand, and I heard her shuffle around before she continued.

'Do you enjoy his company more than ours?' she asked quietly.

'What? No!' I was horrified at the suggestion. 'Zora, I am not interested in humans like *that*. But, as a human goes, from what is available to us, I think he'd be a better ruler than his stubborn, closed-minded, profiteering, murderous father.'

She chuckled. 'In that, I agree with you. I think there may be a way to avoid the socialising, if you have a little time, and if *Black Hind* is ready for service again.'

My spirits lifted a little. 'How?'

'Cor and Eden can search for us,' she said. Cor waddled up to me and flopped on my lap.

I looked down at him. Could they do it? If, between them, they could really identify what we were looking for, it might save us weeks, months even.

'How confident are you?' I asked, trying not to let my hopes rise too far.

'Very. Eden is getting better and better at communicating, more present.' Cor squawked as she said it.

'There's a cost to that.' Ria interrupted as she walked out on the deck to join us. 'Eden and Cor become more entwined. Less separable. Less sane. I'm sorry, I know that's not what you want to hear.'

'No, it wasn't what I wanted to hear,' Zora said gently, 'But, it was something I needed to.'

'Georgie, Sal is asking for you. I think he's heard about your swim.'

'I'll go see him.' I pulled my clothes on and left the three of them alone. At some point, they needed time to talk, and I needed to get a message to Theo after I'd caught up with Sal.

'I need *Black Hind*,' I said as I strolled into his quarters via our back door.

'You need to find the white one,' he replied. 'I'll get Seren to send a message to Safe Harbour.'

'I know. I think we have a plan.' I outlined the idea of using Cor, and Sal listened intently, a gentle snoring interrupting us occasionally from the bed.

Sal agreed in principle to try and scout with Cor, insisting that if the first foray didn't give us anything useful, that we return to the original plan. It was a fair response and I was happy to agree. After all, we both wanted the same thing.

'Then there is the small matter of the King,' I said. Now was as good a time as ever to broach it. We both rode high on the success of our rescue, and carried enough emotional load that maybe, I could get him on board with my plan.

He raised an eyebrow and gestured for me to continue.

'I want to remove him from office,' I said. 'Permanently.'

Sal sat quietly, his hands resting in his lap. I had his full attention, and he had not said no, yet. He sat back and crossed his legs, then rubbed his brows. He was at least considering it. I waited. Rushing to recall *Black Hind* wasn't going to be much different if I waited a few minutes or an hour. While Sal thought through whatever information he had on Anard, I wandered over to the tank. I went to stick my hand in and grab a snack, but it was stripped bare.

'He was hungry.'

Of course, he would have no concept of human food, and it wouldn't be good for his young body. Nor was staying in human form too long. Sal would have to find a safe place for him to regain his strength as well as be himself. Eventually, Sal rose from his seat.

'I agree,' he said. 'I have very little information on Anard, which means if I don't have it, nor does anyone else. He is sympathetic to our cause. How do you plan to do it?'

'Jellyfish soup,' I said. 'You've wanted to use that irukandji toxin for a long time. I know you've been keeping it for a special occasion. It's rare, relatively unknown in this area, therefore fatal.'

'How will we do it?' He opened the door to the tank and watched the jellyfish pulsing with a thin smile on his face.

'I can't risk getting stung myself. As much as I want him to eat one, the chances of getting stung are too high.'

'That leaves us with either chopped jellyfish, in the hope it stings his throat, or injecting the venom extract?' he asked.

I swallowed, fear rising in my throat like a large tide. For this to work, I'd need to carry enough to kill myself as well.

'Just the venom,' I replied.

'I'll have it ready for the day you need it. It may take a few days to properly soak in alcohol and then purify, but it's doable. It won't work in his food, remember. It has to be injected somehow. Take a backup plan. Take poison too.' He strolled over to the window. 'I saw you swimming,' he said, changing the conversation.

'I needed to be alone.'

'You could do that on board.'

'I want to go home, Sal. I want to help you get this done, then go home.'

'Take *Black Hind*, and work out the fine details of the plan. I promise I will try to find the location of your skin. I'll make it a priority hunt.'

'Thank you.'

Sal glanced across at the sleeping child. 'Once we have it,' he said. 'I'll take you both home myself.'

Blue sails skimmed toward us. The speed generated by the new blue foils was more than enough, and as they fitted in the same rig as the white set it made sense for Theo to have rigged them. The red set was too distinctive anyway. The sight of the round black hull slicing through the waves was enough to raise all our spirits. Zora and Ria watched from under a jasmine-wrapped canopy further down the deck. Whatever they discussed had cleared the tension. With the weight of the task ahead, I was glad.

'Shall we go down to meet him?' I called, and they both sprang up, eager to be reunited with our boat.

By the time we had traversed the myriad corridors and passages, *Black Hind* was bearing down on the store-laden deck. Seren had prepared everything she thought we might need. I even saw my repaired black suit poking out of a bag. I had no intention of wearing a full glamour again for a while but she didn't know that, or why we had needed such specific designs. It would be days yet before I was fully recovered from the few short hours I wore it to rescue Gar.

The crew Theo brought with him disembarked for a well earned break. No doubt, he'd pushed them for speed. We loaded the boat, keen to get underway; Ria and Zora filled with some shared purpose since their chat. I knew they'd been showing Cor pictures, but had no idea if a cormorant would perceive a picture as an actual rendering of an object. My role in this was killing. When it came to scouting, I preferred to put my trust in them.

A mere matter of hours after *Black Hind* appeared, we were off again. I hadn't left Sal a good excuse for Gina's absence. I'd just have to trust him to cover my back. I knew he would.

Anard had been recalled to his father's home in preparation for the midwinter celebrations, giving us seven days until the next engagement. I hoped we'd have success by then. Oceans, I hoped we'd found the missing hind.

We dropped anchor a few days later, hidden in a gentle cloak of mist, not far from the second collection on our list. We had enough depth of tide to stay here for a few days while Cor and Eden set to work. They flew dozens of trips, stopping to rest and eat each time they returned. We fed Cor as much as we could catch, but he gave us no suggestion that he had found anything of use. Once Cor had eaten, Zora would ask careful questions, ones that could be directed with a simple peck for response. Occasionally she'd look to Ria.

'Is Eden still okay?' I heard her ask once.

Ria's mouth twisted at the corner. 'Okay is subjective. I don't think they can carry this on for too much longer.'

My heart sank, much as Cor sank to the deck after a particularly long flight.

Again, Zora questioned Cor between his beak-fulls of fish. Cor selected one to give his response.

'Georgie,' she said finally, 'I'm confident that The White Hind isn't here. There's a herd of deer a long way from the water which keep moving. But Cor has landed on each, and Eden has felt nothing. No stirring, no magic. Nothing Cor has seen leads to the possibility that one is in some way different. I'm sorry, I think we need to take a break and move to the next place.'

Mute with disappointment, I nodded agreement and walked to the back of the boat to join Theo.

'We're all trying our hardest, Georgie,' he said.

I knew they were. Maybe too hard, I had noticed the increasing worry in Zora's face as the day wore on. Ria hovered near her.

'I know,' I responded.

'We want you to be able to go home too, you know. I mean, we'll miss you – but Zora told me you are feeling the pull of the sea.'

'Stronger each day,' I agreed. 'It's not about me though, not right now. It's about damage limitation. It's about restoring one small bit of balance in a wild area, preserving it for the future.'

Theo glanced at me sadly. 'It is as much about you and Eden. Before you go back, would you like me to teach you to read?' he asked. 'I'm not sure as much how you might read things under water. Maybe you could keep some things in a safe place on land?'

'Thank you, but I hope we are heading home soon,' I said. It was a kind offer, I just didn't think I'd have time to dedicate to it.

'Come and help me in the galley,' he said. 'They all need a break, and you know they won't stop until we force them.'

Cor shrieked in frustration at something, flapping his wings frantically as Ria and Zora stood back.

'Eden, rest.' I heard Zora say. 'I know you want to do this, but Cor can't fly any more. He's exhausted. I don't know if you can rest, if you can sleep in any form. Please, take what rest you can and give Cor the same. We'll move onto the next place. There's no point in exhausting him to get there a half day earlier.' She hugged the cormorant and then raised a blob of water from the sea – a fish wriggled within it. The bubble burst and the fish fell to the deck, to Cor's evident delight.

Ria frowned at the bird, and worry creased her brows. Zora turned, and Ria's face smoothed instantly, a friendly smile offered in its place.

Was I supposed to see? Was I supposed to act? Eden was determined to find The White Hind. Maybe, a last unfinished business, or just a desperate desire to hold on to their own self-identity for as long as possible by taking control of Cor. I hoped that Eden wasn't pushing too hard.

33

THE GIFTED HIND

Eden and Cor were returning from their second flight two days later when a sleek, white boat flew towards us, skimming the water below them. At the helm, her hair streaming in the wind and fabric billowing behind her like sails, stood Seren.

She didn't leave *Barge* often. As captain and queen in all but title, she was as much a part of *Barge* as Sal. Seeing her here, now, made my guts twist in fear.

She pulled her boat alongside as Cor crashed to the deck, exhausted. Zora rushed to him, shooting a fear-filled look in my direction. Clearly, I was not the only one unnerved by Seren's unexpected presence.

'Is it true?' The words shot me like an arrow.

'I don't know the question, so how can I answer?' I pulled myself upright, my roiling insides readying my body for flight. I had nowhere to run. I was on my boat, with my crew, but an inflamed Seren was making me edgy.

She planted her hands on her hips and stared at me.

'Do *they* know?' she gestured at the crew, and the realisation of her suggestion dawned on me. This wasn't about the murder of the prince. This was about myself and Sal.

Zora rose from the deck, leaving Cor with a few fish and strode to my side.

'If you are talking about the true relationship between Georgie and Sal, yes, we know.'

It was diplomatic, and hid a multitude of truths. I tried to send her a smile of thanks, not entirely sure that it landed.

'If you are talking about her duplicitous nature, then yes, we know.' This from Theo as he took a stance the other side of me.

I half expected Ria to join in, but she merely met Seren's searching gaze and nodded.

Seren stared at me now, looking me up and down.

'That boy – I saw his face as he slept. Clearly he is too young to hide his true nature. What had you rescued? What had I helped you rescue? Tales of sirens and myths are one thing, seeing a real Old One alive, and a young one at that.' She shuddered. 'Sal . . . he told me he was family, he told me you were family. I treated you as such.'

Her mouth twisted, and she gestured helplessly. 'None of you are who you say you are.'

I reached for her hand, and she pulled it back. 'I am still me, Seren. I am the person, people you know. How much did he tell you?'

'Everything. I needed to see it for myself. I need to hear it from you. No lies, Georgina – if that is even your real name. Just the straight truth. Then, I will decide whether to deliver the message I have. Or, whether to get back in that boat and leave *Barge* for good.'

Sal couldn't – wouldn't – cope without her. I had to salvage this for him.

'Theo, can you make some drinks?' I asked. 'Cor could probably do with a break anyway.' I sat, trying to be as unthreatening as I could and gestured for Seren to do the same. She remained standing, her arms now tightly folded. She was more defensive than I had ever seen her. She was hurting.

I dropped the glamour.

Seren gasped. 'Why do you hide your face? You're beautiful.' It was not the reaction I had expected.

I exposed my teeth carefully. 'For many reasons. For Theo's sake, and an easy life. After all, men have a tendency to covet selkies. These teeth are inhuman as well.' I tried to smile reassuringly. Never quite certain if it worked with my pointed canines or if it looked like a grimace.

'And Gina?' she asked.

I slipped into Gina's glamour, and she sighed. 'Well, that answers a million other questions, I suppose,' she said. 'Why are you and Sal here? What are you two really trying to do?'

'Seren, we are trying to rescue a lost spirit, to help the broken land – even if it's one small area we can impact. Then, I plan to go home. You won't have to worry about my presence on *Barge* anymore.'

She tilted her head, her arms still crossed; I was not out of the riptide yet. 'Sal said your skin had been stolen?'

'Not mine, my sister's. I let her take mine to escape and promised I'd find hers – she's pregnant.'

'You didn't tell us that.' Zora muttered.

'You sacrificed yourself? What if we never find it?' Ria asked.

'Then I have new friends and a place to call home,' I said, aware of every eye on me. Theo placed a drink in front of me and a small grin twisted his face.

'I knew it,' he chuckled. Lady Gina, I am pleased to meet you, finally.

He sketched an elegant bow, breaking the tension aboard.

Seren sipped her drink quietly as I left her to her thoughts. Discovering you were working for a pair of Old Ones was news best digested slowly.

Cor waddled over to us and placed his head on my lap. I scratched at him absently as we waited for Seren.

The silence stretched out. When the last mouthfuls of drink had been consumed, Seren finally sat. My heart slowed a little. *Sal, I am trying.*

'I thought about this a lot on the way here,' Seren said. 'Your story matches with Sal's. I believe your objectives align with mine. Neither of you have ever done me or mine anything but good – Sal particularly. Although, maybe I desire him a little less now I know what he is.'

'Shame, you make a good pair.' The words slipped out unbidden, and I froze.

Seren laughed. 'We do make a good team. With time and healing things may be different. For now, I will stay.'

I held back a grin. Maybe now, with the truth exposed, they would find their way to each other afresh. I hoped so. I watched Seren carefully. Her body language was relaxing, and she appeared to notice Cor for the first time. She smiled shakily.

'I have news you need. Prince Anard sent a message that The White Hind is found and resides in his father's collection. A large gift arrived at the celebrations yesterday, including The Hind and several animals not listed on any inventory as far as Sal can see. Either they were hidden from the teams sent to inventory, or they have come from outside Terrania. Prince Anard doesn't know who sent them yet, but fears they may *all* be more than they appear. Someone is trying to gain major favour with his father. He suggests that you attend the midwinter feast to gain access to the court and The Hind before his father sacrifices them all in the name of human safety or revenge.'

'That's all a bit too convenient, ' Zora muttered. I had to agree with her. It stank like rotten crabs. It was also an opportunity we couldn't pass up.

'There must be as many ways to gain entrance at midwinter as fish in a shoal. This is too simple.' I felt uneasy. Prince Anard knew nothing of our plans for his father. We could bring them forward and reclaim The Hind from him instead. I looked down at the exhausted bird on my lap. 'Cor, Eden, you can stop flying,' I said gently. 'We've found it.'

Cor squawked.

'I don't even know what to call you,' Seren said.

'My friends call me Georgie. But in truth, it is a name I stole from Icidro's home. My true name feels lost to me right now, as lost as my skin. Georgie will do, until I feel whole again.'

'I will maintain the charade, for now,' Seren said.

Zora collected the mugs. 'We'd better get back to *Barge* then,' she said. 'I'm guessing no one packed clothes suitable for a visit to the court.'

Oh Oceans, another party. At least it would be easier than a night time raid on this occasion, and I wouldn't have to eat the food. Irukandji toxin would do its work, and we could solve all our problems with a single shot. Well, all aside from one.

'There's one last thing I need to confess to you all,' I said. 'Something I'd rather tell you all away from other ears. Sal and I intend to assassinate the King and replace him with Anard.'

'Glad to hear it,' Seren huffed. 'That's the best bit of news

I've had for days. Let's get this mission underway. I'll see you back at *Barge*.'

With that, she climbed back into her boat, started it up, and it hummed off into the distance.

'I hope you have a good plan,' Theo said. 'Let's get out of here.'

34

IRUKANDJI MEETS THE KING

*Z*ora, Ria and myself disembarked in a quiet cove, trudged through the cool breeze, and joined the flood of people streaming through the outer gates of the King's winter residence for the celebrations.

The King believed he was untouchable, maintaining his grip on power via fear. Human society had passed so far beyond this at one point, yet humans reverted to primitive methods of coercion again and again in history. The high walls were ringed with carrion-topped spikes – traitor's heads mounted as a reminder to all who passed beneath their macabre visages that he would not be crossed. The fake siren would be up there too. By now, crow-eaten and scavenged, it would be entirely unrecognisable. Her beauty lost, but the symbology and the message it sent to the crews still hunting for Old One trophies, unmistakable.

I was melting despite the wind. We had staff uniforms under our ornate musician's outfits – the uniforms smuggled out by Anard. In addition, under both, already heavy, layers I wore the black suit. Long, slender pockets ran up both arms.

One side was filled with Irukandji venom and linked to my needles, while the other held a poison, which Sal had assured me was both fatal and slow-acting enough to allow us time to escape.

I had spent days practicing delivering the contents. We had filled it with dye, and it became a challenge to all in the know, where I had to get a dye into their drinks, or onto their food without them noticing.

As important as this subtlety was the ability to carry out the manoeuvre without getting any on myself. The first few practices were messy. Squid ink and various other dyes stained half the items in my wardrobe now, but eventually, I could reach over and glamorise my hand as I freed the contents. Or, I could deliver it into a glass of liquid. I could pour it with a sauce and scatter it like a dressing – all the fancy features of human food gave me many opportunities for poisoning it.

The biggest flaw in our plan was that, as yet, I had no idea how I would get close enough to the King to actually deliver either poison or venom. I tried to keep my fingers from fiddling with my sleeve tips as we waited our turn in the queue, sweat pouring from my brow.

One of the gate staff reached for my pack as Zora produced a reed instrument from her own with a flourish. She mock-bowed to the woman searching me and began to play. Soft, resonant notes drifted over the noise of the crowd, and completely ignoring the woman searching us, she began to wind her way through people towards the centre of the crowd. I'd heard her play before and was moved then. I had not truly realised the extent of her skill – our searchers were entirely distracted, and Ria and I swiftly reclaimed our bags to slip past them.

The outer courtyard was packed. At midday, the King would address them all from the balcony Zora worked her way towards. She aimed to join the screen-hidden musicians entertaining the milling crowds and sneak into the main hall with them later.

Ria and I needed our own way in, she had proven her ability to hide in plain sight, however, I was far less confident that I could blend in, my height was a distinct disadvantage.

We found a quiet corner and waited. Castle staff wound through the crowds from a guarded hallway. Each laden with enormous platters on their way to the gaily tented bars running the length of the courtyard, then returning empty-handed several minutes later, only to repeat the circuit.

There were no obvious matches for us. All the women were significantly shorter than me, although there was one similar in build to Ria. She was accompanied by a tall, slender young man on this latest trip. I pointed them out.

'They're the best we'll get,' she agreed.

We followed them into the crowd, pushing through in imitation of those jostling them. Ria wore one of my old dresses, sleeve pouches and all. With a venomous grin, she delivered a dose of toxin strong enough to make the recipient appear drunk. The pair managed to offload their trays with only mildly wobbling legs. I admired their determination.

As they attempted to return, their legs buckled. The girl fell first, and the boy rushed to her aid, only to stumble himself. A couple walking past jeered drunkenly before continuing their own passage through the crowd.

'Lisa? Are you okay?' he asked.

She sneered at him. 'I'm just fine, Tom, get back in. I've just twisted my ankle.'

His shoulders dropped, and he managed a few more paces before he followed her lead. Ria and I quickly dragged them from the crowd.

'Are you okay? Can we help?' I asked Tom, but Ria had done a good job. He was entirely unconscious. We pulled them towards the wall, propped them up and placed empty glasses near each. What we really needed now was for everyone to look the other way.

We waited. Ria blended into the wall so that your eyes slid over her, and I hid in a real shadow, tucked as tightly to the wall as I could. Every now and then, someone stopped as if to check on the two staff, but we were solicitous over their care, and spectators soon moved on. Eventually, we heard what we'd waited for.

'Citizens of my fair and powerful country. We celebrate the longest night and together, we will view the morning's sunrise as it heralds the overture of another prosperous year.'

Every head turned to stare upward at the glittering man, basking in their attention. A far stretch from the small and manipulative man who had sat across a table from me those months ago. Here, he held the eye, his clothes shouting even louder than his voice.

We only had a short time before his spectators grew bored with pomposity and returned to their revels.

We removed our outer costumes, Ria swapping hers for Lisa's jacket. She clipped Lisa's pass onto her collar so that it only half showed. I studied Tom's face as we waited, and it was the work of a few moments to align his features over my own. My figure would be harder to cloak, so I took his long, straight-cut coat and traded it with mine. It would have to do.

We followed others back through the guarded archway while the King spouted a rambling speech about nothing and everything, but mostly about himself.

'I can see why you'd want him gone,' Ria whispered. 'I should've had an eye on him too.'

I stole a glance at her. 'You might get the full portion if tonight goes well.'

She nodded. 'It has to. I can feel his spirit-stench from here. Now, get your head down. You are no proud selkie here. You're a serving boy.'

She was right. I studied the floor as I walked. It was so hot in there, I was soon dripping with sweat, my mouth becoming dry with nerves as we travelled deeper into the complex. Ria stepped back quickly as a huge platter preceded the small woman carrying it from a kitchen.

'There you are, Tom!' she huffed. 'You're supposed to be in the main hall. Take this. Now!' Ria stepped back and muttered something incomprehensible as the woman thrust another tray at her. 'Best you help him, or we'll all be in trouble,' she grumbled.

A familiar, slender woman strode towards us, clenching and unclenching her fists as she came. Someone was about to get a mouthful. I recognised the sneer, and the breasts. After all, they had been in my face almost as much as the King's. I tried to study her waist subtly. If he had been successful, would a human female show yet? I wondered how long human pregnancies were, ours were almost a full year, so how much would she show? Every selkie I knew who had been pregnant had chosen to endure the experience in the water for comfort.

She looked a little paler than last time I met her, but she held herself tall, and her fitted clothes didn't appear tight.

Dottrine took one glance at the tray I was holding, and her frustration exploded.

'There it is! The Queen is becoming quite irate at the lack of her favourite foods. That makes The King frustrated and it will pass all the way down the chain to you!' she shrieked. 'You, hurry!' She spun and marched off. I followed Ria as we dashed after the frustrated assistant, and an idea began to form.

Dottrine was similar in shape to me, with two notable exceptions, but it was nothing a glamour couldn't tweak – as long as there was no physical contact. The real question was, how close was she to the King inside the hall.

We scurried along, balancing the over-large trays, floating them over the heads of returning staff. Like by-the-wind sailors on the surface of the sea, they bobbed up and down with the swell of our arms. The noise increased too, crashing out of the room ahead, the volume breaking over us, as we surfed in, following Dottrine.

The room was far smaller than I anticipated – a single entrance and exit the only access. A ring of tables surrounded a central area, where the King was holding court. He regaled his companions with stories of his prowess, gesticulating his arms expressively, and roaring with laughter at his own jokes. Polite titters and chuckles abounded from whichever side of the room he faced. He was a man bathing in his own glory.

I recognised Lady Rene and her son amongst those being dubiously entertained.

'Come on,' hissed Ria.

Dottrine's unbroken stride aimed towards the most deco-rated woman in the room, who wore an entire menagerie on her head. Birds flew, supported on slender wire as they bobbed, whilst the main body of the hat was populated with deer and wolves. To her side, Anard drunk deeply from a glass, iridescent scales glinting in a rainbow of colour from his entire outfit. His arms whispered as they moved, the scales sliding past each other, singing songs of the sea. He looked more regal to my eyes than the pompous idiot cavorting in the centre of the room as though he was the paid entertainment.

'Mother, here they are,' he said as we placed the trays down.

I ducked my head to avoid staring at him, and stepped back allowing Ria to place hers. She slipped in and out smoothly, her face studying everything but his. He glanced at her for a moment, then returned to conversation with his mother. Once again, I was reminded how well he could act.

The seat next to the Queen, for no other in the room could fit that description, was empty, the plate and glasses bare. There was no way I could do anything, subtle or not, with nothing to hide poison in.

I dragged my feet to let Ria catch up to me on our return to the kitchens.

'This way,' she whispered and pulled me down a side corridor. We hid in the darkness for a few moments as others marched past, heavy on the way to the hall, light on the return.

'What do we do now?' she asked. 'He saw me.'

'I become Dottrine,' I suggested.

'Do you have enough energy for that? You can't have too long left?'

'It's not too bad,' I said. 'I'm only doing a face. I'm used to that. I'm relying on Tom's jacket to do all the shaping. I'll be okay to go for a while if I switch.' To make it look like her and plant the seed of possibility that a jealous mistress killed the King, I needed to be convincing. I'd heard her speak to him husky and low. Her clipped speech in front of the family was different. I needed to watch her a little longer. Then, entice him back to his seat, divert his attention, and deliver my treason.

'We need to get her out of the hall.' I said, considering the strategy.

'How long do you need to watch her for?' Ria asked.

Hours, days . . . there would never be enough time to copy every mannerism, to be as close to reality as I could get. We didn't have time for that.

'Can you give me a full course?' It would have to be enough.

Ria nodded slowly. 'I'll get her down this corridor. It gives me time to find a room, or somewhere to hide her in.'

'How will you move her?'

'I'm stronger than I look – consider how much weight I carry with every step.'

I didn't want to think about that. We returned to the kitchen, and resumed carrying trays of food, joining the flow of people winding their undulating way back to the hall.

'Find a dark corner and take up position,' Ria said. 'Be ready to help the closest guests to you. Assist with serving, pour drinks, watch the others.'

I did as she told me, winding my way around the perimeter of the room until I had a good vantage point of the King's table. He was still nowhere near his seat and brandished a glass of drink with vigour.

Dottrine stood behind the empty chair. She glowered occasionally at the absent monarch while his wife relaxed and chatted to Anard. They laughed together, the genuine warmth in their bond apparent for all to see. The Queen ignored the King, no doubt used to the spectacle, and was clearly in no rush to draw him back to her side while more considerate and caring company held her attention.

Eventually, all the tables were served. Ria had re-entered several times, checking I was in place on each occasion. The guests stared at their empty plates, one or two mournfully glancing at the King while they awaited his pleasure. Steaming food began to lose its heat and jugs of soup developed a fatty layer as the liquids sat for just that breath too long.

The Queen eventually broke the deadlock with a discrete cough. 'Our guests, we welcome you to our hall this midwinter, and invite you to dine of our plenty, that you may be sustained through the dark nights ahead. The sun will rise more each day as the night gives way to her warmth. Tomorrow is a new start. Before we know it, our crops will sprout, their shoots bringing hope for a bountiful year ahead.'

I hoped she was right. If tonight flowed as we planned, tomorrow would be a *very* new start.

Cheers resounded and glasses raised around the hall. Dottrine moved the focus of her glower to the Queen. Her furrowed brow and pinched lips masking her genuine beauty under marring lines of jealousy.

An arm waved in front of me, and I rushed forward.

'Soup,' the guest slurred drunkenly. I poured a bowlful, noticing the King finally stride towards his seat.

Dottrine watched him, her sea-grey eyes never leaving him until he finally took his place. I observed her whilst serving those who called on me, trying to take in her movements and her affectations. My subterfuge didn't have to last for long, just long enough.

I was about to kill the King in front of all his people … my stomach began to knot. I needed to stay calm, else my head would be joining those on the gate. My truth exposed for all, and worse, our reality confirmed to those who had not believed in the Old Ones.

The ocean rose in my chest and my heart fluttered like kelp fronds in a fast-flowing tide race. At times like this, I wished I could solidify the glamour a little more, as Sal often did. To hide my true expression with a neutral face was life-saving – or ending in the King's case. I began to slowly move toward the exit as Ria entered. She walked past Anard and the Queen, directly up to Dottrine and whispered something to her.

Dottrine threw her hands up in frustration and stormed from the room. I wasted no time in slipping out after her. Raised voices led me to the corridor that we'd agreed on.

'Why is the bloody cook down here? If she wants to see me that bloody badly, it should be in the kitchen. We are holding a feast!' Dottrine was shouting at Ria.

'She had a falling out with the pastry chef and you aren't going to get your showpiece dessert if you don't persuade her out. Says she won't talk to anyone but you m'lady.' Ria shuffled along, studying the floor.

'You are always in the heart of it aren't you,' Dottrine sniped. 'I may not know your face, but I know the name, Lisa, always sticking your nose in where it's not needed.' She spun as she realised I was following her.

'You had better get back in that hall. Don't think I haven't seen you staring at me.' She sneered. 'You can keep those creepy eyes to yourself in future. Or you'll be fired.'

Ria had her hand on a door handle and motioned as if to turn it, then pulled back.

'Oh, come *on!*' Dottrine cried and yanked the door open. We shoved her in, closing it behind us. Ria stood square in front of it. No one was getting past her now, in either direction.

I stepped up to Dottrine, who searched the empty room.

'Well, where is she?' she hissed.

I reached towards her and gently scratched her with the needle, being careful not to catch any of the fluid on myself.

It was just enough to kill her. Slow enough that we would have time to do our work, and quickly enough that it could be considered that she'd poisoned the King then killed herself.

She spun and hit me. I reeled back in shock – I should have expected it.

I wanted to hit her back, but we needed her unbruised. Dottrine ran for the door. With Ria stood in front of it, it would not budge. She tried to push her, and failed. Ria was as heavy as a column of lead. Dottrine began pounding her fists on the door and shouting.

I didn't let myself think about the rest of the situation. It was too big, the need for the King to die, for Anard to remain unchallenged. Gods, but it was a huge gamble. Anard could be playing us, but every sense I had said that wasn't the case. We had started down this path, and now we would finish it.

'You are going nowhere,' I said and drew her attention by pulling at her jacket.

'You disgusting boy! You think you can have me?' Her voice rose to a shriek, and I was sure that we would be discovered soon. She hit out, her fists colliding with me in dozens of places.

'One or two?' I asked through clenched teeth.

Ria understood what I was trying to ask, as I ducked and readied for another assault.

'Just the one, just her,' Ria replied.

I raised my arm and grabbed Dottrine's nose. No baby, no mercy.

She gasped for air and flailed at me – but not before I'd delivered a dose of the poison from my sleeve.

Her eyes widened as she tasted it, and she spat it back at me.

'What the fuck have you done?' she asked as the venom began to kick in. The strength of her dose leading to leg cramps earlier than I had expected. She buckled to the floor, and as she convulsed, I removed her clothes, switching outfits as quickly as I could.

Sheer terror grew in her eyes at the realisation something bigger was about to happen.

'When can you . . .' I asked Ria, I hated saying it.

'Not yet. Are you ready?'

'I am. If we get this wrong, these innocents will die as well. We need to return their clothes and faces as soon as we can.'

This further revelation brought increased spluttering.

'She'll start bleeding soon.' I said, hoping that the matter-of-fact tone would stop her fighting. This woman was actively trying to usurp the throne in the King's own bed. She was doing no less to the future than I was. Except, I had seen her delight at the killed siren, her encouragement of the King.

I was at least trying to usurp it on behalf of someone who would benefit the world, trying to lessen the impact of humans, to soften it.

Ria moved to one side to allow me out. Only once in the corridor did I perform the final changes to my glamour – a partial body coverage and face.

I strode back to the hall with confidence as I gazed through the sea-grey eyes and defined features at the staff. They scurried beneath my eyes, each intent on being unnoticed. Was Dottrine such an unpleasant person?

I wanted to believe that she was. I needed to. For what we were about to do, she'd suffer less by dying in that room with Ria taking her spirit if it came loose, than she would being tried for the murder *she* was about to commit.

35

IS THERE A DOCTOR IN THE HOUSE?

R hythmic beats carried down the hall; no longer made by the pounding of feet, but the beating of a drum. In the centre of the room a troupe of dancers had taken the stage, their perfectly co-ordinated movements acting out a story, a flick of the head here, a many-legged creature there, a battle of rhythm and motion. Fire shot from the creature's mouth, and the dancing warriors responded. They span and leapt, their heads flicked to the right as one, then they dropped to the floor.

A smatter of half-hearted applause rippled around the room from the diners. The musicians struck up the beat once again and a flute trilled out. The melody grasped at me, drawing me into the music. Haunting and filled with longing, it pulled at my heart with promises of deep water and wonders, of light on waves. It sung of hope in every note. The music carried a magic of its own.

The diners had stopped eating, their fork-impaled food paused half-way to mouths, motionless. It had to be Zora and, she had noticed my entrance.

In the silence, I slipped back to Dottrine's position behind the King. He alone was deeply engrossed in his food, unaffected by the music and barely noticed my return.

The dancers repositioned themselves, and drums picked up the beat. The melody faded into silence and the room exhaled. As though freed from a spell, they continued eating and the new dance routine began.

We had all made it in. As long as Theo and *Black Hind* were in place, it was time to turn this tide in our favour.

The course finished; tables were cleared, and more food was brought in on silver trays groaning under the weight of delicacies. Each selection intricately decorated with coloured syrups and foams. The meat was rich and the scent so strong it made me want to retch, but I held my poise and awaited my opportunity.

'Was there a problem?'

At the Queen's quiet question, the King also glanced back. Would he spot the difference?

'If there was a problem, she would have told me,' he huffed. 'Eat your food and stop worrying. Dottrine manages the staff of this palace like a real Queen should.'

I held my breath, awaiting a venomous response or something that blew my cover. But the Queen's shoulders sunk, defeated. There was more to this exchange than a spat over staff. I held back a smile. She'd be free to manage her own home soon enough.

'Dottrine,' he beckoned me without looking. 'Pour my wine.'

Could it be this easy?

I reached for one of the glass containers trying to brush past his shoulder, but he moved.

'What are you doing? You know I don't drink that one! Have you been drinking?'

I stared about the table in panic. I couldn't come undone over a glass of wine. There was a blood-coloured wine to my left.

I reached for it as he grunted approval – at least, I hoped it was approval.

This time, as I unstoppered it, I added the poison. It would be even slower than Sal had warned with such a diluted dose, but I hoped it would be enough. Too many eyes glanced this way, to scratch him – yet.

I poured the wine and stepped back. For a man in need of a drink, it took him an eternity to take a mouthful.

He took a huge gulp, then sniffed the glass.

'The wine is off. It's disgusting.' He took the lid off the flagon, and swilled more down his throat.

'It's definitely the wine,' he muttered, flinging his glass to the floor in disgust. 'Get me a new one. Now!'

Someone scurried forward to replace his glass as another quickly gathered the glass shards from the floor.

I snatched up the flagon, careful to handle it as far from the neck as possible.

It could take anything from five to thirty minutes for him to start showing symptoms. With the dosage he was now carrying, I anticipated sooner rather than later. I stood in place, holding the flagon, and waited. For a while, it was peaceful, people ate, and the musicians played.

The King twitched as muscles spasmed in his limbs. A cry fell from his lips as he doubled over gasping for air, wheezing from his enflamed throat as the poison began to act. There would be pain in his back soon enough. Sal had told me that it made the skin feel on fire, as though the victim burnt inside his own body. He sounded as though he was choking. I leaned forward and patted him on the back, reminded for a moment of the woman in the Gilded Heaven.

Both the high and low fall beneath the power of the ocean in the end.

I smacked him hard between the shoulder blades as if trying to dislodge some food. I felt the needle catch and had to hold back a grin that attempted to escape despite my nerves.

'What are you doing, woman? Get off me,' he spluttered, and coughed again. I hoped that he felt searing pain, every last bit of it. I wanted to stand on the table – to show the humans we were still here – to glory in the death of someone who had caused and encouraged the hunting of our kind. But, I needed Anard. From the darkest souls, the kindest spirits can be birthed, and we needed this one untarnished.

Instead, as the King hit the floor writhing in pain, as he started to scratch at his own face, I stood and waited for a command.

'Why are you still there?' shrieked the Queen. 'Get the doctor!'

'Yes, Your Highness,' I replied.

A hooded figure slipped from behind the musician screen. I took the flagon with me and followed them from the room.

Despite the drama playing out in the main hall, the staff out here carried on working. Exchanges of worried looks were the only clue that anything untoward was going on.

'Get the doctor to the main hall. Someone is choking,' I said to a passing boy.

He didn't reply, just sped off in what I hoped was the direction of a doctor.

I walked back towards Ria and was joined by Zora. We said nothing, silence remaining my best disguise.

I didn't mind the staff seeing me. After all, we were framing Dottrine, so the more eyes that saw her calmly leave the hall carrying a flagon of wine, the better.

We reached the room where Ria awaited us.

'I'll stay out here,' Zora said. 'Be quick.'

The reek of vomit hit me as I opened the door. Dottrine was curled up in the corner, rocking and staring into space. She glanced up as I entered, her pale skin clammy and soaked with sweat. Red stripes marred her face. The once beautiful sea-grey eyes now red-rimmed and bloodshot as she stared at her own reflection.

I smiled. I should have changed my face, but the shock on hers was worth the risk.

'How?' She stared at me, then bent double in a spasm. 'Please, end it. I can't take any more,' she wheezed. 'You can have him – whoever you are.'

'Have who?' I asked.

'Who else?' She vomited all over the floor. 'Please, kill me.'

I looked across at Ria, who shook her head. 'Not yet.'

'We don't have time to wait,' I replied.

I hated what this woman was doing, what she had encouraged. But that didn't make me cruel. I didn't wish her to suffer as long as she might. More, I didn't want her running for help – well, crawling. It was a wonder that no one had found us yet. Surely it would only be a matter of time before someone wandered in here.

'Do you have enough left?' I asked Ria and tapped my wrist. 'I'm empty.'

'I think so.'

'I cannot make it stop, but I can make it happen faster. We can give you something to numb the pain.'

She nodded eagerly, desperate to ease her passage towards death. Ria knelt by her side.

'I'll help you,' she said. 'Bare your arm.'

Dottrine lifted her sleeve, begging for any mercy we could give her as I poured the wine into a plant pot. It should have no impact on the plant. Ria smoothed her hand across

Dottrines wrist, letting her needles scratch lightly. It would soon deliver a small respite from the pain.

I watched her gasp like a fish out of water and embraced the cloak of dark responsibility falling on my shoulders. 'Are we so much better than her?' I asked.

'As individuals? I can't say.' Ria answered. 'You have darkness in your own soul, but it is tempered with light, like dancing moonlight on water.'

I watched as Dottrine lost consciousness.

'I still can't take her,' Ria said. 'I don't like the risk of leaving a spirit such as hers to break loose, but we need to go.'

I remembered the body in the field when we escaped with Gar and wanted to push her to do whatever she had then, but Dottrine's death needed to be timed right. Our careful dosing should mean the King died first. The fact that she now slept reduced the chance of her attracting help.

We closed the door gently, leaving a pile of discarded clothes and an empty flagon alongside the dying woman.

Then, we left. We walked past the now-empty kitchens and entered the courtyard. Revelling was in full flow as we slipped past the drunk guards who merrily waved us through without a glance.

We joined the crowds, shedding our uniforms along the way. I replaced mine with a subtle glamour while Ria borrowed Zora's cloak. The long bar running through the centre of the courtyard was deeply packed, and the gates flung wide open to allow the people free access. All in all, it was the least secure of the human palaces I had visited. Arrogant in the security of his position, it would no doubt have cost the King his life soon enough. Someone like Icidro – who craved power himself – would have come calling. We'd just sped that along, or so I told myself.

As we meandered along the bar towards the exit, I glanced

back. Someone else was in the doorway now, and there was a distinctly less drunken slant to their posture. She gestured towards the gate.

'We need to get out quickly,' I said.

There were about twenty strides between us and the gate, and twice that for the woman strolling towards it with a bad attempt at nonchalance.

Her voice cut through the air. 'There has been an incident in the main hall. Close the gates.'

A surge of people turned, and voices rose in panic.

'Close the gates?'

'I have to get home tonight.'

'Quick, let's get out of here.'

People who should never be trapped were caught in our snare. Ria ran ahead while Zora and I joined the surge – a tidal wave of people trying to escape. Ria planted herself against one of the huge doors; her feet slowly pushed forwards as they winched the gates closed. Others joined her, emboldened by the sight of a single woman making such a big difference. Little did they know.

The numbers grew and Ria stepped away. The gates jerked forward, but enough people were pushing back to keep them held. We flowed through with the escaping population, remaining a part of that shoal as it fled down the road; faceless bodies moving with the crowd, working our way closer and closer to the edge until, at the next set of thickets, we peeled off and waited for them to pass. The flow of bodies appeared endless. The ground between us and the sea was open sand, our boat hidden from the road, but to reach it, we'd have to risk exposure.

A rattling from down the road alerted us to something in pursuit of the crowd. Quickly, we dived into the bushes.

'Stay close,' I said and dropped a blanket of darkness over

us with my last reserve. It would have to be enough. We pressed close to each other and the ground. Cool moisture seeped through our clothes, and thorns dug into my palms. I could feel them both breathing, so tightly were they pressed against me. Zora was faster than Ria, her breaths snatched in gasps.

The crunch of the vehicle's wheels on the gravel slowed, its inhabitants staring at the road on either side with fierce intent.

'I saw something around here, Get out and look around.'

'Servants said he was ensorcelled by music,' one muttered. 'A hooded mage fled the hall with Dottrine just after.'

'It was the siren come for revenge,' another said.

'He ain't dead yet.'

'That's just what *they* told us . . . he might be.'

Theories abounded as they wandered alongside the vehicle, their mouths as busy as their eyes. I didn't care which rumour they settled for, as long as Anard was not tainted by association.

My body shook with the effort of keeping us covered. Even as close as we were, I could not stretch across us all completely. I couldn't cover all of Zora, and the muffled effect of the darkness faded around Ria's outline.

'Want us to poke the bushes?' one asked.

'Yeah, can't hurt.' A long stick jabbed down towards us, missing Zora by a fraction. Again, it descended, this time making contact with Ria, who didn't flinch as it pressed into her shoulder.

Someone stared in, their breath so close it drifted between the thorns, so close to my face, that I could see the whites around their cold, blue eyes. Thank the gods they hadn't looked a fraction to either side.

The stick withdrew and was about to descend onto Zora

once more when something rustled through the bushes, webbed feet pattered over my body as Cor charged through, exploding out into the midst of the search party. He croaked and flapped in distress, pecking at their feet.

'Ow, fuck!' One shouted. 'Can't be no people in that bush with this bloody great thing. Come on, let's keep going. I still think anyone trying to kill The King would be well gone by now. We've only been sent out so they feel like they are doing something useful. Only one who can help him now is the doctor or his god.'

They moved on.

Under the distant gaze of spike-mounted heads, we strolled to the sea's edge, where our bronze cormorant sat on a rock, preening his wings.

36

FREEDOM

Waiting for news was worse than carrying out the actual assassination. Somewhere, a king might be dying and a prince ascending, but out in the neutral waters, far from the scene of the crime, we would be last to know.

Seren had our staff probing for information between the sheets, but no news had escaped the walls of the King's home since we fled.

'You'll wear a hole in the deck if you keep that up,' Sal said as he rested his hands on the railing. 'We did the right thing, Georgie. We have The Hind, and whatever else Anard frees without further struggle. Fewer people die, change happens faster.'

'I know,' I replied, as we admired the glorious fire-filled sky mirrored on glassy, still water. Fluffy pink clouds floated like jellyfish through a summer sea.

'It's going to be a good day tomorrow,' Sal said. 'I am certain of it.'

'Where's Gar?' I asked. It was rare to see Sal without his small shadow.

Sal gestured water-ward. 'Seren is watching him swim on the back deck. She guards him ferociously. I've never seen that side to her before, almost motherly.' A smile flitted across his face.

'He's a small boy who leaps in the sea in his skin with more independence than any human child of that age. I suppose it must be unnerving for her.'

'Maybe,' he murmured. 'She won't share my bed anymore, Georgie.' He slumped against the rail.

'Give it time. If that's what you really want, maybe you need to talk to her.' The loss of Seren had hit him hard. Maybe hard enough for him to finally act on it if they could mend their trust. If Seren could see he was still the same person.

He stared out at the clouds, and I left him to his thoughts. Some decisions were his alone to make. Once I left, *Barge* would return to being their domain, my name a memory on the wind. Seren was still young enough to bear him a real heir, if he wanted one – if she trusted him again.

So many things we waited on. A death, a succession, and The Hind. A life and stability restored. A skin. There had been no leads on searching for a storm-killed old woman. Even if we'd found the right place, there was no guarantee that the skin would still be there. It could have been cut up to make clothes for all we knew. The thought sent a shudder down my spine and Sal glanced over, distracted from his own brooding.

'Crab scuttle across your bed?' he laughed.

'No, I was just thinking about the lost skin.'

He nodded gently. 'I haven't forgotten, Georgie. But, I fear that if nothing is found soon, you may need to pay another visit to Jake's crews, or accept that it's gone.'

He was right, as much as I wanted to deny it. My only remaining option might be to embed myself in their crew. Or find a way to get one of them to spill more specific details.

'We need the news from Terrania, then we can sail *Barge* north, towards it. If we return The White Hind, we'll be heading towards The Narrows. It could be a good time to make contact.' Sal continued.

The sun had almost drowned and I was about to return to my rooms when something blurred the horizon.

'Can you see that?' I pointed towards the shadowy shape. A huge vessel if we could see it from here.

'Beyond *Black Hind*?'

'Yes.' I narrowed my eyes, trying to make out any distinguishing features. It was not an outline I recognised at all. We watched for a few minutes as it changed course, heading straight for us.

The last of the light had faded by the time the ship anchored alongside. Lights dropping from the deck to bob on the sea indicated the lowering of a smaller vessel, now speeding towards us.

'Should we head down?' I asked, but Sal shook his head.

'Let whoever that is be brought to us. It's too dark to be certain, but if that's not one of the royal ships, I'll eat a cooked bird.'

We sat in the illuminated confines of a hastily erected reception tent and waited for the visitors. Seren had insisted on hiding Driftwood in curtained-off rooms. Ash and Oak were currently attempting to look engrossed in each other whilst lying on sharp implements, and Ivy was making all manner of noises from the area where she lay with Cypress. He glanced at us, mirth dancing in his eyes. I hoped they still had enough focus to respond if I needed them.

Shouted orders preceded our guest. 'Clear the way! Secure the area.'

I'd heard that voice before. It sounded very much like the guard who had accompanied the King on his first visit, his clipped accent heavy with a Territories lilt.

I wasn't dressed with needles but in simple, comfortable clothing and entirely unarmed. I closed my eyes and took a few deep breaths. Sal reached across and squeezed my shoulder gently.

'It will be okay.'

'If they traced me, if one of them lived . . .'

'Then, we will deal with the situation that we face, and no more. Tame the wild storm and be calm,' he whispered as the curtain twitched.

It was him. The guard walked in first, his thick beard announcing its own physical presence as he strode.

'Get up,' he ordered.

Sal raised no more than an eyebrow. 'On my ship, you presume to give me commands? By who's authority?'

The guard grunted. 'The King, of course. Get to your feet, now.'

Sal glanced at me. An almost imperceptible nod and rose to his feet. 'I would suggest that in future you remember that I am in international waters, and your King has no claim on me other than that which I allow him.' He stepped forward. 'A discussion I feel certain we have had before.'

Sal towered over the man, his height further exaggerated by a glamour. The curtain opened, and Anard strode in. He took one glance at the stand-off in the middle of the tent and shook his head.

'Stand down, both of you.' He followed it rather more hesitantly with a subdued, 'That's a command.'

Sal stepped back and the guard threw Anard a salute.

'Yes, Your Highness.'

'Are you here with your father?' I asked.

Anard's face fell. 'No. He was taken ill suddenly at Midwinter. He never recovered.'

'I'm sorry to hear that,' I replied, placing my hand on my heart. 'You must miss him.'

'We think his mistress may have had a hand in his unexpected death,' he said. 'She was found having taken a dose of the same foul poison. She never recovered fully. She lives, but nothing she says makes any sense, and I fear it is a matter of days before she also succumbs. For now, she has been sent to a secure location, where she can be cared for until we decide how to deal with her.'

Sal glanced at me, a single raised eyebrow asking the same thing I wondered. *How was she still alive?* I pushed it to the back of my mind for later.

'So that makes you . . .'

His shoulders drooped and I felt sorry for him. He hadn't wanted this, we'd thrust it upon him. Anard had been happy with his life of isolation and art.

'It makes me King of Terrania.' He glanced to his right, where the guard still hovered.

'Please, give me a moment alone with Lady Gina. I have matters of a delicate nature I wish to discuss with her alone.' I wondered if he was about to repeat his offer of marriage. Was it acceptable to decline a King?

Sal bowed deeply. 'My most sincere condolences, Your Highness.' He clapped his hands, and all occupants of the rooms filed out, followed by Sal.

Anard chuckled. 'I knew you wouldn't be as unprotected as it appeared. You too,' Anard ordered his guard. When the man hesitated, he sighed with exasperation. 'It's Lady Gina, exactly what do you think she is going to do to me? I'll be safe here.'

Once they had all left, he gestured to the most central spot in the room and sank to the floor.

'It's suffocating,' he said. 'They all feel so guilty that he was killed and that they didn't spot anything, that I am being surrounded day and night. I swear they even stand outside the door when I piss. Sorry, Gina, that was crass, but I'm so frustrated.'

I sat next to him. 'You wanted to talk to me alone?'

'Yes, partly for some bloody privacy for a moment, and partly because I have it. The White Hind is aboard that ship. It's white, just like you said, and in poor condition. I've been feeding it and looking after it. They all think I've lost my mind, that it's some expression of my grief. There were other unusual creatures too.'

'Different how?' I leant forward, eager for details.

'Their colour was off, or they were larger than a normal one. After what you said about recognising The Hind, I though they might be special too. You told me we needed to return them, to save our part of the world. So, I've brought them all.'

I felt my eyes widen. 'All of them?' I asked. 'How many are there?'

'Six more,' he replied with a smile. 'Gina, I don't know where they should go. I hoped maybe, you might know. Before that though, will you help me to return The Hind? I want to start this reign right. As soon as it is free, I plan to dismantle all the collections.'

The idea was wonderful, but complete dismantling would do damage too. I thought about Lady Rene's frog house and winced. 'There could be exceptions,' I suggested. 'If the animal is extinct in the wild, like Lady Rene's frogs, they should be allowed to keep that going – for now.'

He nodded. 'That makes sense. The prestige needs to move from the number and rarity of creatures to the success of breeding. I will become a champion of the idea, then the rest will follow. Do you have any suggestions for which creatures I should make my focus?'

I knew exactly which. 'King Anard, you should try to breed lynxes.'

'Lynxes. That feels like a very noble and symbolic gesture. Is there not a smaller, less dangerous creature that needs saving first?' he asked.

'Are you okay?' I asked. 'It seems you are moving pretty fast for a freshly crowned king.'

'You said it was urgent,' he replied.

I had, and it was testament to his newly found purpose that he was acting so decisively and quickly after inheriting the title.

'I took the heads down. All of them,' he said.

I put a hand on his shoulder gingerly, almost anticipating that a guard would leap out at me from behind a curtain. 'It was the right thing to do.'

'I have rescinded the bounty on sirens.'

'Thank you. It's one less place where people can hunt them.' There were still areas outside his boundaries, places like Icidro's and the lands far to the north, but we had to start somewhere. It was a good start. 'I'll come with you,' I continued.

'Just you.' It wasn't a request, but a command.

'Just me,' I agreed. 'When do we leave?'

'As soon as possible. I have left mother in charge of the transition. She grieves less than I expected, but I suppose he has been her husband in name only for years.'

I remembered the slump of her shoulders, a gesture repeated by her son just now, and I felt a warm satisfaction. She was free too.

'I'll get my things packed. We need to return The Hind to the mountain range north of The Narrows. Either transporting it through the town of Orange or the long but quieter ascent from the ocean side.'

'*Barge* can accompany us as far as Orange. But, you travel with me,' Anard reinforced.

My crew wouldn't like this. Part of me wondered if he knew, if this was all an elaborate ploy. Was I walking to my death?

'I will dress more appropriately for accompanying a King.'

'As my friend, not my consort, Lady Gina. Although, that offer still stands,' he replied.

'And, so does my reply.' I laughed. 'How long do I have?'

'Take the time you need. Bring a large trunk. I'll explain why once you are aboard my ship. Do you think Lord Sal would let me have the surveys my father left with you?'

'If you can get into the loc-box, they are yours,' I offered.

Anard rose to his feet, offering a hand to pull me up. I clasped it and attempted a ladylike ascent to my feet. We strolled out of the tent into a ring of expectant faces.

'I'm going to travel to Orange aboard King Anard's ship,' I declared.' He has requested that *Barge* accompany him to Orange, where we will evaluate our next course of action. He wishes to return a lost soul to her roots.'

Sal's face broke into a wide grin and he threw his arms around me. 'We did it,' he whispered in my ear. Then, more loudly. 'Go, pack. Our King needs a friendly ear in times of change. I would not deprive him of the pleasure of yours.'

'As if you could stop me,' I replied, returning the embrace.

Well aware we were performing for our small but very important audience.

As Anard and Sal discussed the loc-box, I made my excuses and went to pack and change my outfit. I'd seen Anard act before, and as much as I wanted this to all be true, there was still a lingering doubt, a small, nagging fear that I would board that ship to find myself a dead selkie.

FAREWELL TO A FRIEND

Anard had not turned on me. His father had not greeted me with death. Everything appeared exactly as he'd said. The Hind greeted me with the bleat of a kindred soul, and I felt every shiver of emotion, of the terror she had endured during her long captivity through our contact. It left me broken and drained. I wanted to push for details, but she did not share herself as her sister had done.

Anard stood guard over me as tears flowed freely, sending his escort away with excuses about wanting to share the beauty of the creatures with me alone.

The other animals he'd transported across the Terranian Sea were a menagerie of oddities. Most were just a rare colouration, but the vulture was different.

He didn't communicate in any form. He allowed me to check his wings, and the buzz of his power tingled through our contact. Eden would have known what he was – the thought came unbidden.

The vulture's flight feathers had been badly clipped, but

with time, he would fly again, to soar over whichever lands he should be a part of.

Huge reptiles, as long as I was tall, also tingled with magic, but I could not open any communication to them. With no links to their lands, I was at a loss. Theo or Zora might recognise their species, then maybe we could work out where to send them. We'd get them all home one way or another.

This collection was a significant donation to Anard's father. Someone had *really* needed his help or support. Once the dust of his passing had settled, the sender was a problem that Anard would need to be wary of.

As we completed our circuit of the menagerie, Anard opened a small door. Inside this room, a heat source hung over an enormous egg. He waved me in, then closed the door.

'Lady Gina, while we're alone I need to ask – you're one of *them*, aren't you?'

This question, again. I knew he suspected, and I trusted him; we needed to keep him on our side. He'd shown no inkling that he knew of my role in his father's death, had not mentioned the uniforms he had sent us to rescue The Hind with, despite the fact I was certain he noticed Ria that night. If he had wanted me dead, I would have been, many times over by now.

'I have Old blood in my veins, yes.' I hoped that would be enough. In the red light, it was hard to read his face, but his nod of acceptance was clear.

'Then, I need you to take this back to your father.'

I stared at the egg closely, unwilling to trust my senses. 'Do you know what that is?' I breathed.

His eyes met mine. 'I believe I do, and *no* king should hold one. If I believe in you and I believe in Sirena, it is but a small step to believe in dragons.'

'May I touch it?' I asked, my fingers already reaching out for it.

'Will it make you go weak and cry again?' he laughed. 'Yes, go ahead.'

I reached for the egg, my heart in my throat. In the warm red glow of the heater, it appeared just slightly yellow, normal, unexciting. There were birds that laid eggs this size. There was no reason to believe it was definitely a dragon.

The leathery shell gave way slightly under my touch, and I had to concede that it was reptilian at the very least. I'd hoped for a communication, some sort of wondrous connection, but nothing happened. I dropped my hands. 'I don't feel anything.' A sense of loss overcame me. For a moment, I had dared to dream.

'Maybe it's too young, maybe it's dead in the shell,' he shrugged. 'Either way, I can't keep it. It needs to be returned.'

'I know just the man to look after it.' Theo would make this his mission. If it was alive, he'd coax it through. Then, we would take it home.

After that, we had not spoken of the animals again. We returned above deck and spent the remainder of the journey watching a pod of porpoises frolicking in the bow waves of our ships. We dined in chill winter air in full view of the crew, but at no other point on the voyage were we alone together. Anard needed his reputation intact – as did I.

Despite his protestations, I was certain there was someone out there who could make him happy, but it wasn't me.

Once or twice in the distance, I caught sight of blue sails atop a dark hull, or a cormorant would fly overhead, circling above us or perching on a rail. It was good to know my adopted family were keeping a close eye on me.

The white coastal houses of Orange appeared on the shore-line, scattered at first, then packed together as we gained on their centre and the enormous dock wall. Whereas *Barge* was huge but relatively low to the water, Anard's ship would tower over the dock. It was entirely unsuitable for the open ocean, and I was glad he had decided not to risk passing through The Narrows. Whilst our lower deck structures could all be sealed and our effective water line raised, Anard's ship was a pleasure vessel through and through, designed for the calm waters of the Terranian Sea. It would ship water with the smallest of storms.

We pulled alongside to a fanfare of music and all the frivolities of the rich.

Attired in heavy, gilded cloth and bearing a long staff – its ornately wrought top decorated with more gold than the average person here would have seen in their entire life – Anard prepared to disembark. I stood alongside, clothed in the intricate red outfit I had worn at our first meeting.

Barge was close behind us, and I was certain that a small boat would be making its way ashore whilst all eyes focused on us.

The forward guard cleared a path through the crowds and fanned out to keep unwanted guests from boarding. Anard and I walked down the ramp with The White Hind between us. He strode with the confident swagger I had seen his father display while I pushed my shoulders back and tried my best to keep The Hind calm, resting a hand on her shoulder and through our contact, assuring her that freedom and her sister were both ahead.

My skin prickled. Somewhere in the gathered masses, someone was staring at me. Gods below – they all were. Why was I so edgy, so nervous? From the back of the crowd came a familiar call. I searched for Cor and found the others below him. They edged along, ignoring our spectacle and getting into position ahead of us. If The Hind were to bolt for freedom, Zora or Ria might be able to calm it. At the very least, Cor could track it.

The pricking of a hundred eyes burned into my back as we escorted The Hind through the town, accompanied by a small group of guards. The guard captain had argued for a full unit, but we talked him out of it, explaining that it would scare The Hind. He hadn't been happy and stomped off, muttering about lawless pirates before carefully selecting a small company to join us. I wondered if Driftwood were also hidden amongst the crowds. The thought brought some reassurance. We wound through the town, past the safekeep, and along the road past the pleasure district towards the tall gates marking the edge of the wild. I had never felt more protected – or exposed.

We'd drawn level with the boarded-up windows of Gilded Heaven when the sensation of being stared at resolved itself into a single focus.

A familiar face, Jake, but not Jake, pushed himself off a stool at Fish's. He swayed slightly as he took in our presence. Fury and greed flickered across his face, no doubt exacerbated by the liquor Fish had been serving.

'This ain't your town, *Prince* Anard. You useless hermit,' he shouted, spittle flying from his lips with each word. 'You're not a tenth of the man your father was, and you'll never be as loved as Prince Ulises – you aren't even man enough to be the shadow of his piss. What the fuck are you doing in my town?'

Anard ignored him at first, raising his chin, and continuing to proceed towards the gates. The guards tightened ranks around us and The White Hind tensed. Her muscles quivered with fear, her ears flicked, they were all too close. I searched for Zora or Ria. They'd vanished through the crowd, far ahead of us, so they must be somewhere around here by now.

Not-Jake called again. 'I think you have something of mine, *Prince* Anard. Thank you for returning her to me.'

'The Hind is under my protection. She belongs to no man,' Anard replied, still walking, not meeting the man's eyes.

'I'm so, very glad you said that. Because it's not your deer I want.' He raised his finger. 'It's *that*.'

I didn't have to look to know he was pointing at me.

'Lady Gina is no man's property.' Anard frowned. 'Leave us, before I have you removed.'

'Oh, I doubt that very much, *Your Highness*. You might call this patch of ground yours, but we don't answer to you.' Several other figures in the bar rose and advanced. They now outnumbered our escort. Beyond them, three hooded figures stepped from the shadow of one of the growing homes, a cormorant waddling after them.

I placed my hand on The Hind, and as hard as I could, I tried to tell her to run through the gates, to the hills. To my relief, she took off, releasing great bounds of power as she ran. Theo, Ria and Zora closed ranks behind it, following it to freedom. I trusted them; if they had left me, Driftwood must be nearby.

'They are friends,' I murmured to Anard. 'She will be okay now. You did it.'

Someone lunged for us. A gun fired. A sailor fell. The guard captain reloaded. The sailors advanced on us, their leader goading them on.

'Take her back,' he shouted. 'She's mine now!'

I stepped towards him, placing myself ahead of Anard.

'This is not your battle, Your Highness,' I said.

'Oh, but it is. He is parading another man's property like she is his own.' The leader slurred and he swayed slightly as he raised his hand to stop the advance. The crews held fire, but weapons remained ready on both sides.

'You do not own me.' I strode towards him with more confidence than I felt. 'I am Lady Gina, daughter of Lord Sal, heir to *Barge*. No other lays claim to me, you're drunk. Go back to your ships.'

'Oh, I think you'll find, I do. Icidro killed my brother, Jake, over you. I've tracked your slippery trail from Icidro to here, and *everything* matches up. I never saw you in person, but it has to be you. You're no lady. You are a bloody selkie, a seal-wife and, as everything of my brother's is now mine, that includes you.' He sneered, licking his lips suggestively.

I froze. He reached into his pocket and pulled out a small handful of silver fur, throwing it up into the wind. My sister's scent, old but distinct, floated faintly on the breeze. It had been kept locked up somewhere so secure that it had retained that scent for all this time. He had the skin.

I daren't turn around. I didn't want to see what was written on Anard's face. All I could think about was the skin, home, and freedom.

Keeping my glamour carefully intact, I continued to advance. 'Anyone can throw fur in the air. Without proof, you could be anyone.'

'You don't deny it?' he laughed. 'You see, Your Highness, you consort with monsters.'

'Gina is no monster,' growled Anard, moving alongside me.

'Whilst I appreciate the backup, you need not get involved,' I muttered.

'This is my land. If we are to protect the hinds, I cannot back down. No matter what you are.'

This was about to get messy.

'If you are truly a selkie, don't you have some kind of legendary curse?' he muttered.

I grimaced. 'Only if I want to die after using it. It's a little like a bee sting – too little, too late.'

Jake's brother had had enough of waiting. He dropped his hand, and the crew advanced, guns trained on me.

'Fuck this,' Anard's captain said. 'I'm not losing two bloody kings.'

Jake's brother crumpled, redness blooming from a gunshot to the chest.

'Get your royal-self back on that ship now. We'll deal with the pirates afterwards.' They closed ranks around Anard, cutting me off.

'Go!' I said. I had one last shell to turn. With Anard out of range, I was free to use everything I had hidden up my sleeves.

'Leave Anard. He's useless. Get the selkie,' Jake's brother gasped from the ground. A shot whistled past my ear. 'Alive, you idiot!'

I ran at the nearest man and stabbed him in the neck. He reached for me as I twisted free. I ripped the skirt of my dress off, and one of them whistled.

'She's keen to get stuck in.'

Free from the fabric, I leapt at another. Flapping wings alerted me to duck as Cor flew into the fray, pecking at eyes and scratching at faces, then retreating upwards, out of reach.

He bought me enough time to dive into Fish's. I ducked through the door and crouched under the bar. Fish looked down. He opened his mouth to call for help and I quickly hissed.

'It was me – I managed to set Rialta free from the Gilded Heaven.'

He reached for a tankard. 'Get out. I'll not have my business wrecked, Lady Gina,' he said quietly.

'Thank you,' I replied. I took a deep breath and prepared the original glamour I had worn to arrive in Orange. I slipped out the back and dropped it over myself, then calmly walked away as the young man who had first walked in many months ago.

Jake's people were scouring the houses, bashing down doors and pulling everyone out. I joined a huddle of residents standing to one side, watching them.

Cor still dived at their fallen leader. Whether Eden had lost control and Cor was now so enraged they couldn't stop him, I was unsure, but they were both my friends. I ran towards them.

'Stupid bird,' Jake's brother said and lifted his gun with a shaking hand. He caught Cor's wing, and the bird spiralled to the floor.

I gathered them up and kicked the gun from the dying man's reach. Not one of his men had remained with him. Loyalty to the almost-dead clearly wasn't their strong point. I held my needles to his throat and his eyes flicked open at the pressure. 'Who the fuck are you?' he asked, then his body fell limp. I hadn't even loosed the poison – the bullet wound had done for him.

I slipped back to the bar, cradling the bird.

Fish leant over it, staring at Cor. 'I remember you, lad, what are you doing back here?'

'My friend needed me.' I said, through gritted teeth, and holding down sobs.

'Aye, that's a brave bird.'

I rose from the stool and left, ducking between houses and changing my face frequently. By the time I finally reached the small house at the end of the docks, I was barely able to walk, and my glamour had faded entirely.

Seren rushed from the building, wrapping me in a cloak and hustling me through the door. 'I've got her,' she called.

Sal rushed down the stairs as I held Cor's limp form towards them. Cor hadn't moved since I picked them up.

'Food, for all of them.' Sal urged.

'Save them.' I whispered before everything went black.

I awoke many hours later in my cabin on *Barge*. Cor was flat out on the bed alongside me, and Sal sat in a chair, his head drooping with exhaustion. I rolled over and reached for Cor, who croaked quietly and shuffled closer.

'Thank you, Eden,' I said. 'You saved me back there.'

'Crok'

'That must have cost you a lot.'

'Crok'

Sal opened his eyes. 'I couldn't get them to eat, Georgie. I tried, really I did.' He sat on the edge of the bed as I pushed myself upright. 'You know it might be time, don't you?'

Tears rolled freely down my cheeks as I held the bird and his unplanned passenger close to me.

'I asked for the others to be sent straight here when they return.'

I didn't trust myself to speak, so I said nothing. We just waited, holding vigil over the exhausted spirit of a lost friend.

Finally, a gentle knock at the door.

'Come in,' Sal called.

Zora, Theo and Ria entered the room. Zora gasped and rushed to Cor.

'What did they do?' she asked, examining the wing and seeing the shattered bones. Her face fell.

'They shot Cor's wing. Eden defended me; Cor attacked the crew, pecking out eyes and clawing faces. Together, they gave me a chance to get free. Kept me free,' I said. 'Zora, Cor has barely moved since. I don't think Eden can step back anymore.'

Sal stood.

'Eden, my heartfelt thanks to you, for all your service.' He bowed deeply and left the room.

Ria moved into the space where he had been, reaching for Cor. 'It is time,' she said.

Theo joined us, and we gathered close to the bird, each murmuring a final word to Eden. A chance to let them know what they meant, how much they'd changed our worlds. Zora gathered Cor to her chest, tears flowing freely.

'Ria—' she gulped, unable to continue speaking.

Ria reached for Cor, closed her eyes and cradled the bird's head gently in her hands. After a few moments, she opened them.

'It's done,' she said and Zora laid the immobile form on the bed.

'Did you feel anything?' I asked, remembering the discussion we had about memories.

She turned to look at me. 'I did,' she said. 'I felt relief. From both of them.'

Zora crumpled into my arms, wracked with soul-shattering sobs.

THE SKIN

We sailed out of port on *Black Hind* the next morning, carrying Cor's body to a small cove around the headland from Orange. Whilst Eden's body had received an ocean burial, we all agreed that Cor's should be closer to the sky. We scrambled up the cliff path to a grassy bank, hunting for the perfect spot. Together, we searched the beach for suitable rocks and carried them up to construct a small cairn of stones over his prone form.

I tried to form some words, to say something important, heartfelt. But as I practised in my head, nothing I could come up with expressed the sentiments I needed to share, at least, not in a human tongue.

I called my emotions in Ocean, filling the air with love and gratitude for the bird who had become so much more to us than we could have imagined. Who had safely carried Eden's soul until they were ready to move on. I poured my emotions into, it letting the world know of his greatness.

Zora waited until I had finished, then withdrew her reed flute from its case and lifted it to her lips. Her haunting melody drifted on the wind to the forested hills rising into their mist-cap. I gazed upward, wondering if the tune carried to the ears of two white hinds. Sisters reunited once again.

She played until, like me, she had said all that could be said without words.

Theo reached into his top and withdrew a single, green feather earring. He worked it through a crack between the stones until it was barely visible.

'I'll never forget you,' he said, resting his hand on the top of the cairn.

Ria smiled. 'That is how they truly live on,' she said.

Our moment of reflection and solitude was broken by gunfire, as a battle begun in The Narrows moved closer toward Orange. Smoke poured from the small boats harrying the royal fleet.

Gunfire rang out again, and another of Jake's boats lost a mast.

I smiled.

King Anard had been fuming over the way his guards had hustled him away from the fight, and it had not taken much persuasion on Sal's behalf to have him send boarding parties onto every one of Jake's ships.

Anard had returned to shore that night, declaring a bounty on the heads of all pirates and left a portion of his crew there as a staging guard until he could send more. Orange would once again become a safe port for traders, and The Narrows, a toll-free passage to all.

He had confiscated every chest, box, and pole from the vessels in port. Several of Jake's ships, which had been along-side in Orange, had been tied together into an empty convoy and towed away for refitting. Then, he had sent his escort into The Narrows. Anard had signalled the start of his reign with a tide of hope, blood and fire.

We watched until the crimson flames died down, and the sea stilled. If Eryn's skin had been aboard one of those vessels, it was now gone forever. I was trapped in this life, my home lost. I let the tears flow freely, for all we had lost, for lives and freedoms.

'We should go back,' I said, as Anard's remaining ships turned to head for port. We didn't move until the last boats had gone from sight.

We clambered down the cliff path, and were about to row out to *Black Hind*, when a red boat shot around the headland with Sal at the helm.

'I've been searching for you for hours!' he shouted.

'We were saying our goodbyes,' Zora called back. She waded out to the boat, and he handed her a bag.

They exchanged words too quiet for my ears to catch, and I watched her back straighten, a defensive posture I had come to recognise. Holding the bag high above the water, she pushed through the waves toward us.

'Theo, Ria. Sal is going to give us a lift back to *Black Hind*.' She stopped an arm's length in front of me and held out the bag.

'Sal wants you to open it alone. Just in case.'

'In case of what?' I clutched the bag to my chest. Every fibre of my body was shaking now. The weight, the feel . . .

'In case it's not yours,' Zora said. 'There was a loc-box on one of the vessels in port. Anard was so certain that it must contain valuables he's had people working on it all night. As soon as he saw what it was, he sent it to Sal.' She gave a small smile and turned from me. Theo and Ria were quick to join her. Sal waved one last time, then the boat hummed out towards *Black Hind*.

My hands shook as I carried the bag along the shore to a group of small rocks. They jutted out into the water and looked perfect to lay on and just *be*. I gently placed the bag on the rocks and loosened the top as I mustered the courage to open it. Before I had even seen the skin, I was hit by the scent.

Oceans, it was her! I wrestled it free of the bag, and spread the silver seal skin over the rocks to check it for damage. Aside from the area, where they'd clipped it, Eryn's skin was intact. I ran my fingers through it, and felt for the opening. It separated with a gentle touch, and I slipped a hand inside. I could slip into it and swim. I could . . .

I held the skin to my face. It was so soft, and my sister's fur glistened in the evening sunlight.

I was free. I could return home to the North Sea with its beautiful, sun-dappled kelp beds, and craggy, wind-swept shorelines. I could sunbathe on that rock again – the flat one that scratched my belly just right. My pulse raced with excitement. I'd promised Eryn that I would retrieve her skin, and I had. Now, it was time to head North to reclaim my own skin. To forget about humans, and the world above the waves. I could return to tranquility – to my home, where the highlight of a day was finding really good food. Where I didn't kill things, unless I planned to eat them. It was time to return to my pack.

Except . . .

I was home already. This little family of disparate individuals – Sal, Zora, Theo, and Ria. They were my new family. Over time, the pretence of being my father had led to a real connection with Sal. I trusted him. He was my pack, and that little boy needed both of our help until he was fit enough to return home. Where I would be the odd female, the one who didn't fit. The black seal of the family.

I sat on the rocks, dangling my feet in the water as wavelets lapped them hungrily, calling me home from afar, and I realised that despite the strength of her call, I didn't want to go home to the ocean to stay. Not yet, at least.

But, North we would go. We would find my selkie pack, and I would swim with them, maybe soon enough that Eryn could birth the pup in her own skin. Then, I would return to *Barge*. My new home with its secrets, obscene luxuries and stink of human.

This time, I would stay by choice, free in the knowledge that I could fish for myself. I could swim as freely as Sal did – on my own terms. As part of both *Black Hind* and *Barge*, I could help the Old Ones. Now we really knew what was happening, Sal and I could change things – things that would affect my family from afar.

We'd rescued three Old Ones together already – not even counting those Anard had asked us to help find their way home. The reptiles and the egg now residing in a warm spot aboard *Barge*. How many more of us would need to be returned to our true homes to affect the balance enough to tip it towards everyone's survival?

As I stroked Eryn's skin, I realised that hiding peacefully beneath the waves would never be enough for me now. I sat for a few moments clutching the pelt to my chest, desperate to put it on and swim. But I would not do that. This journey, this part of my life would be complete, once I held my own skin.

I pushed myself up and strolled back to the boat we had used to land on the beach.

Black Hind rocked gently at anchor as I rowed back out. Zora looked up first as I scrambled up to the rail.

'I thought you might swim back to us,' she said, reaching

over to help me aboard. 'That you'd be desperate to get the skin back on.'

'It's not my skin,' I replied. 'It's Eryn's.'

Theo frowned at me. 'You look happy, but I really thought you'd be flippering to us. I know it's not yours, but if she can wear your skin, why can't you wear hers?'

I shook my head. 'It's the right skin, the one I have been looking for, but it is still not mine. It just doesn't feel right to wear it.'

Ria looked at the pelt I clutched. 'It's not the colour I expected,' she said. 'I thought it would be darker, like your hair.'

Draping Eryn's pelt across my lap, I stroked it as I replied. 'My sister always had pale fur like most of our pack. Mine is black, and it's time to reclaim it. I promised her I would recover this, and I have. Sal, we sail north as soon as that pup is well enough.'

Theo sighed. A body shaking sigh. 'Then you will leave us. I'm sorry. I am happy for you, truly I am. But—'

'We'll miss you,' Zora said.

'You won't need to.' A ring of confused faces surrounded me. Zora's expression laced with hope. I gently placed the skin on the deck and rose to my feet.

'We know there are more Old Ones out there. We have more wild spirits to return, and with Anard on our side, we can make a real difference. I may not have my own skin yet, but I will soon – a lost part of myself finally reclaimed, as I now reclaim my name and identity. My true name is Tellin Dark. I am a selkie of the Northern Territories, and I plan to stay aboard this boat as long as you will have me.'

ACKNOWLEDGMENTS

In an uncertain world, where our human impact is beginning to be felt daily, where the temperatures rise and the floods flow, The Barren feels less of an abstract concept and more of a threat. The world of the Black Hind's Wake is far more relevant than when I first conceived the idea a few years ago.

At that time Georgie jumped fully formed into a short story accompanied by Sirena, and once she'd arrived she demanded to tell her tale – along with that of the leathergill sirens and other Old Ones. So, I complied with her.

As Sirena says to Georgie, 'Remember, Selkie, you cannot do it alone.'

It takes a whole ocean of support to bring a book to life. Diana James, without your unfailing belief in my writing, and your love for my characters in the editorial stages, this book could not have happened. I am so grateful to be able to call you a friend, and cannot thank you enough.

To my family, who lost me for days at a time to the crews

of *Barge* and *Black Hind*, thank you all. Mum and Dad, you asked what I aimed to achieve in the next ten years – we did it a bit sooner than planned! Thank you for helping make my dreams come true and always answering apparently random questions about long distance sailing, racing yacht toilets, and fish stocks. Asa, my Emotional-Support-Human, over the last two years, I've cried over not being able to smell gorse bushes during lockdowns, and hidden away to write. You've supplied the tea, the whisky and the coffee. You've listened to me talk ideas at you, then run off because I solved it myself. But, more than that, you believed in me, pushing me to make this book everything I dreamed it could be, I love you. Natalie, Timy and Georgie, thank you too. For the last few years you have heard more about my books than anything else, and borne it with the patience of true friendship.

Trif book designs has created a wonderful cover, bringing my dreams to life, and the talented Carina Roberts has brought many of my creatures and characters to life in chapter headers. I look forward to working with you both again as we move on to the next adventures in the Black Hind's Wake.

Then, there are a veritable tidal wave of supporters in the writing community. Justin Lee Anderson, thank you for your honest friendship and support. Damien Larkin, Lee Conley and Alex Bradshaw, thank you for being sounding boards and readers, for your patient advice and help, no matter how trivial my questions. Jacob Sannox – your blurb-storming skills and beta notes are legendary. Pam, you helped me get my head around my own writing and see through the words to find the sentences underneath. Andrew, you have been a champion and cheerleader and are forever my first-stop tech guru. Alicia, thank you for the really insightful critique, I hope

I removed the chairs. Tom Clews, your god-book child is finally here, may it now fly free to find readers.

I should also make a special mention of my small, furry writing assistant, Archie. His warm and fuzzy dog-shaped company forms my permanent shadow and our walks always help me to work though problems.

Lastly, thank *you*, dear reader. I hope that you have enjoyed voyaging with the crews of *Black Hind* and *Barge*. If you did, please leave a review. If you'll miss their company, then visit my website for updates and sign up to my newsletter. You'll get a free short story about one of *Black Hind's* crew, before they met, to tide you over until the second book in Black Hind's Wake comes out in summer 2022. I promise not to send loads of mail, just to keep you updated on new releases and maybe share some sneak peeks of the next book's artwork!

www.jehannaford.com

Lightning Source UK Ltd.
Milton Keynes UK
UKHW011242140921
390548UK00001B/50